Praise for Kilómetro Cero

"Kilómetro Cero by James Walter Lee is a sizzling contemporary romance novel, venturing into the realm of steamy encounters that ignite the pages."

—Literary Titan

"Author James Walter Lee has cleverly combined spicy amorous play, soul-stirring proclamations, and the quest for meaning in this unputdownable book."

—Stephanie Elizabeth Long for Reader Views

"Author James Walter Lee weaves a tale that delves into the nuances of age-gap relationships, exploring the challenges and societal judgments that accompany such connections with gravitas and emotional resonance."

—K.C. Finn for Readers' Favorite

"This luscious story is a sexy escapade that features beautiful, powerful people living life in the fast lane. Crackling with energy, Kilómetro Cero pits obligation against desire in a powerful tale of unstoppable lust."

—Jennifer Jackson for Indies Today

Also by James Walter Lee

A House of Cranes
Tooth and Talon

KILÓMETRO CERO

Z

Zennea Press
www.zenneapress.com

This book is a work of fiction. Any references to historical events, real people, or real places are used fictitiously. Other names, characters, places, and events are products of the author's imagination, and any resemblance to actual events or places or persons living or dead is entirely coincidental.

First Zennea Press paperback edition November 2023

Library of Congress Control Number: 2023911874

ISBN 979-8-9885153-0-2 (paperback)
ISBN 979-8-9885153-1-9 (ebook)

Cover design by Ebook Launch

Author photo by James Walter Lee

Interior design by James Walter Lee

In memory of my father, Bo Heung Lee

1

Dressed in one of his best suits, Nick Evers slumped into the cushions of a leather sofa positioned in front of his father's golf simulator. For fun, he turned on the projector when he snuck down to the basement earlier with Autumn. Projected on the fifteen-foot screen was a lush green fairway with a banner off to the side that read Acciona Open de España. Nick drew in a sharp breath. His pants and briefs pooled around his ankles. Autumn Jensen knelt between his open, bare knees. She teased with her lips and tongue, then took him into the warmth of her mouth. The projector fan made a soft whirl. Long-drawn-out breaths passed his lips as he stared at the virtual grassy fairway and the red and canary yellow flag that fluttered in the distance. She flipped her long blonde curls over her shoulder and doubled her efforts. His breath caught and his spine stiffened until he groaned and came.

She sat back on her heels.

"I hope you enjoyed your graduation present."

She took his pocket square from his jacket breast pocket and wiped her lips. He hummed and glanced at her through narrow slits, then off into the virtual golf course projected on the wall. She stuffed the soiled pocket square back into his breast pocket.

"What will you do now?" She asked.

"Sleep."

She shoved his knee.

"No silly. Now that you got your master's degree."

Autumn never questioned him about his career or employment future. She was leading up to something else.

"You know my dad wants me to work at Hale."

"A lot of graduates would kill to work there. You're fortunate."

He wrinkled his lips and sighed.

"I guess."

"What else will you do?"

She sounded like his mother.

"I don't know."

"When are you going to tell everyone I'm your girlfriend?"

And there it was. The question she always led up to. The only one she cared about.

"C'mon Autumn. Why do we always have to go over this? I told you, if I tell anyone, especially my parents, they'll think I'm planning on getting married."

"So? Is that such a bad thing? We've been together for—"

There she goes again. They're not together. They're not an item.

"I'm not looking to get married, no offense."

"But—"

"Or engaged."

She averted her gaze. Outside the door to the golf room, a dull clomping of heels echoed in the stairwell.

"Oh, great," he mumbled.

He froze for a moment, tension abated at the sound of the familiar footsteps. The door handle turned a fraction. Clack. Nick looked at Autumn, then held a finger to his lips, grateful that he remembered to lock the door. A young female voice spoke. "Nick, are you in there? Unlock the door."

He sat up on the sofa.

"Ah, yeah. Gwen, I'll be right out."

Saved by the bell, and an annoying bell at that.

"Everyone's waiting for you."

"Ok thanks. Be right there."

He tilted his head and rolled his eyes. They stared at each other and listened for his younger sister to climb the stairs. Autumn crossed her arms and her lips drew into a tight line. He was unsure what angered her more, his lack of commitment, or how he always escaped her questioning. Clack-clack. The door knob jostled again.

"Ok-ok!"

Nick whispered to Autumn, "Stay here until I go up with her, okay?"

She said nothing, only glared at him.

"Great," he whispered.

He gave her a quick peck on the cheek, stood, zipped his pants, buttoned his jacket, and went to the door. After he slipped out, he shut the door and Autumn behind him. He blocked Gwen as she tried to push past him. She backed away, tossed her sandy-brown curls over her shoulder, and crossed her arms. That moment struck him how grown up his thirteen-year-old sister looked in her party dress. Her age made him consider his own.

"Who are you hiding in there?"

"I don't know what you're talking about, and I doubt you do either."

He put his arm around his sister, turned her to face the stairs, and then led her up. She craned her neck to glance down the stairs at the door when they reached the landing.

"C'mon, let's see if there are any cute boys outside for you to terrorize."

She elbowed him in the ribs before they went the rest of the way up.

~

From the upper patio level, Dr. Richard Evers surveyed the lush backyard of his sprawling Kingswood estate. Deep stone steps created a gentle descent to a second terrace that led to the swimming pool and guest house. Beyond the pool, the lower terrace opened up to a great lawn shaded with mature, towering southern oak, ash, and chestnut trees. A large white catering tent stood erected for the party. Hungry guests, instructed to eat rather than wait for the guest of honor, milled about the food tables fixing their plates of food.

Richard scowled and glanced at his watch for the umpteenth time. Nick was late to his own graduation party. It would be just like his son to stick it to him and embarrass him in front of his colleagues and the important guests he invited to meet his son.

A server came over with a tray of champagne flutes. Richard, Dale Scott, and Jason Knight traded their empty glasses for fresh ones, while Lloyd Reynolds still worked on the one he had.

"Cheers gentlemen. Although this is Nicholas' graduation party, it's also a celebration of Hale's last quarter," Richard said.

The four men dressed in suits and ties raised their glasses, then they all took a drink. Richard took a healthy one.

"Rich, this is quite a party," Lloyd said.

Silver-haired Lloyd Reynolds, a senior executive and veteran of Hale, was older than the other men, and should have retired a year ago. Some would like to see him go, but Richard appreciated the man's wisdom enough to allow him to stay on longer.

"All we're waiting for now is the star of the show."

He offered his friends and colleagues a reassuring smile.

"Where is that fine young man of yours? He always seems on the go. You've got to be proud of him, graduating from Columbia and earning his MBA. I'm sure they have instilled some drive in him," Dale Scott said.

Dale, his old college buddy, who managed all research partnerships at Hale, always offered a hopeful outlook.

"Yes, I'm proud of him. Sometimes he can be all over the place. I hope once he's on the job and has some clear goals, he'll be fine," Richard said.

Hopeful words, but doubt crept in. Maybe he should have let Nick become a model. He had the height and looks, and a casual attitude about everything. At least he would have a job.

"How is Colette? It's a shame that she couldn't be here," Richard said.

"She's enjoying Los Angeles. It's difficult to talk her into coming home. One more year and she'll have her master's like Nick. Hopefully, I can persuade her to come back to Atlanta."

"With a journalism major from USC, I'm sure she could easily land a job here in Atlanta. We've got all the major news outlets and some fine newspapers."

"She tells me her heart will always be in Georgia. It sounded more like a goodbye to me. I guess we'll find out."

"Maybe Nicholas can help with that. I would love to see those two get together," Richard said.

"That reminds me, Colette promised to call him later to congratulate him."

"Great. Anything to get them talking. Is Colette dating anyone?"

"No, no, she's been working hard at her studies."

Dale had a proud smile and lifted his chin. Richard smiled and nodded at the prospect of a romantic relationship between his son and Dale's daughter, Colette. Lloyd waved out toward the great lawn.

"Looks like Helen made me a plate. Excuse me, boys."

Lloyd sauntered off down the steps. Richard felt a gentle tug at his arm.

"Hey sweetie."

He gave his daughter Gwen a hug.

"Did you find your brother?"

"He was in *your* golf room—with the door locked. He said he needed time *alone*."

The way she looked at him, he knew Nick was screwing around, and he had a damn good idea with whom. He huffed at the thought of his son having sex in his golf room with the Jensen girl. Autumn was pretty, but she had no ambition, and worse, she came across as being easy to put it mildly.

Autumn emerged from the house. She looked over toward them, smiled, and gave a polite wave. He smiled and nodded back. Autumn went down the steps to join Nick's other friends by the pool. Richard looked back at Gwen and shook his head.

"Dear, why don't you go look for your mother?"

Gwen wrinkled her face like she did when sent on an errand not of her own making.

"I last saw her down by the tent."

Gwen smiled and hurried off down the steps. He smiled as she sprang off. She must be hungry.

Shouts and laughter caught his attention. By the pool were Nick's rambunctious friends. Drew or Derek. It was one of those two names. The boy laughed and tugged at Autumn's arm and tried to pull her into the pool. Derek, that was the boy's name. Richard quelled the urge to shout down at them to knock it off. Instead, he shook his head, snorted, and wonder where the hell Nick was.

Autumn laughed and squealed wide-eyed as Derek attempted to pull her into the pool. The other guests by the pool watched, but no one intervened. Nick's other friends, who lounged on the patio furniture with their drinks in hand, looked on without a care. Autumn giggled and broke free of Derek's hold, and in he went. Whoosh. Richard huffed and rolled his eyes. After he watched Derek pull himself out of the pool, he looked at the other men and shook his head. His tight-jaw grimace eased into a broad, tight-lipped smile.

"Hello Elizabeth. I'm pleased you could make it."

Dale and Jason held their drinks, turned around, and stepped aside as Elizabeth Bach came from behind to stand between them. Both men smiled and greeted her. Dale gave Richard a brief puzzled look with his eyebrows raised. Several times, Dale cautioned Richard about mixing business with his personal life; especially with such a beautiful, unattached woman as Elizabeth. "That's how empires crumble," Dale once told him when he commented on the perfect shape of her ass. Elizabeth beamed at the three men. Richard snorted and pushed aside Dale's concerns from his thoughts. Elizabeth was a liaison for a partner company to Hale, so that was more the reason to invite her. It was high time Nick started networking. Perhaps a beautiful business associate would get him more interested in Hale. Nick could meet her and start building his network, along with the other business acquaintances Richard invited. That is, if Nick ever showed up in time before everyone left. Jason smiled, turned to Richard, then to Elizabeth.

"What a surprise. Nice to see you, Elizabeth," Jason said.

"Richard invited me."

Dale shielded his eyes from the sun.

"There he is! The man of the hour."

They all turned to look as Nick stood outside the glass patio doors.

Nick Evers walked out onto the stone terrace. He squinted and shielded his eyes as he surveyed the garden party. He wished he had worn his dark wayfarer sunglasses. The gathering was one of the few gatherings in *his* honor. He grinned and pointed an acknowledging finger down toward his friends by the pool. They all waved to him, except Derek, who held up his hand in a half wave. Derek's clothes clung to him and his hair lay flattened to his head. Nick's eyes widened, and he laughed. He recalled a high school party where Derek dove into the pool wearing his private school uniform. Some things never change. His friends clapped and cheered, which drew the attention of the other guests. Blake pumped his fist in the air, then he and Peter whooped. Nick grinned and threw his hands in the air at his friend's joyful acknowledgment.

"Nic-ho-las!"

"Nic-ho-las!"

From the opposite direction, Nick's father's unmistakable voice called out to him in a less joyful tone.

"Nicholas!"

His father stood with his two trusted top executives, and a beautiful, mysterious woman. His father waved him over. They were all smiles. Ready to bombard him with all the news about all the exciting things happening at Hale. Their question, he knew, would be when would they see his smiling face around the office. It made him cringe. This woman, though. She posed a different question.

Taller than his mother, this mystery woman wore dark Jackie O-style sunglasses that hid her eyes. A soft breeze lifted her long, rich chestnut curls that brushed her bare shoulders. She wore a pink and blue stripe sundress that stopped above her knees—and what glorious knees they were. He tried not to stare. Her perfectly plump lips, painted in a pale glossy pink, curved into a soft inviting smile that seemed to suggest something more.

"There's my boy," Richard said.

His father patted him on the shoulder with a heavy hand and gave him a where-the-hell-have-you-been iron squeeze.

"Nicholas, meet Ms. Elizabeth Bach. She is our account representative at Nexgen Biosolutions, a company we partner with."

"Please to meet you, Nicholas. Your father never told me how handsome you are."

The rich and smooth tone of her voice carried with it a poise and confidence, unlike the anxious and uncertain voices of the college girls he knew. She held out her hand with her palm turned down, as if he should kiss it rather than shake it. He took her hand. Her touch felt electric.

"Please to meet you, Ms. Bach."

Her smile widened. The other men looked at her with awe. They adored her. Even his father's eyes were brighter than he had ever known.

"You can call me Elizabeth," she said.

"I think 'Ms. Bach' would be more appropriate," Richard said.

It reminded Nick of the time his father took a glass of Scotch from him, even after he turned twenty-one, relegating him to a simple bottle of beer.

"And Nicholas, of course, you know these two."

He gestured toward Jason Knight and Dale Scott. Both men grinned.

"The graduate!"

Jason Knight's voice boomed. He gave Nick a firm handshake, then patted him on the shoulder.

"You've arrived. Congratulations Nicholas."

Dale shook his hand. Richard put his hand on Nick's shoulder.

"Dale and I were talking about Colette. She's still out in LA, but she said she would call to congratulate you. I hope you two will find some time to chat. She's a beautiful girl, Nick. And she'll be graduating next year with her master's in journalism."

Elizabeth nodded and raised her eyebrows.

"Thanks dad. I'll keep an eye out for her call."

The more his father spoke, the more he felt like a child. He glanced at Elizabeth and tried to gauge her reaction.

"There you are Nicholas," Josephine Evers said.

His mother, Josephine, and Gwen had crept up behind him. Richard took Gwen and held her in front of him. Gwen stared up at Elizabeth with a look of awe. She looked at Gwen and gave her a warm smile.

"Elizabeth, this is my daughter Gwendolyn, and my wife Josephine."

"Hello," Elizabeth said.

"Hi."

Josephine gave Elizabeth a quick handshake, then turned to fuss with Nick's collar. She seemed too preoccupied to give Elizabeth a second glance. After she brushed his shoulders, she found a button undone on his shirt above his waist.

"Mom, leave it."

She fussed with his shirt until she got the button fastened. He smiled as he tried to hold his mother's hands still.

"There."

Josephine stepped back with a look of satisfaction. Elizabeth grinned. He would crumble if she burst out laughing.

"C'mon Dear, you know everyone wants to congratulate you."

"Nice meeting you," Elizabeth said.

"Um. Nice meeting you." Nick said.

His mother then ushered him away.

Abigale Rutherford sat in the shade of one of the magnificent oak trees with Maggie Harris and Faye Young. All were long-time friends of Josephine's. They all wore elegant sundresses. Maggie was the only one who wore a hat. They sat at one of the linen-covered tables set up by the caterer. The three women laughed and gossiped, each with a glass of wine. Nicholas approached in a well-tailored suit with Josephine on his arm.

"There he is," Maggie said.

"Indeed," Abigale said.

"He looks so handsome in his suit. He's going to make all the girls at Hale swoon," Faye said.

"He's making one swoon now," Abigale said.

Abigale batted her hand near her face. The three women laughed.

"And he's my son. God help me," Josephine said.

Her shoulders slumped. They all laughed except Nick, who smirked.

Faye stepped forward and hugged him.

"Congratulations Nicholas."

Maggie followed. She held the top of her sunhat when she gave him a hug to congratulate him. Last, Abigale gave him a hug. She pressed her body into his and whispered in his ear, "Congratulations Nicky," then gave him a kiss on the cheek. She used her thumb to wipe away the lipstick she left there.

"Don't want your girlfriend to be jealous."

Josephine put her hand on her hip and raised her eyebrows.

"Which brings us to the big question. Who *are* you dating now—Autumn?"

"No one mom. Autumn is just a—"

"Ooh. Nick knows what he's doing. Why have a girlfriend? He's all grown up and ready to play."

Abigale crossed her arms, which made her cleavage more pronounced. She then gave him a mischievous smile. He grinned and glanced at the other women, but when his eyes returned, his gaze lowered. A sudden astonished burst of laughter passed her lips in a gasp. It thrilled her to have his eyes on her. It was like jumping into a pool naked. Josephine shook her head.

"Nick, let's go greet the rest of your guests and leave these three to their wine and gossip."

As Abigale watched them walk toward the white catering tent, her mischievous smile returned.

"Mm. Looks good coming and going."

"Oh, stop teasing him like that. You should be ashamed," Faye said.

"I was just doing what you were thinking."

Both women laughed. Maggie crossed her arms and shook her head.

"Oh c'mon, you know I love some innocent flirting," Abigale said.

"Yeah, a little too much. You don't want to encourage him," Maggie said.

Abigale squared and rocked her shoulders.

"Don't I?"

Faye and Abigale laughed. Maggie shook her head, but then laughed along with them.

Nick and his mother met the Reynolds on the way to the catering tent. After hearing stories of his life, told over and over, he needed a drink.

"Hello Josephine, and congratulations Nicholas. We're so proud of you," Lloyd Reynolds said.

His wife, Helen, nodded in agreement. She took Josephine's hands and gave her a proud, heartfelt look. Nick smiled at the both of them. Lloyd and Helen had to be in their seventies. Lloyd should retire, and he and Helen should enjoy their lives instead of him holding on at Hale. Nick snorted. He smirked until Lloyd grasped his hand in an iron grip and shook it with gusto.

"Son, you're going to be great. I can't wait to see you at Hale."

He patted Nick on the shoulder.

"Josephine, thank you for having us, but Helen and I have to run."

They thanked the Reynolds for coming.

"I'm going to get something to eat," Nick said.

"Sure son, go on. You must be starving."

He could eat, but a glass of champagne, a beer, practically anything with alcohol, would suit him right about now.

He entered the tent. At the far end was a minibar, and down the long side were four end-to-end tables of food. He decided the bar would be his first stop, then he saw her. Elizabeth fixed herself a salad and looked up and down the tables at all the food. She wore thin strappy tan heeled sandals with red soles, as if to suggest that danger lurked ahead. His gaze followed her bare heels up the backs of her legs. Her calves had a fit curve that gave them a full mature shape. His gaze stopped at the hem of her dress.

"She's something, isn't she?"

"What?"

He turned and his father stood at his side with a half filled brandy glass.

"Have you heard from Colette?"

"Um, no."

"Maybe you should call her."

"All right. If she doesn't call tonight, I'll call her."

His father took a long drink, then held the empty brandy glass at his side.

"Get something to eat, son."

He watched his father head off toward the bar. When he looked back at Elizabeth, she held a grape between her fingers and a plate of food in her other hand. He watched her slip the grape into her mouth, then their eyes met for the first time without her sunglasses. Her eyes were like crystal blue diamonds.

Nick went to the catering table where Elizabeth stood.

"Ms. Bach, nice to see you again."

"Hello Nicholas."

"Please call me Nick. My friends do."

"You can call me Elizabeth. Although, it might not be a good idea around your father."

He rolled his eyes.

"What about the people close to you? Do they call you Elizabeth?"

Storm clouds formed and darkened the deep blue sea in her eyes.

"I suppose you would have to be one to know."

He received a swat on the back and a pat on his shoulder. His friends Blake and Peter appeared at his side.

"There's the man of the hour. Are you done pressing the flesh?" Peter said.

"Yeah, we want to get out of here so we can celebrate properly," Blake said.

Blake stood on one side of Nick and Peter on the other. They put their arms around his shoulders, looked at Elizabeth, and grinned. Her eyebrow rose as she eyed both of his friends.

Before he could make introductions, a voice shouted behind them.

"Yeah Nick! What do you say we get out of here?"

Derek had his arms around Autumn and Sandy. Their eyes were glassy. His jacket was unbuttoned over his polo shirt. Both wrinkled, but at least dry. He now wore familiar looking swim trunks and sandals he must have found in the pool house. Nick had worn the trunks before, but only for a moment before Autumn stripped him of them. The sandals extended past Derek's heels. Nick smiled and snorted. The casual sundresses the two girls wore made it difficult to tell if there was anything out of place. They could have been fucking around. Derek and Sandy. Derek and Autumn. Maybe all three of them, the way he bragged about having threesomes. Autumn gazed at Nick, her expression stoic, while Sandy grinned.

Nick turned to Elizabeth and shrugged.

"Ms. Bach—"

Her first name he would keep for himself.

"These are my friends."

"This is Blake and Peter, and that's Sandy, Derek, and Autumn."

Derek removed his arm from Sandy's shoulder to take a bow.

"Everyone, this is Ms. Bach. Her company partners with Hale."

Derek snickered. Nick gave him a serious, not-now glare. Elizabeth gave the group a polite smile.

"Nice to meet you all. Nicholas, you have beautiful friends. I hope you all enjoy your evening, and again congratulations."

They watched her walk to the bar, where she got a bottle of mineral water.

"Damn, she's fine," Blake said.

"I *bet* she could teach you some things, and I'm ready to learn," Peter said.

"Seriously?" Sandy said.

Peter jolted, as if he forgot that Sandy and Autumn were behind him.

Nick blurted, "Shut up," then regretted it.

"C'mon Nick. I know you think she's beautiful," Blake said.

"Yeah, okay, but you guys don't have to be rude."

"Someone's got a crush," Sandy said.

Autumn said nothing. Her eyebrows drew in and her face reddened.

"Are you boys going to chase older women now?" Sandy asked.

"You know what they say, 'Aged like a fine wine.'," Peter said.

Blake squeezed Nick's shoulder.

"C'mon, let's get out of here."

Nick and Blake stood at the bar of Chasers, one of Atlanta's popular nightclubs packed with a younger twenty-something crowd. Green and blue neon lights painted the ceiling, while spotlights swept over the crowded dance floor. With little room to move, many of the patrons pumped their hands above their heads to the thudding pulse of music. Blake leaned close so they could talk.

"When do you start at Hale?"

"In a couple of weeks."

"Still not excited?"

"You know the story. It's always been my father's dream for me to work alongside him and eventually run the company when he retires. I'm not sure that's what I want. Everyone keeps telling me I'm nuts."

"Yeah, you're nuts."

"Thanks."

"Dude, you haven't even given it a chance."

"Sure, but I've seen all the pressure my father's under. Not sure I want all that stress."

"Well, you've got two weeks to think about it. Don't let it spoil your night. Look at all these hot girls. Remember when we first came here as freshmen? The women were older. They ate us alive. Now it's our turn."

Nick half chuckled. Three girls approached them and asked if they wanted to dance. Two wore short skirts, one had on tight leggings, and they all had on low-cut tops. They looked like they could be college girls—sophomores, maybe even freshmen.

"Sure."

Nick followed the girl with dark brown hair and blonde highlights. She glanced back often and smiled at him. He smiled back. The girl was shorter than Autumn, less busty, but with an equally athletic body. When he spotted Autumn and Derek dancing, he took the girl's hand and directed them away to the edge of the crowd. Blake and the other two girls melted into the pulsating mob. While they danced, Nick scanned the crowd for his friends, but the spotlights made it too difficult to see. The girl kept her eyes on him and seemed unconcerned about where her friends went. She pushed her body into his as they danced. When the song ended, they clapped, but before either could speak, the next song blasted through the speakers and recharged the crowd. After the fourth song, he was ready to call it a night. His friends, of course, would think he was ill. It was only eleven-thirty. He was ready to slip away and figured he would catch up with them tomorrow. Then the girl leaned into him.

"Want to come over to my place?"

The girl tugged all six feet of him until they stumbled inside her apartment. They kissed on the elevator ride up and along the corridor to her place. He still had a buzz from the drinks at the club, and suspected she did as well, the way she giggled and moved her arms in a theatrical manner. She rushed to unbutton his shirt as they moved through the kitchen to the bedroom. A Georgia State sweatshirt hung over one of the dining room chairs. There were two bedrooms. The door to the first room they passed was half open. It was dark inside, but visible enough to see a landscape of clothes scattered on the floor. Nick tried to recall the faces of her friends. The girl yanked at his shirt.

"Whoa, easy! Slow down."

She unbuckled and unzipped his pants, which fell to the floor. He let her manhandle him, the best she could for someone much shorter. She shoved him, and he toppled back onto the bed. Then she slipped out of her short leather skirt and panties that had PINK printed in block letters around the waistband. She unwrapped a condom and tossed it on the sheets next to him, then she straddled him and ground her pussy against his waking cock. They kissed with open mouths. Her tongue scrapped his teeth, and he tasted her with his. He grew rigid and felt her wetness as she forced what little weight she had down on him. She found the condom on the bed and slipped it over him. After some fumbling, she positioned the tip of his cock inside her. He held her hips and thrust into her. She gasped and dug her nails into his chest. Her moans and cries rose in volume as their bodies collided. She rode him hard, as if to test the elasticity of the condom. He shot into her and held her hips to still her.

She rolled off—no cuddle session, no kissing—then threw on a t-shirt and some pajama bottoms, and left the room. He got up and stumbled to find the bathroom. After he dressed, he found her in the kitchen. The kitchen smelled of fried grease, and there were dirty dishes in the sink. The girl stood at the counter and scribbled in a notebook, then tore out a page.

"That was fun. Call me sometime."

He squinted beneath the bright kitchen light. She folded the paper and handed it to him.

"Yeah, sure."

She walked him to the door, then stood on her tiptoes and gave him a conciliatory peck on the lips. She almost hit him with the door as he stepped out into the hallway. Her muted yet excited voice, followed by laughter, came from behind the door. He took the paper from his pocket. She wrote her name, Kelly, no last name, along with her phone number. He shook his head, straightened his shirt, and tucked it in. There was a text from Blake.

"How'd you make out?"

He shook his head, smiled, and texted Blake.

"Catch up with you tomorrow. I need sleep."

When he got to the street, he crumpled and tossed the paper with Kelly's phone number into the trashcan. He then lumbered to his car and headed home to his parents' house.

2

Nick lie in bed transfixed on the ceiling light fixture. The late morning sun cast bands of light through the open blinds. He forgot to close them when he got home late after leaving the girl from the club. He shifted his leg and knocked a football to the floor. It made a flat thud when it hit the carpet. He scowled, wrinkled his lips, then glanced over the edge of the mattress. His father would have chided him to focus and stop messing around.

What a crazy night. In his early college days, banging that chick would have been the highlight of his evening. Kelly, that was her name. He doubted she remembered his and was unsure if he even gave it. It seemed like there was some bet between her and her friends. He slept with some sorority sisters before and this ranked up there. God only knows what happened to Blake and the other two girls, friends of—Kelly. God help him. He shook his head and chuckled.

He finally got out of bed. His pants, shirt, and socks lie pooled on the floor. He picked up the football and tossed it in the air, then caught it with the same hand. As he gazed out the window, he continued to toss the ball. Almost noon. The world was moving on without him. He hummed, then finally pitched the football onto the bed, went to his desk, and opened his laptop.

He typed Nexgen Biosolutions in the search field, and found the link to the corporate website, then clicked the link for the Atlanta office. The page only listed the profiles for the c-level executives and board members. A couple of faces looked familiar. Maybe they were at one of his father's business dinners. If Elizabeth were there, he would have remembered her. After he scrolled past the profiles and reached the bottom of the webpage, he smirked. He tapped the number on his phone listed at the bottom of the website. When it rang, he stood and sauntered to the dresser.

"Ms. Elizabeth Bach please."

He put the call on speakerphone and stood in front of the mirror that spanned the dresser.

"May I ask who's calling, please?"

"Mr. Nicholas Evers from Hale Biotech."

"Thank you, please hold."

He grabbed the tie he wore for his graduation party, now wrinkled and creased. It hung from the mirror's wooden frame, its knot still made. He slipped it over his head, and it hung down his bare chest to his briefs.

"Good morning, Ms. Bach's office."

"Hello. This is Mr. Nicholas Evers at Hale Biotech."

"I'm sorry, Mr. Evers. Ms. Bach is out of the office at the moment. Would you like to leave a message?"

He stared at his reflection.

"No message. I'm actually calling to schedule a lunch with Ms. Bach. Is she available this week?"

He took his dark, wayfarer sunglasses from atop his dresser and put them on. He then raised his chin and adjusted the knot on his tie.

"The only available day she has for lunch would be tomorrow at one."

Nick smiled at his sunglass-darkened reflection.

"Can you please pencil me in for a lunch meeting at Il Fasto? No need to call me back. I will be at the restaurant for an earlier meeting."

"Certainly Mr. Evers."

After he ended the call, He slipped off his briefs and kicked them so they landed on top of last night's clothes. He checked his look in the mirror, pushed his sunglasses up the bridge of his nose, and swayed his hips and shoulders from side to side. His cock and neck tie swung in unison. He slipped the necktie off and spun it over his head like a stripper and let it fly, then he slipped some swim trunks on and headed downstairs.

Women's voices and laughter from the patio filtered in through the open kitchen windows. Nick poured a small glass of orange juice and swallowed it in a single gulp. As he rinsed the glass in the sink, he smiled at the rich, mature, and confident tone of the women's voices. He strutted out the door to the patio in his swim trunks and dark wayfarer sunglasses, ready to shake things up.

Out on the patio, his mother and her friends Abigale, Maggie, and Faye sat at the table under the shade of the canopy sail. Glasses of ice tea sat on the table in front of them. Their conversation, followed by fits of laughter, told him they had been gossiping. Nothing new. The laughter and volume of their outbursts determined how juicy the gossip. He strolled up behind them.

His mother and Maggie wore modest knit cover-ups over their one-piece swimsuits. Abigale and Faye wore revealing mesh cover-ups draped down their arms with their shoulders exposed. Both Abigale and Faye also wore bikinis and heels, as if they were contestants in some beauty contest. Abigale in pink mules, and Faye in gold strappy sandals. Their laughter subsided when they saw him.

"Oh, hello Nicholas."

His mother wore her caught-in-the-act smile. He grinned and strutted over to where the women sat, then stood next to Abigale, and put his hand on the back of her chair. Abigale peered up, bit her bottom lip and smiled, but said nothing.

"Hi Nick," Faye said.

"Hello Nicholas," Maggie said.

Nick smiled at Faye and Maggie.

"Hello ladies."

"Did you have a pleasant night out?" Josephine asked.

"You know he did," Faye said.

Faye's smile broadened.

"Yeah, it was okay. We had drinks and danced."

"Oh, I miss dancing. Rodger never wants to take me anymore. He's always *tired*," Maggie said.

Maggie wrinkled her face. The other women laughed.

Behind his dark sunglasses, his eyes wandered over the bodies of Faye Young and Abigale Rutherford. Both women were in their early forties, fit, and were two of his mother's younger friends. Maggie Harris was his mother's closest friend. She was in her mid-fifties. Josephine was forty-eight. They celebrated her birthday almost two months ago.

"Well," he sighed, "I'm going to go for a swim and enjoy life before my father chains me to a desk."

They chuckled and smiled at him.

"Better enjoy the pool. Your father has to have it drained this month to fix something," Josephine said.

She waved her hand in the air as if it was no concern of hers.

"Why can't he wait until the end of summer?"

"You know your father—when he's got something on his mind, he doesn't let up."

He felt Abigale touch his lower back, then she slid her hand around his waist.

"Oh Nick, don't despair, you can come and swim at my house," Abigale said.

He crossed his arms.

"Thank you. I might just do that."

"I'm sure the pool won't be out of commission that long," Josephine said.

"Great. I better dive in before they drain it."

Josephine cocked her head and wrinkled her lips. He raised his eyebrows and sauntered away. He still heard them talking.

"Abby, don't encourage him," Josephine said.

"You know Henry never uses the pool. He even seldom sits out on the patio."

"And Henry is often away on business trips."

Nick glanced back. Abigale wrinkled her face and waved her hand dismissively at Josephine, as if his mother made too much of a fuss. Nick sat and splashed his feet at the edge of the pool to test the temperature. Sunlight shimmered off the waves he created.

Nick sat with his friends at the Brick Lane Tavern, a favorite hangout for the group. Two empty beer pitchers sat on the table, along with three plates of appetizers. They picked at the remains of the sweet potato nachos, crispy wonton mozzarella sticks, and bacon-wrapped onion rings. Their glasses of beer sat at various degrees of near empty.

"So, what's on Young Master Nick Evers' agenda for tomorrow? Since he has to make the most of his last days of freedom?" Sandy asked.

She grinned at him from across the table. Her large doe eyes were the most obvious beauty trait she inherited from her mother, Faye.

"I have a business lunch meeting."

"Ooh," Autumn said.

Autumn leaned into the table and drew her long blonde hair over her shoulder and twirled the ends.

"I thought your dad wasn't expecting you to work until you got back from Italy," Sandy said.

"He wants me to hit the ground running."

"Downright contemptuous," Derek said.

Peter chuckled between sips of beer.

"No, it's cool."

"Sounds like you're coming around. Has old Dr. Richard Evers finally gotten to you?" Blake asked.

Nick lowered his gaze as if he were contemplating an item that sat on the table. His eyebrows rose and his lips tightened.

"He has been pretty insistent."

"I'll say. I figured you would have another year or two to decide if Hale was the right place for you."

"Me too, but that's not the case. Maybe I'll stay in Italy and he can wait for the government to extradite me."

They all laughed, except Nick, who gazed at his beer glass. The once foamy head now flat.

"At least Nick can look forward to seeing the woman who came to his party. The one he couldn't take his eyes off of," Sandy said.

She grinned at Nick. Blake sat back in his seat with a euphoric look on his face.

"Ah, Ms. Bach," Blake said.

"Not sure about Nick, but she left an impression on my mind and other places. I think I'm still hard," Derek said.

Derek put his hands between his clenched legs and pursed his lips. Nick shook his head.

"She's pretty, but too old for Nick," Autumn said, "right Nick?"

Autumn smiled, but her eyes told him she really wanted to know what he thought.

Blake sat to his right and Peter to his left, which shielded him from any desperate affections she may have employed.

"You're all being ridiculous. I doubt I'll be dealing with any outside account reps. That would be my father or one of his senior people."

"I wonder if your dad's boning her." Derek said.

Nick's eyes narrowed.

"Easy."

Derek raised his open hands in a gesture of surrender.

"No disrespect to Mrs. Evers, but if I were your father, I don't know… just saying."

Nick glared at Derek. Derek again held up his hands.

Sandy wrinkled her lips and punched Derek in the shoulder.

"Ouch."

"You better miss us when you're away," Autumn said.

He knew she only meant her.

"He will—he will," Blake said.

He nudged Nick.

"Sure," Nick said.

"I hope you have fun in Italy," Autumn said.

Nick sighed.

"Me too, but I'll be staying with my parents' friend's family. It was fun when I was younger. We went skiing and toured the city. Of course, now knowing my father, he'll want Mr. Torino to show me his office and meet his colleagues, not that I'll be doing business there."

"What about their son, Lorenzo? He's around your age, right?" Derek asked.

"Same age."

"I'm sure he knows some clubs and bars where you can pick up some hot Italian girls."

"It's Milan! You know, the city where all the super models work and play. If he can't have a great time there, then I don't know what to say," Peter said.

Nick cocked his head and looked at Peter.

"Sure, I'll just pull out my party invite."

Peter smirked.

"Did you RSVP?"

Nick chuckled, then wrinkled his face at Peter.

Both Autumn and Sandy sat silent, but glared at Peter. Autumn adjusted the bracelets on her wrists and crossed her arms.

"If you want to have a great time, take me with you."

Peter and Blake picked at the remaining sweet potato nachos. They, along with Derek, ignored Autumn's proposal, while Sandy stared at Nick and waited for his reaction.

When he said nothing, Peter jumped in.

"Well, you know, Derek and I would love to go with you and hang out, but no can do bro, *got to work*,"

He smiled at Peter.

"Thanks guys, it's fine. I'll be back before you know it."

He avoided looking at Autumn.

"That's right. Back in no time," Blake said.

"Wow Nick, don't get too excited. Your father can send me instead," Derek said.

They all laughed. Autumn was quiet. Two servers brought their entrees to the table. One took the empty pitchers and appetizer plates.

"Would you like a couple more pitchers?" One server asked.

"Yes," the young men said in unison.

When the server returned, the group filled their glasses, then Blake raised his glass.

"To our dearest friend Nicholas Evers. May he not expatriate to Italy."

"Hear! Hear!" Peter said.

Autumn raised her glass, but only offered a weary smile.

"To Nick," the others said.

Nick raised his glass. They cheered and drank.

Elizabeth parked her car and strutted down the sidewalk to Il Fasto. She had dined there before for both work and pleasure. Il Fasto, a Michelin Star Italian restaurant, a jewel of Atlanta. A good pick Mr. Evers. She smiled as she walked under the covered entrance and went inside.

She stood out of view of the dining room to avoid being spotted. Today she wore a comfortable Veronica Beard jacket and wide-leg pants, with a white and gray striped blouse unbuttoned low but above her cleavage. It was an outfit of serious persuasion, rather than sexy persuasion. Usually she knew the potential client, but in this case, she opted for a serious look. Besides, he had already seen her legs. Another showing might give the young man the wrong impression.

"Welcome to Il Fasto," the hostess said.

"The reservation should be under Evers or Hale."

Everyone who she had lunch with from Hale Biotech made the reservation under Hale, except for Richard, who always put it under Evers.

"I'm sorry, there is no reservation under Evers or Hale."

She cocked her head and smirked.

"Can you please check for Nick or Nicholas?"

"Ah, yes. Here it is."

She raised an eyebrow. The hostess was about to lead her into the dining room when she stopped her.

"Could you do me a favor? Could you please check to see if my party is already here?"

"Certainly."

Again she stopped her.

"He should be a young man in his twenties, tall, dashing, with dark brown hair, sitting alone. Please don't signal or say anything to him."

"Tall, dark, and handsome, in his twenties, and sitting alone."

The hostess' eyes widened. She grinned, then disappeared into the dining room. Elizabeth sighed and glanced several times outside the glass doors. Her wristwatch told her she was on time for whatever this was. The hostess returned.

"Yes, he's there sitting by the window. Shall I take you to him?"

"No, let him sit there—alone."

The hostess raised her eyebrows.

"Oh—can I—"

Elizabeth held up her hand to silence her and then she peeked into the dining room and spotted Nick by the window. He wore a well fitted dark gray suit, white shirt, and a slender deep-teal colored tie. He peered out at the street—presumably watching for her. Her lips curled into a soft smirk. She strolled past the bar and down the narrow hallway that was clad in lacquered ash wood panels to the ladies' bathroom.

At the marble vanity, she touched up her lipstick and fussed with her hair. Two younger women entered. She stepped away from the mirror and pretended to read something on her phone. Neither woman used the bathroom, instead they stood in front of the mirror. They were slender, with long legs. Their elegant printed dresses ended above their knees, and were not indicative of office attire. They withdrew makeup pouches from Chanel and Bottega Veneta handbags. One powdered her nose, the other touched up her lipstick.

"Did you see that guy sitting by the window?"

The young woman's eyes widened.

"Yes, *he's cute.*"

The other young woman's eyes widened, and they both looked like excited school girls. Elizabeth raised an eyebrow.

"He was sitting all by himself. How sad."

The other woman, who freshened her lipstick, pursed her lips into a pout.

"I bet I could cheer him up."

"Should we ask him to join us for lunch?"

Elizabeth rolled her eyes and snorted. She caught the glare of one woman in their reflection. She held up her phone, as if she had been texting someone, and shrugged.

"Sorry, drama."

She stepped out into the narrow hallway and called her assistant Jenna.

"Hey, did you take down Mr. Nicholas Evers' number? Yeah, I know you mentioned he didn't give you a return number. Did it show up on the caller ID? Ok, great. Can you do me a favor and call him to let him know I'm running a bit late? Great, thanks."

She stepped to the end of the narrow hallway and peeked around the corner. She watched him stare out through the tall windows that rose to the ceiling. How sad he looked sitting there all by himself. She suppressed a chuckle at the woman's remark. The bathroom door opened with chatter and laughter, and the two women emerged. Although they maneuvered around her, they seemed oblivious that she was there. She turned her attention back to him. His gaze went to the front of the restaurant, then back outside the windows. The corners of her lips curled into a smile, then her mouth opened and her eyes widened. The two women appeared at his table.

He turned his attention from the window to the two women. His lost puppy dog expression vanished, and he grinned. Perhaps she *can* cheer him up. He motioned with his hands as if to explain something and then examined his watch. Both women turned to one another and smiled. One gestured, probably to her table. He held up his hand as if to ask for a moment, then took his phone from inside his jacket breast pocket. It was a brief conversation. When he ended the call, a serious expression fell over his face, then a brief smile appeared. It was a look of hope.

He slipped his phone back into his jacket. Elizabeth watched with interest. Now for the big question. Will he invite these young, attractive women to sit with him? If he does, would he expect me to join his little business lunch harem? She watched him as he spoke to them. The two women nodded and smiled at him, then returned to their table. She straightened her jacket and walked out into the dining room. She stepped, chin up, with poised strides to his table. He straightened in his seat when he saw her and stood when she arrived.

"Mr. Evers."

Her tone was warm, but all business. He smiled.

"Ms. Bach."

They shared a brief, polite handshake. The two sat simultaneously, like two equally matched gunfighters. He was the first to crack. His shoulders softened.

"It's nice to see you again, Elizabeth."

"Nice to see you as well, Nick Evers. Did you enjoy your graduation party?"

"Yeah, it was good. I enjoyed my time with my friends and met some friends of my father's. Hopefully, I'll establish some new and fruitful business relationships."

She glanced around the restaurant to see if she recognized anyone. Il Fasto was busy at this hour. Patrons filled all the white linen-covered tables. She was relieved not to find any familiar faces. She gazed at the back of the restaurant to where the two young women sat. Both women looked over at them. She made eye contact with them and curled her lips into a devilish smile. The two women turned their attention away. She then returned her full attention to him.

"Is that what this is? Are we establishing a fruitful business relationship?"

He looked down and rubbed the back of his neck before he returned to meet her gaze.

"I hope so."

"It doesn't seem you're quite ready for the job."

"Huh?"

His lips parted.

"I checked with your company. Apparently, you're not on the payroll. Is your father having second thoughts?"

"I'm on the payroll."

"Are you going to offer me your business card?"

He patted his jacket.

"Ah? I must be all out."

"You sure are."

His eyes widened and lips parted. When she laughed, he looked as though he could breathe again.

"Wow, you're tough."

"You have no idea."

"Can we forget about business, and just get to know each other?"

She raised an eyebrow.

"As professionals?"

"As people."

Her lips formed a tight-lipped smile. She considered, at the very least, his pedigree: the son of Dr. Richard Evers, the founder of Hale Biotech. But he's young and cocky. A glimpse into his green eyes and she wanted to get lost there. Her eyes traced his lips. She wondered if he knew how to use them, and not just for kissing. He dressed and carried himself well. But it could all be a façade. She remembered what her mother said about all window-dressing and nobody home. But her mother also told her to *play nice*.

"Sure, that would be wonderful."

She cringed inside at the tone of her own voice. His eyes brightened.

"Great."

Elizabeth maintained a tight-lipped smile.

"Your father said that you're going to Europe before formally joining Hale."

"Yes, my family has old friends in Milan. I haven't seen them for almost ten years. They have a son, Lorenzo, who's my age."

"Sounds fantastic."

"Depends if they'll be in the city. They have a country home, which is—beautiful, relaxing, and extremely boring."

Elizabeth chuckled.

"Isn't that what country homes are for?"

"I suppose. Do you travel much?"

"Yes. Actually, I'll be traveling soon."

"Oh? Where to?"

"Spain. For business, mostly. There was an opportunity to go, so I volunteered."

"Mostly?"

"I have some old friends in Madrid. Like you, I haven't seen them in some time. You can't have all work and no play."

He inhaled as if he were taking in the scent of a flower. His gaze wandered out the window.

"I've never been to Spain."

"You should go sometime. It's beautiful."

His eyes moved as if his gaze travelled down the street and then back before he returned to meet hers.

The waiter appeared. They skipped the starters and ordered drinks and their entrees. When the food arrived, the two younger women passed their table. They said nothing, only smiled at Nick. Elizabeth bet they would have lunch at Il Fasto often over the next two weeks to see if he was here alone. She hoped their asses grew fat. When he looked over at her, he had a curious expression.

"Do you know those two women?"

"No."

Her phone rang.

"Hi Jenna. Okay, yes. Please tell them I'll be there in fifteen minutes. Thank you."

She ended the call and put her phone in her handbag.

"I'm sorry Nick. I have to run. Something's come up at work."

She flagged the waiter, and he came to box her salad.

"Can I see you again?"

"Professionally?"

He said nothing. Instead, his lips bowed into a smile that she found difficult to resist. She opened her handbag.

"Sure, here's my card. My cellphone number is on there as well if you need to reach me directly."

Nick sat at the desk in his bedroom. He scanned some travel websites for Spain on his laptop. Where would Elizabeth stay in Madrid? On most of his father's trips, he recalled him mentioning that business meetings took place in hotel conference rooms close to the airport. Although, if the company he was meeting with was nearby, they would meet at their offices. He shook his head. It was anyone's guess. If he can get Blake on board to accompany him, then it might be easier to sell to his father. His father will be upset that he's not going to Italy, but oh well. He scrolled through a list of hotels. There's no way he could convince Blake to stay near the airport. So where then? This whole thing might fail from the start. Better call Blake and see what he thinks.

He called Blake on his cellphone, but got his voicemail. It was the one he had since he started his graduate studies at NYU. A girl's moans of ecstasy filled his ear, then Blake's voice said, "Kind of busy right now. Leave a message."

His mother must be proud. Nick huffed and rolled his eyes. He smiled as the thought struck him. Maybe he was growing up.

"Hey Blake. I need to ask you something. Call me back."

He ended the call and went back to his search for a hotel. Here's one overlooking the Neptune Fountain or Fuente de Neptuno, close to the Museo Nacional del Prado. Nick spoke the Spanish words aloud, slow and clumsy. Sure, he heard of the Prado, with its famous works of art. He retrieved Elizabeth's business card from his wallet and called her office number. When her assistant answered, he fought the urge to hang up.

"Hello. This is Mr. Nicholas Evers calling. Ms. Bach mentioned she will be away on a business trip and would return near the end of the month. Could you tell me which day she'll be returning? Great, you've been very helpful. Thank you. No—no message. Thank you, and you as well."

He ended the call and entered the dates on the hotel reservation page, then booked two rooms. His cellphone rang.

"Blake, your timing is impeccable."

He put Blake's call on speakerphone, then picked up his football from the floor.

"Oh, yeah? What's up?"

He tossed the football over his head and caught it.

"I've decided not to go to Italy."

"Great, so you can hang out with the gang."

"No. I'm going to Spain instead. Madrid, to be exact."

"Huh?"

"Yeah, change of plans, and I'm inviting you to come with me."

"Really?"

"Yes. Were you asleep or something?"

"No."

"Well, how does that sound?"

"Awesome, but why Spain? Neither of us speak Spanish."

"I figure if I'm going to get away for a week, I would like to go someplace I've never been, and someplace where my father doesn't have anyone to keep tabs on me."

"Sounds adventurous."

"So are you in?"

"I'm in. We maybe in luck. I have a friend who lives in Madrid. His name is Juan Miguel. He went to NYU Stern for a year on their exchange program. I'll call him. Maybe he can hang out with us."

"Cool."

"I'll call you later."

"Later."

3

Behind a broad modern desk in his study, Dr. Richard Evers sat arms crossed and stone-faced. Nick lie stretched out on the tan leather sofa that was against the opposite wall. He gazed at the ceiling like someone waiting for the needle of a tetanus shot to enter his arm. Two settees in the same fashion flanked both ends of the sofa to surround a large square onyx coffee table. It was as though his son hid behind the fortress of furniture.

Richard released a deep sigh.

"Help me understand this sudden revelation. The Torinos are expecting you. Lorenzo was looking forward to spending time with you in Milan. Like you, he's a recent graduate, and he's working as an economist. I suggested to his father that perhaps you two could visit Lorenzo's office and meet some of his friends and colleagues."

Nick said nothing and stared at the ceiling.

"Son, this is how you build relationships. Who knows where Lorenzo's career may take him. These connections, especially with international corporations, can help you both to establish future partnerships. Friendships can mean more if you can benefit from one another."

Nick huffed.

"I thought you understood that concept at this point."

"Doesn't that bother you—to weigh the importance of a friendship based on what someone can do for you?"

"That's life Nicholas. There will be friends that only take from you. Sometimes they take so much that by the time you've realized who they really are, they've already taken advantage of you. They can make you lose trust in yourself."

Nick got up and sat in the middle of the sofa. He met his father's gaze.

"You know Lorenzo. You know his family. They are good people. He may have taken time off work for you. Please consider other people's sacrifices."

Nick rested his elbows on his knees and knit his fingers together. His gaze fell.

"I'm sorry, but I've decided. This time, I want to go to a place of my choosing. It's only for a week. I don't see why it has to be such a big deal."

"Madrid? Why, Spain? Do you know someone there? Someone from school? Is it a girl?"

He glared at Nick, but when Nick kept his gaze lowered, his tension eased.

"So this plan of yours… You say Blake's going with you?"

"Yes, that's right. Blake spoke to his friend who lives in Madrid, and he's going to hang out with us."

"How does he know this fellow?"

"NYU."

"I hope he's not a film student."

Nick half chuckled.

"No. He—Juan Miguel—studied at Stern with Blake."

Richard's shoulders softened. He uncrossed his arms and rested them on the armrests. The tips of his fingers touched the edge of his desk, and he turned his gaze from Nick to look at the shapes of sunlight on the wall.

"Okay."

When he returned his attention to his son, Nick looked up at him. It was the same hopeful expression Nick had when he was little and Richard let his boy have his way. He, in part, wanted to see the outcome of his son's choices, then and now.

"I'll explain to Raphael and Sofia that you won't be coming. I would hope that you would call Lorenzo and extend your gratitude and interest in getting together with him in the future. Extend an invitation for him to stay with us sometime."

"I will. Thank you."

In a room on the hotel's top floor, a panel of sunlight came through the window, stretched across the floor and over the end of one of the two queen-sized beds. One bed remained neatly made, while the other lie stripped bare of all but the mattress cover and pillows. The duvet, blanket, and top sheet lie on the floor in the company of two pairs of jeans, a bra, briefs, panties, t-shirts, and sneakers. The mattress bounced and flexed as its two occupants moved on top of it.

"Oh! Fuck me!"

Autumn threw back her head. Her blonde curls flew and cascaded down her back. Her cries were loud enough for anyone in the adjoining rooms or hallway to hear. Nick held her narrow waist and took her from behind. His hips crashed into her buttocks with each thrust. She clenched at the fitted sheet. The elastic corner came loose and exposed the mattress. She arched her back and lowered her chest to the mattress. He pulled her onto him with increased tempo.

"Oh-fuck, oh-fuck, I'm coming," she cried.

She climaxed, and her sex constricted. With his back arched, he plunged into her one last time. A low groan passed his lips and his body curled over hers. A surge and his warm release filled the condom. They separated. He tumbled on his back while she rolled on her side. She stroked his chest and ran her fingertips down his abdomen, then seized his cock. She stripped the condom from him, repositioned herself, then took him into her mouth. He gasped and grunted. She coaxed one last shot from him. His thick pearlescent stream wet her lips and his abdomen. She tossed the used condom on the floor.

"You know, you don't have to wear those. I'm still on the pill."

He released a soft moan as he lie there. She nestled her body against his body, rested her leg across his leg, and kissed his ribs. Her fingertips circled his nipples, then traced the muscular contours of his chest and abdomen.

"That was good. I need to go away more often."

He ran his fingertips up and down her spine.

"That's not funny. Things don't have to be like this. We could have so much more."

"I told you before, I'm not ready for any type of commitment."

"If we were officially dating, and you wanted to sleep with some other girl, I could look the other way."

He was silent. He rubbed his forehead, then his eyes, and rested his arm over his head.

"No. I wouldn't want that. That wouldn't be fair to you."

"Nick, you know I would do anything for you."

"I know."

"So?"

"I'm just not ready."

"What will you do when you're away?"

"Hang out with Blake and get some clarity on where my life is going."

"You better not fall in love with some Spanish girl."

He chuckled. She tilted her head up and looked at him.

"I'm serious."

He looked into her eyes, but was silent. She sighed.

"Never mind."

Autumn climbed out of bed and tottered to the bathroom. A soft jingle from her pee that hit the toilet water echoed through the open doorway. He closed his eyes as he listened. She returned, climbed on the bed, and straddled him. His head rested on the pillow with his hands tucked underneath. A soft hum passed his lips. She moved her hips and stroked his flaccid cock with her wet sex. When his erection returned, she unrolled a fresh condom over him.

The default ringtone played from Nick's phone on the nightstand. He rolled on his side in his bed and rubbed his eyes, and tried to blink them into focus. The caller ID read unknown and the location, Los Angeles. The ringtone started again. He grunted, then rolled on his stomach and tapped the screen.

"Hello? Oh—Hi Colette. No, it's not a bad time. You're up early. Out for a run. That's cool."

He rolled on his back, tapped the speakerphone button, and rested the phone on the mattress next to his pillow.

"Nick, I'm really sorry I didn't call you on the day of your graduation party. Anyway, congratulations, I'm super happy for you. Now life begins, right?"

"No worries. Thanks. How's things in Cali?"

"It's awesome. I can see myself living here after school. Don't tell my parents, especially my dad."

"Stop the presses. Sweet Georgia Peach Colette kicks the peach to the curb for a—what the hell do they grow out there? Lemons? Oranges?"

"Everything."

They both laughed.

"I have to say, *I do* miss my southern men. Guys here are nice, but different."

"Different like gay?"

"Stop. There are plenty of gay men in Georgia."

"So different as in—they don't want to go down on you?"

"Nick, stop! Well—maybe some aren't so eager for the beaver."

"That's right, you need a good southern man. Someone who loves to hunt and spend time in the bush."

Colette laughed.

"Like you?"

His eyebrows rose and his lips tightened.

"Oh my God, Nick Evers is struck speechless. Don't tell me you changed your ways and straightened up."

He laughed.

"My father would love that. I'm a bit of a hybrid at the moment. Trying to leave behind those spectacular college days, as my father would say, and attempt to act more *professional* and *responsible*."

"Forget about your father. Make yourself happy."

His eyebrows rose, and his lips curled into a smile. He rolled onto his side and glanced at his phone's lit screen.

"Did you get an LA number?"

"Oh, yeah—sorry."

She giggled. He grabbed his phone and added the number to Colette's contact information. Her LA number was now her default number.

"No—it's cool."

Years from now, if he got a new number, what would the location display on people's phones? Would it still be Atlanta, Georgia? There was something liberating about Colette's new LA phone number. He smiled when Colette's name appeared on the screen instead of presenting her as an unknown caller.

"You should come out sometime, to LA."

"Yeah?"

"Yeah. I've got one more year before my dad demands—probably more like begs—me to come back home."

"Your friends here miss you."

"Oh yeah? Which ones?"

"All of them."

"You?"

"Of course."

"Isn't it funny? We weren't close in high school, but now …"

"But now we're adults."

"How is everyone there? Does Sandy still have a crush on you? Is Autumn still chasing you?"

"First of all, Sandy *does not* have a crush on me. If she did, it is so subtle I would never know."

"And Autumn?"

"I see her around."

"Nick, don't be cruel."

He rolled on his back and took in the ceiling's blankness.

"What?"

"Are you still just using her for sex?"

"We have a good time."

"I'm sure you do."

"I can't help that she lusts after me."

Colette huffed.

"New subject. Now that you're finished with school, will you be working at Hale?"

"No, I'm going to run away to Spain."

"Seriously?"

"Seriously. Well, only for a week. I'm going to drag Blake along. He has a friend from college who lives in Madrid."

"So you're going with Blake to hang out with his friend who lives in Spain? Why Spain?"

"*No*. I'm visiting Spain, because I've always *wanted* to go to Spain, and I'm taking Blake with me. He has a friend in Madrid, so we have someone to show us the sights."

For a moment, only Colette's breathing came over the speaker.

"Okay. That's—interesting."

"What?"

"Nothing. I hope you have a wonderful time in Madrid. Will your father expect you at the office when you return?"

"You know him well."

They both sighed and chuckled.

"I'll be in Atlanta in a few weeks. Maybe we can get together."

"Yeah, that would be great."

"It's been a while, Nick Evers. It will be nice to see how you've grown."

"And you. Goodbye Colette."

"Bye, Nick."

He gazed at the ceiling and waited for Colette to end the call. When his phone screen went dark, he flipped it over on its face. If he told Colette about Elizabeth, would she understand?

Richard snorted at the smell of popcorn. He, his wife Josephine, and Blake's mother Tiffany, followed Nick and Blake down the airport's high ceiling corridor.

"Smells like a movie theater," Richard said.

Josephine and Tiffany said nothing and only smiled at him.

The trio trailed behind Nick and Blake. Both young men rolled their large suitcases to be checked, and each shouldered a smaller carry-on. They wore comfortable jeans, t-shirts, and sport coats, and chatted and laughed amongst themselves. Nick looked as excited as the time when he first went off to college at Georgia Tech before attending Columbia for his graduate studies. Richard smiled inside as he watched Nick. Nick and Blake went on ahead to check their bags. Richard waved at Nick and pointed down to let him know where they would wait for him and Blake.

"I'm so excited for Blake. He's never been to Spain. The only other country Samuel and I took him to was Australia. He was only eight then," Tiffany said.

Josephine smiled at her.

"It will be a wonderful trip for the both of them. I wish I could go," Josephine said.

Richard huffed.

"I'm sure Nick would love that."

Josephine swatted his arm. He turned to her with a smirk. Tiffany shook her head at him.

"Our son, or rather, both young men, needs to strike out on their own. It will be good for them," Richard said.

Josephine held up her cupped hand to hide her mouth from her husband, but he heard her.

"He doesn't really mean that."

Tiffany laughed.

"Ouch, that's not nice."

They all laughed.

"Blake tells me that Nick is inspired to visit Madrid. Does he have an interest in Spanish art or architecture?" Tiffany asked.

Richard had no clue what to say.

"Oh yes. Nick enjoys art. He's never been a creative type, at least not in the visual sense, but he enjoys art. Isn't that right Dear?" Josephine said.

"That's right. He enjoyed traipsing around the High Museum of Art when he was a child, and I imagine he's been to The Met, Guggenheim, and MoMA when he was in New York while attending Columbia for his MBA."

He struggled to recall any past mentions by Nick of *any* visits to *any* art museums in New York, yet he smiled at his wife and Tiffany.

"Does Blake enjoy art?" Josephine asked.

"No, I'm afraid not. That's why I was excited to hear about the trip. I'm hoping Nick's interests will rub off on him."

"I'm sure it will," Richard said.

Both women beamed. Nick and Blake returned.

"Blake and I are going to head over to the boarding area, so if you guys want to take off, you can," Nick said.

"We'll grab a drink and wait for your plane to take off," Richard said.

"I love you, dear. Have a safe flight, and call me when you've landed," Josephine said.

Both women hugged the boys, and Richard shook their hands.

"Son, I hope you have a great time, and—of course you already know—I hope to see you at the office when you return. You two have a safe flight."

Nick and Blake strolled off to the boarding area to wait.

"Ladies, how about we get that drink?"

Tiffany and Josephine sat at a pub table on tall bar stools. Outside the airport bar were floor to ceiling glass windows where one could watch the planes take off and land. Richard stood next to Josephine with his arm rested on the back of her chair. The three reminisced about when Nick and Blake were kids. They wondered how their sons would turn out as adults, and were still wondering. Now their boys were off on a new adventure.

Josephine sipped at a flavored sparkling water. When the trio first sat, she told Richard that she would drive them home.

"I'm going to get another beer," he said.

While he waited for the bartender, he glanced out into the concourse. A woman, who wheeled a suitcase behind her, caught his gaze. She wore plaid sneakers with Burberry written in large letters down the sides. Skinny jeans hugged her legs, while an oversized t-shirt with an unbuttoned plaid shirt hung from her shoulders. Her long hair was in a bun. He had never seen Elizabeth dressed in casual clothing, but he recognized her face and confident stride. He tugged at his collar to make sure it was straight, then returned to the table where Josephine and Tiffany sat. Both women were engaged in conversation. He put his fresh bottle of beer on the table and glimpsed over to where Elizabeth stood.

"I'm going to visit the men's room."

Both women continued to talk and laugh, so he sauntered out of the bar toward the men's room, on a path to intercept Elizabeth.

"Hello Elizabeth."

Elizabeth turned, startled at first, then looked reassured when she saw him.

"Oh, hello Richard."

"How are you? Off on a business trip?"

"Yes, I'm headed to Chicago, then off to Spain."

His eyebrows drew together.

"Oh? I mean, that sounds exciting. I didn't think Nexgen Biosolutions did business in Spain."

"Our sister company in Spain handles most of our European relationships. Some representatives here, with former contacts, get to travel for in-person meetings. It's rare that I get the opportunity, so I have to seize the chance when I can."

He nodded.

"What brings you here?"

"My son Nicholas—he's off to Spain as well—Madrid, to be exact. I'm not sure if he has some new found interest in Spanish art, maybe it's bullfighting, who the hell knows. It's hard keeping up with him. Anyway, he's traveling with his friend Blake, who you might have met at Nicholas' graduation party."

She nodded.

"Yes, I met Blake, along with some of his other friends. They are a colorful bunch."

Richard chuckled and smirked.

"I suppose I might describe them that way, as well."

He tilted his head, and his eyebrows drew together.

"Barcelona?"

"Sorry?"

"Will you be going to Barcelona? I thought most of the biotech companies are in Barcelona."

"No. I'll be going to Madrid."

"Oh."

"Sorry, I need to get going."

He glanced over at the bar. Josephine and Tiffany peered at him and Elizabeth.

"My wife and Blake's mother, Tiffany Simmons, are having a drink. I should get back."

"It was nice to see you, Richard."

"Have a safe flight, and hopefully you'll get a moment to enjoy Spain, if you're not in meetings the whole time. I know how that goes."

A text message notification came from her handbag. He gave her a smile and held up his hand in a gesture that he wished not to hold her up any longer. He then returned to the bar and to his wife, Josephine, and Tiffany. While the two women chatted, he glanced to where he left Elizabeth. She stood there with her eyes fixed on her cellphone. No doubt she was reading a text message or an email. He glanced back and forth with his attention split between her and the conversation between Josephine and Tiffany. When he returned his gaze to Elizabeth, she looked in his direction. There was a puzzled look on her face, then she turned and walked off.

"Richard?"

He turned to Josephine.

"Yes?"

"Haven't you been listening?"

"Ah?"

Josephine peered out to the concourse to where his attention had lingered. Her gaze followed Elizabeth as she walked away.

"Perhaps there is someone else that is better at holding your attention."

Tiffany was silent. She looked at Richard, then at Josephine, then turned her gaze to the parked planes outside the window. He said nothing.

"Was that the woman that came to Nick's graduation party? She doesn't work for Hale, does she?"

"Her name is Elizabeth. You met her."

"I know her name."

"She works for Nexgen Biosolutions, a company Hale does business with. And yes, she was at Nicholas' graduation party."

"Why?"

"I'm trying to get Nicholas to meet some people we do business with so he can build relationships of his own. Later, when he starts work, he'll already have some contacts and hopefully it will be less stressful for him."

Josephine wrinkled her lips.

"How thoughtful."

~

Elizabeth took her phone from her handbag. There was a batch of new email and several text messages. The most recent messages were from an unknown caller. The location, Atlanta, Georgia.

The message read, "I am waiting to board my flight to Madrid. This is a little crazy, I know, but I want to see you. Nick."

She stood in the middle of the concourse. After reading his message, she looked up toward the bar where Richard Evers went. He sat at a table with two women. Before she turned away, their eyes met. She walked away down the concourse, then tapped her phone to see the next message. It was from Jenna. She wrote to wish her a safe flight, and to contact her if she needed anything while she was away. She deleted Jenna's message and then looked at the last message. It was from Rafael Sanchez. She stopped and peered back, but the bar and Richard were no longer in sight.

Rafael wrote, "My dear Lizzy. I wish you a safe journey. I look forward very much to see you again."

She smiled.

"Me too."

She kept Rafael's message, and created a new contact for Nick, then she looked at the list of messages and the names who sent them. Nick was no longer an unknown. The corners of her lips curled up. She read his message again. When she looked up, she caught her reflection in one of the airport shop windows. There was a certain smile that had been missing for some time. Her eyes narrowed, and she shook her head, then walked on.

Nick stepped onto the balcony of his hotel room that overlooked the Fountain of Neptune. Beautiful flowers bordered the fountain, which sat at the center of a roundabout called Plaza de Cánovas del Castillo. A pleasant breeze brought a smile to his face. The foreign architecture of the surrounding buildings brought on excitement and a sense of adventure. Somewhere in this unfamiliar country and this unfamiliar city, he would find Elizabeth. She had yet to reply to his text message. Stay calm, he told himself. He had things to do to preoccupy his time, like to unpack, contact Blake, and most important—figure out breakfast. After he took some pictures from the balcony with his phone, he called home. His mother was relieved to hear that he had a safe flight and arrived at the hotel without issue.

He felt obligated to call Autumn, and he hated himself for it. Maybe Colette was right. He called Blake instead.

"Hey, you up? Yeah, the hotel is very nice. Me too. We'll get used to the time difference. Do you want to get something to eat? Okay, great. I need a shower too. If I'm ready before you, I'll knock on your door, otherwise come get me. Okay, later."

He ended the call, went back inside and tossed his phone on the bed, then dug through his suitcase to find something to wear. As he did, he moved his clothes to the dresser and hung up his sports coat. After he showered, he stood naked in front of the full-length mirror. His dark, uncombed, wavy hair stood up as he flexed his chest, arms, and abs. He looked forward to visiting the fitness room and pool later. As he brushed his fingers through his damp hair, he raised his chin and tilted his head, undecided if he should shave. A text alert came from his phone on the bed.

The message was from Elizabeth. It read, "Hi Nick. Are you following me? What happened to Italy? Did you make it safe to Madrid?"

He huffed and smiled.

He texted her, "Safe and sound in Madrid. I'm staying at a hotel close to the Prado. I can see the Neptune Fountain from my room. Where are you?"

Nick tapped the Send icon, then regretted questioning her whereabouts. His lips tightened and his eyebrows drew together. He stood there with his eyes fixed on the message thread.

In the hotel restaurant, bright sunlight came through the glass domed ceiling. White marble tiles covered the floors and there were Corinthian style columns that stretched upward. White linen covered the tables, and mahogany stained chairs with comfortable cushions filled the dining room. An aroma of sausages and ham came from a buffet. Blake and Nick filled their plates with scrambled eggs, sausages, croissants, and danishes, then sat at an empty table.

"Juan Miguel texted me back," Blake said.

He spoke between bites.

"He's working, but he'll meet up with us later. He knows some clubs where we can meet girls."

All Nick could do was chew and nod until finally he could speak.

"That's great. How's your room?"

"It's awesome. I can't wait to bring some girls here."

His eyebrows rose as he peered at Blake over his glass of orange juice. Blake sipped his coffee and glanced around the dining room.

"Looks like it's going to be local girls. No hot tourists here, just a bunch of old retired folks and a few families. Little kids, ugh."

Blake looked like he was in pain. Nick chuckled.

"Oh Blake. I can't take you anywhere."

Both young men grinned.

"I think you've had a little too much of Autumn. You forgot how to have fun."

"Yeah, Autumn has been texting me. Not a lot, just annoying messages."

He shook his head.

"Don't worry. I'm your wingman. I've got your back. Juan Miguel will come through for us. We're going to have one hell of a time."

A vision of Elizabeth came into Nick's thoughts.

"I think so too."

"Good."

Blake tapped the top of the table with the bottom of his fist, grinned, then something caught his eye, and a serious look came over his face. Nick turned to follow Blake's gaze. A young woman on the restaurant's wait staff was replenishing some of the food items at the buffet. He laughed and shook his head.

"What? She's pretty."

"Please don't get us kicked out of here."

Blake wrinkled his face. Then they both chuckled.

"Since you dragged me kicking and screaming to this beautiful country, where, I might add, neither of us speaks the local language, what's the plan?" Blake asked.

"I would like to walk around and see what's what. We are close to the Prado Art Museum. We should check it out."

"I would like to do that, but I have to ask, have you gotten a new appreciation for art? Frankly, I'm surprised. The only art museum you visited while you were in New York was The Met."

"Yeah, I guess I wasn't interested then, but now I want to learn more about art and other things."

"Really? Do tell."

"Maybe it's all the hounding my father put me through, to grow up, you know."

Blake sipped his coffee and sat quietly, then the corner of his lips turned upward.

"Okay, do you want to tell me *why* we are really here? And don't give me the same philosophical answer you would give your parents. I mean, what are we *really* doing in Spain?"

Nick turned his gaze from Blake and stared out into the dining room.

"I'm looking for something."

A text alert came from Nick's phone.

The message was from Elizabeth. It read, "I'm in Chicago."

4

Nick, Blake, and Juan Miguel waited at the packed bar for their drinks. Colorful strobe lights pulsed over the crowded dance floor and music thundered in their ears. It was a stark comparison to the earlier part of their day. They skipped a visit to the Prado, wandered about the city, got lunch, then ended up back at the hotel for a swim. At the pool, they met an older Belgian couple, who were the only other English-speaking guests. Afterwards, they used the fitness equipment in the hotel's mini gym, and just hung out and waited for Juan Miguel to text Blake. All the while, Nick waited for a text, or anything, from Elizabeth. He glanced at his phone. Nothing. When he looked up, he was relieved that Blake was busy talking to Juan Miguel. Last thing he needed was for Blake to further chide him over waiting for a text from Elizabeth. Someone touched his arm.

"Hola."

A girl with long dark hair, who wore black tight shorts and a white lacy top that exposed her midriff, smiled at him. He smiled back.

"Hello."

"Hablas español?"

"No, sorry."

"Hi, I'm Stella."

She held out her hand.

"Hi, I'm Nick."

Her hand was more delicate than he imagined.

"American?"

"Yes, sí, I'm American."

"Would you like to dance, Nick?"

"Ah, sure. One moment."

She nodded. He turned and grabbed Blake's shoulder. Blake turned around with a drink in each hand.

"Blake, I'm going to dance with Stella."

"Wait, what, Stella? How? What about your drink?"

Blake held up the drinks.

"Save it for me, or drink it yourself."

"Yeah, okay, great. Hey, find out if she has any friends."

He gave Blake a quick wave as he followed Stella to the dance floor. They snaked through the crowd. She stopped, threw her hands in the air and swayed to the music. She danced better than most girls he had been with. He moved the best he could on the packed dance floor. She twirled a few times, then faced him. She held her arms high over her head. Sparkling bracelets slid down her forearms, and her long dark hair swayed as she moved. She was a beautiful girl, thin with an angular face, big dark eyes, and full sensual lips. She gave him a coy smile. He smiled back at her, but Elizabeth pervaded his thoughts.

They clapped after the music ended. She leaned close to him and touched his arm.

"You are a good dancer."

"No, you are a good dancer."

She laughed. The music exploded through the speakers again. She smiled, put her hands in the air, and moved her hips. He joined her. After the song ended, he took her aside before the next song started.

"Do you have friends with you? Other girls?"

"Sí."

She held up her hand for him to wait. He pointed back to the bar where he left Blake and Juan Miguel. She nodded. He worked his way through the crowded dance floor. Juan Miguel and Blake grinned at him. Blake shook his hand, then handed him a drink.

"Well? I've been standing around here like your personal waiter. You better have some good news."

"She's going to find her friends and meet us here."

"She's sexy. I hope her friends are, too."

He sipped his drink and scanned the crowd for Stella. It was difficult to see with all the flashing strobes. When Blake turned away to order another drink, Nick checked his phone. There were three new text messages from Autumn, but nothing from Elizabeth. His lips tightened into a straight line and his eyebrows drew together. Did he owe Elizabeth anything? He was out with his best friend, having a great time. Why not have a great time? He stuffed his phone back into his pocket.

Stella appeared. She bounced light on her feet towards them, followed by two other girls. Juan Miguel spoke to the girls in Spanish and introduced them.

"This is Marissa. This is Isabella. And this is Stella."

After he introduced Nick and Blake, they smiled and nodded at the girls. Stella was the shortest of the three girls. Marissa was thin like Stella, but with softer features. She had shoulder-length brown hair and wore a black crop top with jean shorts. Isabella had brown hair with blonde highlights and wore tight black pants and a black spaghetti strap crop top. She was bustier than the other two girls and looked the most athletic. Blake's eyes fixed on Isabella.

"I explained you are my friends visiting from the United States. They are excited to dance with some Americans," Juan Miguel said.

"Cool," Blake said.

"Cool," Marissa said.

The three girls laughed. Blake held up his glass to toast them.

"Juan Miguel. Ask them if they would like a drink," Blake said.

They nodded and Juan Miguel gave their drink order to the bartender. When everyone had their drinks in hand, they did an official toast to the evening and new friends. Juan Miguel directed the group to some tables near the dance floor. There, both foreign speaking parties exchanged questions, while Juan Miguel interpreted. Stella shared glances and smiles with Nick. Blake seemed most interested in Isabella, but her attention was on Nick. Most of Marissa's questions were about Blake. Since Juan Miguel knew Blake from

NYU, many of his answers in Spanish ended with laughter. It was uncertain if any of the three girls were into Juan Miguel. They spoke to him the most, but their eyes were on Nick and Blake. They seemed to treat Juan Miguel as a host or translator and only flirted a little with him.

"You like my country?" Isabella asked.

She only looked at Nick.

"Yes, it's beautiful."

Isabella nodded and smiled.

"How long will you stay?"

"For the week," Blake interjected.

Juan Miguel interpreted. Isabella nodded and all three girls smiled.

"Dance?" Stella asked.

Stella looked at all three men.

"Yes?" Marissa added.

Marissa gazed at Blake. Blake grinned.

"Sí," Blake said.

Marissa took Blake's arm. Stella motioned for Nick to join them, but he held up his hand to let them know he was going to sit this one out. She made a sad face, while Blake put his hands up in astonishment.

"Vámonos," Juan Miguel shouted and joined them.

They all headed to the dance floor. Isabella stayed behind with Nick.

"You don't want to dance?" he asked.

Isabella shook her head and sipped her drink. He nodded and drank. Her shoulders rocked to the music. He took out his phone and scanned his messages. His jaw knotted. There were eight new unread messages from Autumn, even after he texted her earlier. He skipped past her unread messages. Below her messages were ones he read earlier from his mother and his sister, Gwen. Further down were two messages from Derek and four from Peter. He looked at Elizabeth's last message again. It only read, "I'm in Chicago." Below was the reply he made this morning, which read, "Chicago? What about Madrid? Are you still coming?"

He wrinkled his lips, and when he looked up, he met Isabella's gaze.

"Girlfriend?"

Her lips curled into a coy smile.

"Oh, no-no. No girlfriend."

He rotated his head left and right. Her eyes brightened.

"Sorry, my family."

"Ah, sí, familia."

She smiled and nodded. He glanced once more at his text message to Elizabeth, then he put his phone away.

"Come, dance," she said.

He finished his drink. Then she led them to the dance floor. He glanced around to find Blake, but it was too difficult, with all the undulating bodies lit only by the sweeping strobe lights. She tugged at his arm. He turned, and she was already moving to the music.

They danced for two songs, then returned to the table to find their friends there. Blake grinned and appeared in deep conversation with Stella and Marissa. Both girls had puzzled expressions. Juan Miguel sporadically jumped in to interpret. There were nods and smiles on both sides.

Isabella held his hand as Nick led them into the lobby of the hotel.

"One moment," he said.

He held up his hand to tell her to wait in the lobby. He went to the men's bathroom, relieved himself, then peered at his reflection in the mirror above the sink. His face glistened oily and the tips of his hair clung together with sweat. His eyes and mouth drooped from all the drinks he had. There were new messages on his phone, but only one interested him. It was an earlier message from Elizabeth. It read, "Made it to Madrid. Breakfast, tomorrow? Meet me at the Más Sí cafe. I'm bringing my friend Gabriella. Be there at nine."

"Fuck."

His shoulders slumped, and his head listed to the side. He glanced at his reflection. Isabella was waiting.

Her eyes brightened, and she smiled when he returned. He noticed her better in the bright light of the lobby. She stood there in tight black pants and a formfitting black crop top with spaghetti straps. Her chestnut-colored hair with blonde highlights hung over one shoulder and descended below her breasts. She held her silver clutch handbag in front of her.

Fuck, she's beautiful. How could he say no? He sighed, took her hand, and led her to the registration desk. The young woman behind the counter wore a white blouse, opened at the collar, and a black jacket. Her dark hair held tight in a bun. She looked up and smiled at them.

"Hello. Sorry, no hablo español."

He looked at the young woman's name tag. It read, "Camila."

"No problem. How can I help you?"

"Camila, could you please arrange a cab for her? Also, could you tell her I'm feeling sick and need to rest?"

Camila looked at both of them, and a subtle coy smile appeared on her face.

"Your room number, please."

"Room 506"

"Your name, please."

"Nick Evers."

Camila glanced up and smiled at him.

"Very good. Thank you, Señor Evers. I can certainly help you."

"Thank you, Camila."

Camila spoke to Isabella in Spanish. Isabella's lips parted as she listened.

"Oh," she said.

Isabella wrinkled her face and put her hand on his midsection. He first nodded, then shook his head in frustration. She again wrinkled her lips, then nodded.

Camila opened a door behind the registration desk, poked her head in, and spoke to someone in Spanish. Isabella wrote her phone number on the small hotel pad, then tucked the folded paper in Nick's breast pocket. She brushed her hand over his chest where she had placed the note.

A middle age gentleman in a hotel uniform came through the door behind the registration desk. He pulled down on his vest that had ridden up and smiled at them. Camila further explained the situation. He held out his arm and gestured for Isabella to follow. Isabella hugged Nick and kissed him on the cheek. She then followed the man out to the street, where a cab waited. After she got in, the man from the hotel closed the door, and the cab drove off. Nick huffed. Blake would think that he was ready for the priesthood. He turned to Camila.

"Muchas gracias, Camila."

"You are most welcome, Señor Evers."

She smiled at him. He shambled to the elevators. His head was still light from the drinks and dancing. A shower would do him good. He took his phone out and opened the most recent text message. It was from Blake. It was a thumbs-up emoji. He shook his head and chuckled. The elevator doors opened, and he got in.

When Nick got to his room, he stripped off his clothes and sat on the bed in his underwear. He listened to two voice messages, both from his mother, asking for him to check in. He rolled his eyes. Why does she need more than a text message? He looked at Elizabeth's text message again. He fought the urge to text her again and put his phone on the nightstand.

A knock came at the door. Blake, you dog, did you forget to pack condoms? Stupid question. He went to the door and opened it part way. Camila, from the front desk, held a packet of antacids and a bottle of water.

"Señor Evers?"

"Oh, hello, Camila."

Her blouse was unbuttoned and open down to her cleavage. Her lips were glossy and there was a sheen from below her neck to the tops of her small breasts, as if she had applied some cream. The fringe of a purple lace bra peeked out from behind her blouse.

"I brought you something for your stomach."

"Oh? That's very thoughtful of you."

She smiled and held up the bottle of water and a packet of tablets. He opened the door further and took the items. Her gaze traced down his body.

"Is there anything else I can help you with?"

Her words had a seductive tone. He glanced at her breasts and when he looked up, their eyes met.

"I'm fine for tonight. Thank you, Camila."

"Sleep well, Señor Evers."

He closed the door and watched her from the security peephole. She strutted away in her high heels. Her jacket and short shirt fit her body well. The way she moved, it was as though her rump waved at him. He put his back to the closed door, shut his eyes, and exhaled.

"Fuck. Maybe I am ready for the priesthood."

5

Elizabeth sat across from her friend Gabriella at the cafe Más Sí. A breakfast of coffee and chocolate con churros sat on the outdoor bistro table.

"Your friend Nick and his friend Blake will arrive soon, yes?"

Elizabeth looked at her watch.

"Let's hope so."

Gabriella cocked her head and raised an eyebrow.

"Yes, Nick will be here, along with his friend Blake."

She smirked at Gabriella.

"Is Nick your boyfriend or only your lover?"

Elizabeth tightened her lips to keep from spraying her coffee.

"Gabriella! He's much younger than I am."

"So."

"So, I don't think it's a good idea to get involved with such a younger man."

Gabriella took a churro and dipped it into the cup of chocolate sauce.

"I would."

She held her mouth open in a seductive O shape, then slid the dripping chocolate covered churro into her mouth. Elizabeth laughed.

"Of course you would."

She bit off a piece of the churro, licked the chocolate from her lips, and struggled not to laugh and choke. Elizabeth wrinkled her face as if she tried to refrain from another burst of laughter, and waited for her to swallow. When she regained her composure, her smile and bright eyes departed.

"Why are you meeting him, then?" Gabriella asked.

"His father is the founder of a company I do business with. I'm trying to play nice."

"So, this is for business?"

Elizabeth shrugged.

"I suppose."

She fumbled with the bracelets on her wrist, then she sipped her coffee.

"Does he know that? He's travelled all the way to Spain to see you."

She swallowed a sip of coffee, turned her gaze away to the cobblestone street and watched the few cars that drove by, then sighed.

"He's infatuated, that's all."

"That is quite an infatuation, to travel to another country—to chase you. Couldn't he wait for your return?"

"Yes, of course."

She spotted two young men across the street, one taller than the other. The taller one had dark hair and wore a casual gingham button-up shirt and tan colored slacks, while the shorter one had on a solid white polo and light gray joggers. Both wore sunglasses and sneakers.

"There they are."

Gabriella looked up as the men crossed the street.

"Oh mío, Lizzy. Which one is Nick?"

"He's the taller one with dark hair."

"I see your concern. That one could be a big problem for you, or no problem at all."

"Don't get carried away."

Gabriella laughed.

As the two young men strolled up the block, Gabriella toyed with the ends of her long dark hair and ran her fingers down the neckline of her cream-colored silk blouse. She opened the collar to expose her cleavage.

Elizabeth smirked and rolled her eyes at her.

Nick hid his eyes behind dark wayfarer sunglasses, but he had a delightful smile, and not an overly anxious grin, which she watched for. Maybe there is some sincerity there. She stood to greet them.

"Hello, Nick."

"Hello, Elizabeth."

He took off his sunglasses. She looked into his eyes and found nothing but sincerity. He gave her a polite hug and a kiss on the cheek.

She glanced at Gabriella, who beamed. Nick turned to Blake.

"This is my best friend, Blake. Elizabeth, you both met at my graduation party."

She nodded. Both she and Blake smiled and said hello. She then gestured to Gabriella, who stood.

"This is my dear friend Gabriella."

"Hello," Gabriella said.

She stepped forward and kissed Blake's cheek, then turned to Nick and kissed his cheek. She grinned at both young men. Their eyes widened, and they grinned.

"Yeah, they do that here," Elizabeth said.

Gabriella laughed and nodded at their confused expressions.

"Shall we sit?" Elizabeth said.

"Please join us for some coffee and chocolate con churros?" Gabriella said.

Both women gestured toward the table like two game show models. Blake grinned.

Gabriella gestured to the waiter. Both women sat. Nick sat next to Elizabeth, and Blake next to Gabriella. Elizabeth smiled and glanced at Gabriella, who grinned at the two young men. She tensed inward at the bright playfulness in her friend's eyes. The waiter brought more coffee and churros with chocolate sauce. Blake tried the churros.

"This is very good."

"This is a typical breakfast in Spain."

Gabriella grinned, and spoke to Blake like he was some child she had taken to the zoo, and was now rewarding him for good behavior. He nodded while he dipped a churro in the chocolate sauce. She sipped her coffee and laughed while he ate. When she shifted in her seat, crossed, and extended her legs, Elizabeth noticed Blake tilt his head. She assumed his hidden gaze was on Gabriella's long bare legs.

"It's great to see you again," Nick said.

He gazed at Elizabeth as though they were the only two people at the table. Her lips curled into a subtle smile.

"Nice to see you, too."

"Nick, what do you do?" Gabriella asked.

Gabriella touched Elizabeth's arm as if to apologize for her interruption.

"I recently completed my MBA, and I'll be starting a new job at a company called Hale Biotech in a couple of weeks."

"That sounds exciting. What will you do at Hale Biotech?"

"I'm not sure yet, but I hope to manage partner relationships."

A coy smile appeared on his lips as he glanced at Elizabeth.

Gabriella nodded with her eyebrows raised.

"How about you, Blake?" Gabriella asked.

"Like Nick, I recently got my MBA. I'm not sure where I'll land. I have submitted my resume to a few places."

She nodded.

"It's an exciting time in your life, after years of school. I'm sure you both will do well."

She smiled and looked over at Elizabeth.

"What do you do, Gabriella?" Nick asked.

"I'm a journalist for a newspaper here in Madrid."

"That's cool," Blake said.

"So, how did you meet Elizabeth?" Nick asked.

"Lizzy worked with a friend of mine, Antonio."

"Oh?"

He glanced at Elizabeth with a puzzled expression.

"We are all dear friends. I'm so happy to see Lizzy again. It's been too long."

"Will you see Antonio while you're here?" Nick asked.

He refrained from calling her Lizzy, which she was grateful for.

"I don't think so."

"Oh, you should. He would love to see you," Gabriella said.

She gave Gabriella a tight-lipped smile, then brought her attention to the two young men.

"Have you two been enjoying Madrid?"

Blake's eyebrows drew together, and he rubbed his eye under his sunglasses.

"Are you all right, Blake?"

"A late night perhaps." Gabriella said.

Gabriella smirked at him. He snorted and pushed his sunglasses up the bridge of his nose.

"Yeah, Nick and I have been adventuring. Drinks and dancing. My friend Juan Miguel, who I knew from NYU, lives here in Madrid. Anyway, we had a great night. It was crazy."

"Oh? Sounds exciting. Did you dance with lots of girls?" Gabriella asked.

"Oh yeah. It was unbelievable."

Through the wire mesh tabletop, Elizabeth saw Nick kick the side of Blake's foot.

"Yeah. Um. We had a good time, but we were tired from the flight and time change, you know, so we didn't stay out too late," Blake said.

"So, the big question for you ladies is, are we going to hang out today?" Nick asked.

"Sorry, I have things to do, but I enjoyed meeting you both," Gabriella said.

"We just got here. Can you stay a little longer?"

Nick looked at Elizabeth.

"No, I'm afraid not," she said.

Blake rubbed his chin, as if he were confused.

"Today isn't good for me either. I have meetings," Elizabeth said.

She spoke to Nick as if he was the only one listening.

"It'd be nice if we can get together before we head home," Blake said.

He shifted his gaze from Elizabeth to Gabriella.

"Sure, I think that's possible," Gabriella said.

She smiled at him, then glanced at Elizabeth.

"We'll see," Elizabeth said.

"I would really like to see you while we're here in Madrid," Nick said.

He only looked at Elizabeth. She could see the want in his eyes.

"I should be able to move some things around. How does tomorrow sound?"

His face brightened.

"Sounds wonderful."

Both women stood.

"Adiós," Gabriella said.

"Please stay and enjoy your coffee and chocolate con churros. Nick, I will text you later with a time and place for tomorrow. Adiós boys," she said.

Both women strolled down the sidewalk. She fought the urge to hurry or glance back, as she was certain Nick was watching.

~

At the outdoor cafe, Más Sí, Nick and Blake watched Elizabeth and Gabriella stroll down the sidewalk until they were out of sight. Neither one glanced back at them.

Blake bit into a churro and wrinkled his face.

Nick slipped on his sunglasses and drew his eyebrows together.

"I have to say, that was short, and chocolaty sweet," Blake said.

Blake pushed the plate of churros away from him. Nick's jaw knotted. He motioned for the server, then held up his wallet. The waiter waved his hands as if to say there was no cost and pointed down the street in the direction where Elizabeth and Gabriella went.

He left a tip anyway, and both he and Blake crossed the street. At the corner, he spotted the two women. He waited and hoped that Elizabeth would glance back, but she never did. Blake nudged him and both men walked on.

"Fuck, Nick. Elizabeth's friend Gabriella is super hot. Did you see those legs? Tell me you saw her legs. Fuck!"

They strolled down the cobblestone sidewalk, Nick with his hands in his pockets. He sighed.

"Stop, just stop. I'm getting a headache."

"What? What's with you? Don't tell me you're growing old on me."

"No. Fuck, no."

He struggled to form even a tired smile. Blake gave him a sympathetic grin. He shook his head and laughed.

"Never mind. It's great that you find Gabriella attractive."

"Attractive? C'mon. I could be her sex slave if she wanted."

Nick rolled his eyes.

"What? You're telling me you don't want to fuck Elizabeth? C'mon. I know you."

Both stopped on the sidewalk. Nick crossed his arms.

"Okay-okay. Yes, I want to sleep with Elizabeth."

"Sleep with?"

"Yes, there's a difference."

"Is there?"

"Blake, all the girls we hooked up with in college were one-night stands. Elizabeth is different."

Blake raised his eyebrows.

"Are you telling me you're in love with her?"

"I don't know, but there's something about her."

"Geez."

Nick said nothing. He shoved his hands back into his pockets. They walked again up the block.

"Is this going to conflict with us having fun here?"

"No, of course not. I wouldn't drag you with me, just to have you watch me sit around and pout in some other country."

"Good."

Both men walked in silence until they reached the crosswalk and waited for the signal to change.

"I say we have a nice, casual day. Check out some sites and chill. Later we can go to a different club tonight. What do you think?" Blake asked.

"All right. You still haven't told me how things went last night."

"Since you rousted me awake this morning to meet your girlfriend, I was going to make you beg. However, since I met my future wife and dominatrix, I will reveal what went down last night."

"Elizabeth is not my girlfriend, and I doubt very much that Gabriella is a dominatrix."

"Please, Nick. I am a man of little hope. Don't squish my dreams."

"Yeah, okay."

They both chuckled.

"Well, let's have it."

"Marissa and I got a cab back to the hotel."

He punched Blake's shoulder.

"Ouch."

"Yeah, I got your text message. Okay, go on."

"Since we didn't speak each other's language, we had to employ *the language of love.* We kissed and fucked. Then she left. One word I could understand was universidad, university right? At least, I think that's what she said. College girls, I love 'em."

Nick chuckled.

"I guess you still have your college charm."

"Always."

"What about you?"

"Nothing much to tell. We danced some more, then I took a cab back to the hotel. Got a text from Elizabeth and the rest, you know."

Blake wrinkled his face.

"Lame. Are you sure you're not growing old on me?"

"Shut up."

They came to the corner where the side street met the large roundabout with the Neptune fountain at the center.

"We're close to the hotel. Let's get a proper breakfast."

"All right."

Nick sat with Blake and Juan Miguel at a club with a live band. The three young men wore button-up shirts and jeans. This club had a more sophisticated atmosphere, that was both laid back and intimate. No crazy strobe lights hung from the ceiling. The only bright lights lit the stage where the band performed. A fair amount of patrons filled the dance floor, but there was ample room to move around. The place reminded Nick of some clubs back home with great live music and a comfortable atmosphere.

He touched the paper in his pocket with Isabella's phone number, while Blake and Juan Miguel chatted. An urge came over him to ask Juan Miguel to call Isabella. As that urge became stronger, he slipped his finger from his pocket and sipped at his drink. He smiled as he watched his friend. Blake was always on the hunt for girls. There was a hungry look in his eyes. Several times, Blake leaned toward Juan Miguel to ask him something. Patience, Blake. Nick smiled to himself.

"Hola."

He turned around and a beautiful woman in a black dress stood there.

"Ah? Hola."

"Soy Luciana, cómo estás."

"I'm Nick. Ah? No hablo español. Sorry."

"Americano? Nice to meet you."

"Yeah, I'm an American. How are you? Luciana?"

"Yes, Luciana. I'm good. Thank you."

He shook her hand, then Blake and Juan Miguel appeared at his side. Blake looked stunned.

"Oh, Luciana. This is Blake and Juan Miguel."

"Hello," she said.

"Hello," Blake said.

"Hola," Juan Miguel said.

Luciana and Juan Miguel spoke in Spanish, while he and Blake looked on. Their conversation often ended with laughter. Her laugh was rich and musical, and her smile reminded Nick of Penelope Cruz.

"What did she say?" Blake asked.

"She asked how I know you and Nick. I told her we went to NYU together. Then I told her that Nick is a close friend of yours," Juan Miguel said.

"That's it? Then why all the laughter?"

Juan Miguel shrugged and smiled.

Blake glanced at Nick and shook his head.

"Nice to meet everyone," she said.

Every time Nick glanced at Luciana, her eyes were on him. They ordered more drinks. She expected her friends, but they were late. She saw Nick, and he looked like someone she would like to have a drink with. They told her how excited they were to visit Spain and Madrid. She expressed her sadness at their limited stay and wondered if they would ever visit Barcelona, her hometown. Although she spoke some English, Juan Miguel helped to translate when needed. She said she was a flight attendant for Iberia. They nodded and explained that they had recently graduated from business school. She looked in her early thirties.

Blake ordered drinks for everyone. Luciana sat between the two Americans, while Juan Miguel stood with his drink in hand at Blake's side. She crossed her legs and her foot brushed Nick's shin. She smiled at him every time their eyes met.

"Nick, what do you like most about Madrid?"

He rested his elbow on the counter of the bar and looked off in thought. His lips curled into a smile.

"I think I like the people the most. The beautiful Spanish people."

He glimpsed at Blake, who nodded and smiled behind her. It was Blake's signature reel-them-in look and gesture.

"That is very sweet."

She got a text message.

"My friends are not coming."

Her lips turned down. Blake motioned to Nick.

"Excuse me, Luciana."

They walked to an open spot near the dance floor.

"Look, this place is nice, but there's not a lot going on here, if you know what I mean?" Blake said.

He looked over Nick's shoulder, presumably at Luciana. Nick turned around. Juan Miguel sat on the stool next to her, and they were chatting. Nick shrugged.

"Marissa texted me. Her and Stella want to meet up with us at another club. She said that Isabella might show up later. She also said that you sent Isabella home in a cab. What's up with that?"

"I wasn't feeling well. I think it was the drinks. When we got to the hotel, I got sick, so I sent her home. What else could I do?"

He hated to lie to Blake, but his friend needed to ease off the gas.

"Okay—okay. I understand. I spoke to Juan Miguel, and he said he'll take us to another club if we like. That's what I would like to do. Do you want to come with us or hang out with Luciana? You might have better luck here, since I can't promise Isabella will be there."

"Are you trying to ditch me?"

"Seriously, Nick. I finally got a break. You're usually the one to go home with the girl. Also, I don't think your heart is in it, or maybe your heart is someplace else. I won't say where, but I think you're wasting your time."

"It's all good. I want you to have a great time, and I definitely don't want to stand in your way or drag you down."

"Are you trying to make me feel guilty? Are we both going to go home with our dicks in our hands?"

Nick laughed.

"No—hell, no. I'm just saying you and Juan Miguel should meet up with Marissa and Stella and have a great time. I'll be fine."

Blake chuckled.

"Sounds like you're trying to get rid of me."

"I am. There's nothing here for you, unless you want to drink, hangout, and enjoy the music with your old buddy."

"Eh—no, not tonight. Thanks for understanding. Have a great night, whatever that might be."

"You, too. Catch up with you, mañana."

Blake returned to the bar, where he spoke to Juan Miguel. Juan Miguel spoke to Luciana. They smiled and shook hands with her, then waved to Nick before they departed.

Luciana put her elbow on the counter of the bar, tilted her head, then ran her fingers through her dark brown curls. When her eyes met his, she raised an eyebrow and her lips curled into a tight-lipped smile. She pulled an open barstool close to her. He sat down and they ordered more drinks.

"Why didn't you go with your friends?"

"My friends are interested in partying and meeting girls. They also wanted to dance."

"You do not want to meet girls and dance?"

Her tone was playful.

"No. I don't feel like dancing or meeting other girls. I am enjoying your company."

She smiled.

"Oh? That is nice."

He smiled.

"It is."

Their knees touched. Her knees between his as they sat facing each other. She took his hand and placed it on her thigh. He expected to feel her smooth bare leg, but she wore sheer stockings and the texture surprised him. She glanced around the immediate area, then took his hand and moved it up her thigh. At the top of her stocking there was a new texture, one of swirling lace. Beyond that was her smooth, warm flesh. He glanced around to see if anyone saw them. As he did, her breath and her lips were on his neck. He turned and their lips met, wet and open.

He leaned back to look into her eyes. His thumb slipped in the fold of her leg near her hip, the one that would lead to a more intimate conversation. After a moment of contemplation, he gently squeezed the back of her thigh and her calf before removing his hand. She leaned toward him.

"Nervous?"

His eyebrows rose.

"No."

"What's wrong?"

"I'm thinking of someone."

"Wife?"

"No-no. No wife."

"Girlfriend?"

"No, not exactly."

"I have a boyfriend. In Barcelona. It's okay if you have a girlfriend."

She raked his evening stubble with her fingertips, then moved her hand to his knee and leaned close so their faces were a breath apart.

"I have to fly out in the morning."

Her breath, warm and soft as she spoke, carried the scent of apricots.

"Will you stay?"

Nick touched her cheek, and he closed the narrow space between them so their open mouths met. Her nose brushed against his nose. The kiss was deep and wet. She grasped his arm to hold him in place, but he drew back and ended the kiss. Both gasped when their mouths separated. Her eyes sparkled.

"Stay, yes?"

He closed his eyes, and the breath went out of him.

"I can't."

"Esto es Loco."

When he looked at her, she looked away. Her gaze was one of hurt and disappointment. He raked his fingers through his hair.

"I'm sorry. I want to—I want you, but I can't."

Her gaze softened. She touched his cheek, and he kissed her palm.

"This woman—must be special."

"She is. I should go."

He stood and kissed Luciana on the cheek, and their lips met one last time. She smiled and nodded with a look of surrender. Then he departed.

6

Elizabeth and Nick met at the rooftop restaurant above the hotel where she stayed. The afternoon sun blazed overhead in a cloudless sky. They sat at a shaded table under a canvas canopy.

"How was your night out with Blake?"

She lifted her wineglass, took a slow sip, and gazed at him over the top of her glass. He ran his fingertips over the tablecloth seam, and appeared lost in thought.

"It was good."

"Oh? Is that all?"

"Um, sorry. I feel like I've been babysitting Blake. All he wants to do is drink, dance, and sleep with as many girls as he can."

"And that doesn't appeal to you?"

"No."

"Why not? Are there not beautiful girls here? You're an exceptionally handsome young man. I'm sure it can't be *too* difficult for you to find someone to share your bed."

He snorted, then took his wineglass and drank. She waited. After he put his wineglass down, he sighed.

"When I texted you to tell you I was coming to Spain, it was to see *you*, and not to run around Madrid chasing girls."

Her eyebrows rose.

"I'm flattered, but don't you think that's a little extreme?"

He gazed out at the tops of the buildings. A gentle breeze rustled the canvas canopy above their heads and caressed their skin. She brushed her hair from her face and flipped it over her shoulder.

"I couldn't wait for you to return to Atlanta."

She sipped from her wineglass. His boyish fascination with her, albeit sweet, was troubling. He was too good looking to be a stalker. The two young women at Il Fasto back in Atlanta would have gone home with him.

"So, there is some urgency to the matter?"

"Yes. Can't you understand?"

"Enlighten me."

She smirked. His eyebrows drew together.

"Ever since I met you, you're all I think about."

Even though it was a cliché, she still smiled inside. He traveled here for her, as Gabriella pointed out. No man has ever chased her to another country, and some of them had the means to do so. She sat quietly and gazed into his piercing green eyes. The corner of her lips curled into a delicate smile.

"That's very sweet, Nick. I am very flattered, more than you will ever know, but the fact is, I am much older than you. You should be with someone your own age, or younger. You have a life of ease with everything laid out in front of you."

His lips tightened and his hands balled into loose fists at the edge of the table.

"You sound like my father. He relishes telling me, as often as he can, how *great* my life is, but to me it hasn't even started. You don't understand. The moment I met you, I didn't know what I wanted. All the things given to me were things I didn't ask for. I don't know how else to explain it."

Yikes.

She wanted to gulp down her glass of wine and yell for the server to bring a bottle. A fire burned in his beautiful green eyes.

"Say something," he said.

She peered at the table as if she hoped to find some philosophical answer written there.

"Are you sure you're not just infatuated with me?"

"Elizabeth. I'm sure."

A slow, meditative breath escaped past her lips, then she met his gaze. His age still posed a question of uncertainty. If they were going to do this, they were going to do it her way.

"Nick—"

She exhaled.

"Nick, I'll confess. When we met, I thought you were very dashing, very spirited, but like other people's perception of you, I also thought you were immature and spoiled, but—"

"Yes?"

"—but there was something about you that moved me."

He smiled a soft smile of hope.

"When we met for lunch, I thought you had a crush, and nothing more. Now—well, now, I can see this is something else—something more. Do I feel the same way about you as you do about me?"

She beamed inside, but struggled with how she might answer her own question. The hurt that all this could bring coiled inside her. He waited for her answer.

"Yes."

He gazed at her with a contemplative expression. His face softened, and he raised his eyebrows, then his lips curled into a gentle smile.

"What do we do now?" he asked.

"We enjoy the rest of our lunch, then go for a walk, and see where that takes us. But let's not talk about this any further."

His smile faded.

"Okay."

She raised her glass of wine, and he did as well.

"To sharing a wonderful day and exploring possibilities," she said.

His smile returned. A sparkle in his green eyes drew her into his gaze.

"I'll drink to that."

They ate and discussed how she came to live and work in Spain before she moved back to the United States and eventually to work for Nexgen Biosolutions. Then they discussed his life, his father, and Hale Biotech.

"You know, Richard, your father is a visionary and even a genius. Creating a biotech company that grew from a small independent research lab is extremely impressive. I won't go on, I'm sure you've heard the story over and over, but I think any frustrations you have toward him, put them aside and give him and Hale Biotech a chance."

He nodded and sighed.

"My friends say the same thing."

"You have smart friends."

She gave him a warm smile.

"That might be a stretch."

They both laughed. His smile lifted her heavy heart.

"Have you been to the Puerta del Sol?"

"No."

Her lips curled into a thin smile.

Elizabeth and Nick strolled down the cobblestone sidewalk. The stone buildings on either side had shallow balconies. They passed several tall, black, ornate iron gates. She surrendered to her desire to touch him, and halfway down the street, she took his arm. He held his chin higher and his green eyes brightened.

The street ended and opened up to an expansive space with broad sidewalks filled with pedestrians. Monolithic broad stone buildings lined the edge of a great cobblestone semicircle. A glass domed entrance to the metro stood at one end of the plaza. Shops lined the bottom floors of the buildings. She smiled inside as he took in the historical square. After a moment, she tugged his arm and led him across the street.

"This is the heart of Madrid, where major streets of Spain originate. Over there is a zero plaque marking their starting point."

His gaze spilled into hers.

"Could this be our starting point? This moment I mean."

Sunlight caught his green eyes, and gold glittered within. She wet and parted her lips. He put his hand to her cheek and kissed her. His lips were softer than she imagined. There was a mature determination in his kiss. His warm hand slip around her waist and then she was in his arms. She caressed his angular jawline. It was as though she had touched his face before, perhaps in a dream, but this was no dream.

"Yes, Nick. *This* can be our starting place."

They strolled around the square. She laughed at how taken he was by the statue of The Bear and the Strawberry Tree. Tourists and locals alike sat on the stone ledges surrounding the monuments. Most strolled, but a few hurried off, like one businessman in a suit with a look of stern desperation. Nick and Elizabeth reached the crosswalk, then strolled back to her hotel.

Tomorrow, she promised him an evening out. They would go out for drinks and tapas, and maybe even dancing. She instructed him to dress up, and to come up to see her room, since he bragged about his room's splendid view of the Fountain of Neptune. It warmed her heart that he enjoyed Madrid. They shared a brief kiss before the cab whisked him away.

In front of the hotel room's full-length mirror, Elizabeth examined her outfit. She wore a sleek black Cult Gaia cocktail dress, and everything underneath: bra, panties, garter, and stockings—Agent Provocateur. Even though she had no intention of leaving the room, she slipped on her prized black Christian Louboutin heeled sandals. The dress, the lingerie, the shoes, she packed for such an occasion, but it never occurred to her she would dress her sexiest for a much younger man.

She fussed with the ends of her hair, then flipped her long curls so they settled down her back. A knock came at the door. She gave her reflection a devious smile and narrowed her eyes.

When she opened the door, Nick stood in the hallway with a bouquet. He wore a navy sports coat with a white shirt open at the collar, cream-colored slacks, and dark brown oxfords. She recognized the flowers as some she had seen in the hotel shop downstairs. Printed on the paper wrapped around the stems was the hotel's logo.

"Yes, Señor. May I help you?"

She raised an eyebrow, and he glanced down at his outfit.

"Pardon me Señorita. A gift from a man who wishes to make your acquaintance."

She gestured for him to enter. He stood with the bouquet like a nervous prom date and took in the room. She fought not to laugh, but surrendered a smile instead. The room was a mixture of modern and traditional. It was an elegant off-white colored room with broad crown molding. He stepped between the small sofa the size of a loveseat and the coffee table. After he sat the flowers on the table, he turned to the kingsize bed with a button tufted fabric covered headboard. Soft music and fresh air entered through the two sets of floor-to-ceiling shutters that lay open to equally tall doors, each to a shallow balcony.

"This is very nice."

"Sorry, it doesn't have your view."

"It's better," he said, "Cozy."

Her lips curled into a smirk.

"Are you saying that you would favor me over King Neptune?"

"Of course."

"The only thing is, I don't have a trident to defend myself."

"I would never want you to feel that you have to protect yourself against me."

"That makes two of us."

He straightened, which made him appear taller.

"You look very handsome."

"And you look lovely."

She smiled, but cringed inside. It was a compliment given to her by his father, Richard Evers, on more than one occasion. She pushed it from her thoughts.

"Thank you."

"So, what should we do tonight since you know this city?"

"From your short time in Spain, you might have noticed that things don't get started until later in the evening. I thought we could enjoy each other's company. Maybe even play a *little game*."

"A game?"

After yesterday's kiss, her confidence grew, but she still needed to test him.

"It's a physical one. Are you up for it?"

"Yes."

"You'll do as I instruct. No complaints, no questions."

"All right."

"Take off your shirt and jacket."

He did.

"Take off your shoes and socks."

His lips parted, but he remained silent.

A devilish smile formed inside her. He looked calm and curious. The view of him in only his trousers had raised the temperature in the room. He went to unbuckle his belt.

"Not yet."

His eyebrow rose.

"You said you want to be with me. Do you really know what that means?"

Her fingertips glided over his chest. His lips parted.

"I want to know you—all of you."

"Oh? What if you don't like what you find?"

His Adam's apple rose, then fell as he swallowed. He moved to embrace her, but she held his arms, and he lowered them back to his sides.

"I don't care about anything else. I'm not afraid of any secrets you have."

As her gaze descended his body, she ran her fingertips over his shoulders, then down his spine. His muscles rippled under her touch. Her fingers traced his waistline to the front, then up over his abs. At the sharp curve of his chest, her fingertips paused on his nipples. His breath, slow and deep, swelled his chest. She sat on the edge of the sofa and crossed her legs.

"Kneel."

As he knelt before her, she straightened her leg so that the toe of her shoe touched his midsection.

"Take off my shoe."

He unbuckled the thin strap at her ankle, then he cupped her heel and slid the strap off. The corner of her lips turned upward at his attempt to cop a feel. She pressed her toes into his erection. He drew in a slow breath.

"Now the other shoe."

The sound of music that filtered into the windows earlier had stopped, as if everyone paused to listen.

"Kiss the top of my foot."

His eyebrow rose. She straightened her leg, and he bent forward. He took her foot in his hand and kissed her instep. The warmth of his lips sent electricity up her leg, but when he inhaled, her eyes narrowed. Naughty boy. She found it unimaginable that someone like him would enjoy sniffing girls' feet. Maybe she woke something within him.

"Enough," she said. Her tone hushed, but firm.

His legs remained folded under him, but he straightened his upper body. She again eyed the bulge at the front of his trousers, and further drew up her skirt until the welt of her stocking was visible. He licked his lips.

"Come closer."

She slipped her stocking foot between his legs, and wiggled her toes and raised her foot, then she pressed her instep under his crotch, first delicate, then firm. He inhaled and his eyelids lowered. She pressed her toes against his erection. His eyebrows drew together and a soft groan passed between his lips. She raised her skirt higher to expose her garter.

"Undo the clasp."

Her words were soft and dreamlike. He undid the clasp and the elastic strap contracted under her skirt.

"Take off my stocking. Do it slow."

He carefully took hold of the top of her stocking and pulled it down, exposing the flesh of her thigh, inch by inch. She had never seen a young man his age move with such care. Although it was a test of temperament and patience, the manner he seemed to savor the experience intrigued her. The stretched, coffee-colored stocking darkened as the nylon fabric collected down to her ankle, then toes.

"Hold my stocking to your lips."

Expressionless, he did as she instructed. She watched as he drew in a deep breath, then another, then his breath caught when she pressed her toes into his crotch.

"Lower your trousers."

He rose on his knees, unbuckled his trousers, and lowered them to the floor. His engorged cock flexed diagonally, the tip almost cresting the band of his briefs. A dark, wet spot marked the location of the head of his cock. She moved to the edge of the sofa, braced her stocking foot on the lip of the coffee table, and opened her legs so that he had a full view of her panties.

"Come closer and take my toes into your mouth."

So far, he had been obedient. He made no signs of resistance or objection. She slipped the tips of her fingers alongside the seam of her panties, then raised her bare leg and pointed her toes at him. His tongue slipped and played between her toes and his mouth sucked at her as though he were enjoying a fast melting ice cream cone. Her sex clenched between her thighs. She took in a sharp breath.

"Very good."

Inside, she melted and struggled to maintain her composure. She hung her bare leg over the sofa arm. Her legs spread wider.

"Now kiss and lick me here."

She pointed to the back of her thigh. He kissed her there. His lips were warm and soft, and his tongue made small wet circles.

"Now here."

She touched higher on her inner thigh. His back and shoulder muscles flexed as he bent forward, and he put his hands on the sofa.

"Careful. Keep your hands to yourself, mister."

He tried to hide a brief smile. She narrowed her eyes. When he kissed her upper thigh, her lips pursed as she tried to hush a soft purr. It seemed he was doing his best to give it back to her.

"Stop. Put your face between my legs, but no touching. Close your eyes and breathe me in."

His eyebrow rose.

"Would you like to continue, or would you like our evening to end?"

Her harsh tone made her cringe inside. He positioned his face between her legs, closed his eyes, then breathed her in slow and deep. His steady, warm breath penetrated her wet panties and electrified her sex. She bit her lower lip. Her flutters became spasms, and her juices ran wet to her anus. She slipped two fingers under her panties and worked her fingertips into her slick folds. Her knuckles came back shiny and wet.

"Open your mouth."

His eyes remained closed, and he parted his lips. She slipped her fingers from her panties. Glistening wet strands stretched between her fingers. She slipped them into his mouth.

"Taste me."

He licked her fingers clean.

She fingered herself again and fed it to him. He opened his mouth, ready for more, and she gave him more. Her clit throbbed as she watched him savor her.

"Stand."

His eyelids lifted as if he awoke from a deep sleep. They stood, and she turned her back to him.

"Unzip me."

As he unzipped her dress, she slipped the straps from her shoulders, and her dress pooled at her feet.

"Clasp your hands behind you."

She turned and faced him. Her breasts were bare. Her stiff nipples ached for attention. His eyes toured her body before they met her gaze. A coffee-colored stocking remained on her one leg, held up by a mint green polka-dot garter. There was a sparkle in his green eyes, and his lips curled into a smile. Her eyes narrowed.

"Kneel, then remove my panties and kiss my back."

She turned away from him and imagined he would have kissed her back without her instruction, but she still felt the need to guide him. He slipped her panties down her legs and to the floor, then planted soft kisses on her lower back and buttocks. A tingle traced up her spine. Thoughts of his expression seeing her naked ass caused her lips to curl into a devilish smile, which she vanquished before she turned around.

He moved closer, on his knees, and looked up at her with patient eyes, but the subtle lick of his lips gave away his desire. She sat on the couch and spread her legs. One stocking clad and one bare. She then touched herself.

"Look at my pussy."

He licked his lips and gazed at her sex.

"Lick my panties."

He looked up at her.

"Look at my pussy and lick my panties."

He rolled her panties inside out to expose the crotch and brought his tongue to the fabric. She stroked herself. The head of his erection protruded from the top of his briefs. Her eyebrows drew together, and she licked her lips at the sight of his cock. The head of his cock was red, engorged, and the shiny tip oozed.

"Come here. Kiss me."

She spread herself with both hands, and with one finger drew up the thin velvet flesh to expose her clit. He left a soft kiss, and his heavy warm breath tickled the hairs on her pubis.

"Now your tongue."

With his tongue he asserted pressure below her clit, then up and over, then back down again. Her sex fluttered and clenched inside. She released a soft hum. She wanted to lift her hips and grind her sex on his tongue and lips until his mouth was wet with her juices.

"Put your finger inside me."

"Mm. Good."

"Now, another."

"Mm. Yes."

"Press your fingers toward your tongue, and move them side to side."

"Oh. Yes. That's it."

She sucked in air through her teeth. Her hips shook and spasmed.

"Oh-fuck. Oh—fuck!"

She dug her fingers into the sofa cushions, lifted her hips, and came in a sudden stream into his mouth and on his neck and chest. Her body spasmed. She collapsed onto the sofa cushions, and he knelt there with parted lips and wide eyes.

"Come here and put your hands behind you."

She traced her fingertips around the waistband of his briefs. When she reached the head of his cock that protruded, she made circles to spread the clear pre cum over the tip. The muscles of his torso hardened like stone, and he released a soft groan. She slipped down his briefs to reveal his engorged cock. She bent forward, and they kissed. As their tongues tangled, she stroked and tugged at his cock. He grunted, his shoulders stiffened, and his back curled toward her. Ribbons of pearlescent come jetted from him, one stream, then another. He came on her breast, her abdomen, and her stocking clad leg. He curled into her arms, with his head on her shoulder, then his body shuddered. The game was over. He had played fair and did as she asked. She took his hand and led them to her bed. They slipped under the sheets and she spooned behind him. Her hands explored the muscles in his chest and abdomen. She stroked his cock. He stiffened in her grasp and released a heavy shuddered breath.

"Ready so quick. I'm impressed."

She purred in his ear, which made him further swell and harden. He rolled onto his back while she retrieved a condom from the nightstand drawer. After she stroked him a few times, she mounted him. She moved slowly at first, with his hands at her waist. She placed one of his hands on her breast as she moved on top of him.

Music from the street, once again, came in through the open balcony doors. With one hand, she braced herself on his chest, and with the other, she touched his bristly stubbled cheek. He kissed her palm and fingertips. Her hips rose and fell. They exchanged soft moans.

Her thighs trembled. He steadied her. Her lips parted and her cries drowned out the world around them. She clutched and squeezed his chest, her knees drew in tight against his ribs, and then she came.

He sat up and kissed her neck. She put her arms around his shoulders, his face buried in her long, dark chestnut curls. Flesh to flesh. Their hearts thumped in one beat.

"My God!"

Her words released in a gasp. He tightened his embrace and kissed her neck, then her ear.

"So good," he whispered.

She climbed off of him, disposed of the condom, then slipped back into bed. This time, she curled into his arms with her back to him. She caressed his hand and gazed off into the murky shadows of the room. A feeling of fulfillment came over her, and her heart felt lighter. This could be something—something special.

She listened to his soft and steady breaths, then he mumbled.

"Who are you?"

7

Slivers of sunlight pierced the room from the gaps around the shuttered balcony doors. Nick stretched his arm to the side of the bed where Elizabeth had slept. The sheets were cool and empty. She warned him last night that she had an early morning meeting. He grabbed her pillow and covered his face. The scent of her perfume lingered on the pillowcase. He rolled the pillow off of him, then rubbed his eyes and looked around the shadow cast room. After he sat perched on the edge of the bed to get his bearings, he went to the sofa, where his pants lie folded, and retrieved his phone. He had messages from Blake, his mother, Autumn, and Elizabeth. He read the only one that mattered to him.

Elizabeth's message read, "Buenos días. I had an extraordinary evening. Please sleep in as long as you like. I will catch up with you later in the day."

He smiled as he read her text message. The urge to jump back in her bed and wait for her return tempted him. He closed her message and looked at the list of new ones. Out of courtesy to his mother, he read her text message.

Josephine Evers wrote, "Call me Nicholas. I need to know that you're safe and well."

His smile faded. He closed his mother's message and decided he would rather call her from the cab than ruin the mood with any chiding from her. He dropped his phone on his folded pants, then went to get a shower.

Nick walked across the lobby of the hotel where he was staying. He felt light on his feet, as though he could dance. Then someone called out to him.

"Señor Nick Evers."

He turned and a young man who had to be around his age waved from behind the registration desk.

"Yes?"

The young man held up a letter.

"You have a letter, Señor."

He wrinkled his face.

"A letter? From whom?"

He walked over to the registration desk. It was an envelope with the hotel's logo and address where Elizabeth was staying.

"A woman dropped it off earlier."

"When?"

"I am sorry, I do not know. It was waiting when I arrived."

"Then how did you know it was a woman who left it? Did you see her?"

"No Señor. I was told it was a woman who left it for you. Someone from the hotel staff wrote your room number on the envelope."

The young man pointed to the handwritten room number on the envelope. It was *his* room number. He had a difficult time imaging her writing him a love note. Then again, yesterday evening surprised him in the most delightful way. Anything was possible with her, he was certain of it. He slipped the envelope into his pocket.

"Muchas gracias."

"Yes, of course, Señor."

Nick dropped his jacket on the bed. He opened the doors to the balcony to let in the fresh air and sounds of the street below. He wished there was music that would filter into his room like it did in Elizabeth's room, but there were no clubs nearby, only the sound of traffic. A band of sunlight came into the room and stretched across the floor. He took the envelope from his pocket and sniffed. No perfume. After he opened it, he wet his lips.

Dear Nick,

We had an extraordinary evening. Thank you for indulging me in our little game. You were very much a gentleman. It was wonderful to watch you sleep. You looked content with your sweet smile. I struggled this morning with whether I should write you this letter. I think you know me well enough now that you see how much I prize my independence. It's been one thing in my life that has always kept me sane and protected me from deep emotional entanglements. There have been some in the past, which took me a long time to recover. I can't say if we pursued this course we're on if it would lead to disaster, but there is something inside me that says it will. I have to listen to my gut and caution myself against any folly my heart may consider. So I must end this and save us both. I know this is not what you wanted to hear, but I believe it is the best for both of us. You'll find love, a grand love, and in time you'll forget about me. I cherish the moment we shared, but I too must move on and live my life.

Elizabeth

His heart sank and his stomach turned. Her words blurred to tear-filled eyes. He questioned his decision to come to Spain. Worries he held at bay in the back of his mind came to the forefront. Worries she would never believe how smitten he was. They played a game—her game. He did everything she asked. He crumpled her letter and threw it across the room. It rolled under the sofa. When he closed his eyes, a tear spilled over onto his cheek.

He retrieved his phone from his jacket pocket.

Blake's new text message read, "Apparently, someone had a great time."

He texted Blake, "I'm back in my room. Where are you?"

Blake's text response read, "I'm hanging out on the rooftop lounge. Come on up, it's nice up here."

He texted Blake, "I'll be up shortly."

Blake texted twice, first a thumbs-up emoji, and the second message read, "Wear your swim trunks, there's a pool and bar up here!"

He glanced at his mom's message, wrinkled his lips, then tapped the phone icon and listened as it rang.

Nick walked through the covered bar with its few patrons and out onto the rooftop terrace. The vibrant blue noon sky had few clouds. The city's rooftops looked like an endless sea of reddish-brown ripples. He squinted, then slipped on his dark wayfarer sunglasses. Spaced around the patio were large tropical plants in beautiful stone vases. His flip-flops snapped against his heels as he ambled toward the pool. He spotted Blake in his swim trunks and sunglasses at the end of a row of patio chaise loungers. Blake raised his glass and grinned when he saw him. A young woman in a white bikini with shoulder-length brown hair swam in the pool at the opposite end. When she reached the edge of the pool and braced herself there, he saw it was Marissa. Her hair was lighter than what he remembered, but the club was dark when they first met. When she saw him, she waved and shouted.

"Hola."

He waved to her and smiled despite his mood.

"Hola."

He had left Elizabeth's crumpled message in the room. He was going to show Blake, then thought better of it. Nothing mattered.

"Hey buddy. How's it going? We're just chilling by the pool. Beautiful day. What say you, my good man?"

Blake took a sip of his drink and looked up at him. He sat on the lounge chair next to his friend. Blake grinned as he watched Marissa swim and play in the water. Judging by Blake's smile, he was in love, or at least deeply smitten.

"I see you had another great night. Marissa too."

"Sí-sí. Muy bueno. She has today off, so she's going to spend the day with me. I would invite you to tag along, but you know things are progressing."

Nick raised an eyebrow.

"Do I hear wedding bells?"

Blake held up his hands in a halting motion.

"My dear man, let's not get carried away."

Nick chuckled.

"That's cool. You two should have fun together. I'll be fine."

"Thanks buddy. I knew you would understand. I'll have Marissa see if Isabella is free tonight. Maybe we can all go out, if you have nothing planned—something perhaps with Luciana? How did you make out with her, anyway?"

Nick wrinkled his face.

"It was nice. We got more drinks and hung out at the club a little while longer. She had an early flight to catch, so that was it."

"I'm surprised. She seemed so into you. Did you dance with her?"

"No."

"Okay? How about your lunch with Elizabeth? Did she at least let you pay this time?"

"That's a lot to talk about. I don't want to spoil your day."

Nick watched Marissa. Marissa pulled herself out of the pool and rung out her hair. She traipsed, dripping wet, around the edge of the pool. Her wet white bikini did little to hide the dark area of her areolae that circled her stiff nipples. Further down, her bikini bottom clung to the contours of her sex. She stood alongside Blake's chair as droplets ran down her body. She seemed not to care how her swimsuit clung to her, unlike the girls Nick knew who would tug and pick at their crotch. There was no attempt to adjust her swimsuit. He tried not to ogle her. She grinned at him. He adjusted the front of his swim trunks and bent his knee to hide his crotch. When she straddled Blake, they kissed deep. Her tongue visibly flicked in and out of his mouth. She ground her crotch against his. The front of Blake's swimsuit rose. Nick turned his gaze to the shimmering ripples in the pool. Jeez, get a room.

"More drinks, por favor," Blake said.

Marissa stood, holding Blake's empty glass.

"Nick, what would you like to drink?" Blake asked.

"Same, whatever."

Blake held up three fingers. Marissa smiled and nodded, then she slinked down the side of the pool. Blake had a wet spot on the crotch of his swim trunks where Marissa sat. There were also droplets on his chest and sunglasses. Nick shook his head and chuckled, then they both laughed.

"I'm glad you're having a great time," Nick said.

Blake's smile faded.

"Yeah, but that's not the reason for our trip. It's supposed to be for you. So what happened? You and Elizabeth had lunch. Did you eat something that didn't agree with you? Did you vomit on her?"

Nick rubbed his face.

"God, no. That would have been much easier to deal with."

"Ah? Oh—kay."

"Lunch was perfect. I finally told Elizabeth how much I liked her. After lunch, we went for a walk to this incredible square called Puerta del Sol."

"Been there. Marissa and Stella took me."

"Whatever. I need you to listen."

"Go on."

He pinched the bridge of his nose, then continued.

"Anyway, it was perfect. We shared our first kiss, then I walked her back to her hotel. She told me to go back to my room and dress up for an evening out, to get drinks, dance, whatever."

"Whatever?"

He nodded.

"When I got back to her hotel, I got her flowers and went to her room. No drinks, no dancing, but some amazing whatever."

Blake cocked his head.

"The whatever, whatever?"

Nick raised his eyebrows.

"The whatever."

He peered at the shimmering ripples in the pool.

"Okay, so you two fucked. Do I have to torture you for the details?"

He huffed and smirked at Blake.

"So I spent the night. She left in the morning for an early business meeting. I was on cloud nine until I got back here. There was a letter from her at the front desk. Essentially she said, thanks, but this would never work out."

Blake was quiet. Nick glanced over at him.

"Sorry. I'm speechless. God, that's fucked up."

"Yeah."

"What are you going to do now? We've got two more days here."

"I thought about going to her hotel and confronting her. Let her tell me face-to-face that she doesn't want to be with me."

"I don't think that's a good idea. Maybe you should give her some time. We'll all be back in Atlanta in a few days. You could probably use the time to think."

Marissa returned with three glasses cradled in both hands. Nick jumped up to help her. He took one, then she handed Blake his. She sat at the foot of Blake's lounger and put her arm around his bent leg. Nick smiled at the both of them, then raised his glass.

"Cheers."

"Salud!" Marissa and Blake said.

They drank.

~

There had been no calls, no phone or text messages from Elizabeth, since Nick received her note from the hotel front desk. The finality of it was unbelievable. It was unclear if she wanted him to chase her. It seemed like another test. The hotel phone in his room rang and shook him from his thoughts.

"Hello?"

"Hola señor Evers. Cómo estás? Te espera una noche maravillosa. El señor Simmons solicita tu presencia para una noche increíble con…," a female voice said.

"What? Wait-wait. Did you say, Mr. Simmons? Blake? No hablo español."

There was laughter on the other end of the line.

"Hey, buddy. Are you dressed yet?" Blake said.

A lip smacking noise came through the receiver.

"Vamos, darse prisa," a female voice said.

He assumed it was Marissa and shook his head and laughed. There was laughter on the other end of the line.

"Nice, real nice. Yeah, I'll be ready in twenty minutes."

"Marissa says that Isabella will be there. We're going to keep you at a two-drink limit. Isabella doesn't want you getting sick this time," Blake said.

Blake's jerky laughter sounded as though Marissa were tickling him. Nick rolled his eyes.

"Yeah, okay. I'll meet you two in the lobby. Okay, see ya."

"Adiós."

He hung up the phone. Fuckers—literally. He chuckled to himself. At least Blake was having a good time.

He got a quick shower and was drying off when his cellphone rang. It was his default ringtone. He sauntered from the bathroom to the bed, where he left his phone. Colette's name appeared on the screen. It was her LA number, but he had yet to assign any specific ringtone. He put the call on speaker so he could dry off.

"Hey Colette."

"Hi Nick. How are you?"

"I'm enjoying all that Madrid offers."

He scrubbed his hair dry with the towel.

"Oh. I'm sorry. I thought you were back in Atlanta. I'll let you go."

"No-no, it's fine. I'm getting ready to go out with Blake. He met someone here. Her name is Marissa."

"Ooh, and you?"

"No, this is more of a contemplation of life or an existential journey for me."

He ran the towel over his chest and around his back.

"So the answer is, no. Seriously, Nick? Girls come after you and you don't even have to try. Are you hiding in your hotel room, or are you dressing up as a priest?"

"I'm sure that would make them come after me more, wouldn't it?"

Colette laughed.

"Yes—yes, it would."

Nick laughed. He stood naked in front of the mirror as he dried himself. What would she think if she could see him?

"We're going out tonight. Blake's friend, Juan Miguel, took us to some clubs, but he can't make it tonight, so we're on our own, and neither of us speaks Spanish."

He chuckled.

"When have words gotten in your way?"

"Seriously though, Colette. It's nice being here, away from my father. I'm glad Blake is having a great time, but I've not been in the mood to party. Maybe it would have been better if I went someplace quieter, so I could think."

"That doesn't sound like you."

If he stayed in Atlanta, all he would do is think about what Elizabeth was doing in Madrid.

"Nick, you there?"

"Yeah, sorry."

"Well, I think you should enjoy yourself. If you won't give yourself permission, you have mine."

"Thanks, mother."

Colette laughed.

"Are you still in California?"

"No, I've come back early to Atlanta. That's why I called."

"Oh. That's cool. Blake and I will be back in a couple of days. Let's get together."

"Yes, Nick Evers, let's."

"Anyway, I've got to finish getting ready to meet Blake and Marissa. It was nice hearing your voice."

"Yours too. See you soon."

"Bye Colette."

"Bye."

He waited for her to end the call and smiled at the silence between them. It was as if she hoped he would say something more. She finally ended the call.

8

Nick and Isabella rushed out of the club and onto the cobblestone sidewalk. His arm rested on her shoulders and her arm wrapped around his waist. A night of dancing left their sweaty faces shiny and their clothes clung to their bodies as they stumbled under the streetlights. Blake and Marissa left the club an hour earlier to go to his hotel room. There was a line of white cabs down the block with red stripes.

"Thank you. Gracias. I needed that."

He smiled with his eyes closed and his head tilted back as he took in the night air. Uncontrollable laughter escaped him. She beamed at him with her arm still around his waist. He gazed into her dark brown eyes, and then their lips met. His mind and body felt equally present. It was like when he kissed Elizabeth in the square. Isabella held his face in both hands and kissed him deep. Her lips were fuller and softer than anyone he had ever kissed. His tongue flicked against hers.

"Mi casa, sí?"

"Go to your place? Yes. Sí."

He smiled at her. She waved her hand high in the air to catch the attention of one of the cab drivers. They stood near the edge of the cobblestone sidewalk while crowds of people that were out enjoying the evening shuffled around them. He smiled inside at the couples with cheerful faces that passed by on the sidewalk. Across the street, he spotted Elizabeth. His body tensed. When he glanced at Isabella, he was grateful her attention was elsewhere. Elizabeth was with a tall man with dark hair, maybe in his late thirties or early forties. He looked like a Spaniard. She had her arm looped around his. They wore formal clothing. Maybe she had an evening business meeting. She wore dark stockings that might have been the same ones she wore the night they were together? He wondered if she miss her panties he took from her room. He huffed.

A white cab pulled to the curb where Nick and Isabella stood.

"Nick?"

She tugged his arm.

"Oh? Yeah—sorry."

She got in and slid across the seat. He glanced across the street once more, but Elizabeth had disappeared into the crowd. He got in the cab, and they were off to Isabella's place.

~

Elizabeth and Rafael strolled down the cobblestone sidewalks filled with tourists and locals. They passed a line of white cabs that sat waiting for potential fares from the club across the street.

"Lizzy, I can't tell you enough how delighted I am to see you again."

He had first given her a chiding yet playful look when they met for the evening.

"It's been a long time. Thank you for such a wonderful dinner. I've missed Spain, Madrid, and all my friends here."

"Have you spoken to Antonio?"

She lowered her gaze to the cobblestones as they walked.

"No."

"Oh? I'm sure he would love to hear from you, and more so, to see you."

"Yes. I know."

"He has never married, and he does not date anyone. I've only seen him with various women from time to time. He is a man, you know. As for his heart, I believe he is lonely."

"That's his choice."

Her tone was sharp.

"Is it?"

He was silent. As they walked on, she squeezed his arm to ease any tension and assure him that no harm was done.

"Tell me about this young man you mentioned over dinner."

She sighed and looked up at the streetlights, then tugged at his arm.

"There's not much to tell."

"Your eyes, earlier, said otherwise."

She half chuckled.

"Oh, Rafael. Not much escapes you."

"Lizzy."

His voice was firm.

"Okay. His name is Nicholas, or rather Nick. His father is the founder of a large biotech company that the company I work for does business with."

"Oh? Hm."

She glanced at him with narrow eyes and a smirk on her face.

"Something you want to say?"

"So this young man, Nick, you are in love with him, but you are worried about your job?"

She coughed.

"Don't be ridiculous."

"Am I?"

"Yes."

He tugged at her arm that was wrapped around his, but when he glanced at her, she turned her gaze away.

"Fine, Lizzy. Don't confess that you are hopelessly in love with this Nick, like you were with Antonio."

"You're being far too dramatic."

"Am I? Don't forget your many tears you brought to me over, Antonio. Will you now bring me tears over this, Nick?"

She was quiet. The streets thinned of pedestrians and few people passed them as they walked on. She drew in a sharp breath.

"I don't know what to think or feel about Nick. He seems obsessed with me. God, he's ten years younger than I am! Why are we having this conversation?"

"There must be some feelings. That—Lizzy—is why we are having this conversation."

They stopped under the streetlight. She peered down at their shoes.

"I toyed with him, but he seemed to enjoy it. His patience wore me down and I slept with him. I thought that would be enough for him to realize that we could have nothing more than a sexual relationship. I want more than that, or nothing at all."

"I see. What happened?"

"I wrote him a letter telling him we could never be."

"Why not talk to him and make him understand?"

"Hah."

His eyes widened.

"He won't let go. I just know it."

"Why do you believe that? Does he chase after you? Stand outside your window like Romeo? Call your phone incessantly?"

"No."

His eyebrows drew together and his lips parted, then he shrugged.

"He cried the night we were together. Like someone lost, then found."

"Hm."

"The first time we met, he acted as though he had a simple crush on me, nothing more. Then he calls my assistant and arranges for a business lunch. I go. It was a pleasant lunch, more personal than business. I found him delightful, and he's very handsome, so I flirted a bit. I'll admit."

"And now? He is here in Spain. In this very city."

"His parents were sending him on a vacation to Italy, but he came to Spain instead. Before his flight, he texted me saying that he hoped to see me in Madrid."

"And he has."

"You're not being very helpful."

"Lizzy, I am now hearing the details. I've had no time to form an opinion, but I have a question."

"Yes?"

"What if he is deeply in love with you? Does anything else matter?"

She wrinkled her lips.

"When you were a young man of twenty-six, could you imagine yourself being with only one woman?"

"I was never in love when I was twenty-six. So, I can not say."

She cocked her head.

"Don't you understand what I'm saying? Nick is at the point of some drastic life changes. He needs a casual girlfriend and not someone like me in his life. Besides, I don't need a boy."

"So, what you are saying is that you need a man? Perhaps like Antonio?"

"No. Not that either."

"Why? What was wrong with Antonio? You never told me anything. Only that you two wanted different things."

"We did, and that was everything. I wanted my life."

He snorted, put his hands in his pockets, and shrugged.

"Okay, I understand Antonio can be inflexible, but what about Nick?"

"There's something sweet about him. I don't get the impression that he would try to control me."

"But you fear he might hurt you, being a young man, as you say."

"The hurt. I can deal with that kind of pain. What I can't deal with is losing myself. Do you understand?"

She took his arm, and they both walked along.

"Yes, Lizzy—I do."

The cab dropped Isabella and Nick off on a quiet narrow street among unending columns of residential flats with no alleys between them. He paid the taxi driver.

"Hola Isabella."

A voice came from above. Isabella waved up at the balcony, where a shirtless middle-aged man waved back. The man leaned on his elbows over the black wrought-iron railing with a cigarette between his fingers. There were other balconies occupied with people enjoying the night air.

Nick followed Isabella into the building. She chatted in Spanish with an old woman as they rode the elevator to the third floor. The old woman could have been her grandmother, but she stood closer to him, which dispelled that notion. The woman stared at him. He offered a polite smile, but then kept his gaze on the illuminated numbers above the doors. When they got off the elevator, Isabella turned to the old woman before the doors shut.

"Buenas noches."

The old woman said the same, but she only looked at Nick. He gave the old woman a friendly smile, but was relieved that she remained in the elevator car. Guilt crept in, manufactured by the old woman's sideways glances. Isabella took his hand and guided him down the hallway. Faint music and voices came from behind closed doors. She stopped in the hallway.

"Aquí estamos."

He gave her a smile, and his eyes widened. She unlocked the door; they went inside and she switched on the lights. Her flat was one large, narrow room. The ceiling was high. There was a small kitchen to the left with a table for two, a closed door to the right, which could be a closet or laundry room. He raised his eyebrows when he peered into the shadowy doorway from the living room. Enough light filtered into the room to see that it was the bedroom. In the living room there was a beige sofa, a bright red easy chair, and two tall doors that opened to a balcony.

"Perdón."

She smiled at him and stepped gracefully, like a dancer, into the living room to open the doors to the balcony and let in the night air. He followed her into the living room and stood by the sofa.

"Come? Ven, ven."

She motioned for him to join her on the balcony. He did. She held his face and kissed him. He took her into his arms. Again, the softness and fullness of her lips surprised him. He only held her three times this evening, a brief friendly hug when they met up at the dance club, once in the street, and now on the balcony. She had brushed up against him when they danced, and as provocative as that was, this was more intimate.

Marissa must have told her more about him from speaking to Blake. He wondered if she knew about his father and his father's company. Maybe. He doubted Blake mentioned Elizabeth and hoped that was the case. There were no tense moments this evening between them. He gazed into her dark chocolate brown eyes like a cliff diver preparing to leap and trusting the depths of the water below. They kissed. Deep and wet.

She led him back inside and gestured for him to sit. He sat on the beige suede sofa while she went to the kitchen. He stretched his arm across the sofa back and smiled at the framed black and white poster of New York City's Flatiron Building. On the opposite wall hung another framed black and white poster. A photograph of James Dean. He chuckled. The rebel without a cause.

"El vino?"

She held out a glass of red wine for him. Its bubbles made it look more like a mixed drink.

"Gracias."

He waited for her to sit.

"Salud," he said.

"Cheers," she said.

Their glasses made a crisp chime when they touched.

"Mm. Bueno," he said.

"Tinto de verano. Is good, sí?"

"Yes, sí."

She tilted her head and ran her fingers through her long dark brown waves to the blonde highlighted ends.

"Te gusto? Nick, do you like me?"

"I do. Yes. Sí."

She slid closer to him on the sofa. They held their glasses of wine and kissed.

"Perdón me."

She sat her glass of wine on the floor at the side of the couch, then disappeared into the bedroom. She turned on a light, and only half closed the door. He eased back on the sofa and drank the wine. A breeze came in through the balcony along with low Spanish speaking voices and an occasional low growl of car tires on the cobblestone street below. For the first time, he felt no pressure from anyone, even himself. As he listened to her in the other room, his smile inside surfaced. He stretched out his legs and drank.

When she came out, she stood in the doorframe. She had freshened up her makeup, changed her clothes, and removed her shoes. With her bare heels on the floor, she appeared more vulnerable. Maybe it was the change in her height. She wore a stretchy white ribbed tank top and a pair of lightweight pink cotton lounge shorts. Her top contoured to the shape of her breasts and did nothing to hide her nipples. Her hips led to long, slender bare legs and delicate feet.

"Is this okay?"

He stared with his lips parted.

"Yes."

She laughed at his expression, retrieved her glass of wine, and sat next to him. He felt self-conscious and slipped off his shoes. They sipped their wine. He pointed to the poster of the Flatiron Building.

"Do you like New York?"

"Ah, sí New York. Mm. Someday."

"Sí, someday."

He sat his glass of wine on the floor and rubbed his hands together like he was washing them.

"Ah? Baño?"

"Sí, in there."

Light from the adjoining bathroom spilled into the dark bedroom. From the window on the opposite wall, streetlights cast shadows across the ceiling. He went in and closed the door. The sound of his stream echoed off the tiled walls. It reminded him of the bathrooms in one of Autumn's father's hotels, where he and Autumn met for sex. He splashed water on his face and wondered if coming here was a mistake. Isabella is a nice girl. He questioned if this night was only about sex. He doubted if he could give her anything more. When he opened the bathroom door, she stood next to the bed. The lights were out in the living room.

When he went to her, she put her arms around his neck, stood on her toes, and angled her chin upward to kiss him. He held her waist. Her lean midriff—flesh, muscle, ribs—shifted warm and alive under his touch. She unbuttoned his shirt and let it fall to the floor, then she went and turned out the bathroom light. Her hands came around him from behind and unbuckled his belt, and lowered his trousers to his ankles. She left soft kisses on his back. The light was dim when she stepped around him. She swayed as if dancing to slow music that only she could hear. She lifted her tank top below her breasts, gazed at him, then pulled her top off. Her nipples were stiff and raised. She flipped her hair and tossed her top somewhere in the shadows.

He stood there in his briefs. Their lips met. Her firm breasts and tone body pressed against his and he lifted her into his embrace. His cock swelled. She ran an open palm from his cock to his lean midsection. She directed him to the corner of the bed, where she removed his briefs. His heavy, stiff cock angled toward her. She urged him into a seated position, then knelt between his knees. She grasped his cock and gave the head a playful lick. There was enough light from the window that he could see her face when she looked up at him.

"You like?"

He swallowed and licked his lips.

"Sí."

His breath caught as her tongue inched up his cock. She cupped his balls in one hand and stroked him with the other, then licked the head of his cock, and took him into her mouth. He braced his arms back on the mattress. She worked him to near agony. He sucked in a breath through clenched teeth, then grunted.

"Wait."

He held her wrist as he teetered on the edge of climax.

"Please—please. Por favor."

The light was too dim to tell if she was angry or confused. He pulled her up between his legs, then kissed her rougher than he intended, but she responded by slipping her thigh over his. She straddled his leg and stroked him as they kissed. He stopped her. She went to the nightstand. After she fumbled through the contents of the drawer, she held up a condom packet and jiggled it between her fingertips.

She unwrapped the condom and touched his shoulder to suggest that he lie down. Instead, he took the condom and placed it on the nightstand. He then knelt at her feet and caressed her lower legs, her knees, and her thighs. His hands slipped under her shorts to squeeze her buttocks. She gasped. He kissed her stomach. Her body was more toned than Autumn's. He shook the thought of Autumn from his mind, but he wanted to fuck this girl like he fucked her. He grasped the bottoms of her shorts, slid them down her legs, then placed kisses from her navel to her smooth shaved sex. A soft hum passed her lips.

After she reclined on the bed with her legs open, he grasped her hips and pulled her to him. He was about to put his mouth on her, but kissed her inner thigh instead, as he and done with Elizabeth. She moaned. When he reached the top of her thigh, he hovered over her sex, and breathed her in. She smelled of spice, perhaps her perfume, a hint of sweat, and her feminine scent. He released a slow, warm, heavy breath. A low hum passed her lips. He kissed the velvet line that hid her labia. The next time, his tongue slid between her slit and into her delicate folds. She was wet, her sweet honey clung to his tongue.

There was less flesh to her sex, as there was to Elizabeth's. He pushed the comparison from his mind, and pressed his tongue into her folds and dipped into her sweet hole. Her moans intensified. He slithered his tongue upward and kissed and licked her clit. His finger slid inside her. She flexed her buttocks to raise her pelvis and press her sex to his lips. He created slow circles and her hips rocked. Her breathing became heavy.

"Oh Dios! Oh Dios!"

Her body shuddered. She grasped his head, pressed his face between her legs, while she climaxed. Her juices flowed to his awaiting tongue. Her legs lie limp in his arms. He kissed her thighs, then she sat up on her elbows.

"Oh mío."

She caught her breath and released a burst of giddy laughter. He smirked at her and she playfully bit her finger. She laughed as she ran her fingertips over his wet lips.

She grasped the condom from the nightstand and took his hand to guide them onto the bed. After she rolled the condom over his cock, she straddled him and kissed his chest and neck. Their lips and tongues met. She tasted of sweet summer wine. She tilted her pelvis and rode her clit over the length of his shaft. His thick and swollen cock divided her wet folds as she moved her pelvis forward and back. She slipped her hand between her legs and directed the tip of his cock inside her.

With her hands on his ribs for balance, she rose upright and took his entire length inside her. Her head tilted back and her lips parted. He held her thighs. She pressed her elbows against her ribs, which made her breasts more pronounced. He groaned as she pivoted her hips on each rise and descent. He caressed her thighs to waist, to ribs, to breasts. A surge grew from his anus, to scrotum, to cock. He flexed his buttocks and held on as long as he could. The muscles in his lower back clenched, and his chest hardened to stone. She cried out each time their bodies collided. He held her waist and raised his hips in a final upward thrust, which lifted her off the bed. His cock electrified as he filled her.

"Oh, fuck!"

He groaned deep. His own voice surprised him, or it may have been the room's acoustics. She made soft moans and sighs. Her muscles relaxed, and she moved in a slow, dreamlike rhythm. He covered his eyes with his forearm and sunk into the pillow. His body spent. Her weight left him. The mattress jostled as she fell and rolled to lie next to him. She muttered something in Spanish, then removed the condom from him. He peeked under his arm.

She climbed off the bed and went into the bathroom. He heard her toss the condom into the trash, and he squinted when she turned on the bathroom light. She was bent over in front of the sink with her legs parted. He rolled on his side and propped his head up under his arm. She wiped between her legs and washed her hands. She then sat on the toilet in the far corner of the bathroom behind a narrow partition, with only her knees in view.

There was an urge to pee, so he lumbered to the bathroom and leaned against the doorframe while he waited for her to finish. He combed his fingers through his hair and listened to her pee. He enjoyed listening to Autumn pee after sex, and he smiled now as he did then. When Isabella appeared, her expression was less joyful.

"You okay? Bueno?"

She shrugged with a tight smile. There was a hint of tension, maybe fear, in her eyes. She waved her hand dismissively, patted his chest, and stepped around him. He went and relieved himself, then found her sitting cross-legged on the bed.

"Por favor vaya."

He stood there naked with his hands open. She tossed his clothes at him.

"Ah?"

He put his trousers on without his briefs. Party's over. He picked up his shirt and buttoned it. She glared at him.

"Por favor?" he said.

"Go," she said.

Her door made a loud clunk that echoed in the hallway. It reminded him of the New York apartments he had been to. When he made it to the street, he hissed out a slow breath. He peered up at the third floor, not sure which balcony belonged to her flat. He shook his head and took out his phone. There were several text messages from Autumn, one from Blake, and one voice message—from Elizabeth.

"Hello Nick. I would like to see you. Meet me at the restaurant Deseo Estrella tomorrow at 2 p.m. If you can't make it, I'll understand."

He considered deleting her message, instead he put his phone back in his pocket. She got what she wanted—him moving on, or at least trying to. He shook his head, then glanced up the cobblestone street. It was well lit, but quiet, with no taxicabs in sight. He walked in the opposite direction of the cab that drove them earlier and hoped he would find one of the major streets.

9

Elizabeth sat in Deseo Estrella, one of her favorite restaurants. It was a cozy little bistro and bar with rich wood panels and exposed brick walls, simple wooden chairs, and tables covered in pale yellow linen tablecloths. She sat in a private corner, away from the windows, but with an unobstructed view of the people passing by on the sidewalk. She glanced out often and hoped to see Nick when he arrived—that is—if he ever did.

The server, a middle-aged man with noticeably dyed hair, too dark for his pale complexion, came by with a bottle of wine. Before he could ask, she nodded. He turned over the empty wineglass on the table, filled it, and sat it next to the full glass of ice water that had been sweating droplets onto the linen tablecloth. She rotated the wineglass by its stem and continued to gaze outside the window. She wrinkled her lips. He was late.

"Miss? Are you waiting for someone?"

Nick stood there in a green gingham shirt open at the collar, with one or two buttons unbuttoned more than usual, cream-colored trousers and tan loafers. His hair was a beautiful mess, wavy and finger-combed, as if he had just returned from a ride up the coast in a convertible. He had also taken on a light golden tan.

"Hello."

The dryness of her voice surprised her.

"Elizabeth."

His tone was flat and cautious.

"Please, won't you join me?"

He sat across from her. She gestured to the server, who returned with a bottle of wine and a pitcher of water. While their glasses were being filled, Nick took in the restaurant. She held up her hand before the server could speak.

"Un momento por favor."

The server nodded and left them. Nick glanced at the wineglass before him. When his gaze met hers, he looked away.

"Thanks for coming. I wasn't sure if you—you didn't leave a text message or—never mind, I'm happy you're here."

Her words trailed off to a whisper. She picked up her wineglass and drank.

He sighed, then his gaze met hers. The tension in his eyes and the tightness of his lips were the only things in contrast to his otherwise comfortable appearance.

"Sure. It's good to see you again, Elizabeth. What's on your mind?"

His voice was flat and detached.

"I'm sorry, I wrote you the letter. It was too hasty. I'm not used to having my feelings flying around like birds that have escaped their cage."

He lowered his gaze and shifted the glass of wine in front of him, then released a heavy breath.

"That's an interesting way to put it. You always impressed me as a woman who was bold and decisive. As successful as you are, don't you have to be a person who takes risks and makes *the leap*?"

She knew he meant faith, but right now, faith eluded her. She shifted in her seat.

"Yes—yes, I suppose. But it's good to know where you're going to land, so you don't risk getting hurt."

He stared at the wineglass and rotated it in both hands as if he were examining it, while he turned his head subtly from side to side. A soft, whispered breath passed his lips.

"I love you."

Her eyebrows drew together.

"What did you say, Nick?"

He cleared his throat.

"What are we doing here, Elizabeth? What is this?"

She looked away.

"I don't know, Nick. This is all unfamiliar territory for me."

His eyebrows drew together, and he cocked his head.

"I'm trying to process everything—my feelings—everything."

She peered into his eyes. They were a deep green pasture of possibilities.

"I need time."

"Okay."

The server returned. She ordered a salad despite her lack of hunger.

"Nothing for me."

He looked at the server and turned his head from side to side. After the server left, she felt the need to reach for Nick. She put her hands on the table, but they never passed her wineglass.

"Are you not hungry?"

"No, I've got to go. Blake and I have to head to the airport. We'll be flying home early this evening."

She waited for him to ask her what she was going to do, or when she would return to the United States, but he was silent.

"I hope you and Blake have a safe trip home. I'll see you in Atlanta, and we can figure things out there."

They stood, shared a brief polite hug, and she kissed his cheek.

"Nick?"

"Yes."

"You can call me Lizzy."

A tense, tight-lipped smile appeared on his face, but the pain in his eyes remained. As he walked away, she hoped he would turn around, rush back, and take her into his arms. Instead, she watched him leave, then waited for him to pass by the restaurant's windows, but he never did.

There was no going back now. Elizabeth stood in front of the door to Antonio's flat. In the past, he usually left the door ajar. Rather than knock, she stared at the peephole and wondered if he watched her from the other side. She raised her closed hand to tap on the door, but it finally opened and there he stood. Her lips curled into a soft smile when their eyes met.

"Hello Lizzy."

He had the same beautiful rugged face of a fearless bullfighter. His chestnut colored eyes held a steely gaze, and his long shoulder length wavy black hair, now accompanied by strands of gray. He was barefoot and his clothes were loose-fitting. He wore an untucked, faded blue shirt with oyster shell buttons and tan linen trousers. All he was missing was a straw hat and a sandy beach to stroll on.

"Hi Antonio. May I come in?"

He bowed his head, stood aside, and held the door for her. Her heels clicked on the entranceway tiles. She slipped past the kitchen and into the living room. It was almost as he left it when she last saw him. There were new books and a new picture or two. The plants and flowers, of course, were different because he lacked the skill to keep them alive. Her lips curved into a soft smile of remembrance. She turned around, and he stood there with his hands in his pockets.

"Your place. It's as I remembered."

"I'm pleased—and you—you *are* as I remembered."

His voice was rich and familiar, and his Spanish accent was dangerously sexy. Her eyebrows rose, then fell, and her lips tightened. She went to Antonio, and they shared a brief hug and a polite kiss on the cheek.

"I was pleased to get your call. It's been a long time. How are you, Lizzy?"

"I'm well. Very busy."

He raised his eyebrows.

"Oh? What brings you to Madrid?"

"Business."

"I see."

"Will you be staying long?"

"I'm actually flying back to the United States tomorrow morning."

"Ah. Then we must not squander the time we have. Sit, please. I'll get us some drinks."

"That would be nice."

He hurried off to the kitchen. She glanced at the modern leather sofa, to the leather club chairs, and to the rug on the living room floor. Every place she could think of was one where they shared a passionate moment. She put herself in an unfair situation by coming here. She could have easily met him for lunch at any restaurant and he would have come. Clattering from the kitchen woke her from her thoughts. She sat in one of the two leather club chairs. He returned with two glasses of deep-red sangria, with slices of lemon, lime, and other various bits of fruit. They made a quick toast to her visit, then he sat on the leather sofa across the glass and chrome coffee table from her. She drank, then nodded.

"Very good."

He smiled and sat casually with his legs crossed and his arm over the back of the sofa. He pinched at the leather seam that ran across on the top of the sofa cushion.

"I saw Rafael."

"Oh?"

"He tells me you never married and don't have a girlfriend."

"Are you here to rectify that?"

She cocked her head and wrinkled her lips.

"You can tell Rafael my life is none of his business."

"I think he worries about you."

He snorted.

"He has nothing to worry about."

"Doesn't he?"

"We all made our choices, Lizzy. You chose. I chose. What is the saying, like ships that pass in the night?"

"Have you moved on? Have you found someone? Are you happy?" she asked.

He looked toward the balcony. The breeze animated the tall sheer drapes.

"As much as we desire, there are some things that are not meant to be. Isn't that right, Lizzy?"

She drank and her gaze lowered to peer at the glass of sangria she held in her lap. She was silent.

"Well, the past is the past. You are here. That is all that is important. Let's not dig up old ghosts."

Elizabeth smiled and stifled a chuckle. She knew he meant bones.

"Let's drink to that. No old ghosts," she said.

She held her glass up to drink, but laughter overtook her. He raised his eyebrows, shook his head, then laughed. They raised their glasses and enjoyed the sangria. She took a lengthy swallow.

"Oh," he said.

He went to the kitchen and brought out the pitcher of sangria. After he filled her glass, he left the pitcher on the coffee table. He had a manner in which he always sat comfortable, casual, and inviting. That made her want to be close to him. She drank the sangria and wondered how many she would need to quell her nerves.

"Have you seen any of your friends?"

"I had lunch with Gabriella. I think you met her once or twice."

He cocked his head and looked off in thought.

"The journalist, beautiful, yes?"

She smirked at him.

"Yes, she's a journalist."

He raised an eyebrow and smirked at her.

"And, yes, she *is* pretty."

His chin rose, and he grinned.

"Are you interested in her? Shall I arrange a lunch date? Of course, I'll have to warn you, she likes younger men."

He laughed and drank.

"No, I've finally come to a peaceful place where I can work and enjoy my life without considerations. I suppose, much like what you have."

There was a bitter tone to his words. She drank, and he sighed.

"It's beautiful outside. Shall we go out on the balcony?"

"Yes, please, let's."

His balcony looked out over a quiet enclosed courtyard, unlike many that faced the street. The breeze lifted her long, dark curls. She intended to put her hair up in a bun, to suggest her visit was a friendly one and nothing more, but she relished the way he looked at her, and she needed that. She wore heels for the same reason, and could have opted for comfortable sneakers or loafers. The heels were ones he got for her years ago. Another misstep, or not. The sangria eased her tension and quieted second thoughts. It also made it easier when he put his hand on her lower back. She wore an oversize casual top with a scoop back over her tight black capris. His touch was warm. Electricity travelled down her spine, into her hips, and settled between her thighs. Soon she would be wet, she was sure of it.

The breeze caught his hair. He was ten years older than her, the same age difference between her and Nick. He smiled at her. His dark shoulder-length hair flowed in the wind, while his shirt gaped open to reveal defined ridges where muscles met bone. He was an older man, but far from decrepit. He was the type of man who could ride in on a stallion, sweep her up, and ride off with her. She smiled inside.

"I miss these moments, Lizzy."

The warmth of his hand on her back was intoxicating. The sangria had softened her senses. She leaned in and kissed him. She stumbled, and he took her up in his arms. It was a familiar embrace, one filled with undeniable memories that lingered and haunted her. His kisses were always deep, but he never put his tongue in her mouth. She never knew why, but she took it as a kind of gentlemanly respect, which she admired.

"That was quite unexpected," he said.

"I'm sorry. I guess I was caught up in the moment."

Her eyelids were heavy and dreamy.

"No apologies necessary. We have history. Good history. I believe. Good memories. Yes?"

"Yes, of course."

They looked down into the courtyard. An old woman sat on a bench talking to a small wiry-haired dog that lie at her feet. Since they kissed, he now held her around her waist. She watched the old woman stroll away with her dog.

"Come inside, Lizzy. I want to make love to you."

She knew and felt his intense gaze without having to look at him. His warm hand covered hers as she held the railing. She nodded, and he led her inside.

~

A breeze joined them in the bedroom from the open balcony doors and animated the long sheer drapes in a dreamlike undulation. Their clothes lie strewn on the tiled floor. Elizabeth's arms curved above her head like a ballerina as she lie on her back. Her legs bent at the knees as if captured at the height of a dancer's leap. Antonio flowed in and out between her legs like the tide. Her feet caressed his calves. He savored her body with long, engaging thrusts as he did the first time they had sex. It was as though he wanted to know her body completely. Now, it was as though he never wanted to forget.

His steady, slow tide rose to a storm that sent waves crashing to her shores. Her body shifted among the sheets and pillows each time he plunged into her. Her cries carried to the tall ceiling. Their moans joined in a duet. He groaned and huffed in breaths like a pearl diver who had dove beyond his limits. Then his body stiffened and shook as his seed spilled into her.

They lie naked on their backs. Both gazed transfixed at the ceiling. She pondered the cracks like a fortune teller ponders lines in a palm. Their bodies lie wrecked like two lovers who leapt off a cliff to die together. His chest rose and fell like a receding tide. Silver strands adorned his wiry chest hair that circled his nipples and ran down the center of his abdomen to his navel.

"I never imagined for the rest of my life that you would ever let me touch you again, the way I wanted to touch you."

His words were shaky.

"I know," she whispered.

"Lizzy—"

"Wait. This moment, as wonderful as it was, was just that—a moment, a onetime thing. You see. I've found someone, but I never properly ended things between us. At least not in a fair way."

"So this is your goodbye kiss?"

He snorted.

"You know Lizzy, we could have been spectacular together. We both love to travel. We could have experienced so many incredible things—together."

She swallowed. A tear pooled at the inner corner of her eye. She held her eyes shut and wiped it away.

"I know. We could have experienced wonderful things, but not with the love I needed. One that will allow me to be free and to be myself."

"Do you think any man can give you that? I think not. Men will always feel the need to possess women, especially the ones they love."

"Maybe—maybe not. This man I've met is younger and more progressive. He doesn't need to control me. He sees me as an equal."

"So that is it? Was I just your captor? Your older lover with outdated views on relationships?"

She turned on her side with her back to him.

"This man. This younger man, you say. How long do you think he will to care for you? Ten years? Twenty years? Fifty years?"

He snorted. She sighed as she lay facing away from him.

"He told me he loves me. I believe him."

A sigh hissed past his lips.

"And I—I think I love him."

He huffed. She turned to lie on her other side to face him, but he sat on the edge of the bed with his back to her. He struck a match and lit a cigarette. He made a hissing sound when he took in a long drag. It was the sound she remembered when she last saw him. When she left him and Spain for the United States. It was the sound of someone witnessing tragedy unfold before their very eyes.

"I'm sorry I've come. This was a mistake."

She stood and dressed. He said nothing. He stayed at the edge of the bed, his back to her, as he smoked his cigarette. Perhaps he peered outside, or perhaps his eyes were closed. She was unsure. No other words passed between them when she left.

When she crossed the courtyard, she glanced up at his balcony. The doors were open. One drape fluttered outside the doorway as if to wave goodbye. She expected he might come to the balcony to watch her as she left, but the balcony was empty. When she got to the street, she hailed a taxi. When it pulled to the curb, she took off her heels—her prized black Christian Louboutin heeled sandals, the ones he had gotten her—and put them in the trash. She then slipped barefoot into the taxi.

10

Josephine sat with Nick, alfresco, at a French bistro in downtown Atlanta. Although the restaurant's tables had large square umbrellas to shade its patrons from the bright sun, they wore their sunglasses. She beamed across the table at him. She was excited to take her son to lunch and chat about his time in Spain. Hopefully, he would tell her about his future at Hale Biotech, but she was most eager to find out who was in the running to be his wife, if there *was* one.

"I'm so happy you're back home. Everyone's missed you so much."

She leaned toward him and rubbed his forearm. He smiled.

"You know your father. All he's been doing is working. He's been making all the necessary arrangements for you to start. He picked out a nice office space for you and even hired an assistant."

"Why do I need an assistant? I thought I was going to be *the assistant*, at least until I got some time in."

"He wants to throw you in the deep end and see how you make out."

"Great."

"You'll do fine. You got Dale, Lloyd, and Jason to watch over you."

"Sure."

He took a drink of the white wine spritzer his mother ordered for the both of them. He brushed his fingers through his hair. Her lips tightened.

"You look tired."

"Yeah, the time difference."

"Shall we order you some coffee?"

"No, I'm good."

She reached over and held his forearm.

"So tell me, how was Spain, and how much trouble did you and Blake get into?"

He chuckled. She raised her eyebrows.

"Madrid was nice. The hotel and rooms were excellent. The nightlife was crazy."

He paused.

"Hm. Sounds like you could have done all that here. Did you take in any culture?"

"Oh yeah. The food, the people. We visited Puerta del Sol. It's an amazing square, where the major streets of Spain originate from."

She drank her wine spritzer. A subtle smirk appeared on her face.

"Good. What else? Did you go to the Prado museum? What about any of the cathedrals? There are other squares as well, like the Plaza Mayor."

"Mom, you've never been there. How do you know?"

"First off, I love art and you know I wouldn't have missed an opportunity to visit the Prado. The rest, I read in travel guides, which I wish you would have paid more attention to. It doesn't sound like you got much out of your trip. Let me guess, you and Blake were drunk all the time? Did you two go around making fools out of yourselves? Did you have parties in the hotel rooms? I'm sure your father and I will find out when we get the bill."

"Relax. We went to some dance clubs that Blake's friend took us to, but other than that, we just hung out. The hotel had a beautiful rooftop patio with a pool. Blake and I took advantage of that. The food was great and walking around the city was wonderful."

She took off her sunglasses. She believed him. He never lied to her, he only withheld information. She suspected that's what he was doing now.

"Nicholas, take off your sunglasses."

He removed his dark wayfarers and sat them on the table. Although the umbrella provided shade, he squinted at the bright sunlight.

"Blake met a girl. Not sure how serious it is, but they—sorry, her name is Marissa—hung out a lot. She's cool. Not sure what Blake really thinks. He hasn't told me anything yet."

She nodded.

"And you? Did you meet someone, perhaps one of Marissa's friends?"

He sat back in his chair and met her gaze.

"Not exactly. I danced with some of Marissa's friends. They were nice, but there was the language barrier."

She laughed.

"You don't have to explain that part to me. Your father and I speak the same language, and we still have difficulty communicating."

He raised his eyebrows and his lips wrinkled.

"Have you seen Autumn yet? She came over a few of times. We had lunch on the patio. She cares a lot about you. I need to know. Are you serious about her?"

"Ah—no. We're just friends."

"Son, I would say you're a little more than that."

"I guess, but neither of us are dating anyone."

"She is."

"Huh? Who?"

"You."

"No, she's not."

"That's not what she told me."

He crossed his arms and huffed. She held up her hands in a motion of surrender.

"Okay. It doesn't matter. That's good to hear. Your father and I like her. We just don't love her. We both think you need to be with someone else. Someone more on your level."

"You mean, Colette?"

"Colette is an incredibly smart and driven young woman."

She cocked her head. He gazed off, and a coy smile appeared on his lips. She followed her son's gaze, which was cast at a table with two women in sun dresses having a casual lunch. They looked in their thirties or early forties.

One of them must have noticed him. The woman smiled briefly at him before she returned her attention to her friend. Josephine poked at her salad.

"Have you thought about Colette?"

His gaze returned, but his smile faded.

"Oh, yeah, sure."

"She came back early from California. You should call her."

"Yeah, I know. She called me when I was in Madrid."

"She did? Nick, that's wonderful. What did you two talk about?"

"She asked how I was enjoying Madrid, and that she was back in Atlanta and we should get together."

"Oh Nick, that's excellent."

She leaned over her salad with her fingers knit together.

"Yeah, I'll call her later."

She grinned. Richard will be happy and relieved when that happens.

"Mom? What if I was interested in someone who was older than me?"

Josephine sat upright. She huffed and brushed her fingers through her hair at her shoulder.

"Nick, you can't be serious?"

He gazed at the two older women.

"Oh, I don't know. What if I am?"

She followed his gaze.

"Nicholas. As intriguing as that may be for you, I see no future in that endeavor."

He looked at her. His face was flat and serious. She hoped it was one of his pranks.

She drew her chin inward and her shoulders stiffened.

"Is there an older woman trying to seduce you?"

A brief raise of his eyebrows and her mouth dropped.

"It's not Abigale, is it?"

"Stop."

"Faye?"

"Mother?"

"Well, I know it can't be Maggie. She's too dull for you."

"And what if it was her?"

She wrinkled her lips and cocked her head.

"Nick, we both know which of my friends are always vying for your attention. I don't mind them flirting with you. That builds a young man's confidence, but I don't want you fucking any of them."

"Mom!"

She sat back in her chair with her arms crossed and waited for him to further explain himself.

"So, you're diametrically opposed to me having an older girlfriend?"

She shifted in her seat.

"Son, I am opposed to any form, way, shape, type, you want to call it. It's not right. I don't even like the idea of you having a one-night-stand with an older woman. What brought this on, anyway? Don't you get enough sex from Autumn? Her father owns those two hotels that you two are always messing up the beds. Sure, give me that look. I know *all* about your little adventures at the Ramada Inn and the Microtel."

He pinched the bridge of his nose and sighed.

"I hope you know. Your father and I give you a lot of leeway. Look at Peter and Derek's parents. Their parents are much stricter."

"And Peter and Derek both revolt. They drink, they screw around. They don't care."

Her shoulders fell. She put her hands on the table and raised her eyebrows.

"Sure. I agree, too much discipline can have negative effects. Your father and I wanted you to make your own decisions, and we hoped they would be good ones. If you ended up making any bad ones, we would help you correct them. This fantasy of being with an older woman should remain a fantasy. Trust me Nicholas."

She searched Nick's eyes for acknowledgment that she got through to him. The tension in his eyes faded, and his tight lips curved into a conciliatory smile.

"Okay."

While Nick ate his salad, she looked over at the table with the two women. The one that smiled at her son, laughed and chatted with her friend, then twirled the ends of her long curls around her finger. Her eyes snuck glances toward Nick until she noticed Josephine's glare.

Blake waited at the ground floor bar of Breezes, an upscale club in downtown Atlanta. He sipped a vodka tonic while he watched for Nick and texted back and forth with Marissa. Marissa should have been asleep since it was almost 3 a.m. in Madrid. Nick's mother, who knew the owners of Breezes, arranged for Nick and his friends to have a private table upstairs that overlooked the dance floor. Everyone waited upstairs for him to arrive. Blake texted Marissa goodnight.

"Blake Simmons!"

He looked up and Colette Scott stood in front of him with a smile. Her long, dark, honey-blonde hair with bleached tips had a style that made her look as though she spent the day at the beach. She wore a black off-the-shoulder long sleeve top with white skinny jeans and heeled sandals.

"Whoa!"

She laughed and held his arm.

"Hi Blake, how are you?"

He slipped off the barstool and held his arms open. They hugged.

"Wow Colette, you look fantastic! California is very agreeable with you."

She nodded and chuckled.

"Thank you. Yeah, I love it there. It's been a while. You're looking good, Blake. Something in your face. You're not engaged, are you?"

He laughed, then raised his eyebrows.

"No, but I've found someone I really like."

He looked around as if he was about to impart a secret.

"There's only one problem…"

"She lives in Spain?"

She drew her chin in and grinned at him. He raised an eyebrow and tilted his head. She took a hold of his arm.

"Don't be mad. Nick told me. Marissa, right?"

He smiled.

"No, that's cool that he told you. Yes, her name is Marissa. She lives in Madrid. I swear, I left my heart with her when I left Spain."

"Awe. Blake, you're going to make me cry."

They both laughed.

"Let me get you a drink."

"Where is everyone? Josephine Evers said you, Nick, and a few friends were going to be here tonight. She even got a car to bring me here. Is there some surprise going on?"

"Ah? She arranged a private table upstairs for the gang. Peter, Derek, Sandy, and their dates they brought with them are all upstairs, hopefully not drinking too much before Nick can get here. Of course, there's you, me, and Nick. I'm not sure if Autumn is coming."

Colette held her clutch handbag in both hands. She nodded with a tight lip smile. He pointed at his drink, and she nodded.

"Sangria."

He gave her a thumbs up and ordered her one. When she had her glass of Sangria, he texted Nick to let him know they would be upstairs.

"C'mon, let's go up."

When they got upstairs, Colette hugged Peter, Derek, and Sandy, while they each introduced their dates. Blake forgot their names from the time he left them upstairs until he returned. He was grateful to hear them again. Sandy's drink was near full, while Peter and Derek both had liquor-filled stares and empty glasses in front of them.

"Blake, how come you didn't bring a date?" Derek asked.

"I'm good."

Blake smiled at Colette. Peter followed Blake's gaze. Peter pointed back and forth between Blake and Colette.

Colette and Blake chuckled, and both spoke in unison.

"No, we're just friends."

"Anyone hear from Nick?" Derek shouted.

He looked over at Blake, who shook his head, then checked his phone for any text messages. There was only one from Marissa. It was a picture of Marissa lying in bed, blowing a kiss. Blake smiled. When he looked up,

Nick arrived at the table. He held up his phone and glanced over at Blake. Blake nodded.

"Got your message. Thanks."

Nick went around the table, hugs and handshakes. When Nick came to Colette, he gave her a longer hug. Blake smiled. He liked Autumn, but there was something about her that was too desperate. Hm. Nick and Colette looked good together. He hoped Nick had gotten over Elizabeth. Nick glanced at him. He raised his chin and grinned. The server came over and everyone ordered more drinks. Nick pointed to what Colette was having and ordered one of those. Colette moved to sit next to Nick.

As the night went on, Nick and Blake told everyone about their time in Spain. The girls, Sandy, Colette, Shannon, and Charlene, left the table to use the ladies' room. That left Sandy's date, Roger, a lanky redhead, behind with the boys. Blake was happy he remembered Shannon's and Charlene's names. At least he hoped so. Derek said that both girls were roommates attending Georgia State University. Blake and Nick laughed when Peter said that. They picked them up at Starbucks. Peter has better luck over lattes than at any bar or club. Derek has picked up girls at the laundromat. Both Blake and Nick shared glances. They laughed and shook their heads at their friend's stories. Roger chimed in. He mentioned he met Sandy at the library. Blake wrinkled his face. They all laughed anyway and Roger, red-faced, joined them.

Blake's smile faded. When he looked at Nick, Nick's eyebrows drew together and he tilted his head.

"Hey Autumn," Derek said.

Nick turned around, stood, and gave Autumn a hug. Blake, Peter, and Derek also stood.

"Hi Autumn," Blake said.

He watched Nick as Nick spoke to Autumn. Their faces were close to each other. Autumn crossed her arms and her lips tightened as she peered up at Nick. He bent down to whisper into her ear. Her gaze looked strained. He waved the server over and got a drink for her. Autumn sat where Colette was sitting.

Peter leaned close to Blake.

"What's that all about?" Peter asked.

Blake shrugged.

"I guess she didn't get an invite."

When the four girls returned, Colette smiled and gestured for Autumn to stay sitting next to Nick. She grabbed her drink and sat at the other end of the table next to Blake. He smiled at her. He then glanced at Autumn. She laughed at a joke Derek told, but her face looked tense as though someone had slapped her. Nick finished his drink and was working on his second. Blake snorted and shook his head. When he looked at Colette, she was staring at him.

"Oh, sorry, what did you say?"

"Do you know if Nick and Autumn are dating?"

"No, they're not."

"Then why does Autumn look pissed?"

"I don't think she got an invite for this little gathering."

Colette's eyes widened, and she nodded.

"What are you two conspiring at down there?" Nick said.

Blake's lips parted. He glanced at Nick and Autumn.

"Blake was telling me about his new girlfriend," Colette said.

Colette laughed as she tugged at Blake's arm. He gave her a dirty look.

"Sorry, that was his announcement to make."

She held her hands up in an admission of guilt.

Peter and Derek looked confused, which made their dates, Shannon and Charlene, look confused. Nick pointed at Blake and laughed, then everyone joined in as Blake held up his hands in surrender. Blake caught Autumn's sideways glance at Colette. Colette seemed not to notice or care. Autumn moved her chair closer to Nick. Blake snorted, then wrinkled his lips when he saw the defeated look on Nick's face.

"I don't know about everyone, but our good friend Nicholas Evers has his first day at work tomorrow. Isn't that right, Nick?" Blake said.

Blake held up his glass. Nick looked up and smiled at him.

"That's right."

Everyone held up their glasses.

"To Nick's first day. May he not be terribly hung over. First impressions are important, they say," Blake said.

They all laughed and drank. Nick turned his head side-to-side and smirked at him.

"Thanks for the toast. I'm so happy to see you all again. Let's get together soon. I need to get some sleep."

Nick smiled at Colette. Autumn held his arm and looked to be chastising him on their way out. Outside, Blake turned to Colette.

"Can I give you a ride?"

"Thanks, but Nick's mom arranged a car for me. There they are. Thanks for a fun night, Blake. Good luck with Marissa."

Colette gave him a hug and a kiss on the cheek. Then she traipsed off to a large black sedan that was parked by the curb to pick her up. He watched her. She moved well in heels, as though she had been to her fair share of exclusive California parties. It was easy to see why Nick's parents wanted him to date her. Funny thing was, she appeared as though she could take or leave him. Blake put his hands in his pockets and raised his eyebrows as he watched the black sedan drive off with Colette. He was unsure where Nick and Autumn went. He waved to Peter, who held hands with Shannon. Or was it Charlene? They got into Peter's car and drove off. He walked up the block to where he parked.

"Blake!"

Derek, Sandy and their dates called after him. He waved without a glance back and shouted over his head.

"Good night!"

11

"How are you making out?"

Nick swiveled around in his padded executive chair. His gaze and wandering thoughts returned from the sea of cars in Hale Biotech's parking lot. Dale Scott stood in front of Nick's new desk. A prickly heat rose around Nick's collar.

"Mr. Scott. I didn't hear you come in."

Dale chuckled.

"Better get used to it. You think I'm sneaky? Your old man moves like a ghost around here. And Nicholas, please call me Dale."

"Thanks for the advice—Dale. Please call me Nick."

"All right Nick. Looks like they got you all set up here. Now you just need something to do before boredom sits in. Am I right?"

"Yes, I suppose."

"Then follow me, son."

When he came from behind his desk, Dale put his hand on his shoulder.

"I've got a couple of meetings I would like you to attend. Afterwards, you can give me your opinion over lunch if your father doesn't steal you away. How does that sound?"

"Sounds great."

They went down the hallway, past the elevators, and into the stairwell. They descended the steps one floor, emerged in the hallway, then slipped into a frosted glass enclosed conference room. Along the way, Nick received a few quick greetings and well wishes. The meeting in the conference room was already underway. Dale motioned for the presentation to continue while they slipped around the side wall, stood, and listened. The representative of a smaller lab was promoting their specialized facilities in the attempt to win a contract with Hale.

After everyone left the conference room. Dale spoke briefly to one of his colleagues who sat in the meeting from the beginning. He wanted to be filled in later with the details. Dale glanced at his wristwatch.

"We've got a little over ten minutes. Pour us both a cup of coffee and grab me one of those bagels."

"Sure."

He got a coffee and bagel for both of them, and they sat at the conference table.

"I would like to see the labs and the research facilities."

"Oh, you will. I know your father wants you to first get acclimated to the business side of Hale. He's going to count on you making some big decisions that may affect the entire company. As for the labs and actual research, unless you're a scientist like your father, it's difficult to have one foot in one world and one foot in another. Most of us can't. That's why he's the boss."

He smiled at the respect in Dale's eyes. Through the frosted glass wall of the conference room, he noticed a small group gathering in the hallway. Dale noticed too, and they hurried to finish their bagels and coffee. Dale brushed his hands together as the door opened. Angela, Dale's assistant, held the conference door while the group ushered in. Two Asian men with stoic faces entered, one distinctly older than the other. A tall, slender white man with a beard and a polite smile followed them. Trailing behind the men was the most beautiful woman he had ever seen. She wore a navy jacket with a matching pencil skirt, a white button-up collared shirt and black pumps. Her long, dark chestnut colored curls flowed over her shoulders. He had to be mindful to close his mouth.

"Mr. Scott, the folks from Nexgen Biosolutions are here. This is Dr. Nakamura, his assistant Mr. Kim, and, of course, you know Mr. Jennings and Ms. Bach. Can I get anyone anything?" Angela asked.

There were only mumbles and no clear demands. Angela smiled.

"Great. Have a wonderful meeting."

She left the room and closed the door. The frosted glass door gently slid shut on soft, close hinges. Dale stepped forward to shake everyone's hand and to introduce Nick. When they got to Elizabeth, Nick held his breath.

"… and this is Ms. Bach, who you met at your graduation party."

Nick smiled.

"How could I forget?"

Her eyebrow rose.

"Good to see you again, Ms. Bach."

"Mr. Evers."

She held out her hand, and he shook it. Her handshake was stiff, but when he looked into her crystal blue eyes, he had to remind himself to breathe. The three men from Nexgen Biosolutions clapped and woke him from his trance. They congratulated him on obtaining his MBA from Columbia University. Everyone settled into their seats. Dr. Nakamura discussed some newer technologies that Nexgen had been working on. Mr. Kim sat quietly with prepared documents so Dale could further discuss Nexgen's proposal with the rest of his team. Mr. Jennings sat with his fingers knit together and only jumped in from time to time to mention the financial benefits. Nick struggled to take everything in. He wanted to gaze at Elizabeth the whole time. The few moments when their eyes met, she gave him a squinty-eye, tight-lip smile, like one an adult would give a child before ice cream was served.

"Nicholas, do you have any questions?" Dale asked.

His eyes widened, and he sat straighter.

"Ah, no. I'm very fascinated, but I don't want to talk out of turn. I would rather first get my bearings."

"Sensible, with an abundance of caution, just like his father."

Dale patted him on the shoulder. The men chuckled, nodded, and smiled. Elizabeth sat there with her hands folded in her lap and a soft smile on her face.

"Thank you all for coming. I will go over the materials that Dr. Nakamura and Mr. Kim are leaving with us. Let's all grab lunch sometime soon," Dale said.

The men nodded. Elizabeth smiled at both Dale and Nick.

Everyone funneled out of the room and into the reception area in front of the bank of elevators. He watched her as she followed her colleagues. She never gave him a second glance.

"Careful."

Dale grabbed his arm, and he jumped.

"She's a looker, isn't she? But she's too much woman for you."

"Huh?"

"Ah, nothing."

Dale squeezed his shoulder.

"C'mon, while we're here on this floor, let me introduce you to some of the good folks in our accounting and financial departments."

Dale turned him around to guide him down the hallway, away from the elevators. Angela stopped them to take the binder and folder that Mr. Kim brought for Dale and his colleagues to review.

"I'll put these in your office. Will you two be needing lunch ordered?"

"Thanks Angela. No, ole Nick and I are going to dine out, unless he's got a hot date and going to kick this old man to the curb."

Dale laughed, and Nick shook his head and chuckled.

"That would be great. I look forward to it."

Angela smiled and hurried to catch the elevator. Nick watched her hurry off so he could see Elizabeth before she left. She was still there, but now talking to his father. The other three men, Dr. Nakamura, Mr. Kim, and Mr. Jennings, must have gone ahead without her. His father was smiling when he spoke to her. His father put his hand on her arm. Nick's eyebrows drew together. His father looked pretty relaxed and comfortable, an expression rarely seen on the man. As Nick and Dale headed down the hallway, his father caught up to them.

"Gentlemen, sorry I missed the Nexgen presentation."

He gave Nick a broad smile and a wink.

"How's your first day going, son?"

"Great. I sat in two meetings with Dale, and my office has everything I need."

Dale nodded and smiled.

"Yeah, I'm going to take Nick around to meet some folks here, then we're headed out to lunch. Care to join us?"

Richard looked at his watch.

"Sorry, I've got a few meetings myself, and an off-campus lunch meeting as well."

Dale nodded. Nick smirked and said, "Don't forget to breathe."

Richard squeezed his arm, then hurried off toward the elevators.

"The man never sits still."

Dale chuckled.

"Tell me about it."

All he could think about was Elizabeth. She was cold and all business, but friendly to his father. The smiles they shared looked more personal than professional. Now his father hurried off in the same direction as Elizabeth. He would check his father's schedule with Cynthia, his father's personal assistant. Maybe she knew where his father was having lunch.

The hostess in a Bavarian outfit greeted Nick and Dale. Dale grinned as soon as he saw her. She wore a copper colored bodice with a steep neckline that half covered her breasts. A white short sleeve blouse with puffed out shoulders covered the rest. Her skirt was a dark navy with little flower patterns down the front. She carried two menus and was about to guide them into the packed dining room toward several open tables near the windows. Nick spotted his father at a table by the windows.

"Dale, do you mind if we sit over here? I don't want to sit in the sun."

Dale wrinkled his lips, and his eyebrows rose.

"Okay, yeah sure."

The table he pointed to needed to be cleared. The hostess waved for the busboy. After they settled and ordered their drinks, Nick excused himself to use the men's room. From behind a lattice partition, he peered through the narrow spaces. His father held a glass of wine and laughed. A pillar blocked his view of the person who sat across from his father. He returned to his table. Dale glanced around the restaurant.

"I have to say, Nick—interesting pick. It's cozy. Very German. Looks like a great place to entertain clients. I'll mention it to your father."

He grinned. Nick smiled and raised his chin. Great, he'll will want to know why we, too, drove across town for lunch.

"Yeah, sure, but I don't think my father likes German food."

Dale gazed with squinted eyes at some of the busty waitresses. Nick shook his head and chuckled. Dale was probably twenty years older than him. He shrugged.

"What? I'm not dead yet."

They both laughed. Nick raised, and eyebrow. Dale smirked.

"All you young guys have all the fun. It's an exciting time in your life. You better enjoy it."

"I'll do my best, sir."

"Sir? Fuck sake, might as well bury me now."

They laughed. Mr. Dale Scott was an okay guy. Not as stuffy as he imagined he would be. Certainly not like his father. They ordered some sandwiches, and Dale talked him into ordering a beer. He stopped Nick right away when he tried to order a soda.

"You can't drink a soda at a German restaurant."

Dale had the waitress bowing with laughter. She beamed at him. He had much more charm than Nick gave him credit for. Dale could sleep with her if he wanted. Nick shook from his thoughts the image of Dale fucking the waitress in some back corner of the restaurant's kitchen, or maybe even in the ladies' room. The waitress winked at Nick. He smiled at her, but felt nothing. After she brought their food and drinks, then departed, he gave Dale a questioning glance.

"I have to say Mr. Scott. *Dale*. It's hard to imagine you as Colette's dad. She's so focused on life, like my father. You, you're laid back and easygoing."

"Thanks. It's not always easy. I work hard, and I'm serious, but I need to blow off some steam. Your dad is a great guy, but sometimes I think his screws are too tight."

Dale's eyebrows rose and his lips wrinkled before he took a drink of his beer.

"You won't get any argument from me about that."

"Since you brought up Colette, how was your night out?"

The argument with Autumn crept in.

"It was good, but my friends were there, so we didn't get to talk much."

"Maybe just the two of you can get coffee, lunch, or even dinner sometime."

Hope floated in Dale's eyes.

"I'll call her and we'll figure something out. It's nice that she's back in Atlanta."

Dale smiled and nodded.

"Yeah, her mother and I are happy to have her home."

While Dale ate, Nick glanced to where his father sat. His father nodded, then turned and tilted his head as if to look up at someone next to the table. The pillar obstructed the view. Then Elizabeth appeared. She headed toward the bathrooms. His chest and stomach knotted. He watched how his father looked at Elizabeth as she strutted to the ladies' room.

"Not hungry?"

He unclenched his fist under the table. Dale had finished half his sandwich and held the other half in one hand and his beer in the other.

"Sorry, thought I saw someone I knew."

Dale nodded as he chewed. Nick ate and glanced around as though he was taking in the ambience. He saw Elizabeth before she disappear behind the lattice partition that led to the bathrooms. He wanted to know what was going on. When he last saw her in Madrid, he wanted to control the conversation, and he felt he did. Seeing her at the office and now at the restaurant, everything descended into a fog. What made matters worse, Cynthia, Nick's father's personal assistant, told him that his father had canceled his lunch meeting. Lucky for him, Cynthia overheard where his father was going for lunch. This was no business lunch his father and Elizabeth were having. His stomach continued to knot. He wanted to wait outside the bathrooms to confront her. His fist pressed into the seat cushion. The waitress came by and seemed genuinely concerned that he hardly touched his food and drink.

"Is there something wrong? Can I get you something else—maybe?"

"Ah? No, I'm good. I guess I wasn't that hungry."

Dale smirked at the waitress.

"Don't mind him, he's allergic to delicious."

Dale and the waitress busted out laughing. Nick screwed up his face. They laughed some more, and all he could do was shrug.

"Can I at least box that up for you?"

The waitress had a sweet inviting smile, a familiar one, where he was certain he would later find the girl's phone number tucked in his bag of food, or written on the inside lid of the takeout container.

"Sure, that would be great."

He smiled back. The waitress took his plate. He watched his father pay the check, then he walked to the entrance of the restaurant and stood there. Shortly after, Elizabeth appeared. Neither Richard nor Elizabeth saw them. He was relieved that Dale sat facing away from the entrance. Before Elizabeth and his father left the restaurant, they shared a brief kiss. It was awkward, but lips met. His heart sank.

12

The hollow coo of a mourning dove came through the open window. At the full-length mirror, Nick contemplated his naked reflection. He filled his lungs and pumped up his chest, then squeezed his midsection. That usually made him smile, but not today. He knit his fingers behind his head and scowled at himself. His eyelids rimmed with red from a sleepless night.

The kiss Elizabeth and his father shared only brought on the worst imaginings. It was difficult to contemplate the game they were playing, and worse, for how long. She seemed to make light of his devotion to her. As for his father's devotion to his mother, that was a joke, and an unfortunate joke on his mother.

Outside the bedroom window came the faint sound of the garage door opening. His sister, Gwen, giggled. Their mother said something. Car doors opened and closed with a thunk. An engine made a soft growl. The garage door closed, then silence.

The house sat empty. The best time for a swim. One problem. Workers had drained the pool. He scowled, then took his dark wayfarers from the nearby corner of his dresser and slipped them on. After a moment of consideration, his lips curled into a devilish smirk. Fuck them all. He was going for a swim.

~

Nick drove up the curved brick driveway and parked off to the side of the five-car garage. One bay door was open, and a white Mercedes convertible sat parked inside with its top down. Abigale's car. She had to be coming or going. He smiled when he read her license plate: *CHEEKY*. He rang the doorbell, and stood there in his swim trunks, a tank top, canvas loafers, and dark wayfarer sunglasses. The drive over with the windows down left his hair windswept and made him look like he came from the beach after a day of surfing. The warm sun on his shoulders and the gorgeousness of the day helped to return some of his old self-confidence.

The door opened and there stood Abigale Rutherford in a pale pink sundress with a white sash tied around her waist. White strappy heeled sandals showed off her painted toes.

"Nicholas?"

She straightened up as if she was preparing to take the dance floor in a ballroom dance competition. He smiled at her, and her eyes brightened.

"Hello Abigale."

Only a handful of times he called her by her Christian name. All were after he turned twenty-four, and none of those times were ever in front of his mother or father. She looked him up and down, then she glanced around the driveway as though she expected to see his mother.

"Um? Hi."

"Sorry for stopping by unannounced, but I don't have your phone number. You said I could swim in your pool. Is this a bad time?"

He tilted his head. It was a tease, as if she had been cruel not to give him her phone number. Not that he ever needed it before today.

"Ah—no-no—sure, it's fine. I—I was going to do a little shopping, but—no, it's fine. You could have had your mother call or text me. Does she know you were coming over?"

His lips curled into a coy smile. He took off his dark wayfarer sunglasses.

"No, she doesn't know. Do I need her permission?"

His one eyebrow rose. Her lips parted.

"Shall we call her and let her know I'm here?"

"No, don't be silly. Come on in."

He had only been to the Rutherford's home a few times. Most of the time, his mother had her friends over.

"You have a beautiful home."

He glanced around with little interest, then fixed his gaze on her. He savored the way her hair flowed and swayed down her back, the subtle roll of her shoulders, the pressure in which her hips and ass went taut with each step, as she led him through the house to the back patio, and to the pool.

"There are towels in the bathhouse. Can I get you something to drink? A water, or ice tea perhaps?"

"Sure, anything."

She went to the small outdoor refrigerator at the patio cooking space and brought back a bottle of water.

"Aren't you going to join me?"

She seemed conflicted, and bit her lower lip.

"Change into something more comfortable and join me."

He gazed into her eyes and offered her a warm smile.

"All right. I think I'll get something to drink as well. Can I get you a drink too, besides the water, I mean?"

"Sure. Whatever you're having would be great. I'm easy."

He sauntered off to sit on one of the lounge chairs next to the deep end of the pool. He took off his shoes and tank top, then adjusted the waistband of his swim trunks so they sat at his hip bones. When he heard the patio doors open and close, he smirked, then dove into the shimmering blue water. He pushed off from the bottom and swam across the short side of the pool. He then swam back across, pulled himself out, and reclined on the lounger. Droplets from his body fell through the weave of the lounger and spattered on the patio stones beneath him. He rested his forearm across his eyes to shield them from the bright sunlight. Deep, sleep-deprived breaths passed his lips. Thoughts of Elizabeth crept into his mind, and he pushed them out. Each breath brought him closer to sleep.

A soft clink of a drinking glass being placed on the small glass-top table woke him from his thoughts. From under the bottom edge of his forearm, he could see her bare legs and feet. He admired her painted toes. He glanced up from under his arm.

"Oh, thank you."

He sat up and swung his legs to the side. She wore a white string bikini tied in bows at her hips and around her back and neck. The triangular patches of fabric covered her intimate bits and nothing more. The only attempt at modesty was her knit cover up that dropped over her shoulders and half covered her breasts. As bold and flirtatious as she was, she never wore such a revealing bikini to his parents' house. Even in her more modest swimsuits, he fondly remembered them being cut high on her hips and narrow enough in the crotch to see how well-groomed or shaven she was. He admired her young forty-something, taut, childless, and fitness-conscious midriff. She stood there with a smile; drink in one hand, suntan lotion in the other. She wore similar dark wayfarer sunglasses, and he took it as a nod to his sense of style. There was a hint of the delicate floral scent she wore. He picked up the fruity pink drink from atop the table.

"It's a cocktail made with watermelon, lime, vodka, and club soda. It's good, try it."

He took a sip from the straw. Pieces of fruit floated at the top of the glass. It was strong. His eyes widened. She burst out laughing. He held up the glass to examine its contents.

"Good, right?"

"Very good. Thank you."

He tilted his head.

"Aren't you going to sit with me?"

"The sun is too oppressive at this end of the pool. I like to sit at the other end. You can join me if you like."

Two large, freestanding umbrellas shaded the table and loungers at the other end. She glided gracefully in long strides alongside the pool, down to the other end. Through her knit cover up, he made out glimpses of her buttocks. He watched her all the way until she sat on a lounger and took a sip of her drink. She looked over at him and gave him an inviting smile.

He put his wayfarers on and grabbed his cocktail, then sauntered over to where she sat. He sat on the lounger next to her.

"Better?" she asked.

"Much."

He took a sip of his drink.

"Are you going to get in the water?"

"Maybe, we'll see."

She smiled at him and tilted her head. After he took a drink, he took his sunglasses off, then got into the pool at the corner, where quarter circle steps descended into the shallow end. He descended the steps until he was waist deep, then lowered his body into the water up to his neck.

"Ah."

He grinned and turned around.

"You have a nice pool."

"Thanks."

He swam at an easy pace to the other end, then held onto the edge, and glanced over at her. She took a couple of casual sips of her drink and rested her glass on the table, then applied some lotion to her legs. There was enough shade at her end of the pool, so she took off her sunglasses and sat them on the table next to his. They looked like they belonged together. He sprinted the length of the pool, flipped in the shallow end and raced in a sidestroke to the far deep end. When he reached the edge, he hung on to catch his breath. He wiped the water from his eyes and ran his hand over his forehead and through his hair.

At the corner of the pool, she sat on the bottom step so that the water came to her shoulders. She had moved their drinks to the edge of the pool, as if to invite him to come sit next to her. He wiped the water from his mouth and licked his lips. He climbed out of the pool, turned toward the shallow end where she was, and dove in.

He swam underwater until he reached her. A flash of legs and her white bikini bottom was what he saw before he surfaced. He smiled as his head popped out of the water, but he kept his body submerged to his shoulders to match hers. He rubbed the water from his face and hair.

"Impressive."

"Thanks. I like to see how long I can hold my breath."

She raised an eyebrow. He moved to the side of the pool and put his arm up on the edge. Since she already had her hair and makeup done for an afternoon out, he avoided asking her if she was going to swim. The ends of her curls were wet, but her makeup remained pristine. They sipped at their cocktails.

"You said your husband doesn't use the pool. Why is that?"

"He's not that adventurous."

"Okay? But don't you have an indoor pool as well?"

"Yes, with a hot tub. He likes to entertain when he's home. Sometimes I think our pools are more for show than anything."

She brushed her hair aside. Her lips closed around the straw and she sipped her cocktail. He watched her lips, her neck as she swallowed, her hand movement, her hair, and thought about Elizabeth.

"How was your trip to Spain?"

He was about to speak, then took a sip of his drink first.

"It was exciting. We only visited Madrid."

"We? Oh, that's right, you took your friend with you."

"Yes, Blake went with me."

He chuckled.

"What?"

"I think he found a serious girlfriend there."

"Oh?"

"Blake has a college friend from NYU who lives in Madrid. He took us to a few clubs, and we hung out. Anyway, Blake hit it off with a girl he danced with the second night we were there, and they were inseparable the rest of the time."

His words trailed off. The only thing he wanted to talk about, regarding Spain, was Blake's time there.

"Oh, and what about you? I'm sure you had lots of girls vying for your attention."

She sounded like Elizabeth.

"None of them interested me."

"So Blake got the cutest one? I find that hard to believe."

She took a sip of her drink and flipped her hair over her shoulder. He wrinkled his lips and gazed off at the shimmering ripples of water. He exhaled into a sigh.

"No, there were plenty of beautiful girls. I guess I wasn't interested."

"Oh? That doesn't sound like you."

She sipped the last of her cocktail. His glass was near empty.

"Would you like another?"

He met her gaze, and his tight lips curved into a soft smile.

"Sure."

The way the sun lit her eyes made them glitter. He watched her climb the steps out of the pool. Her long wet curls stuck to her shoulders and back as she emerged, then her waist, then her near bare buttocks flexed as she moved her hips. The water clung to her body as even it desired her. His lips parted at the sight of the thin white strip of her bikini that disappeared between her ass cheeks. She bent down to pick up their cocktail glasses, her wet bikini hugged her sex and her nipples stood pronounced like two little landmarks on her bikini top. She smiled and looked pleased at his expression.

"Don't go anywhere."

He gazed at her as she strolled off in the sun with their glasses. Her wet skin glistened. None of the younger women he had ever known moved like her. She moved like a goddess. She moved like Elizabeth. He slipped his hands under the water and grasped at the front of his swim trunks. He was harder than ever. So much so, his testicles drew tight. He released a heavy breath and licked his lips. After she went inside, he went to the pool house and waited.

Inside the Rutherford's pool house, there were several wicker club chairs and a wicker sofa, all with printed tropical patterned cushions. At the center was a glass top coffee table. There were two changing rooms with wooden slat doors, a bathroom, and behind a walled partition were two elegant marble walled showers. Nick stood naked with his back against the shower wall, eyes held closed, and head back against the cool marble. His skin prickled, and his heart thumped as he waited.

From the other room came the subtle clinking of drinking glasses being placed on a glass tabletop.

"Nick?"

Abigale's soft voice carried into the marble showers. He drew in a sharp breath.

"Nick?"

He stepped out from the showers. Her eyes went wide and her lips parted when she saw him. Their freshly made cocktails sat on the coffee table. If they were still in her hands, he imagined she would have dropped them.

"Abby."

Her gaze was down at his cock. He would have never called her Abby in front of his mother. He stepped toward her.

"Abby. Come here."

The commanding tone of his voice surprised him. She remained frozen, but her gaze rose to meet his. He came closer until he stood in front of her. She covered her eyes with both hands, her elbows covered her breasts.

"Oh, Jesus, Nick!"

He seized her around the waist. She twisted in his arms, a faint attempt to free herself. She lowered her hands from her face, but kept her forearms up to shield her chest. He pulled her close and kissed her. She tensed at first, then she parted her lips to allow his tongue to enter. She brought her arms up around his neck and slipped her fingers through his hair. He loosened the bows from behind her neck and back. Her arms tensed when he slipped off her bikini top. He pulled her closer. Their kiss deepened, and she tugged at his hair. He carried her to the wicker sofa.

Her hair pooled around her face and shoulders. He gazed at her. Her small, firm nipples crested the tops of her large breasts. She closed her knees and covered her crotch.

"Nick?"

Her voice was a dry whisper.

"It's okay Abby. Don't be afraid. I'm just going to fuck you."

She raised her eyebrows and sucked in a breath through parted lips. He untied the bow at her left hip. Her chest rose and her midsection tightened. She moved her hand from her crotch and pulled the bow tied at her right hip. She opened her legs, and he knelt between them, then he slipped off her bikini bottom. Her intense gaze made him smirk inside. After he peered at her well shaven sex, he closed his eyes and brought the crotch of her bikini bottom to his face. She drew in a sharp breath. When he brought his lips close to her sex, he smelled the perfume she had sprayed above her pubis. It was the same floral scent he detected earlier. She must have applied it when she went to the house to get them another cocktail. It was inconceivable that it would have lasted after her being in the pool. She smelled incredible, and he gave her a devilish smile before he applied his tongue to her clit.

The slick juices from her folds coated his tongue like warm honey. Her midsection flexed and her hips shuddered when his tongue pierced her opening. He glided his tongue upward to draw circles over her engorged clit that rose like a pearl from beneath its fleshy hood.

She released deep moans followed by heavy breaths. Her legs opened wider, and she grasped and tugged at his hair to pull his open mouth onto her sex. He gently inserted his fingers, first one, then another, and applied them as Elizabeth had taught him. Her body shook and her buttocks flexed as she came.

"Oh-oh-oh, Nicholas—oh Nick, oh Nick."

Her pussy squeezed his fingers that were inside her. He stroked his hard cock, then pressed its length to her folds to tease her. He moved his hips so that the head passed over and massage her swollen clit. Her eyebrows drew together and her lips parted. When her gaze caught his, her tongue darted out and circle her lips. He pressed the tip of his cock to her slick, wet opening. She peered into his eyes with a fiery gaze. He found the want that was missing in Elizabeth's eyes. Her delicate flesh yielded, stretched, and embraced his thick cock, as her tight hole took all of him. He moved slowly to savor her every inner contour. He wanted to give her what he wanted Elizabeth to have. She gasped as she took in his entire length.

He flexed his buttocks as he plunged deep into her. Her sweet cries rose to the rafters of the pool house. He grasped her hips. His pelvis slammed into hers. Her cries rose until she replaced his name with the Lord's.

"Oh fuck me Nick, oh Nick—Oh God—fuck."

Her nails dug into his arms. Each inward thrust, her pussy tightened. He was certain her cries carried beyond the walls of the pool house. Perhaps even the neighbors heard her cries of ecstasy. His testicles tightened, and he grunted.

"Fuck Abby, I'm going to come."

"Come on my belly. Come on me, baby."

He slipped from inside her. Long, thick streams of pearlescent semen spewed forth with each throb of his cock and painted her body from the notch of her neck to her pubis. His balls pressed against her wet, ravaged sex. He massaged her clit with the head of his cock. As he did, his come dripped and mingled with her wet juices. He lowered his body onto hers. She raked her nails down his back and over his ribs before grasping his buttocks and pressing her pelvis into his. His cock throbbed between their bodies.

He rested his head on her shoulder. Her long curls tickled his face and he could smell the scent of her perfume. He kissed her shoulder, then her lips. When he braced himself over her, she gazed at him with dreamy eyes and a soft, sated smile.

"That was wonderful. Oh God, that was wonderful!"

He laughed. She threw her arms above her head and turned her head from side to side.

"Oh my God, Nick, what did we just do?"

She laughed some more and covered her face with both hands. Her thighs slid along his ribs. His lips formed a weary smile.

A keen awareness crept into focus. At Henry and Abigale Rutherford's home, in the Rutherford's backyard, in the Rutherford's pool house, on the Rutherford's wicker patio sofa—he had fucked Henry's wife and his mother's friend. Metaphorically, he felt he fucked himself. He stood, his cock now limp. He looked down at her. She looked younger, lying there on the patio sofa. Or maybe he felt older. He felt empty, like when he slept with Isabella. He wondered if she would put him out as well. Her fingers travelled up his thigh and stroked his limp cock. Beautiful Abby. She was not, nor could she ever be, his Lizzy.

"This can never happen again, do you understand? Tell me you understand, Nicholas."

Her tone was jovial yet stern. She sounded like a parent chiding a child. At that moment, he hated her. This woman, his mother's friend, dick tease, had gotten what she had wanted all along. He, a once adored teen, now a young man, was finally ripe for the picking, and had been plucked. His lips wrinkled and drew into a tight line. She stroked the length of his limp cock. Semen seeped from him.

"Never-never can this happen again."

Her tense and worrisome gaze met his as she stroked him. His gaze travelled down her body. Her breasts, her nipples, her abdomen glistened with his come, and her navel was a pool of his semen. His cock stiffened in her grasp. He more than agreed with her declaration that this shall never happen again, but his body and her actions were having a different conversation.

"Yes—I understand."

Abigale put her bikini top on. Her breasts and abdomen still glistened wet with his come. She deftly tied the bows behind her neck and back, and pushed at her breasts until she centered her nipples under the triangular bits of fabric. Her small but hard nipples poked through. He licked his lips. It disgusted him at how much he wanted to fuck her again. She stood there for a moment, bottomless, then turned and bent down to pick up her bikini bottom. He had a clear view when she bent over. Her thighs and labia glistened, wet and ready. Her slow movements suggested she wanted him to tear off her bikini and take her again. While she finished tying the bows on her bikini bottom, he went to the shower and put on his swim trunks. When he returned, she waited by the pool. She left their cocktails on the table in the pool house, as if they were going to be back to enjoy them. He gathered his things by the pool. He pulled his tank top over his head and slipped on his canvas loafers. She gave him a tight-lipped smile, but they both said nothing when they went to the house.

He watched her climb the stairs with her long, beautiful, poisonous legs.

"Goodbye Nicholas. It was nice having you over."

She never turned around to look at him, not even before she disappeared upstairs. Her cool demeanor emphasized that today was a onetime deal. He wrinkled his lips. The doorbell chimed. He glanced out the narrow side window. His mouth opened, and his eyes widened. The doorbell chimed a second time. He hurried back to the kitchen. The front door opened. In haste, he slipped into the side dining room, instead of out the patio doors to the pool. A voice echoed from the grand foyer.

"Hello?"

13

Josephine Evers turned into the Fall River Estates.

"She's going to be so happy," Gwen said.

She beamed and shimmied her shoulders while buckled in the passenger seat. Josephine smiled as she navigated the large Mercedes SUV up the winding, tree-lined road.

"How do you know if she'll be home?"

"I don't. I called her, but only got her voicemail. Anyway, it will be our little surprise for her, okay?"

She smiled over at Gwen. Gwen grinned and gave her mother an exaggerated nodded.

They passed mini-mansion after mini-mansion, before turning onto Goldwyn Lane. The street ended in a cul-de-sac, where three veritable mansions stood tucked away in beautiful wooded lots.

"What if she's not home?"

"We'll just leave it on the entranceway table with a little note."

"Um, okay? But I wanted to see her excitement."

Gwen bounced in her seat as Josephine turned into Abigale Rutherford's stone driveway.

The driveway curved gently to the right, then sharply to the left. The grand house rose before them with its five-car garage. One of the bay doors was raised and a white Mercedes convertible sat inside with its top down.

"Looks like she's here."

"Yay."

Josephine parked near the doorway, not expecting to be long.

"That looks like Nick's car."

Gwen pointed near the trees at the end of the large garage. Josephine turned off the engine. Her eyebrows knit together and her lips tightened. Gwen unbuckled her seatbelt and opened the door.

"Honey, stay here."

"Huh?"

"Close the door."

Gwen did as she was told.

"What's wrong?"

"Just stay here, please. I won't be long."

She opened the tailgate and fumbled through the shopping bags.

"It's on the right side, Mom."

"Got it, thanks, dear."

As she went to the front door, she glanced over at the blue BMW. Like Gwen, she was certain it was Nick's. She sighed, then her eyebrows drew together. He should have told her his plans. The situation made her dizzy, and she felt the start of a headache. A feeling of intrusiveness kept her from opening the front door, so instead she rang the doorbell and waited. Nothing. She never had to wait before. Unsure how long she should wait. She rang the doorbell a second time. When she tried the handle, it was unlocked. She turned back to make sure Gwen stayed in the car. She held up her hand to inform her she would be quick. Gwen nodded and looked down. Apparently, she found something more important to hold her attention. Josephine went inside.

"Hello?"

Her voice echoed in the entranceway with its marble floors and high ceiling. When her gaze rose and followed the curved staircase upward, she looked away and refused to consider that Nick may be upstairs with Abigale. Her shoulders tensed and she took in a deep breath.

"Hello? Abigale? Are you home?"

The Rutherford's house was sprawling. It confused her where to look and even if she should. She told Gwen she would leave a note and the shopping bag on the entranceway table and that would be that. There was a beautiful bouquet of tulips in an elegant crystal vase that sat at the center of the entranceway table. The flowers invited her to leave the gift there and be on her way. Something tugged inside her. She sat the shopping bag on the table in front of the flowers. As Nicholas' mother, she felt she had the right to know. True, Nicholas was twenty-six and old enough to make his own decisions, whatever they may be. Oh hell, Jo! She admonished herself. Fuck sake, Nicholas still acts too immature and has a lot to prove, especially in Richard's eyes. Her shoulders stiffened. He needs Richard and me to make sure he starts off on the right foot. She raised her eyebrows at the heated conversation that went on inside her head. She restrained herself from shouting her son's name like a crazed woman who lost their child at the supermarket.

"Abigale, Dear? Hello?"

She walked down the hall toward the kitchen. Her heels sounded loud as they struck the marble floor. When she went into the kitchen, the counters were a mess. A knife laid across a cutting board with bits of watermelon and slices of lime, an open bottle of vodka, and a capped bottle of seltzer. There was also a container of strawberries that looked untouched. It was unclear to her why it gave her any relief that there was no whipped cream or chocolate, her memory of what she and Richard ate the first night they made love.

"Abigale?"

She huffed.

This is ridiculous. Footsteps echoed from down the hall, the staccato of heels similar to her own.

"Oh, hello Josephine. I didn't hear you come in. I was upstairs."

Abigale wore a sundress and heeled sandals. She had her hair up in a ponytail.

"Hi, sorry for barging in. Gwen and I—actually Gwen—found the top you wanted."

"Oh, that's so sweet. Where is Gwen?"

Her eyebrows drew together, and she turned as if to search for Gwen. She looked a bit too undone, with only her dress and heels. She usually wore a bracelet, or a necklace, or both. At least she wore her wedding ring. It was unimaginable, Abigale not wearing her wedding ring with that enormous rock.

"She's in the car. We were only going to pop in, but then we saw Nick's car. That is, Nick's car?"

"Yes, it is. He surprised me. I remembered my offer for him to swim here. I didn't think he would take me up on it."

She chuckled.

"So he's out back?"

"Yes."

"And what's this? Did he mess up your kitchen?"

Abigale glanced at the counter. Josephine's eyes narrowed when she noticed the damp ends of her hair.

"Oh no. That was me. I made a cocktail for Nick to enjoy by the pool. I was going to make myself one when I came down. Would you like one? You really should have Gwen come in."

"No, thank you. We're going to get going."

"Did you want me to get Nick for you?"

"No-no, I'm sure I'll see him at home later, as long as he doesn't have plans with his friends."

She chuckled. Abigale nodded and smiled. The two women walked to the front door. Josephine gestured to the shopping bag she left on the table. Abigale thanked her, and they shared a brief, polite hug.

"There's some lotion you missed."

She pointed to the spot near her own collarbone.

"Oh? Thank you."

Abigale made no move to check for herself.

"Thanks for stopping by, and thank you for picking up the top for me. That's so sweet of you both."

"Let me know how it fits."

"Oh, I'm sure it'll be a perfect fit."

Josephine had the suspicious thought that Abigale might model the top for Nick, with nothing else on *but* the top. She walked to the SUV. Gwen sat up in the car seat and waved at Abigale, who stood in the doorway. She got behind the wheel and gave Abigale a quick wave and a smile before she and Gwen drove off.

Nick approached Abigale as she came through the front door. The soft growl of rubber treads faded as his mother's SUV drove down the stone driveway. Abigale closed the door. She went to the entranceway mirror that hung on the wall. She licked her fingertips and wiped near her collarbone. Then she turned toward him. Her eyelids were heavy and her smile victorious.

"I think the coast is clear now."

His lips parted. He wanted to say something, anything, but nothing came. She walked down the hallway to the kitchen, her heels clicked on the marble floor. He watched her until she disappeared, then he walked out to his car.

Nick's swim trunks and tank top sat clumped in the corner of his bathroom. He had kicked off his canvas loafers earlier, and they lay in awkward positions outside the bathroom. One shoe lay upside down, feet away from the other.

He braced his hips against the vanity as he leaned over the sink to scrutinize his face in the mirror. Although he shaved earlier, an early evening stubble bristled under his fingertips. He held his fingertips to his nostrils. His eyelids half closed as he inhaled. Abigale had climaxed on his fingers and he had not washed them since. He slipped his fingers into his mouth. His cock stiffened against the cool porcelain vanity. Thoughts of being completely inside her, and how his cock must smell of her sweet cunt juices, brought him to greater arousal. He stroked himself with a gentle grip, like that of her pre-climaxed pussy. The more he thought of her smugness, having him like he was some country club waiter, the tighter and rougher he stroked himself.

His shoulders flexed and curled forward as he reached climax. He continued to stroke himself even after he had nothing further to release.

She had a run at him, enjoyed herself, and that seemed to be that. She used him, but he came willingly and literally. His reflection sickened him. He pressed his hand against the mirror to brace himself, then he spat on the thick pearlescent clumps that sat at the bottom of the basin. He turned on the water and watched it all disappear.

After a shower, he returned to the sink. Droplets of steam coated everything, like dust over forgotten memories. He swiped the condensation from the mirror. The spot he cleared made him look like he was inside some icy prison. He wanted to forget the day even happened. It would be easy to go see Autumn, who has been sick for his attention. Something inside him wanted to see her, but not for sex. He knew Autumn would do her best to comfort him, even at her own expense. Blake or Colette would sit and listen to him. Both were always ready to lend a thoughtful ear. The mirror steamed up again and he could no longer see himself.

He brought his fingers to his nose. Abigale's scent was gone. He wished something, anything, of Elizabeth's had stayed with him. He wanted to believe what Elizabeth told him at the Puerta del Sol. She talked about the city's square being the center of Spain and told him that this could be their starting place. Maybe it was the moment. Maybe the sun was in a special place in the sky that made things right.

In his bedroom, he kicked one of his canvas loafers out of his way. His phone's screen lit up. He had left it home all day. There were various voice and text messages from almost everyone except for his father and sister.

He had played the voice message from his mother that she left hours ago.

"Hi Nick. Would you like to join Gwen and I for lunch? Text or call me within the hour. Love you, Bye."

He swiped the message to delete it. There were two voice messages from Autumn.

Autumn's earlier message was, "I really need to see you. I'll be at the Ramada. Meet me at six."

Autumn's message from last night, "I need to know where we stand. Are you seeing Colette?"

He swiped both messages and deleted them. He snorted when he saw Blake's voice message. Blake never leaves voice messages. He hit play.

"Hey pal. We've got to get together today. My parents are having guests over for dinner, so I can't go out tonight. Maybe we can grab a coffee. Call me when you get this."

He rubbed his temple, then wrinkled his face. Blake left a similar text message as well. He texted Blake.

"Hey Blake. Coffee sounds great. When? Where?"

Nick hit Send, then glanced at the remaining list of people who texted him. None interested him. Another voice message awaited. It was a significant one, the only one, one he saved for last out of anticipation and terror. He swallowed, then played the message from Elizabeth.

"Hello, Nick. I've been meaning to call you. I'm sorry I haven't called sooner. Sorry for being so aloof. I don't want anyone to know there is anything going on between us."

It seemed nothing was going on between them. Their one night together, and the few meals they shared, was not much of a courtship. He wrinkled his lips and continued to listen.

"At least, until we both have contemplated all the ramifications. I hope you understand. That doesn't mean I don't want to see you. In fact, I've been thinking a lot about you."

His eyebrows rose, but his lips remained in a tight line. He remembered their kiss in Madrid, but would never forget seeing her with his father at the restaurant. The muscles in his jaw tensed. He was angry for his mother's sake, but she had in the past given his father space to make a fool out of himself. This time, though, his father would not have what Nick hoped belonged to him. He huffed. With reluctance, he typed Elizabeth a text message instead of calling her. He was afraid of what he might say.

"Hi Elizabeth."

He wanted to type "Lizzy," her suggestion, but fear kept him at a distance.

"I've been thinking a lot about you, too. I understand the work situation."

He snorted.

"Anyway, I hope we can see each other soon."

He wanted to mention the kiss at the restaurant.

"Call or text me when you're available."

He tapped Send, then noticed an earlier text message from Colette.

"Hey Nick. We didn't get to talk much when we were out with your friends. Do you want to get together, just you and me?"

He read her question a second time. All he could find in her words was sincerity. He typed a reply.

"Sure, when?"

An alert appeared at the top of his phone. He tapped it. It was a text message from Blake.

Blake's message read, "5 p.m. Starbucks."

He replied, "See you there."

14

Nick sat in the Ramada Inn parking lot for nearly half an hour after he had coffee with Blake. Now he rode the elevator to the top floor. Autumn's dad usually kept the rooms on the top floor vacant for personal out-of-town family or guests. The floor was the least used and smelled the least moldy. The elevator came to a stop, and the brushed aluminum doors opened to a spiraled green and purple patterned carpeted floor. He caught his reflection in the large horizontal wall mirror that hung opposite the elevators. The rims of his eyelids were red, and his eyeballs felt heavy in their sockets. He walked in a daze down the hallway. The last door, where a window looked out on the parking lot, was the room where he and Autumn often met for sex. He took out his wallet and searched for the room key card Autumn gave him two years ago. He found it and inserted it into the security slot. The little green light flashed, and he turned the knob.

A single curtain panel hung drawn. A harsh band of sunlight crossed the room. The television was on and the sound of cackling cartoon characters almost masked a familiar moaning. He silently closed the door. Is sounded as though Autumn had gotten a head start. She had pleasured herself before while she waited for him to walk in on her. It excited her. His lips were dry and sore, but he licked them anyway. Sex was the furthest thing from his mind. On one of the queen-size beds with its golden comforter still in place were two naked bodies, one mounted atop the other. The lovers, caught up in their grunts and moans, were slow to acknowledge his presence. Autumn was on her knees and elbows, with Derek behind her. He gave her two good thrusts before he noticed Nick.

"Oh! Fuck!"

Derek pulled out of Autumn. His cock bobbed like a spring as he flailed his limbs and he threw himself to the side of the bed. He looked as if he expected Nick to attack him in his nakedness. He tore at the comforter to cover himself. Autumn stood by the side of the bed. Nick held up his hand as if to hush them.

"It's okay. What you two are doing is okay. I'm not mad or upset. I'm sorry I disturbed you."

Derek's eyes were wide, and his mouth hung open. Autumn looked confused. Nick walked out and gently closed the door. The door lock made a muted click. As he neared the elevators, a metallic clunk of a door handle sounded behind him, then came the pattering of bare feet on the hallway carpet.

"Nick—Nick, wait."

He turned around and Autumn ran toward him, naked. She covered her breasts as she ran, then stood fully exposed in front of him. He stared into her eyes.

"Say something, Nick."

"Autumn, I already said all that needed to be said."

He walked to the elevators, and she followed.

"No, wait a minute. What does that mean? Are we through?"

"I got your message. You told me to come by at six. You showed me what *you* wanted me to see."

He pushed the button to call the elevator. Tears ran down her face.

"I wanted you to feel anger and jealousy, like I always do. I wanted you to scream and tell me I'm a whore. I wanted you to show anything for me, any fucking sign that you cared for me at all."

Her words trailed off.

"Please Nick. Don't you care about me?"

The elevator doors opened, and he stepped inside.

"I'm sorry Autumn. I should have never let things go on this long."

She cupped her eyes and wept. He thought she might follow him onto the elevator, but as the doors narrowed, she fell to her knees on the spiraled green and purple patterned carpet. The elevator car descended, and he stared at his distorted reflection in the brushed aluminum doors.

When Nick got to his car in the hotel parking lot, he bent over and retched, but nothing came up. He got in, fired up the engine, and sped out of the lot. He wished Autumn would have moved on long ago, when he refused to commit to being her boyfriend. When he went to New York for school, he was sure she would find someone new. Maybe she had been seeing Derek all the times when he avoided her. Things with her were a mess, but they paled compared to the news Blake had dropped on him earlier. One of the latest calls Blake got from Marissa was that Isabella told Marissa she was pregnant and said it was Nick's. She told Marissa about the broken condom.

An alert came over his phone. It was a text message from Colette. He had hoped it was Blake offering to take him out for drinks, so he could numb the turmoil in his head and face things tomorrow. He read Colette's text message, while he waited at the stoplight. It was her reply to his last message.

"Great. I'm available at 9. Dress casual. Let's go someplace chill. I'm in the mood for pizza or a cheeseburger. Come get me at my parents'. Don't be late!"

Chill sounded good. He needed to escape now more than ever. A quick glance at this watch told him he had time to go home and drown himself, or if he could pull himself together, hang out with Colette. Well, Richard and Josephine, some child you bet on. Time to move your chips over to Gwen's table.

15

Populated with a thirty-ish crowd, The Capital Bar and Grill, was a place Nick had never been to. The atmosphere was more refined than where he usually hung out with his friends, and carried a serious, *adult* mood about it. When he met Colette's gaze, she looked like someone watching a live comedy routine, poised and ready to laugh at the joke when it arrived. She giggled.

"Huh?"

"Nick. You act like this is the first time you've ever been to a restaurant. I know your father is strict, but he doesn't keep you locked in the basement, does he?"

He laughed. He was almost certain it was out of madness. The last time he spent in his parents' basement was when Autumn gave him head in front of his father's golf simulator. He snorted. Colette had a look of sincere interest. He wanted to unload his day on her, but that would have been true madness.

He imagined the conversion going something like…

"Oh, Colette, let me tell you about my day…

First, I banged my mom's friend in the bathhouse near her backyard swimming pool…

Wow, that was a teenage fantasy finally fulfilled, but I think it was better for her than me…

Then I found out the girl I slept with in Spain could be carrying my child…

My friend Autumn, who I have this friends-with-benefits thing going on, well she fucked my other friend…

I walked in on them—oops…

Who knows, they could be fucking now…

My father kissed the woman I'm in love with…

Yes, I even told her I loved her, crazy right? Anyway…

The woman is older than me, but… "

He snorted and shook his head.

"No, he doesn't lock me in the basement, but maybe he should. It's just … I've never been here before. This place is nice. Cozy, yet mature."

Colette tilted her head and chuckled. He glanced at the menu.

"Okay? Hopefully not too mature. I don't think they have a senior's menu. You don't want one, do you?"

He chuckled, smiled, and shook his head. She smiled back. He got their server's attention, who brought a third glass of beer for him. Colette's first glass of wine glass was nearly full. The server took his empty glasses, and they placed their orders. Her eyebrows rose when he took a drink.

"Tough day?"

He chuckled.

"What? What is it, Nick?"

"I'm off to a decent start at Hale, which should make my father happy. Your dad is cool and easy to work with. He also seemed pretty happy about us going out tonight."

"Oh yeah. He's been talking about you a lot. Singing your praises, in fact."

Nick frowned and raised an eyebrow.

"Don't be so doubtful. You'll do well. Also, it doesn't hurt to have your father running the company."

"Sure-sure, but what do you really think, and I don't mean the future of my career?"

She ran her fingertips through her dark honey blonde curls and twirled the bleached ends around her finger. She had a tight lip smile and looked at him with her pale blue eyes from behind the curls that fell across her face.

"I don't know. Probably nothing you haven't already heard before."

"Really? I always thought of you as someone who was very insightful. You *are* a journalism major, after all."

"All right."

The corner of his lips turned up and his eyes brightened. She drank, and over the top of her glass, she gazed into his eyes.

"Well…"

She paused. She looked down at the table as if there was a crystal ball for her to see into his future and to tell her what type of man he would turn out to be.

"I think you're sweet and kind. You're smart and driven when you want to be."

"I don't know, Colette. Sounds like yesterday's news."

"Ha-ha. What do you want me to say?"

"I don't know. I'm sorry, I'm being ridiculous."

They both drank and avoided each other's gaze. He finally turned to her. She looked off towards the swinging doors to the kitchen. She was beautiful, and had definitely taken on that California girl look with her curly sun kissed hair with the blonde ends. Her makeup was light and natural, no harsh dark lipstick to contrast with her fair skin. He fell into her pale blue eyes when her gaze met his. Her moon shaped eyes when she laughed, or when she had a broad smile, made him smile both inside and out.

Their food came, they ate, and they chatted about college, family, and friends. His head was light from the beers he drank. She was always easy to be around and never pressured him. He drank for other reasons, but owed it to her to be attentive and upright. When the server came around, he only asked for his water glass to be filled.

She tilted her head and looked like she had something on her mind.

"What?"

He smiled at her. She shrugged.

"It's—it's so easy to talk to you, and be around you. Don't you think?"

His lips curled into a subtle smile.

"It's you. You're easy to be around. You don't stress me out, like most everyone else."

She chuckled.

"I guess that's good, isn't it?"

"It's great. I enjoy talking to you. Not to suggest anything, but my parents offered us the use of the lake house if you want to hang out after dinner."

There was a sparkle in her pale blue eyes. Her lips were soft, unsmiling, and her face had a look of joyful contemplation. She had only one glass of wine and sipped at her glass of water with lemon wedges that swirled at the bottom. She sat her glass on the table.

"Sure, that would be nice."

Colette's parents' friends would say, which she had overheard before, that Colette was dutiful. Her parents wanted her to explore a relationship with Nick, so in trusting their judgement and wisdom, she was open to the idea. Nick was, after all, tall, handsome, and intelligent. He seemed interested in her, at least as a friend, and that was a good start.

Nick went to the kitchen to open a bottle of wine, while Colette reclined on her side next to the fireplace with a big, plush pillow behind her. She sent her parents a courtesy text message telling them she may not be home tonight and to not worry. Also, she mentioned that dinner went well, and that she was still out with Nick and they may stay the night at his parents' lake house. She imagined their faces when they read her message. Smiles abound. She chuckled softly and turned her head from side to side.

When Nick returned, Colette took a glass of wine from him. He sat his glass on the stonework at the foot of the fireplace, and grab one of the oversize pillows, hugged it, and reclined on his stomach near her. At first, he peered into the fireplace and looked lost in thought. She smiled at him. The fireplace produced a warm orange glow on their faces. It was romantic, even though he had only flipped a wall switch to start the fire in the gas fueled fireplace. He turned on his side toward her, his arm cocked to support his head. He took his wineglass, swirled the liquid, then took a light sip. This was the most comfortable he looked all night. She raised her eyebrows. Maybe it was the alcohol. She was fine driving them to the lake house, but she worried he would fall asleep as soon as they got there. She had no expectations other than to continue their conversation.

"How's the dating scene in California?"

"Depends on who you hang out with. I spent most of my time focusing on my classes."

"Sounds boring."

Colette tilted her head and narrowed her eyelids.

"I have a group of friends, just like you. We hang out and have a good time. I always kept things casual, no serious relationships. That made it fun and less stressful. I think it's best that you share each other's intentions. Do you agree?"

He looked off into the fire.

"Oh yeah, for sure."

After he took a drink, his lips tightened. She ran her fingers through her hair.

"So what are your intentions, Nick?"

"I thought we discussed that over dinner."

"What are your intentions regarding me?"

"Oh."

"Yeah."

He smiled, but his gaze remained transfixed on the fireplace. She scowled and her lips tightened.

"Are you okay?"

"I like you a lot Colette, but I've got tons of shit going on that I need to figure out."

"Oh?"

She took a drink and stared at him.

"I ended things with Autumn. She hung on for far too long, and all that time I used her. I didn't think I was, but she made it easy and I got comfortable."

He peeked out of the corner of his eyes at her, then returned his gaze to the fireplace. She took in a deep breath.

"That was the mature thing to do. I applaud you, though you took a long time doing it. Will you still try to be friends with her?"

"I don't know if that's possible."

"You seemed to have resolved that. You said 'tons' plural. What are the other tons?"

She inspected her fingernails. This pry it out of him psychiatric session was getting old. She wondered if he needed patient confidentiality from her to get him to talk.

"Nick, it's okay, you can tell me. I won't judge you or reveal your secrets to anyone."

The corner of his lips turned up.

"I know. You've always been a good friend."

He said *friend* like it was a foreign word. He turned to her and met her gaze. There was a sadness in his eyes and he wore a tight lip smile. She raised her eyebrows. He exhaled a long slow breath as if he were about to make an Olympic ski jump and risk life and limb.

"All right. On my trip to Spain with Blake, I hooked up with this girl. She is a friend of Marissa's, the girl Blake is having a long distance relationship with."

"Does this girl you hooked up with have a name?"

She took a drink and glanced at him over the top of her glass.

"Her name is Isabella."

She nodded, then swallowed.

"Anyway, Isabella told Marissa that when we had sex, the condom broke. She said nothing to me that night. Now, she thinks she's pregnant."

"By you?"

"I guess."

She rolled back onto her elbows with the oversized pillow behind her. He took a drink. She looked off toward the kitchen. He had left the lights on there.

"Pretty fucked up, huh?"

She wrinkled her lips and raised her eyebrows.

"Yeah. Hm?"

"Hm. What?"

"You should wait until you're totally certain. Can't you get a paternity test?"

"How would I do that? She lives in Spain."

"I'm sure there's a way. You should check into it."

He fumbled with his empty glass, sat up, then stood. She watched him head back to the kitchen, then she glanced into the fire and thought about an abortion she had almost two years ago. He had started his graduate program in New York when she had her abortion in California. It was the darkest time in her life. She was uncertain if she would ever tell him about it. Noise from the kitchen drew her attention. Silverware chimed from a pulled drawer. A moment later, he returned with a fresh bottle of wine, then first topped off her glass and filled his own.

"Thanks for listening, and not freaking out on me."

She chuckled.

"Oh, I'll leave that to your parents. Does anyone else know?"

"Well, Blake told me after speaking to Marissa. As for what went down with Autumn, that happened earlier today. You're the only one that knows."

"Jesus, Nick."

He nodded. They drank and glanced at one another. She inspected her glass of wine.

"How come you never asked me out?"

"I guess you were too smart and nerdy for me."

She wrinkled her lips and tilted her head. He chuckled.

"Sorry, it's true. I felt intimidated."

Her lips curled into a smile. She stretched out her leg and tapped his shin with her foot.

"You know there's more to it than that. I wasn't hot enough for you."

His lips turned down and his head turned slowly from side to side as if he were considering her statement. She put her barefoot on his thigh and nudged him.

"C'mon, you know it's true."

He raised his hand in surrender.

"Okay-okay, you were a little awkward, but everyone grows into the person they'll become. You've become a beautiful woman."

She continued to push on his thigh with her foot.

"And you're smart and sexy."

He put down his glass of wine and took her barefoot in both hands. She pushed gently within his grasp.

"And you're kind and understanding."

He rubbed her arch, then he focused on her heel and toes. Her eyelids became heavy. She took a sip of wine, then smiled at him with a soft, tight-lipped smile. He held out his hand to gesture that she give him her other foot. She did, and he rubbed both of her feet. She wore capris and his hands ventured up her calves to give them a squeeze, then back down to her heels.

"Mm. I think getting things off your shoulders has worked out better for me than you."

She took a drink, then sat her wineglass on the stone base of the fireplace. She then drew her arms up behind her head and her eyelids closed. He cleared his throat.

"I'm not sure about that. I feel much lighter telling you about my messy life. Would you want to be with someone like me?"

"Mm. I find it attractive in a man who will acknowledge his faults and try to correct them. We all make mistakes. It's what you do after that counts."

He slipped his fingers under the cuff of her capris and cupped and rubbed her knee, then the back of her leg. She smiled with closed eyes. He was quiet.

"You can't go backwards and change things. We can only go forward. Mm. Yes. I mean, yes?"

She hummed and moaned softly. Then, after a moment, her eyelids opened to slits and found him peering off into the fire. Her hand covered his to interrupt his massage. When he turned to her, she moved on her knees, then straddled him. She looked into his eyes, brushed her long curls from his face, and kissed him. His lips were softer than she imagined and electrified hers until a sign lit up in her mind—Nick Evers—it read. His hands slipped up Colette's thighs, and he held her at her waist. She touched the side of his face and his stubble bristled against her palm. The scent of wine was on his breath, mixed with a hint of his cologne.

They kissed, soft and brief, then longer and deep. She felt him swell beneath her. She pulled her top over her head until she freed her tangled curls. Her breasts were heavy and filled her bra cups. She wore a revealing lacy blue-gray bra she hoped he would like, and he did, judging by the soft dreamy smile on his face. Their lips met again, and she unbuttoned his shirt. When she worked his shirt over his shoulders, she pushed him back onto the pillow, then she unbuckled his linen shorts and slipped them off of his long tan legs. He wore boxer briefs. His erection was apparent. She touched him outside of his briefs. He lifted his chin and closed his eyes. He caressed her thigh with his fingertips. She slipped his briefs down, his cock exposed, hardened with a subtle arc that pointed up toward his navel. She tugged his briefs down his legs, past his ankles, and freed him of them.

He hummed and muttered something incoherent after she had taken him into her mouth. She straddled his leg and curled her body over him. With each pass of her lips, his head and thickness swelled. His skin was velvet over stone, with a distant salty taste of the sea. As she stroked him, it fascinated her how his cock fit within her grasp. She admired the length, color, and contours of his cock. Soft moans passed through his lips.

She brought her arm behind her and unlatched her bra. Her full, tan-outlined breasts fell free, and she tossed her bra on the floor. His eyes remained shut. He lifted his hand and Colette guided his touch to her breast. He was gentle, which surprised her. No awkward pinching and groping. Her lower back tightened when his fingertips found her nipples. She stood and removed her capris, then slipped free of her matching lace panties. She smiled as he watched her through heavy half-closed eyelids, like a child unwilling to give in to sleep.

She lowered her body over his. She tilted her pelvis so that her bikini groomed bush brushed against his testicles and the base of his cock. He rested his warm hands on her thighs. She inched up his body until her wet sex kissed the head of his hard cock. Her hips moved, and she ground herself against him. Each tilt of her pelvis brought her clit in contact with him, and electricity arced up through her body. She explored his sculpted abdomen and chest with her fingertips. Her long curls lay over his skin as she kissed his nipples, and when she looked up at him, he watched her with a curious, dreamy gaze.

"That's very nice," he whispered.

She bent over him, her breasts flattened against his chest, and their lips met. She slipped her fingertips between their bodies, aimed his cock, and eased him inside her. After she rose and braced her hands on his chest, her chin lifted and her lips parted. They both drew in audible heavy breaths. With each movement, she took him deeper. Her heavy breaths turned to moans and moans turned to cries.

He curled into a slouched seated position. His hands touched her breasts, then held her at her hips as she fucked him. She put her hands over his. He groaned.

"I'm going to come soon."

He put his hands on her buttocks and she could sense that he was about to pull out. She huffed between breaths.

"It's okay. It's okay. I'm on the pill."

She took his hands, and their fingers interlaced. She eased him back on the floor and held his hands above his head. Her body stretched out over his like a jockey riding him to the finish line. Her hips rose and crashed down, taking him in short, but deep, strokes. He grunted.

"Oh, fuck."

She rode him harder until his cock spasmed and he filled her. Now she needed to come with him still inside her.

"Make me come."

She released his hands, and he grabbed her hips, then she lifted herself to give him room to move. He thrusted upward. His cock churned his come inside her. She tilted her pelvis and flexed her buttocks to allow his aim to touch her inside, where she most desired. Her climax rose and cascaded down, then her muscles clenched his cock and threatened to expel him. His flesh and bones sunk into the carpet. She moved in a slow rhythm like the flutter of a jellyfish. As their heavy breaths receded, he withered inside her. His thick semen saturated their pubic hair. She remained straddled on top of him and rested her head against his chest to listen to his heartbeat.

The morning sun broke over the tree-line and cast a warm glow over the lake house. Nick stood on the dock. His forearms rested on the wooden railing. The dark blue remnant of night departed as its companion of light arrived on the horizon with oranges, reds, and violets. Two lovers forever chasing one another, a brief kiss, a touch, then a goodbye. It was some silly fairytale he heard.

He gazed out across the shimmering ripples and took in the lake air. Hours earlier, while Colette slept, he checked his phone. There were no new messages from Elizabeth. A dull, distant tapping sound came from behind him. He turned toward the house and Colette stood inside the glass patio door. She tapped on the glass to get his attention. She had the bedsheet wrapped around her. They had slept on the floor downstairs, so they would be close to the kitchen. They talked hours after their lovemaking, and with little desire to cook, snacked on crackers or whatever they could find, and drank more wine.

She waved, then pressed her open hand to the glass. He waved and motioned for her to join him to watch the sunrise. She smiled, but turned her head from side to side, then released the sheet that covered her. It slid down her breasts, past her triangular patch of golden blonde pubic hair, and pooled at her feet. She turned around and gave him a view of her backside, then she disappeared into the morning shadows of the room. He smiled to himself, then ran back to the house.

~

In his bedroom, Nick lie in bed with his feet on the pillows and his head at the foot of the bed. He gazed at the ceiling fan as the blades turned slow and hypnotic. His overnight getaway with Colette gave him a lot to think about. She proposed they be exclusive, to satisfy their parents' frequent queries, and hopefully end Autumn's pursuit of him. She had taken a risk with her proposal, by assuming that he throughly enjoyed the sex with her, at least, over what he could get with Autumn. He voiced no distinction, but he did, in fact, enjoy having sex more with her. So her assumption was correct. It baffled him why he held back from her. He wrinkled his face and felt around the sheets until he found his football. He tossed it over and over toward the ceiling, each time he got closer to the fan's blades.

Elizabeth had left a text message. The next day after work, he was to meet her for dinner at a Brazilian steakhouse. He looked forward to air out all the things that had been troubling him. Foremost, the kiss she shared with his father at the German restaurant. He tossed the football toward the ceiling, but this time the fan blades caught it, and launched it. The ball thudded against the wall, and crashed down on his desk, slammed his laptop closed, then bounced out of sight.

"Nick? Nick, are you okay in there?"

His mother's voice came from behind the door, then a knock followed.

"Come in."

She opened the door.

"I was down the hallway and heard a noise. What happened?"

"Nothing. I was just tossing the football around."

Her lips wrinkled and her eyebrows knit together.

"You need to stop playing around."

He waved and motioned for her to leave his room.

"Nicholas, I need to talk to you about something."

"Yes mother. It's about Colette, right?"

She drew her chin in, and her face softened.

"No, I already spoke to Irene Scott, and she filled me in. We're all thrilled that you two finally went out and had a great time."

"Okay."

"I want to talk to you about going to the Rutherfords to use their swimming pool."

"Okay."

She stood in the bedroom doorway with her arms crossed. He rolled his eyes toward the ceiling and watched the ceiling fan blades as they turned. There was a dark mar in the white paint. The football must have clipped the ceiling.

"I don't want you using their pool. Abigale is too much of a flirt, and I don't want her coming on to you. God knows, Henry is always away. It wouldn't surprise me if she was having an affair. She gets bored so easy."

He raised his eyebrows and pursed his lips.

"Do you care if she's having an affair?"

"Yes, of course. That would ruin her marriage. I doubt Henry would stay with her."

"How do you know he's not having one of his own?"

He turned to his mother. She put her hands on her hips.

"I don't. Anyway, if Abigale is having an affair, I don't want it to be with you. Do you understand?"

He wanted to laugh. That was what Abigale told him.

"Yes mother. I understand."

"Good. Even if she wasn't married, you're much too young for her."

He snorted.

"Got it. Close my door, please."

"All right. That's settled. I'm happy we got to talk."

She closed his bedroom door. He put his arms up with his fingers knit together and rested his head on his hands. He thought about Colette's other proposals. One was a hypothetical. If they got married, she half-joked and was half-serious, they could run off together to California and make a life of their own without the baggage of Atlanta. It sounded tempting. He wondered how long that idea had been brewing in her head. They knew each other well enough. They had been friends since they were teenagers. Maybe she understood their compatibility more than he did. Her suggestions made sense, and her feelings toward him made him smile. Had she been waiting all this time for him to reach the same conclusion?

16

The Brazilian steakhouse Elizabeth chose was more upscale than Nick imagined. Its exterior was modern, with broad stretched canvas awnings for outdoor luncheons. The interior had a high, cream-colored ceiling with masculine, broad, dark wood, paneled walls. The grinning hostess led him to the table where Elizabeth sat. They shared a brief, polite embrace. He made no move to kiss her, he only pressed his cheek to hers. After seeing her kiss his father, he wanted an explanation, if there was one.

"Hello Elizabeth."

"Lizzy, please. How are you?"

He had thought about Colette, and his amazing time with her. He questioned why he even came tonight, but something inside compelled him to.

"I'm—good. How are you?"

"Great."

They both sat. There were two glasses of wine already on the table. Her glass was half full. He smiled and gazed at her, and then at her glass.

"I hope you don't mind. I ordered a glass of wine for us. They have a variety of beer, if you would like one of those instead, or perhaps a mixed drink?"

"No, this is good. Thank you."

He picked up his glass and had a few of sips to catch up to her. The frustration he felt toward her made him feel justified for not asking how long she had been waiting. She turned her glass in her hands as if she were contemplating something. Beneath the table, her foot brushed against his leg. He peered into her crystal blue diamond eyes and surrendered.

"Were you waiting long?"

She sipped her wine, then turned her head subtly from side to side until she swallowed.

"No. Maybe ten minutes."

Her voice was soft, warm, and with a welcoming tone that he ached for.

"Good."

He glanced around the restaurant and took in its atmosphere. The dining room filled with an aromatic scent of grilled beef and chicken whenever the kitchen doors opened and servers entered and exited. Steam hung in the air. The servers leaving the kitchen carried long vertical skewers with cooked meat out to the tables. He raised his eyebrows and his lips parted, which made her chuckle.

"This is nice."

Their table had a view into the kitchen, where they could see the cooks and waitstaff busy at work.

A familiar woman's voice in a musically haughty tone said, "Oh, hello Nicholas. What a delightful surprise."

His body stiffened. He turned and, sure enough, Abigale Rutherford stood there at their table. She grinned and tugged at the man who she had her arm looped around. The man appeared in his thirties, taller than her, but shorter than Nick, broad shoulders, athletic. A tattoo on his neck rose above the collar of his shirt. He had dark hair with olive skin and tightly groomed facial hair. He turned to them and grinned. His bright white teeth lit up his face.

"This is Bruno, a friend of mine," Abigale said.

Nick stood and shook Bruno's hand, then Abigale stepped forward and Nick gave her a polite hug.

"My-my, the game is certainly afoot," Abigale whispered into his ear.

She smirked and gazed at Elizabeth when Nick stepped back. He gestured toward Elizabeth.

"This is Elizabeth. She is a friend of mine. Elizabeth, this is Abigale."

A sense of pride crept in. The friend part was a work in progress, and one he hoped to get beyond. He refrained from mentioning to Elizabeth that Abigale was his mother's friend. She stayed seated and offered a warm smile.

"Very nice to meet you both."

She first addressed Abigale and then gave Bruno a nod and a smile. Nick's jaw tightened when he saw the way Bruno looked at Elizabeth. He knew Bruno was dying to touch her, to kiss or shake her hand. He chuckled inside when Elizabeth made no move to offer her hand.

"And you as well. Enjoy your evening," Abigale said.

Her tone carried a stain of sarcasm, and her nostrils flared. Abigale took Bruno's arm, and they strolled away. Nick sat and looked across the table at Elizabeth. His eyes were wide and his eyebrows raised, then he quickly covered his mouth as he burst into laughter. She stared at him with a shocked look on her face.

"What was that all about?"

Her words tumbled out.

"That woman is a friend of my mother's."

"Oh?"

Her eyes widened.

"The guys she's with—Bruno. I can tell you is more than just a friend."

"Ah. I sensed that might be the case."

"Yes, ah indeed. Abigale's husband, Henry, travels often for work, so while the cat's away, the mice will play. Isn't that how it goes? Of course, Henry is older than Abigale and he himself is a big flirt, if you were to believe my mother. So who knows, maybe he doesn't care."

"She's a beautiful woman. Why wouldn't her husband care?"

"Trophy wife."

"Nick, that's cruel."

"No Lizzy, it's true."

She grinned when he said her nickname. The way her eyes lit up made him smile.

"Is she going to give us any trouble?"

"Trouble how? We're only having dinner. Besides, Abigale is the one who's married, and she's out with a good looking younger man, who *is not* her husband. Also, she lives close to my parents', and you made me trek all the way across town to have dinner with you. So why did she travel all the way across town to *this restaurant* to have dinner with *Bruno*?"

Her lips wrinkled, and she nodded.

"What do you think of her with a younger man?"

He straightened up in his chair. He saw the comparison she made.

"Knowing what little I know of her, she probably wants the thrill of being with a younger man. As for him, no idea what he's after. Sex? Money? Both?"

"You know, I'm not rich, right?"

He cocked his head and gazed into her eyes.

"You're rich in how you live your life, and the passion you have for it."

Her eyebrows rose and her lips parted.

"Hm."

"Hm?"

"That's very nice of you to say."

Her gaze lowered, and she touched the base of her wineglass. When she glanced around the room, her lips pulled to the corner of her mouth.

"What is it?"

"Your mother's friend glanced over toward our table."

"Did she?"

"Yes. I don't like her."

"Do you want to leave?"

"No, I can hold my own."

"What do you mean?"

"You know she is interested in you."

Her gaze returned to meet his.

He half chuckled, then snorted.

"Really? How so?"

She stared into his eyes and licked her top teeth and lips with the tip of her tongue. He shifted in his chair.

"Stop. You're teasing her, right?"

She laughed as if he told the funniest joke. He fought to keep his composure, but failed and grinned at her.

"Stop. Now I know you're teasing her."

She smirked at him.

"Just having some fun. Why do you care? Will she tell your mommy about us?"

"Ouch. Is that a shot at my age?"

"No, sorry, of course not. I've known older men whose mothers still control their lives."

She wrinkled her face and raised her shoulders.

He chuckled.

"My mother isn't that way, thankfully. My father, on the other hand—"

His eyes strained, and the weight of the question he carried until now was more than he could bear. She spoke before he could.

"That's good to hear."

Her words were slow, and he could see his anxiety reflected on her face. He took in a deep breath, followed by a slow exhale.

"Lizzy, I need to know something, and I hope you'll be honest with me."

She leaned forward is if he was about to impart some secret, and the distance between them was crucial.

"Okay?"

"What kind of relationship do you have with my father?"

"Excuse me," their server said.

They glanced up at the young man who arrived at their table with tall skewers of sizzling sirloin impaled on them. She beamed. They straightened up in their seats and removed their hands from the table. The server sliced the beef from the skewers and put it on their plates. They asked for more wine before he left. She ran her fingers through the ends of her long curls. Her gaze was tense. When her eyes met his, he raised his eyebrows to echo his inquiry.

"All right. Richard, I mean your father, has always had a thing for me."

Her eyebrows rose. Tension crept into his shoulders and neck. Their bodies leaned into the table like two sides of an open drawbridge, preparing to meet in the middle.

"Ever since I took over the Hale account at Nexgen Biosolutions, and met with him, he wanted to arrange more business lunches and dinners. First, he would meet with the team, then eventually, only me. I felt flattered, because of his reputation, but I knew he was married, and I didn't want to get involved."

She shrugged her shoulders. Her expression was one of disinterest. A simple explanation, as it appeared to her, neat and clean. He clenched his knee under the table.

"Will you excuse me for a moment? I'm going to use the men's room."

She nodded. She cut into her strips of tender sirloin as he stood and left the table.

Elizabeth ate slowly while she waited for Nick to return. She glanced across the dining room to where Abigale and Bruno sat. His arm lie across the table as if he wanted to touch her. Elizabeth snorted. Abigale smirked and batted her eyelashes at Bruno. Elizabeth rolled her eyes. Abigale stood and walked across the dining room toward the ladies' room. When she got closer, Elizabeth turned her attention to the food on her plate.

"Hello again. I hope you're enjoying your evening out with Nicholas. He's such a fine young man."

She looked up at Abigale and acted surprised to find her standing there.

"Yes, I am. Thank you."

"Has Nicholas told you I am a friend of Josephine's, his mother?"

"Yes, Nick mentioned that."

Abigale's smile broadened. The woman seemed pleased that Nick mentioned her in his conversation. She glanced around the restaurant, and when she returned her attention to Elizabeth, her smile faded.

"I'm surprised, no let me take that back. Nicholas typically likes his women younger, but lately he seems interested in sampling a more mature and complex bouquet."

She picked up Nick's glass of wine, swirled the deep red liquid, and put it to her nose. Elizabeth watched her aghast, and her thighs flexed, ready to pounce. Abigale raised her eyebrows and shrugged, then returned his glass of wine to the table.

"Clearly, his tastes are evolving. They're still crude and lack refinement. He's young though, but he's intelligent and clever. I have no doubt he'll figure it out."

Elizabeth's jaw tightened, but she managed a pinched smile.

"I too have no doubt Nick will figure things out."

Her tense smile turned into a smirk.

"It seems your date has other plans."

Abigale turned, and they both watched Bruno as he smiled and laughed with the cute young blonde server, who waited on Bruno's and Abigale's table. Abigale turned to Elizabeth and waved her hand in the air as if it was of no significant matter.

"Excuse me," Abigale said.

She then strutted off toward the restrooms. Elizabeth exhaled and took a generous drink of wine. What a cunt. She glanced over the top of her glass and caught the blonde server at Abigale's table slipping Bruno what was probably the girl's phone number. She huffed out a chuckle and shook her head.

"Hello Nick," Abigale said.

She caught him after he exited the men's room.

"Oh, hello Abigale."

"Abby. Call me Abby, dear. I rather like it coming from you. Except, not around your mother. We wouldn't want to get her all worked up, now would we?"

The way she smirked at him, it seemed she would like something else coming from him, but the way they left things left a bitter taste in his mouth. His eyebrows knit together.

"No, of course not."

He felt she was trying to appease him with her use of their nicknames, Nick and Abby.

"Oh, and you're welcome to swim in *my pool* anytime. I was hasty with my words."

"Hm? No. Abigale, I think you were right about what you said. About that being the last time. Wouldn't that be the wise thing to do?"

She smirked and raised an eyebrow.

"Let's not ruin the start of a beautiful friendship. Besides, what you have out there is a dead end."

She ran her fingertips down his jaw to his chin. Her gaze penetrated his. She slipped something into the breast pocket of his sport coat, then slinked around him. She smelled good, there was no denying it, intoxicating even. Her scent lingered in his nostrils. She slipped into the bathroom, her short dress with those long, silk-clad legs. He was sure she knew he was watching. He dug into his pocket. It was a book of matches with the restaurant's logo on the face. He flipped it open. Written inside was a phone number, no name, Abigale's, no doubt. A trash bin was right there, next to a potted palm tree. He stared at it for a moment, then he slipped the book of matches back into his pocket.

He looked at his phone. He had it set to silence any calls or notifications. There was a new message from Colette. It said, "Hey." He closed his eyes and held his breath for a moment, then exhaled and went back to join Elizabeth.

17

Elizabeth turned into an entrance lined with well-groomed boxwood shrubs and a colorful array of various flowers. A sign with scrolling gold letters read Lakewood Estates. The headlights of Nick's car reflected in her review mirror. Before she drove into the garage, she reached out her window and pointed to the lot where he should park. She waited outside her garage. As he crossed the street, she smiled at his long, purposeful strides. A little unease slipped in, now that she made it known to him where she lived. It had been years since she invited a man of romantic interest to her place. The last time turned into a stalker situation. Thankfully, Nick was no stalker. She grinned when he walked up to her. He tilted his head and his eyebrows drew together.

"You didn't think I knew how to cross the street, did you?"

He glanced up and down the row of condos. There was a look of surprise on his face.

"C'mon, silly."

She took his hand, and they both went in through the garage. Inside, she had him wait in the kitchen while she turned on some lights. Her condo was contemporary in style, with hardwood floors and some throw rugs here and there. The kitchen had granite countertops and elegant crystal lighting. A partial view into the living room displayed her taste in modern furniture: a leather sofa, two leather-covered chairs, and a sleek coffee table. There were two large framed landscape photographs on opposite walls, pictures of the same location but different views. His eyebrows rose and his head bobbed in a slow nod.

"You have a nice place."

"Thank you. Make yourself at home."

He stepped into the living room and went to the pictures.

"This place looks familiar. Where is this?"

"Those are the Machu Picchu ruins. They're from my trip to Peru. I had them enlarged. One I took at dusk, and the other at dawn."

"Really? That's impressive."

She chuckled. He returned to the kitchen.

"Thank you. By the way, there's plenty to drink in the refrigerator, and I have a leftover cheese platter, if you want a snack."

She braced the wall and slipped off her heels. She could feel his eyes on her. When she turned around, he had the refrigerator door open and was bent over as if he prepared to climb inside. She put her elbows on the island's granite countertop, braced her chin in her palm, and watched him with curiosity. Her eyes drifted lower to his backside. Her nostrils flared and her lips curled into a smile. She went to his side.

"Can I help you find something?"

"Do you mind if I have a beer?"

"Get us both one."

He closed the refrigerator door and held two Belgian pilsners. She took two glasses from the cabinet, and he poured.

"Did you want to ask me something over dinner?"

"Huh?"

A dark unease had ebbed and flowed from his face the entire evening. There hung an unasked question. He wanted to know something. She could see it in his eyes and in the tenseness of his face. He needed to be certain of something. She would wait for him to ask if he was able. She stared at him and waited.

"Ah? No. Why?"

He avoided her gaze, filled a glass of beer, and handed it to her. She raised an eyebrow. Okay?

"Thank you. Let's take our drinks into the living room."

He followed her. She moved without a sound like a ghost in her stocking feet. His leather bottom loafers made soft taps on the hardwood floor behind her. A man chasing his muse. She wondered if he still felt that way about her.

"Why don't you take your shoes off? You'll be more comfortable."

He slipped off his loafers and put them to the side of the sofa. They both sat, took sips of their glasses of beer, and placed them on the coffee table. She moved closer to him.

"Tired? You look as though you've got the weight of the world on your shoulders."

He chuckled with strained eyes.

"Was it the woman at the restaurant, Abigale?"

He put his arm up on the sofa's back behind her. He rested his other hand on her knee.

"No. She's something, though, isn't she? No-no, not her. My parents have been pushing hard for me to date the daughter of one of their friends. A girl I knew since we were teenagers."

"Oh? Was she at your graduation party? Was she one of your friends?"

"No. She goes to USC, and couldn't make it for my graduation party."

She nodded.

"Let me guess, your father has issued you an ultimatum? He can be pushy in his business deals."

His lips tightened, and his eyebrows drew together. She had touched a nerve. She raised her chin as though she finally understood.

"You asked me if I had some relationship with your father. I don't, but he persists. I can see something about that still troubles you."

"What does that mean, exactly? He persists."

He moved his hand from her knee and rested it in his lap.

"A man wants what he wants. With your father, and with his success, failure doesn't come easy. A man like him is always looking for a solution. Don't you trust me?"

He tilted his head, and drew in a slow breath, then peered at his glass of beer on the coffee table. She imagined the gears turning in his head.

"Yes, of course I trust you. Let's not forget, I grew up with the man. I know he can be a stubborn prick."

She moved closer until her shoulder rested under his arm and against his ribs. She raised her chin and their lips met. His lips were soft and moist. His stubble bristled when she ran her fingertips down his cheek. She rested her head on his chest and listened to his heartbeat.

He stretched out his legs under the coffee table, and she felt his tension ebb under her touch. He returned his hand to her knee, and as they sat there, the world seem to turn a little slower. She sat up and they enjoyed their drinks.

"Tell me more about this friend of yours. The one that goes to USC. The one that your parents are fond of."

He took a sip of his beer, sat his glass down, and cleared his throat.

"Her name is Colette. She's a nice girl. I've known her since we were teenagers. Her father is Dale Scott, who you know from Hale."

She nodded and held her glass of beer with both hands in her lap.

"Dale is a great guy. My father likes him. Our families get along well. So, naturally, they want to get their kids together. When we were teens, I wasn't interested in her. She was more of an awkward nerdy type."

"And now?"

"She's definitely changed since college. She's pretty, and no longer awkward. Next year, she'll be getting her master's degree in journalism. I'm sure she'll have a great life ahead of her."

"But not with you?"

His shoulders pushed back into the couch, and his eyebrows knit together.

"I don't think so. We're different people. Besides, she wants to live in California. I can't see myself leaving Atlanta unless there was a strong enough reason to tear me away."

His gaze bore into her. Within his green eyes lie possibilities, an offer of love and relationship. He looked at her as though he posed a question, and was searching her eyes for the answer.

"The world is a very big place. You would stay in Atlanta for family? For Hale Biotech?"

"I have commitments to both, but I don't want either to rule my life."

"Would you ever choose someone over family, career, or even fortune?"

"For love?" he asked.

She looked down into her glass of beer that she held in her lap. The foamy head had since diminished to a thin ring that clung to the inside of the glass. She met his awaiting gaze.

"Yes. Would you? For love?"

A soft, tight lip smile appeared on his face. He looked away. Now it seemed it was his turn to stare blankly as if to ponder the carpet, the coffee table, or his glass of beer. She raised an eyebrow and held her breath. She was unsure if he realized the price of love.

"You realize that could mean giving up Hale Biotech, and possibly being shunned by your family. Could you live with that?"

His eyebrows rose, then descended into a scowl. She wrinkled her lips, and she spoke before he could answer.

"Whatever you decide to do, I'm sure you'll give it some careful thought."

His shoulders slumped, and he looked relieved to not have to provide an answer. He picked up his glass of beer and took a drink.

"I think I know my family and what they can—"

His assertion started off with confidence, but faltered with uncertainty.

"Tolerate?"

In a low voice, she provided the word they both despised. Acceptance would be a battle, and most likely an ongoing one, full of bitterness and spite.

"Yes, but what I meant was, or rather what I hoped to say was, that they would come around to accept whoever I loved and chose to be with."

"I'm pleased you feel that way. What about Hale? What if your father cut you out?"

"I don't know. Hale has always been my father's true love."

He paused. Maybe he was seeing something for the first time, or accepting a long held realization.

"I see what my father created, but I don't love the company like he does. He loves Hale more than his own wife. My mother, bless her soul for putting up with him. I could never do that."

She stared at him. Her lips curled into a soft smile. There is more depth and dimension to Nick Evers, certainly more than he lets on. She took their glasses and sat them on the coffee table. She then peered into his eyes. The possibilities remained. She pressed her body against his, and he took her into his arms. They kissed. The exchange was gentle, wet, and electric.

His green eyes looked bright with promise. He leaned toward her and their lips met again. With parted lips, their kiss deepened and their tongues reacquainted. His eyelids opened heavy and dreamy. She rose to her feet, and took him by the hand, then led him to her bedroom.

Nick slipped off his sports jacket and tossed it on the floor, while Elizabeth sat on the edge of the bed. The corners of his lips flattened to match her stoic expression. When he unbuttoned his shirt, her breath left her. He tugged his shirt free from the waistband of his trousers and dropped it near his sports jacket.

Her eyebrow rose at the sight of his thick chest, broad shoulders, and lean, defined midsection. She struggled to believe that someone who looked like him would be insecure around her. He unbuckled his trousers and dropped them on the floor before he slipped off his socks. He stood in his briefs, but he might as well have taken them off, too. The fabric stretched and formed around his erection. A faint hum passed her lips.

His intense green eyes darkened with anticipation as he stood there and waited for what was to come. She slowly drew up her skirt until the lacy tops of her thigh-high stockings were visible. She watched his gaze lower to peer at her stocking feet, then up her legs to the tops of her stockings, where she slipped her fingers under and slid them down her legs. His lips parted and the tip of his tongue wet the corner of his mouth.

She tossed her balled up stocking on top of his clothes. A memento. She assumed he had taken her panties the night they were together in Madrid. The memory brought a smile, which she kept inside her. She shifted and rolled onto her other hip, then further raised her skirt and slipped off her other stocking. He stood there and took in her seduction. His cock stretched the front of his briefs. She tossed the second balled-up stocking.

After she stood and turned away from him, she held her long curls over one shoulder to expose the zipper at the back of her dress. A wordless gesture and request. He cleared his throat, which made her lips curl into a soft, private smile. He unzipped her dress and ran his hands over her shoulders and down her arms. Electricity flowed to her fingertips. Her dress slipped down her body, and after some gentle movements of her hips, it was on the floor. She turned around and held his face while she brought her lips to his. His kiss felt sensual, purposeful, and determined.

His bulge protruded and pressed into her belly. It was torture not to tear off his briefs and mount him, but a slow seduction would be her gift to him. She reached behind her and unclasped her bra, then let it fall down her arms and to the floor.

He kissed her breasts and cupped them in his hands, then sucked on her nipples until they reddened. Her back arched, and a low hum escaped her parted lips. He lowered himself to his knees and kissed her belly, then slid her panties down until they were at her feet. She stepped out of them. He cupped her breasts and pinched and tugged at her nipples that slid between his fingers. His breath on her sex caused droplets of her juices to crawl down the inside of her thigh.

She moved back onto the bed and propped herself up on her elbows while he remained on his knees. When she opened her legs, the inside of her thighs were wet. He crawled up on the bed with his head and shoulders positioned between her open legs like a tiger stalking low in the underbrush. When their gaze met, she gave him a coy smile with a raised eyebrow.

His tongue licked her clit in abbreviated strokes, then he applied longer ones that descended into her slick folds, and teased at her opening. A surge within her caused her body to flex and her hips to rise. She pressed her sex to his lips and tongue with an eagerness for firm and vigorous attention.

His mouth and chin glistened wet with her sweet nectar. He ran his tongue over his lips before he went back to work on her. There was a fire inside those green eyes. A fire she had stoked.

She squeezed his hand on her abdomen and took a fistful of his hair. He must have sensed her approaching orgasm, and applied his tongue more fiercely to her clit. Her buttocks clenched, and a tremor shook her hips down to her thighs. He rose after her body settled. She moved to the edge of the bed to strip him of his light blue briefs. His cock pointed upward, fully engorged, when she freed him. She took him into her mouth. He groaned as she sucked and stroked him. She grasped his firm ass cheek, that hardened to stone as her mouth moved over him. Heavy breaths passed his lips. She was careful not to bring him to climax. Her fingertips massaged the velvety skin of his scrotum.

They moved onto the bed. She retrieved a condom from the nightstand drawer. After she rolled it over his cock, she got into a kneeling position at the headboard. She glanced over her shoulder as he positioned himself behind her. His lips descended her spine with kisses, then he squeezed her buttocks as if he were testing the firmness of fruit. She raised her rear off her heels and arched her lower back. He parted her buttocks and entered her with one effortless stroke. Her mouth opened and a low, deep moan escaped.

This was a position she loved and dreaded. It made her come quickly and with such intensity, especially with the right lover. Once Antonio knew this, he used it to his advantage to keep her passion for him ignited. The last time she slept with him in Madrid, they made love face-to-face. It would have been too much to cloud her judgement otherwise. Now she had a new lover, and hopefully more.

"Oh, fuck!"

He held her hips and took her in long strokes. The angle of his thrusts ignited her body. During their night together in Madrid, the sex was wonderful, but she was on top and in control. She needed to know what kind of lover he was. Now she knew.

"Fuck me!"

He clutched the headboard with his hands next to hers as his hips crashed into her buttocks. His outward thrust brought him close to slipping outside of her, then he filled her again. Her moans rose to cries, then she came. Her sex clenched around his cock. He kept his pace, and she rode each climax one to the next. A flood of her orgasm eased his efforts, allowing him to take her deep and quick. She sensed he was getting close. He paused, perhaps to catch his breath, then he grasped her hips and drove his cock into her with greater intensity. His breaths became shorter until he grunted.

"Oh, fuck—fuck."

He sunk deep into her with his hips tight against her buttocks. His cock spasmed again and again inside her until his body curled over her in a great arc. His heart thumped against her back. Eventually, they rolled onto the bed and let exhaustion take them. During the night, half asleep, she watched him visit the bathroom. She smiled inside when he crept back into bed.

She rose early to shower and dress for work. The sun had yet to open its one great eye. The lights were still on that lined the sidewalks and streets. He slept with his body turned toward the wall, away from her. She crawled from the bed as to not disturb him. Low hums passed his lips as he exhaled. She picked up his sport jacket from the floor, and laid it over an armless chair in the corner of the room. Something fell from the pocket. It was a matchbook from the Brazilian steakhouse. Written inside the flap was a phone number with no name. She glanced over at him. He was still on his side, in a deep sleep. Her eyebrows drew together. She slipped the matchbook back into the pocket of his sport jacket.

18

Nick sat on the edge of the bed and attempted to rub the sleep from his face. She was gone. An unsigned note sat on top of the dresser. It was a simple direct message, void of any romance. An appreciation for last night, a desire and suggestion that they should talk more, and a mantra: Rise early and set about to make an impression on the world. Her words brought on a smile. He showered, dressed, then sauntered out to the living room, where he found his loafers and slipped them on. When he went to the front door, the morning sun brightened the entranceway.

The front door, with its semi-private, decorative, oval window, darkened by a shadow that approached like some spectre. He had already squeezed the door handle, and the door swung inward. His father stood on the porch. Both men stared at one another.

"Nicholas?"

"Father? What are you doing here?"

"Nicholas, since you're the one standing inside, I believe that question is more appropriate for me to ask you. Well?"

He might have smirked like other times when his father caught him doing something his father disliked. His father's jaw muscles flexed. It was the onset of an approaching shouting match.

"I'm seeing Elizabeth Bach."

A dreaded pride burned inside him. His face heated and his skin prickled. The declaration was only one of a few in his life where he stood up to his father.

It was easier to let his father guide him. He usually appreciated the guidance. It absolved him of having to make his own decisions, but then he often had to live with the choices his father made, with a disregard for his own desires.

"You can't be serious? She's too old for you?"

His father's eyebrows drew together, and he huffed. He chuckled with a haughty and dismissive sneer. Nick's shoulders tensed, and his eyebrows knit together.

"You haven't answered my question."

They glared at one another, then his father snorted.

"I'm here to fetch Ms. Bach for a morning breakfast meeting."

Nick huffed.

"Interesting. That's the best you can do?"

"Nicholas, if you have something to say, say it, but if you have an accusation to make, you better think carefully before you make it."

"When Dale and I went to lunch, I saw you kiss Elizabeth. Why don't we talk about that?"

"I think you need to get your eyes examined."

"So you're denying it?"

"There is nothing to deny. I'll catch up with you later at home."

His father went down the porch steps and strode across the street to his car. Nick watched and waited until he drove off, then he went to his car, where he sat for a moment to think what to do next. He sent Elizabeth a quick text message.

"I ran into my father. He was standing on your porch when I was leaving. He said he stopped by to take you to breakfast. I want to believe in you and me, in us. Help me."

After he tapped Send, he looked at his list of new messages.

Blake wrote, "Let's get together tonight. I spoke to Juan Miguel and Marissa."

Nick replied, "Sure."

Colette wrote, "I want to see you. Can we get together?"

He rubbed his eyes and pinched the bridge of his nose. His eyes burned. He saved Colette's message and went to the next one. It was from Autumn. His thumb hovered over her name, then he tapped it.

She wrote, "Can we talk?"

His eyebrows drew together, and his lips tightened. He deleted her text message.

~

At the Brick Lane Tavern, the mid-week evening crowd was lighter than usual. Nick and Blake sat on stools at the bar with beers on the counter in front of them. They dressed casually in jeans and polos. Tabby, one of the friendly bartenders who knew them, glanced towards them from time to time to see if they were ready for another. Nick gave her a smile and a wink. He chuckled inside at the thought of the many times Blake flirted with her. It got him nowhere.

He swiveled on his stool to face Nick.

"Okay, I got Juan Miguel to meet with Marissa to find out what is going on with Isabella."

Nick held his beer bottle as it sat on the counter, but waited to take a drink. His eyes burned and the tension in his shoulders had never left since he arrived. He raised his eyebrows and stared at Blake.

"Anyway, Juan Miguel tells me that Isabella told Marissa that she missed her period, and Marissa said that Isabella has also been with one other guy. It didn't sound all dramatic, like what Marissa first told me."

"You sure?"

"Yeah, yeah."

"But what if she finds out that she's pregnant? How will I know if—"

Blake grasped his shoulder.

"I wouldn't stress. Juan Miguel and Marissa both think that Isabella doesn't want a baby. So, if worse comes to worst, then she can get rid of it. I believe abortion is legal in Spain."

"Jesus. You make it sound so—"

"Easy? Of course, it *isn't* easy, but I don't think it's the end of the world."

"Might be for me, if word got around."

"Trust, my friend. If you can't trust me, then who can you trust?"

Nick laughed, then drank his beer.

"Everyone's getting together later. Are you going to stick around?"

None of his other friends had yet to arrive, which he was grateful for. He glanced at his watch, then patted Blake on the shoulder.

"Thanks for checking into things. I'm going to take off. I'll hang out with everyone another night when I'm less of a zombie."

Blake raised his bottle of beer and nodded.

"You bet, buddy. See you around."

He was tired of explaining things. Blake said nothing about Autumn and Derek. He wondered if anyone would tell Blake tonight what happened. He hurried out the front door to his car. As he crossed the restaurant parking lot, a car door slammed shut behind him.

"You asshole."

The voice crackled, yet sounded familiar. He stopped before he reached his car and turned. A few cars down the row, Derek moved out from the driver's side of his car. His eyes were sharp and vengeful, his face a twisted mask of tension. He looked like a demon under the stark light of the parking lot lamps.

"Derek?"

"You're an asshole, Nick Evers."

Derek stood tense, and his posture suggested an impending physical altercation.

"What are you talking about? The last time I saw you, you and Autumn were going at it."

"She can't move on. You won't tell her in no uncertain terms that *it*, whatever *it* is between you two, is over. Everyone knows you two weren't dating, yet she kept faithful to you."

"Did she? Was that what I saw?"

"She used me to piss you off. I always knew you didn't give a fuck about her."

He scowled, and his lips tightened.

"She can make up her own mind. I told her all along that I didn't want to be in a relationship."

"Then why did you keep fucking her? Was that really all she was to you?"

He looked beyond Derek at the evening traffic.

"That's a good fucking question. I don't know."

He hated himself, but was sure Derek wouldn't see that. Derek moved closer and pushed up his shirt sleeves.

"Yeah, you don't care about much, do you?"

"What's it to you?"

"Because I love her."

The blood drained from his face. If Derek wanted to hit him, he would let him. Both Derek and Autumn flirted in the past, but he must have mistaken those moments for them goofing off.

"Why didn't you make a move? I wouldn't have stood in your way."

Derek huffed. He glanced away briefly.

"I did. I tried hooking up with her a few times when you were in New York, but nothing came of it. She always talked about a future with you. Now, even though she's thrown it in your face and you walked away, she still believes that you'll come back to her. She wants you any way she can have you, and you're letting her look like a fool."

Nick sighed.

"I'm sorry Derek. If I would have known, I would have pushed her away."

"Why don't you push her away now? Or are you saving her for a good time when you have no other options?"

Nick turned his head slow from side to side.

"That's low."

Derek raised his chin and crossed his arms.

"Tell me it's not true."

He sighed.

"I'll talk to her."

"I hope that's all you'll do. You've played with her life long enough."

Derek stalked away without another word. He watched him enter the Brick Lane Tavern. It was anyone's guess what he would say to Blake. He took his phone out and wrote a text message to Autumn, then deleted it. There was still no reply from Elizabeth. He read Colette's text message again, then sent her a reply.

He wrote, "I would like to see you too. Let's get together tomorrow night."

He tapped Send. There was a voice message from his father. He played it.

"Nicholas, we need to talk. I've made plans for us to have lunch tomorrow, providing you'll be coming to work. Dale was looking for you. I told him I sent you on some errands. See you tomorrow."

He deleted his father's voice message, then he got a new text message alert. Colette replied to his text message with a smiley emoji. Her message brought a weary smile to his face. All he wanted now was to sleep.

At the Briarwood Country Club, Nick sat at a private corner table in their less formal dining room. White wicker chairs with tropical print cushions surrounded honey oak tables. Ceiling fans with blades shaped like palm leaves rotated at a lazy pace. It was early. Club members filled only a few tables for brunch. Light clinks of silverware and china, and muffled chatter echoed in the otherwise quiet dining room. He waited for his father to arrive. An untouched glass of ice tea sat in front of him beyond a plate topped with a triangular folded cloth napkin.

Outside the window, down the soft shouldered hill, three golfers stood on a practice putting green. He watched them putt to one of the seven holes. His father's voice carried across the dining room. Richard Evers usually spoke louder than necessary. Nick's lips curled into a smug smile, but his expression turned stoic when his father arrived at the table.

"Great, thanks, Cynthia. No—no, that's fine."

Richard Evers looked at his phone before he slipped it into the breast pocket of his suit jacket.

"Hello Nicholas. Sorry I'm late. I had to shuffle a few things around."

His father looked at him only after he sat down.

"That's fine. I got here a few minutes ago."

"Great, so you haven't ordered yet."

His father waved for the server. The server arrived with an ice tea, which he assumed his father ordered on his way to the table. They placed their lunch order and waited for the server to depart. He watched his father as he took a drink. Richard gave a thumbs-up to the server, who Nick assumed had been watching from across the room. He rolled his eyes, and wished they spiked his ice tea, as well.

"So, what did you want to talk about?"

Richard snorted. He sat straight in his chair and crossed his arms.

"I feel bad about how we left things. I don't want you to make poor decisions out of spite. Anyway, I had a lengthy discussion with your mother, and we both concluded that you need to have your own space, and I don't just mean metaphorically speaking. Since Hale owns an apartment complex near the airport for foreign or specialty contract employees, Crest Tower is the place. I can arrange for you to get an apartment there, at least until you find one for yourself."

Nick's eyebrows rose.

"So you're throwing me out?"

"Nicholas, you're twenty-six. It is time for you to ween yourself off of my tit, spread your wings, or grow a set of balls, whichever you prefer, and make your own way. You're already making your own decisions that will shape your life. Onward, I say."

Nick chuckled and shook his head.

"Unbelievable."

"What? You thought this time would never come."

He huffed and tilted his head as he glared at his father.

"Ok—Crest Tower—fine. When do you want me to move out?"

"I've cleared your afternoon and had the necessary arrangements made. We can enjoy our nice casual lunch, which is a luxury for the both of us, since we rarely get the chance, then you can head to the house and a moving crew will be waiting to load your things onto a truck and get you settled at Crest Tower this afternoon. Cynthia informed me that there are three vacant apartments. You can take your pick. I would have picked one for you, but that wouldn't allow you to choose, and since we're talking about making choices, I'll leave that to you."

"How magnanimous of you."

"Indeed."

The server brought out their lunch. His father took a bite of his grilled chicken sandwich and chewed with vigor. Nick waited for the server to leave. He watched his father eat.

"What about Elizabeth?"

His father finished chewing and washed things down with a sip of ice tea. After he cleared his throat, he met Nick's gaze.

"Well, Nicholas, that is entirely up to you. My hope would be that you wouldn't throw your life away."

His father looked as though he might carry on talking, but silenced himself. Nick relaxed back in his chair.

"I've been talking to Colette. Thanks for letting us use the lake house."

His father stabbed at his salad.

"Sure-sure, anytime. With Colette, of course. That girl is going places."

The change in his father's mood and tone caused a soft smile to bud on Nick's face.

"We're supposed to have dinner tonight."

His father stopped eating and looked at Nick. His eyes widened, and he nodded slowly. He dabbed his napkin at the corners of his mouth.

"That's splendid. You could show her your new apartment, maybe christen it even."

He nudged Nick's elbow. An uncertain smirk crept across Nick's face.

"Oh, I almost forgot. The apartments at Crest Tower are semi-furnished. The furniture is nice, but may not match your style. You'll have to figure that one out later. See Nicholas, choices."

"Thanks."

"You got it. Have you decided where you'll be taking Colette for dinner? I can set you up with a reservation at say, Il Fasto. She likes Italian, right? Hell, everyone loves Italian."

"That would be very nice of you."

"You got it, Nicholas. Unless, of course, you think I'm pushing in?"

He held up his hands as if Nick had a gun pointed at him.

"No, that's fine. I appreciate it."

"Good."

The mid-week dinner crowd at Il Fasto was fairly light. Nick's father had secured one of the two private chef's tables. From their table, they could see out into the main dining room and watch the other patrons. They could also gaze into the kitchen and observe the elegant food being prepared by the energetic kitchen staff. While Colette peered into the kitchen, Nick looked over towards the large bank of windows. It was dark outside, and the streetlights had come on. An older couple sat at the table where he first had lunch with Elizabeth. The older man and woman laughed, ate, and appeared content with one another. It made him smile.

"Happy thoughts?"

She jolted him from his reverie. He turned to find Colette with a smile and bright eyes.

"Yeah, sorry. What a crazy day."

"So you're moving from your parents' house?"

"Moved."

"Already?"

He nodded.

"That's crazy."

She took a sip of wine and peered at him over the top of her wineglass.

"My father doesn't waste time. When he has his mind set on something, he wants it done right away."

Her eyes widened.

"I guess."

She held her glass of wine close as if she had prepared to take another drink. Her eyes remained wide with astonishment.

"You guessed right."

He raised an eyebrow and smirked at her. They both chuckled. He raised his glass of wine.

"Anyway, it's done. So let's toast to our evening out, compliments of my father."

They touched their glasses together. He winked at her.

"I hope you're super hungry."

She grinned at him. Aromas of well seasoned grilled or braised meats and melted cheese wafted from the kitchen. One of the kitchen staff brought their entrées to the table. The head chef in a white culinary uniform with sleeves that ended at his upper forearms addressed them as Ms. Scott and Mr. Evers. They looked at one another with wide eyes. He tried to imagine who gave the restaurant her last name, as Victor, the restaurant's owner, and most of his staff, knew Nick. It was personal. He wanted to believe that Cynthia, his father's personal assistant, added that touch, but even if she did, it would have been under the direction of his father. He sighed, but as he watched her excitement, the weight of the day fell from his shoulders.

After the server filled their wineglasses, they ate like giddy teenagers. Halfway through their meal, he chuckled at her.

"What?"

"I was thinking about what you said."

"What did I say?"

"We're you joking about us getting married?"

She sat silent, but had a tight lip smile. He worried she might spit her food out in a fit of laughter, which would be terrible to do in front of the chef and kitchen staff. His eyebrows rose and his lips tightened. He wanted and hoped for a serious answer. She finished chewing, took a drink of wine, then tilted her head as if she were contemplating his question.

"Well—"

She gazed at him. Her lips curled into a soft smile. He tried not to smile for fear the conversation would turn into a joke.

"I was implying that since we know one another well and we get along, that a future with you would be most likely—wonderful. Our parents see something there as well. I know you hate to give them credit. Also, we've determined that we are sexually compatible, so there's that as well. Does that scare you?"

He ran his fingers through his hair.

"No-no. I was curious, that's all."

"Curious? How so?"

"I wanted to know how serious your suggestion was."

"Are you telling me you are considering it?"

He smiled and gazed out into the dining room, to the table where the old couple sat, where he and Elizabeth had lunch. The couple had left and the table now sat empty. He returned his gaze to her.

"Possibly."

"Hm? Possibly?"

He chuckled. She took a sip of wine, then crossed her arms.

"Explain."

"I thought you explained it well."

"That was *me* being pragmatic. I've never known *you* to be pragmatic."

"Colette, please give me some credit."

She waved her hand.

"Done. Credit granted. Please explain yourself."

He chuckled.

"I like how you wave your hand like some genie. It's adorable."

She crossed her arms. He held up his hands in surrender.

"Okay, okay."

His smile faded. He gazed into her pale blue eyes. She wrapped one of her honey blonde curls around her finger as she waited for his answer.

"In all seriousness, I agree. We would make a good couple."

"Then it's settled. I will await your proposal. No pressure, think it through."

He smiled at her.

"I have and I will."

She beamed, then she wrinkled her face.

"I don't think genies wave their hands. Don't they nod their heads?"

She nodded her head twice, quickly. He laughed and fell back in his seat.

After they finished their entrées, they ordered tiramisu and mascarpone cheesecake and some appetizers to take with them. As they waited for the food to be prepared, he went to the men's room. He had several new text messages. Tonight was going well with Colette. He fought the urge to look at any of them, except for one. There was a new message from Elizabeth.

She wrote, "Hi Nick. I'm out with your father to clear the air. No worries. Can I see you later tonight?"

His eyebrows drew together, and he cocked his head. He hoped she knew what she was doing. A heavy breath passed his lips, and he glanced at his reflection.

"Tough day? Oh, yeah? Me too. What the fuck are you going to do now? I don't know. You?"

He muttered to himself, rubbed his forehead, and considered pleading insanity. He pocketed his phone and headed back out to Colette. She smiled at him when he returned, and he smiled back, but he could tell she saw something in his eyes.

"What's wrong?"

"Family drama. I'm sorry, I have to run to my parents'. Nothing too urgent. Can we get together tomorrow?"

"Yeah, sure."

Her eyebrows drew together.

"I hope everything is okay."

"Oh, yeah. It's fine."

She shrugged, and her lips curled into a subtle smile.

"I'm excited to see your new place tomorrow. Thank you for a wonderful evening."

"It *was* wonderful, wasn't it?"

"Yes."

One of the kitchen staff members came to their table with the boxed desserts and appetizers and thanked the young couple for allowing them to be of service. He drove her home. Their boxed desserts and appetizers sat on the backseat.

19

Across town at the French restaurant, Coquelicot Rouge, Elizabeth Bach and Richard Evers followed the hostess to their dining table.

"Please do not think too much of my agreeing to have dinner with you. I know we need to talk, but that's *all* we're going to do."

"My Dear, that is all we ever do."

"Richard, I mean it."

"Of course. Did I mention you look lovely this evening?"

When they arrived at their table, he stepped in front of the hostess and insisted on pulling out her chair to seat her. She gave him a stern gaze. The hostess's eyes widened and darted to her, then to Richard.

"Enjoy your evening."

The hostess smiled, then strode her way back to the front of the restaurant. They both ordered wine, which came promptly. She had a grateful smile when the server placed the glass of wine in front of her. The cabernet cavalry had arrived. She took a healthy drink.

"It surprised me to see Nick at your place. How did all that come about?"

Richard held up his hand as if to suggest that she wait a moment. He then tilted his head, as if he were pondering something.

"Actually, *when* did all that come about? Let's start there."

She held her glass of wine and stared at him with a smirk. He waited. She made him wait longer. She turned the stem of her wineglass with her fingertips.

"Nick was interested the first time we met at his graduation party. You remember, don't you? I still don't know *why* you invited me. A lapse in judgement, perhaps? Anyway, kismet has *her* own way of sorting things out. I get boy crushes from younger men all the time, but I never imagined I would have a crush on a younger man. Nick is quite special."

He took a drink of wine, then peered into his glass.

"This glass has a spot on it."

Richard waved to the server, who brought him another glass and filled it at the table. She watched him with a coy smile on her face. One word came to mind—buffoon. After he took a couple of sips and the glass was to his satisfaction, he brought his attention back to her, like an old man who finally found his spectacles.

"Yes, Nick is quite something. Of course, it is neither here nor there. I can't have you dating my son."

She crossed her arms and straightened up in her chair.

"Richard, it isn't up to you. Nick is capable of making his own decisions, and he needs the chance to make them."

"You sound like his mother, and you're—"

It never escaped her that, before formally meeting Josephine, Richard always avoided saying his wife's name. Nick's graduation party was the first time she met Josephine. The way the woman acted, she was sure she suspected Richard of having an affair, and her cool demeanor toward her was a sign she suspected her as the *other* woman. Elizabeth's lips tightened, and she tilted her head.

"Don't you dare say I could be his mother."

His face reddened. He took his glass and drank. His eyes wandered around the restaurant.

"No, of course, I wouldn't say that, but you are considerably older than he is."

She stared right through him. He shrugged, cocked his head, and raised his eyebrows.

Before either could speak, their server arrived. Both donned a polite smile and listened to the server recite the evening's specials. They placed their orders. He ordered the lamb, while she ignored his protests to indulge herself, and instead, she ordered a simple salad. After the server left, she excused herself to use the ladies' room.

She stood at the marble vanity and scanned the messages on her phone. She read Nick's last text message, then replied.

She wrote, "Hi Nick. I'm out with your father to clear the air. No worries. Can I see you later tonight?"

After she sent the message, she checked her makeup in the mirror. She thought about hanging out in the bathroom long enough for the kitchen to prepare Richard's lamb. Later, she could then pop out, have her salad boxed, or eat it in his company if she must, but then make a quick get-away. She groaned as she fussed with her hair, then she fluttered her eyelids and rolled her eyes. A trio of women entered the bathroom. They smiled into the mirror at her reflection and her reflection smiled back.

She returned to the table. The server had poured him another glass of wine. She took her seat across from him. He held his glass in front of him as if he wanted to make a toast.

"I would like to toast Nicholas."

Elizabeth raised her eyebrows, and her lips tightened, but she took her wineglass and held it up.

"To Nick."

Her voice was hollow. He smiled at her.

"To Nicholas and Colette. They are having dinner tonight, and I'm sure he will show her his new apartment afterwards. It could be a very romantic evening."

She lowered her glass and struggled not to throw her wine in his face.

"What game are you playing?"

He took a drink of wine, then sat his glass on the white linen-covered table.

"I had lunch with Nick. We talked. He told me he was going to have dinner tonight with Colette. Also, he has moved out of the Evers homestead and spread his wings to soar to more exciting climes. I'm excited for him. Aren't you?"

Her eyes burned. She imagined if there was a moment for her to see red, this was it. Richard, with his stupid grin. This dinner date was over. She reached for her handbag.

"Well, hello Richard. Oh? Hello to you too. It's Elizabeth, right?" Abigale said.

Abigale and her husband, Henry Rutherford, stood alongside their table.

"Ah? Abigale, what a wonderful surprise."

Richard stood to kiss Abigale's cheek. He then shook Henry's hand.

"Henry, great to see you."

"Richard, the pleasure's mine."

Henry was a short stocky man with broad hands. He shook Richard's hand with vigor. Abigale patted Richard's chest.

"Josephine always tells me you're too busy to join us for dinner. It seems she's quite right. You are indeed a *very* busy man."

Abigale grinned and winked at Elizabeth. Richard's face turned red. A gentleman at another table called out Henry's name. Henry turned and recognized the man, then waved.

"Richard, that's a good friend of mine. Can you spare a minute to come over to say hello?"

He smiled and stood.

"Um? Certainly."

He looked at Elizabeth, who glared at him, then at Abigale, who shooed both men away. Abigale took Richard's seat.

"Okay, honey, dish. Did you first tuck in young Nicholas and now you're working on seducing his old man?"

Abigale took a sip from Richard's wine glass. Elizabeth cocked her head and wrinkled her lips. Abigale held Richard's wine glass as if she had claimed it, then her eyebrow rose and her lips curled into a devious smile.

"I have to say this is getting interesting. Have you worked out how you'll get both father and son to fuck you at the same time? Oh, how exciting? Which one will go where? Will you suck off one while the other takes you from behind, or will you take both cocks—one in the ass and one in the cunt? I vote for one in the ass and one in the cunt. Depending on the size, it can be scary at first, like you're going to be torn apart, but then… Well, it's a bit like skydiving. You scream all the way down—but when you land—you want to go right back up again."

She laughed, and glanced at the plate of food in front of her, then turned her nose up at Richard's lamb and buttered some bread instead. Elizabeth snatched up her handbag, stood, and strutted out of the Coquelicot Rouge.

Nick parked in the guest lot across the street from Elizabeth's condo. He glanced at the message he sent to let her know he could see her tonight. She had yet to reply.

The boxed appetizers from Il Fasto permeated the cabin of his car. Colette refused to take them. She wanted him to take them to his new place, so they would have something to eat tomorrow. She said she would bring over some sandwiches or a pizza to go with the meatballs and the tiramisu and mascarpone cheesecake.

He started a new text message, then wondered if he should call her instead, but feared the call would go to her voicemail. His lids closed, and he rested his eyes. The aroma of the boxed meatballs in the back seat made it too difficult to think. Trees blocked his view of her condo, so he got out of the car and walked to her place.

The condo windows were dark when he crossed the street and walked to the front door. The street and sidewalk were quiet. He climbed the porch steps. There was a dim light inside, probably from the kitchen counter accent lights. He checked his phone again. Nothing from her. Worst case, she was in there with his father. His body became rigid. He pressed the button for the doorbell.

After a couple of unanswered rings, he turned around, huffed, and then headed back to his car. He switched spots after a few cars left so he could see through the narrow walkway gap between the bushes. He could now see her garage door, but not the front door. The wait weighed on him, and he reclined his seat back and closed his eyes. He could still smell the meatballs and flatbread, but the aroma had faded since the food had grown cold. As he waited and peered through the gap in the bushes, his eyes became heavier and he drifted off to sleep.

He woke to the sound of car doors being shut. Two women stood, chatted and laughed. They parked several spaces from him. Both women wore cocktail dresses and heels and carried small clutch handbags. They looked like they had just come from an evening out. He snorted and glanced at his watch. It was minutes to midnight. He had been asleep for almost an hour. Fuck. He rubbed his face, then ran his fingers through his hair and rubbed the back of his neck. He watched the two women stroll up the walkway toward the condos.

Car lights came around from the direction of the entrance to the development. He blinked his tired eyes. As the car rounded the curve and came closer, the car's shape and the silhouette of its driver looked familiar. He was certain it was Elizabeth. Her garage door opened, and the car slowed. He hurried from his car. She pulled her car into the bay and the garage door closed when he reached the edge of the parking lot. He sauntered up the walkway to the street. Grogginess had yet to release its hold on him. He yawned as he crossed the street, then walked up the sidewalk to her front door.

There he stood again, at her front door, but this time he knew she was home. No additional lights were on besides the accent lights he saw earlier. He almost pushed the doorbell button, but decided to first check his text messages. Nothing. Curious, he sent her another text message.

He wrote, "I'm on my way over. See you soon."

He chewed his lower lip, then tilted his head from side to side to loosen the knot in his neck. Too many questions raced through his thoughts. He pushed the button to the doorbell. A car drove by on the street behind him. Its lights caught him on her porch like some burglar. His whole body stiffened. After the car passed, he looked around. The street and the sidewalk in front of the condos fell silent again.

Shadows moved on the walls inside her place. A light came on in the living room, then he saw her shape come to the door. He blinked when the porch light came on. She appeared at the side window, then the door opened and she stood there in a black silk robe that fell mid thigh. Her legs were bare, and she wore no slippers. He glanced at her painted toenails.

"Hi Lizzy. Did you get my messages?"

"Nick?"

She stood in the doorway. He waited for her to invite him in.

"Is everything okay? You didn't reply to any of my messages. I was afraid to call, since you told me you were out with my father. Where were you? What did you do? What was there to talk about?"

She crossed her arms and held her robe closed.

"We met for dinner to discuss my relationship with you. No surprise, your father is vehemently opposed. He told me about you and Colette, and how you two are building something special. He doesn't want me to ruin things for you."

The knot in his neck returned.

"What? That's none of his fucking business."

"Perhaps not, but were you out with Colette?"

He huffed.

"Yes. I explained the situation to you. I'm trying to play along, to calm things down, to—"

"And what about Abigale? Are you playing along with her as well?"

"Huh?"

"The book of matches from the Brazilian steakhouse you had in your pocket fell on the floor in my bedroom. There was a number written inside, but no name, so out of curiosity, I called the number. I got Abigale's voicemail."

He felt a prickly heat rise and settle on his face.

"Wait, she put that in my pocket."

"Oh, I bet she did."

"I was going to throw it away."

"But you didn't. Maybe she or your friend Autumn can be your fuck buddy when you don't have any other place to stick your prick."

"Lizzy."

"Elizabeth."

His shoulders slumped. She glared at him.

"I was afraid this was going to happen. Getting involved with you was a huge mistake. I worried you were too immature, or couldn't stand the heat if things got serious. I don't think you realized how much of an uphill battle it was going to be for us, especially where your father is concerned. He has a lot to protect, and he will do everything he can to protect it."

He stood with his hands out to his sides.

"But—I care about you."

"That maybe true, but I never felt sure of your commitment. I really liked you, but until you're done whoring yourself out, maybe you shouldn't be in a serious relationship."

"Elizabeth, that's not fair."

"Goodbye, Nick."

He held up his hands.

"Elizabeth, wait."

She closed the door, then turned off the light in the living room. He watched her fade into the shadows of her condo. He clenched and raised his fist to pound on the door, but the hour was late and she had made up her mind. His hand dropped to his side. As he stumbled back to his car, his heart felt heavy.

It was after midnight when he got in. Nick stood at the kitchen island in his Crest Tower apartment. He microwaved the leftovers from his dinner with Colette and drank a Spanish beer he picked up on his way back to his new place.

Scattered around the living room and the bedroom were boxes of his belongings. He put his casual clothes in the dresser that came with the apartment and hung shirts and business attire in the closet. The new place was void of any smell of smoke, which was one thing that made him happy. One of the other vacant apartments, the most desirable one, one on a higher floor, had a better view, but smelled of smoke and ash. The building manager told him they could clean it after he moved in, but the move left him with no energy or patience. The last vacant apartment faced the expressway. His new place at least had a view of a small park with winding paths that gave him something pleasant to look at, and a place to go for a run when he needed to get out.

He opened a bottle of San Miguel 1516, a pale lager he grew fond of during his trip to Spain. He then sauntered out onto the balcony, leaned against the railing, took in the night air and the view, and sipped the beer. Lights lit the walkway in the park behind Crest Tower. He watched a lone jogger. After Elizabeth pushed him away, he wanted to run—run away from everyone. A couple walked their dog on the sidewalk that bordered the park. They stopped to hug and kiss. The dog sat on the sidewalk and waited. He finished his beer in two long swigs, then went back inside.

When he returned to the kitchen, his phone screen sat lit. There were new text messages. He never read the ones he got earlier, other than the one from Elizabeth.

Colette wrote, "Can't wait to see your place tomorrow. Sweet dreams xo."

Her message made him smile.

He replied, "Thanks, sweet dreams xo."

When he saw who the next message was from, he wrinkled his lips.

Derek wrote, "When are you going to talk to Autumn? How long are you going to drag this out?"

He was about to reply, then deleted Derek's message. There were several messages from Blake.

Blake's latest message, "Been trying to reach you. You can delete my voice message. It's the same as this text. I'm guessing you can't answer your phone. Apparently, Isabella is pregnant, and she wants to have the baby."

Blake's next message, "No one can find the other guy Isabella was with. Maybe you should do a paternity test. Then you'll know either way."

Blake's earliest message, "Derek hates you. He says you ruined Autumn's life. I don't want to be in the middle. Talk to them, please."

He huffed and shook his head, then closed his eyes and pinched the bridge of his nose.

"Fuck."

He replied to Blake, "Thanks. I'll catchup with you later."

He had to contact Autumn at some point. Tonight, though, was not a good night. Elizabeth's rejection would put him right in bed with her. He went to the bedroom, undressed, got a quick shower, then put on some pajama bottoms and fell into bed. As long as the day had been, sleep eluded him. Soft yellow light came through the bedroom window from the street below. The ceiling fixture cast a long shadow, like a charcoal smudge on the ceiling, made by a giant's thumb. He missed the ceiling fan in his bedroom at his parents' house. When he watched it rotate, he could think.

Lizzy. Elizabeth. He felt he no longer knew her, and wished he could stop thinking about her. He rubbed his face and tugged at his hair. The ache in his chest returned.

Isabella. He tried to forget her after she threw him out. If she were carrying his child, he would have to talk to her, and they would have to figure out things.

Colette. He snorted, and his lips curled into a subtle smile. She surprised him. She seemed understanding when he told her about Isabella. It had to be more than her feeling compassion for his situation. She slept with him afterwards. He expected Autumn could live with it, but Colette, no.

Then there was Autumn. He rubbed his eyes. He felt his body desperate to surrender to sleep, but restless thoughts churned in his mind. Autumn-Autumn-Autumn. He sighed. Things went on too long. She wanted it. He let it happen. At first he felt led by her, and he was fine with that. Now he realized he could never give her what she wanted. The rest of his friends saw it.

He felt around and found his phone that lay on the bed next to him. He knew what he needed to do, but apprehension kept him from sending a text message to her. She would ask where he was, then she would be at his door, then in his bed, even at this hour. He had to do something. Tomorrow he would contact her, but not before he spent his day with Colette. Things were going well with Colette. He wondered if he could love her. In all his father's fucked up wisdom, maybe his father was right. He needed to find out, and he knew any conversations with Autumn would sour his day with Colette.

20

Nick watched Colette from across the stacks of decorative baskets and floor furnishings. The store smelled of spices from the incense the employees burned at the checkout counter. Colette stared, engrossed in the various wall art, from photographs to painted and printed canvases. Whenever she glanced his way, she would smile. He smiled as she contemplated a picture. She slipped her curly honey blonde hair behind her ear. It was almost as if she had done it, so he could see her face. A woman wearing a blue apron that covered her blouse and fell over the front of her jeans asked him if he needed any help. She stayed close by and grinned when he caught her watching him.

He stalked Colette up and down the short aisles. She picked up things here and there and he was curious what she selected to adorn his new apartment. He avoided crowding her and wanted all the decisions to be made solely by her. He made it a game. She looked his way and curled a finger to suggest he come hither. He held his hands behind him and raised his chin, then sauntered up to her.

"Yes, Dear?"

He talked through his teeth like some British aristocrat. She laughed.

"What do you think about what I've selected so far?"

She showed him the three pictures she selected: two black and white photographs, and an abstract painting that looked like fruit. He raised his eyebrows and nodded.

"Very nice. For the living room?"

"Yes. Something to get you started."

He inspected the two framed photographs. One was of the New York City skyline rising out of the fog. He thought about the Flatiron Building and the picture Isabella had on the wall in her apartment. The second photograph was more vivid and with lots of contrast. It was a picture of some palm trees. The sky behind the trees was intense enough that the trees looked like silhouettes. Very California. He raised an eyebrow. She scanned the pictures the store had mounted on the wall.

"I'm still not sure what would look good in your bedroom. I think you could also use a vase or two, maybe one for the dining area and one for the living room."

"Hm. Sure."

He looked at the framed photographs. There was a photograph of the Machu Picchu ruins, like the one in Elizabeth's condo.

"How about this one?"

She tilted her head as if she were imaging how the picture would look on his bedroom wall. She shrugged and smiled at him.

"Hm. Yeah, it's nice."

"What?"

"I don't know, Nick. It kind of reminds me of a cemetery."

"Really?"

"Never mind. I'm sorry. It's beautiful. Let's get it."

He cocked his head and wrinkled his lips. But she already told the shop girl that they wanted the picture added to their purchases. He glanced at the picture one more time. Maybe it was a kind of cemetery. She picked out a few more items and when they were ready to check out; she held her hand out with a smirk on her face.

"Card please."

He handed her his credit card, then he signed the printed store copy of the receipt. After they loaded his new home furnishings into her parents' Range Rover, he backed her against the SUV, and pinned her there. She gazed up at him and bit her lower lip. The breeze caught a few of her honey blonde curls, and they fell across her face. She brushed them away without breaking eye contact with him. He stroked the backs of her arms. She touched the sides of his face, and her lips parted as she ran her thumb over his lips. They kissed. Soft, wet, and deep. Her breath was delicate and anxious. He wrapped his arms around her and lifted her onto her toes. He pulled back from her so he could look into her eyes. Her pale blue eyes, the color of the sky. The color of hope and possibilities.

"C'mon, let's do something fun."

She raised her eyebrows.

"Ah? I think I would rather do this."

He laughed, and she smiled.

"C'mon, it'll be fun."

"Ok?"

He took her hand, and they went back inside the mall. They strolled and shared smiling glances at one another. Twice she tilted her head and wrinkled her face at him, not in anger or frustration, but curiosity. Other shoppers flowed around them like waves, as if they were a ship at sea on a determined course. They stopped in front of Cartier. The jewelry store had a handsome marble exterior. They still had their fingers entwined. She tugged at him.

"Nick?"

"Let's look at rings. I would like to know what you like."

She drew her chin in and raised her eyebrows.

"Rings? As *in* engagement rings?"

"Yeah. What do you think?"

"Ah? Are you trying to ask me something?"

"Yes Colette, I'm trying to find out what types of rings you like. Is that okay?"

"Okay? Yes, that's okay. And—is that it?"

She gazed hard into his eyes.

"Yeah."

He chuckled. While he still held her hand, he gently swung their arms.

"Don't stress. This is supposed to be fun. C'mon."

He grinned and tugged at her. She shifted in her stance as if struck with tremendous shyness. He pulled her into his arms and smiled at her.

"Do you want to leave?"

She shook her head, no.

"Are you going to be okay?"

Like a little girl, she nodded, and her lips curved into a faint shy smile. They held hands and went inside.

Elizabeth struggled to get her thoughts together. She made a few calls earlier in the morning, but lacked attention for much else. She had Jenna cancel all of her off-site meetings for today and instructed her to reschedule the meetings wherever they fit best on her calendar. With her office chair reclined and her arms crossed, she glared out the window. Richard, that self-centered, egotistical asshole. Abigale, that bimbo with her fake tits. She huffed. Nick said he loved her. She pretended not to hear him. Why? His declaration was more than a crush and more than some juvenile craving. She was numb. Colette? She only knew what he told her about the girl. A young woman, a college girl, going to school in California. She knew Dale, but she never met his daughter. Dale was a good guy. If that was any indication of the type of girl Colette was, Colette would probably be good for Nick. Elizabeth sighed. She pondered an equally important question. Did she really love Nick? She peered out the window with a tense gaze at the nearby buildings and the streets below. Her eyebrows rose, and the tension eased in her face. She was sure of her feelings, which scared her, and that's why it hurt to hear Richard talk about Nick. She was unsure what to do, and if she should do anything at all. The last thing she wanted to do was ruin his life.

Jenna poked her head into Elizabeth's office.

"Elizabeth. I'm going to lunch now. Did you need anything?"

She swiveled her chair to face Jenna, then she straightened up in her seat.

"How about I take us to lunch?"

Jenna's eyes widened.

"Ah? Okay."

"Great, do you like Italian?"

Jenna grinned.

"Sure, everyone loves Italian."

Elizabeth chuckled.

"Great, how about we go to Il Fasto?"

"Whoa. Are you firing me?"

"C'mon, don't be so melodramatic."

"When am I ever melodramatic?"

"Never. Never mind. Let's go."

Elizabeth and Jenna sat at a window table at Il Fasto. It was the same table where she and Nick first had lunch together. She sat where he had sat on that day. She smiled as she watched Jenna, who looked around the restaurant and took in its elegance. Her lips parted and her eyes were wide with excitement. She failed to convince Jenna to join her for a glass of wine, so instead two ice teas with lemon wedges sat on the table in front of them.

"This place is so nice. It's like we're having a holiday lunch. I definitely have to tell Kevin about it. Maybe he'll take me here for my birthday."

Jenna ran her fingertips over the white linen tablecloth at the edge of the table. Elizabeth squinted and her lips curled into a tight-lipped smile.

"You two would have a wonderful time, and how could he say no to taking you here for your birthday? He could also bring you here for Valentine's Day, but get a reservation well in advance."

After she spoke, she felt a twinge of embarrassment for giving Jenna advice about reservations. Jenna had made plenty of them for her, for professional and private occasions.

"Great idea."

Jenna beamed and sipped at her ice tea. Both women looked out at the sun splashed sidewalk and the lazy traffic that passed by. When Elizabeth met Nick for lunch, he had stared out the same window. She knew now that he watched for her to come up the sidewalk. She remembered how handsome he looked in his well fitted dark gray suit, and that sexy slender teal tie. His breathless Christmas-day smile, and bright green eyes with endless depths of desire. Desire for her. When they sat together, she waited for him to be all charm, smug and cocky, but that never happened. He was thoughtful, sincere, and although subtle, made his interest in her known. They both had moved well beyond that day. They found moments of bliss, which felt like dreams, but then they awoke to harsh realities. He tried to get close to her. She blamed herself and her ambivalence. Her eyebrows drew together.

"Are you okay?"

She fluttered her eyelids, shaken from her reverie, then threw on a smile.

"Sorry, yes. I'm fine."

The server arrived at their table to take their order. After the server left, Jenna was about to speak, but Elizabeth cut her off.

"Tell me about Kevin. How are you two getting along?"

She touched her chin and gave Jenna her best bright-eyed, inquisitive look.

"Oh, Kevin. We're doing well. We're still saving to get a house together. At least that's the plan. I tried to convince him to share an apartment with me so we can save, but he still likes his space. He says he doesn't want to be far from work."

She shrugged and drank her ice tea. Elizabeth raised her eyebrows, then she picked up her glass of ice tea and glanced at her as she drank. They both sat their glasses down at the same time.

"Couldn't you both find a new apartment instead of deciding whose place to live at?"

"That's what I said. I even told Kevin I didn't mind commuting if it was going to be such a big deal. What else can I do?"

She tilted her head and stared at Elizabeth.

"I thought you said that you two were doing well."

Jenna straightened up in her seat, and her eyes brightened.

"We are, really. I'm just making too big of a deal out of it. He's good to me. He's going to be my happy-ever-after. I just know it."

The corners of Elizabeth's lips turned down, and she raised her eyebrows.

"Oh? How do you know?"

"He loves me."

Elizabeth tilted her head, pinched at her earlobe to separate her curls from her earring, then glanced outside the window. She wished she had walked up the other sidewalk so Nick could see her the day they first had lunch together. If she had, she wondered if he would have smiled at her. She believed so.

Colette beamed each time she tried on the next engagement ring that caught her eye. It was like watching a child see Santa Claus, over and over. The array of rings, bracelets, necklaces inside the glass cases made Nick dizzy.

"Have you two set the date?" The saleswoman asked.

Colette's eyes fixed on the ring that was on her finger. Nick had yet to pop the question. He tilted his head and sighed.

"Oh, I don't know. I'm not sure she even likes me."

"Honey, you can get me *that* ring, and I'll like you."

The saleswoman's eyes widened, and she laughed. He chuckled. They both looked at Colette, who was in her own little world.

"They're all so beautiful."

"Thank you, dear."

The saleswoman smiled at her with moon shaped eyes. Nick glanced at the rainbow colored stretchy bracelet on the saleswoman's freckled wrist. Attached to it was the key to the display cases. He looked at Colette.

"Well, which one do you like?"

She held up her hand at an angle, so the ring caught the light. Her eyes brightened.

"I think—this one."

Her words came out as if she were in a trance. Nick and the saleswoman lifted their chins as if in awe of the ring on her finger. He took her hand and held it flat over his as he inspected the ring.

"Very nice. It definitely suits your style. Is it heavy?"

"No."

She shook her head no, then slipped the ring from her finger to let him feel its weight. He held the ring in his palm, then pinched it between his fingertips and brought it up to his eyes to inspect the diamonds.

"It is beautiful."

She gazed at him. He was certain that she held her breath. He gazed into her eyes, then he lowered himself to one knee. Her eyes widened, and she gasped.

"Colette Angela Scott, will you marry me?"

Everyone in the store seemed to stop what they were doing and turned their attention to Nick and Colette. The saleswoman who showed the rings to Colette held her clenched hands to her chest. Her mouth hung speechless, as she, along with everyone, and most of all Nick, waited for Colette's response.

She nodded and smiled before she could speak.

"Yes."

He slipped the ring back onto her finger. He stood, and they kissed and embraced. Everyone in the store clapped and cheered. Shoppers who walked outside Cartier gazed in with looks of confusion. After everyone settled down, the saleswoman looked at Nick. She smiled, but she had an anxious look in her eyes.

"We'll take it."

The saleswoman exhaled and held her chest.

"Wonderful."

Colette trembled. Her hands covered her mouth as she stood next to him. He put his arm around her waist to steady her. The ring size matched hers, so she could have it that day. She refused to have the saleswoman clean it.

"No, it's perfect. I don't want to take it off."

Other customers congratulated them as they left the store. She drove on a cloud to his new apartment so they could setup the new furnishings and celebrate their engagement. Every time they stopped at a traffic light, she glanced at the ring. It glittered in the sunlight. The only thing brighter was her smile. He smiled inside and out when she glanced over at him. Her life had taken a giant leap forward. He hoped his had, too.

21

Nick's phone sat on the kitchen island next to a pizza box with a half-eaten pizza. It was his and Colette's celebratory lunch. She left after she helped decorate his new apartment and a bout of blissful sex. He was relieved to be alone. She made it difficult for him to think.

On his phone, Autumn's contact profile stared up at him. It might as well have been sharp shards of glass or a snake, something that needed to be handled with care. Autumn was just like his father. They both fought to get their way, even if it cost them personally. She had sacrificed her dignity for being with him for as long as she had. It was difficult to tell what she had gained. Attention, affection, sex, definitely lots of sex, but no commitment from him to be her boyfriend. He watched Blake date and break up with plenty of girls. Yet, he avoided committing to a single, exclusive relationship. Sure, there were girls, but they came and went until he met Autumn. He blamed his father for his unrelenting criticism. He knew his father had held his nose when Autumn was around. His father never told him how he felt about Autumn, but he could see it on his face.

He tapped the phone icon. A dull droning ring came through the phone's speaker. It rang for a long time. He wondered if she was there, or merely contemplating whether she should answer. He expected her voicemail message to play at any moment.

"Hello."

Her voice sounded low and childlike.

"Autumn?"

"Hi, Nick."

"Did I get you at a bad time? Were you sleeping?"

There was a pause. A faint yawn came through the speaker.

"No-no. It's fine. I'm up."

"I'm sorry I haven't called sooner, but I needed some space. I hope you understand."

"I'm sorry too. Derek and I—that was me losing my mind. I'm not with Derek, if you're wondering."

"You know, Derek loves you. He confronted me and was prepared to get into a fistfight over you."

There was a pause again. He could hear her breathing. It was slow. Maybe she had been crying.

"He said it before that he loves me. When you were away in New York. Derek wanted me to be his girlfriend. I told him no. He's just a friend. I don't feel that way about him."

He ran his fingers through his hair and squeezed the back of his neck.

"Nick?"

"Yeah, I'm here."

"Okay, good."

"Listen, Autumn. We had some great times, but—"

Soft sobs came over the phone.

"I was a total jerk. I should have never let things go this far. It was totally unfair to you. We need to stop seeing each other. We can't—I can't go on playing around with you. You deserve better."

"Nick. Don't."

There was a tender pain in her words.

"I'm sorry, Autumn."

"Nick?"

"Goodbye, Autumn."

He tapped the screen to end the call. He braced his hands on the countertop of the kitchen island and lowered his head. Tears tickled his cheeks and ran down to his chin. There was no way he was going to tell her he got engaged today. That would have to come later. He hoped to tell her soon. The longer he waited, the better the chance she would hear it going around and not from him. He turned off the lights in the kitchen and living room, then lumbered to the bedroom. As he lie in bed with his arm tucked behind his head, his gaze fell on the framed photograph of the Machu Picchu ruins Colette hung for him. He snorted and turned his head slowly from side to side. His eyes moved around the picture. He wanted to touch the stone walls, to know what they felt like, and to know that they were real.

Colette and Nick agreed to keep their engagement a secret until they had a chance to first tell their parents. He was sure Dale would give his blessing, but he wanted to ask formally as a matter of tradition and courtesy. She wanted him to have the opportunity and told him she would wait until he was ready. Afterwards, they both planned on telling their parents in person, her parents first, then his.

He took the rest of the week off from work. He was sure his father sensed something. His father was all too agreeable about him being away from the office. With all his new free time, Colette wanted to spend the day with him, but he told her he needed to take care of some things, and he wanted to see Blake. She agreed, which surprised him. If she were Autumn, she would have insisted on tagging along.

As he came up the sidewalk, he saw Blake sitting near the window inside Starbucks. When he got inside, they shook hands, and Blake patted his shoulder.

"So nice to see you. Thanks for all your help with Isabella. I've been thinking a lot about your suggestion to get the paternity test. Regardless if the other guy ever turns up, at least I'll know for myself if the child is mine."

"I think it's the right thing to do. Marissa and Juan Miguel have been an immense help. They've suggested that we all get on a call, or at least you, Juan Miguel, and Isabella, to hash things out. Juan Miguel can interpret for you. I think you want absolute clarity on all the details. I wouldn't talk to Isabella without him."

He glanced down at the table and nodded as he listened to Blake.

"I think you're right."

"Damn, right! What are you having? I'll get it while you sit and think."

"Just a grande Americano, thanks."

He gazed out the window while Blake headed to the counter. He needed closure with Elizabeth, whatever that meant. Whatever his father said to her did the trick. She was out of his life. "No worries," she had said. He shook his head. She should have never had dinner with his father. It frightened him how much he still wanted her. None of the sticky points mattered. He would have her any way he could. He supposed that was how Autumn felt about him, and yet he denied her.

He raked his fingers through his hair and gave Blake a weary smile when he returned with their drinks. Madrid was six hours ahead of Atlanta time. Marissa and Juan Miguel would be available after work, so Blake and Nick would call around noon. Nick and Blake planned to get lunch afterwards, some place where Nick could get a drink. He was sure he was going to need one.

After they had hung out for a while and chatted, the inevitable had arrived. He gazed at his empty paper cup on the tabletop and turned it with his fingertips.

"Ready?" Blake asked.

He nodded. Before they left Starbucks, Blake text messaged both Juan Miguel and Marissa to make sure they were available. Marissa would contact Isabella. When Marissa and Juan Miguel got back to Blake, they knew they were all set. Nick and Blake went to Blake's car to have a quiet place for the call. Blake called Juan Miguel first. Marissa had gone over to Juan Miguel's, so they only needed to call Isabella.

Blake leaned toward Nick with his elbow on the center armrest. He set the call to his speaker so they both could hear. Nick had to endure the moment of playfulness between Marissa and Blake before they would call Isabella. Everything had happened fast. He was engaged! He should be beyond joyful. As he listened to Blake and Marissa carry on, he wondered if those two would get married. Nick never thought to ask what was on Blake's mind, and here his friend was taking care of *his* problems. He considered how poor of a friend he had been to Blake. What an inconsiderate asshole. He must have grumbled something, because Blake glanced over at him. He shook his head and gazed out the side window. Their conversation continued until Juan Miguel called Isabella to add her to the conversation.

He listened as Juan Miguel, Marissa, and Isabella spoke in Spanish. When Marissa mentioned his name, Isabella's tone changed and there was hesitation in her words, as though she chose them carefully.

"Isabella checked into the paternity test. Her and Nick would have to wait nine weeks before the test could be done," Juan Miguel said.

His shoulders stiffened. Nine fucking long weeks. Although he told Colette they could get married right away, he now planned on convincing her to set a date sometime beyond nine weeks. He still was uncertain what he would do if the child was his. He had no clue where it would leave him and Colette, their engagement, and their future. The only certainty was uncertainty. It still struck him how easy she was to talk about his situation when he first brought it up. He wanted to believe her and hoped she would feel the same way if matters took a dire turn.

The call ended with an amicable agreement between Isabella and Nick. They would wait and do the paternity test after nine weeks. She made it clear she would have the baby regardless of who the father was. She wanted to be a mother, and that was important to her, husbandless, not withstanding. He wondered if she knew of his family fortune and was hedging her bets that the child was his. He hated himself for thinking of such things. Regardless, he wanted to help her to some degree, even if the child wasn't his. Blake snorted.

"That went pretty well, wouldn't you say?"

He felt Blake watching him as he peered out the front window.

"Yeah, I guess."

"Calm heads. I was expecting some shouting. You got lucky, my friend."

He met Blake's gaze. Although his eyes burned, he managed a weary smile.

"You're right. Thanks for all your help. If Marissa and Juan Miguel are ever in town, I want to show them a good time. It's the least I can do."

Blake grinned.

"Marissa is coming in a week or two after she makes arrangements at work."

Blake must have noticed his look of surprise.

"What? How long do you think I can be away from that girl? What am I, some kind of monk?"

They laughed. He never thought of Blake as the abstinence type.

"Are you telling me you and Marissa are exclusive?"

"Yes."

Blake answered without hesitation, which caused him to raise his eyebrows.

"Oh? She must have done something to you."

"She did. It's funny though. Out of the three girls—Isabella, Stella, and Marissa—Marissa was the quietest one. You know, I usually go for the loudest girl."

"That would have been Stella. I remember you eyeing Isabella, but she wasn't having anything to do with you. She didn't even dance with you."

"Yeah, that was fucking cold. She didn't even get to see my moves. It doesn't matter now, things worked out and I couldn't be happier. Maybe my taste in women has changed."

Nick raised an eyebrow, sighed, then nodded. Elizabeth slipped into his thoughts. She was unlike any woman he had ever been with.

"Derek told me you talked to Autumn and finally ended the sexcapades. She's crushed, but Derek is happy. He thinks, he now has a shot with her. He's an idiot, but oh well. Anyway, I thought it was about time you moved on from her. She's a nice girl, but you two weren't going anywhere."

Nick snorted at the thought of Derek chasing Autumn.

"So what's going on with you and Elizabeth?"

"I don't know."

His own answer surprised him. After all, he already committed himself to Colette.

"I really don't know."

"She's a mystery."

"That she is."

He got out of Blake's car, and after he got to his own, he followed Blake to wherever they were having lunch.

Colette sat on the sofa with her bare feet tucked under her. She held a pint of ice cream in one hand and a spoon in the other. The faded red USC crop-top she wore showed her midriff, and white jean shorts showed her bare legs. Sunlight poured into the curtain-less living room windows of Nick's Crest Tower apartment. He was in the kitchen cleaning up. They had ordered sandwiches for lunch from Brewsters, a deli down the block. He folded the top of a bag of sweet potato chips and put them in the cupboard, then smiled over at her. She watched him move about the kitchen as she slipped half spoonfuls of ice cream into her mouth from the pint container. He flipped the dish towel over his shoulder and leaned against the island counter.

"We should talk more about setting a date. I think we both thought sometime soon, but maybe we should have something more concrete."

She swallowed and stuck her spoon into the ice cream.

"Oh? Yeah, sure. What were you thinking?"

"You have another year at USC. Maybe we should wait until after you graduate."

She raised her eyebrows. They never got around to discussing where they both might live, after they were married.

"I thought we would get married before I was done with school, then I can have you out west with me and we both can enjoy California."

"What about my job at Hale? You know my father won't go for that."

She looked down at the coffee table and stroked her neck. She kept her gaze there for a moment and said nothing. Finally, she looked up at him. He crossed his arms and his lips tightened.

"I thought, or had a feeling, you wanted to get away from Atlanta, at least for a while. California is really nice. Los Angeles is great. Will you consider giving it a chance? We can be husband and wife, no more dating. We can figure things out after we've been there for a while. I know you would love California."

There was a softness in her voice. He sighed and raised his eyebrows. His arms remained crossed, but the tension in his shoulders softened. His breath left him with a heavy sigh.

"I don't know. I have to think about it. Also, as much as I hate the thought, I'll have to talk to my father."

"I think he'll go for it. And if he gives you any trouble, then *I'll* talk to him."

He wanted to laugh and stifled a chuckle.

"Really?"

"Once you get your degree, can't you work at a news outlet or newspaper here in Atlanta? All the big networks are here, too."

"Sure, but that's not the point. You should live in a place that makes you happy and feels right for you. That's how I feel when I'm in LA."

He rubbed his chin and stared out the living room window from where he stood in the kitchen. There were a few times when he visited Los Angeles with his family, but only as a boy and as a teenager. He disliked it then. He never expressed, to anyone, how he felt about Atlanta. Georgia and Atlanta held special places in his heart.

"What about family? Your family is really nice. Good, easy-going people."

"Yeah, they're very understanding. They don't pressure me to do anything that I feel isn't right for me."

He wrinkled his lips. Elizabeth felt right to him. He raised his chin and snorted.

"The way your father treats you, I would think you would want to be anyplace but here."

She slinked seductively to the kitchen, one thumb hooked in the pocket of her shorts. Her other hand held the ice cream container up as if she were modeling it for some sexy advertisement. She slid the container of melted ice cream onto the granite countertop, then pressed her body against his and pinned him. She took the dish towel from his shoulder and hooked it around the back of his neck and held both ends. He peered into her pale blue eyes, and she peered into his.

"Nick. I know what I want. This feels so right, even as fast as things are happening. I won't bully you about leaving Atlanta. We should talk more about it, but let's give it a rest for now."

She pulled him down and their lips met, full and wet. Her lips tasted like cool strawberries and cream. He put his hands on her hips. She leapt and wrapped her legs around his waist, and he carried her to the bedroom.

They helped each other out of their clothes and laughed as they stumbled around. He picked her up and laid her on the top of the bedspread. Her honey blonde curls fell about her face, and she brushed them away. The two thin gold chain necklaces she wore pooled in the recesses of her neck and collarbones.

She smiled at him when he climbed between her legs. He knelt there and touched her. His fingers slipped into her wet velvet folds. Her eyelids drew down, and she watched him with a dreamy gaze. When he put his mouth on her, his nose rested on her pubis and his tongue dashed over her clit. She hummed and moaned. They found each other's hands and their fingers knit together.

He moved forward and scooped up her legs onto his shoulders. She squealed playfully when he took her by her hips and pulled her close to him. He was erect, long and thick. His abdominal muscles were tight and defined. She stroked him. His cock lay on her stomach, the tip wet and pointed at her navel. He moved his hips, dragging his cock over her until she lifted her butt off the bed and he eased inside her. Her eyes widened and her lips parted. With each deep thrust, she sucked in a breath.

His rhythm was mechanical, yet he tried to stay in the moment. He pushed away invading thoughts and soldiered on until he came. He was unsure if he made her come. It used to be a matter of pride. He felt numb. As he lie wrapped in her arms with his head on her chest, he listened to her heartbeat race, full of life.

After she showered, she left him with a quick kiss goodbye. He was still lying stretched out naked on the bed, his hands tucked behind his head. He would see her again tonight at her parents' house. They invited him over for dinner. They would use the opportunity to announce their engagement and show her parents the ring. Later that evening, the plan was, they would drive to his parents to tell them the good news as well. He was sure everyone was going to be happy, almost everyone.

22

It was late in the evening when they pulled into the driveway of his parents' home. There was a familiar-looking Porsche parked in the driveway, but Nick was uncertain who it belonged to. Earlier, they had a fabulous dinner at Colette's parents' home. It elated both Dale and Irene Scott to hear the news of their daughter Colette's engagement to Nick. The couple now hoped to pass the news onto his parents. They dropped in unannounced, but they were hopeful his parents would be home.

He held her hand and glanced once more at the Porsche before he pressed the button for the doorbell. It struck him as odd. They could have gone inside. He still had a key to his parents' house. He struggled to recall if he had ever rang the doorbell, even as a joke. She grinned at him as they waited.

The door opened and his mother, Josephine, stood there, wide-eyed.

"Oh, Nick. Oh, hello, Colette. What are you two doing out here? You could have come in."

"Well, mother, I don't live here anymore."

He smiled, to avoid seeming sarcastic. His new apartment, and his engagement, made him feel more distant from his parents than ever before.

"Come on in. Don't be ridiculous. My son—ringing the doorbell—that's madness."

Josephine smiled and gazed at Colette. When they went inside, his mother looked them up and down. He wore a dark blue suit with a sharp-pressed, white button-up shirt that was open at the collar. Colette was in an elegant white cocktail dress, with a gold belt that matched her long honey blonde curls that cascaded over her shoulders. Tan heeled sandals adorned her feet.

"You both look stunning."

His mother's eyes were wide, and she looked eager to hear what they had been up to. She gazed at Colette, but before Colette could say anything, Nick spoke.

"You look very nice too, mother. Are you having a dinner party? We're not interrupting, are we?"

Colette looked at him as though she worried coming there unannounced was a bad idea.

"No-no, don't be silly. We had Henry and Abigale over for dinner."

His shoulders and back tensed.

"Oh, maybe we should go."

Josephine gave him a long look, but then she turned when the clicking of heels on the marble tiles came from down the hall.

"There you are. Richard sent me to make sure you weren't fighting off some home invaders," Abigale said.

Her eyes widened, and she grinned when she saw Nick.

"Oh, my goodness, it's Nicholas. And who is this beautiful young woman?"

"This is Dale Scott's daughter, Colette. These two have been dating, but we're not supposed to talk about it."

She winked and nudged Abigale with her elbow.

"You missed such a lovely dinner your mother put on. Of course, we're having drinks now, and that's equally nice," Abigale said.

Josephine touched Abigale's elbow.

"She's absolutely right. Come on back and have a drink with us. Your father and Henry are going to send a search party for their wives soon if we don't stop lollygagging here in the foyer."

Abigale laughed and nodded. Nick looked at Colette and she shrugged and smiled.

They followed his mother and Abigale down the hallway to the large family sitting room. He struggled to keep his gaze from the bend in the back of Abigale's legs, the areas of exposed flesh of her heels and shoulders, her buttocks that flexed as she moved. She moved naturally in a sexy manner. The only manner he had ever known. He glanced at Colette and she turned to him and smiled, then wrapped her arm around his. He was relieved that her gaze was elsewhere.

When they got to the family room, Richard and Henry were no longer there. His mother's and Abigale's drinks sat on the glass coffee table, and the cherry end table where they had left them.

"I bet they've gone down to Richard's golf simulator," Josephine said.

A light came from the side hallway that led to the stairs down to Richard's man-cave. Nick raised his eyebrows and wrinkled his lips. He and Autumn fucked there a few times. Once they almost got caught by his father. The only other time was when Gwen went looking for him on the day of his graduation party.

"Where's Gwen?"

"She's staying the night at a friend's."

Abigale smirked at Colette. Josephine waved at everyone to take a seat.

"Why don't you all have a seat and I'll get some drinks, since our bartender has abandoned us."

They all chuckled. Nick went to the bar.

"Mother, why don't I take care of that? I see your wineglass is full. Mrs. Rutherford, how about you? Need a top off? Colette, what would you like?"

Josephine picked up her glass of wine and smiled at him.

"Thanks Dear."

He went to where Abigale sat at the end of the sofa. She held out her glass to him. When he grasped it, she continued to hold on to it.

"Richard made me some silly concoction, which wasn't bad, but I'd prefer a gin and tonic."

She raised her voice and laughed. Colette and Josephine chuckled. She ran her finger over his palm while they both held onto the glass.

"Nicholas, can you make me one I'm really going to like?"

Her voice trailed off, and she finally released her glass. She smirked and winked at him.

"Sure, Mrs. Rutherford, anything for you."

He smirked at her, then looked over at Colette.

"Some wine, like what your mother's having, would be nice."

He went to the bar to prepare the drinks. He watched the three women from behind the counter. His mother looked at Abigale for a moment with a tense look, which quickly turned into a tight smile. She then turned her attention to Colette.

"Colette, dear, tell us what you and Nick did this evening."

"We had a really nice dinner at my parents' house, then took a drive, and here we are."

She looked anxious as she sat on the sofa with stiff shoulders and her hands in her lap. She had taken off her engagement ring and kept it in her handbag, waiting for the right moment to show it to everyone. He fixed Abigale's gin and tonic first, then poured a glass of wine for Colette. After he brought out both drinks, he went back and grabbed a bottle of beer for himself. He sat next to Colette on the sofa.

"Don't you two look like a pair? You look real nice together," Abigale said.

"Don't they? We've been trying to get them together for so long," Josephine said.

Colette raised her eyebrows and had a sheepish smile on her face. Nick wrinkled his face at his mother.

"Mother."

"Sorry, Nick."

"You're dressed so nice, and thought so much of your parents to come on over and have a visit with us old folks? That's so sweet."

Abigale laughed.

"Old folks? Josephine, dear, I hope you're not lumping me in."

Abigale played with the ends of her hair. Josephine tilted her head and glanced at her, then waved her hand as if to dispel any assumptions.

"Course not."

Josephine and Colette held their wine glasses and took occasional sips. Abigale brought her glass to her lips and watched Nick as she sipped her gin and tonic. He glanced away, but every time he looked her way, their eyes met, and her lips curled into a self-assured smile.

"We thought it would be nice to stop by since we've been dating. We haven't visited either of our parents much, Nick and I—together—that is," Colette said.

She held her glass of wine in her lap above her white dress, then seemed to think better of it and placed the glass on the coffee table. Nick put his hand on her back to help calm her nerves.

"That's right."

He took a sip of his beer. His mother sat forward, a broad smile on her face. She held her glass of wine and her other arm rested across her lap.

"That's so sweet," Abigale said.

She tensed her face into a squinty-eyed smile, then took a sip of her gin and tonic.

The snickers and chuckles of grown men came from down the hall. Richard and Henry appeared, drinks in hand. Both men wore button up shirts open at the collar, dress slacks and oxfords. Their smiles broadened when they saw Nick and Colette.

"Hey-hey, it's Nick and Colette. Great to see you both. What a delightful surprise," Richard said.

Henry stood alongside Richard and gave both of them a nod and a smile. Richard went to them and gave them both a hug. Henry came over to shake their hands.

"Wish you could have joined us for dinner. So what brings you over to visit the old folks?"

"Oh, stop!" Abigale said.

She rolled her eyes and chuckled. Richard glance over at her with a confused look on his face. Josephine laughed, then shook her head and waved at Richard not to pay any attention to Abigale.

"Now that you're here father, Colette and I have an announcement."

Josephine's eyes widened. Abigale sat up. Nick put his arm around Colette.

"Colette and I are engaged."

Everyone beamed, except Henry and Abigale. Henry offered a warm smile. Abigale smiled, but a slight disappointment shone in her eyes. Richard and Josephine hugged Nick and Colette, then Colette put her engagement ring on to show everyone. His parents looked impressed. They all commended him on how well he did with the ring.

"I had a little help."

He glanced at Colette, who smiled and leaned her head against his shoulder. Abigale cupped her elbow and drank her gin and tonic. His mother's head tilted with every ooh and ahh. He wondered if his mother would eventually cry. His father squeezed his shoulder.

"You did it, son. I'm so happy for the both of you."

"Thank you."

He smiled at his father and did his best to hold on to every bit of positive energy. He tried to avoid Abigale's gaze, but his eyes strayed to her, anyway. She gave him a tight-lipped smile. Before his gaze left her, she winked at him. Richard hurried to the bar and opened the champagne. Josephine handed out the glasses of bubbly. They all toasted the young couple's engagement.

Nick smiled and glanced around at everyone. Abigale's tongue flicked out to lick at the corner of her mouth. Her gaze briefly penetrated his before she turned her attention to Richard and Josephine.

"The champagne is wonderful."

She shrugged her shoulders in delight, but had yet to take a sip. Richard and Josephine nodded and smiled at her. Although Henry smiled as well, he held his glass as though he would have preferred it to be a tumbler with Scotch or brandy.

"Nick, I am so impressed with you. I mentioned to Henry and Abigale how you're off to a great start at Hale, and now—well, now you're engaged."

His father glanced around the room, prideful, like a man who finished building an entire city. Nick smiled and tried to feed off of his parents' joy, but felt starved instead. Anticipation hung in the air. The next obvious question asked was when was the wedding. They gracefully dodged the inquiry, telling everyone they were still discussing things. No one asked Colette if she was pregnant. Nick was grateful. He would be most grateful when the night was over and they could get out of there. Henry grabbed his arm.

"Nick, any thoughts on where you two might go for your honeymoon? To me, that's the most fun part of getting married. Hell, I don't care much about the ceremony," Henry said.

Henry glanced at Colette with a nervous look, as though he hoped not to offend her. Her attention was on Josephine. Nick chuckled.

"No, I hear you. I'm all for getting away and having fun than dealing with the stress of a wedding day."

"It'll go faster than you think. You'll be fine, and soon enough you'll have your toes in the sand and a drink in your hand."

Henry patted his shoulder and beamed at him.

Before his parents poured more champagne, Nick spoke up.

"Father, Mother, Mr. and Mrs. Rutherford, we're so happy to announce our engagement to you, and we're grateful for your support, but we're going to head out now. Thank you for letting us crash your evening."

He took Colette's hand. Richard and Josephine wrinkled their faces as though he were being absurd. Henry smiled at the couple and nodded. Abigale smiled and sipped her gin and tonic. Her untouched glass of champagne sat on the table. Josephine took Colette to the kitchen to get some food for them to take home. Nick went down the hallway to use the bathroom. Before he could pull up his trousers, the door opened.

"Whoa."

Abigale leaned back against the closed door with her hands behind her. She flicked the door lock, and it made a crisp metallic sound. In the mirror's reflection, her gaze was low, as if she were hoping to get a peek. Her eyes rose to meet his. He raised his eyebrows, zipped up his trousers, and buckled his belt.

"Can I help you?"

Her lips twisted into a coy smile.

"Why Nicholas, I sure hope so."

He cleared his throat and turned to face her. She went to him and pinned him against the vanity. Her breasts pressed firm against his chest, and her bare thigh between his legs and into his crotch. Her lips were so close she spoke into his mouth.

"Nick, you've stirred something inside me."

Her breath puffed against his face, and her perfume filled his nostrils. She was intoxicating. He struggled to hold on to his senses.

"I'm engaged to Colette."

His words came out hollow and feeble.

"Oh? And I'm married to Henry. So what's your point?"

"Aren't you worried someone will catch us?"

"Not if you fuck me fast."

She took his hand and slid it up her skirt, so his fingers sank into her moist panties. He tried to pull away, but she held his hand there. She stared with hungry eyes into his eyes and grinned when he touched her and his lips parted. She massaged her clit with his fingers still on her. He exhaled a slow breath, and she ran her fingertips over his parted lips. Her fingers were wet and slick from touching herself, and smelled of her scent. She ground her crotch against his fingers and teased him until he slid them under her panties and touched her wet folds. She gasped. Her lips parted and her tongue licked at her teeth. She gasped a second time when his finger slipped inside her.

"We've got to stop. This is madness."

He withdrew his hand from under her skirt, and she grasped both of his wrists. She spun around so her back was to him and placed his hands on her hips. She then hiked up her skirt and pulled her panties to one side over her left ass cheek. With her buttocks mashed against him, she rolled her hips in a circular motion. His cock firm inside his trousers.

"Uh, Abigale?"

"Abby."

"Uh?"

"Hurry Nick, we're going to get caught."

He closed his eyes, unbuckled his belt, and lowered his trousers and briefs. His stiff cock rested between her toned buttocks. Before he could do anything, she reached around and directed him inside her. Her wet cunt engulfed him. He put his hands on her buttocks as she moved. It felt as though she would swallow him whole. Her breaths came heavy each time she took his cock inside her. Unarmed against her, he put his head back and tried to relax.

"Nicholas, when you're ready to come, I want you to come on my ass."

She must have heard his breathing and wondered if he was getting close.

A knock came at the door. Still inside her, he held her hips firm.

"Nick, are you in there?"

It was Colette. His eyes went wide. He glanced around the bathroom.

"Um? I'm going to be a while. Something is bothering my stomach. Can you give me a moment? No one will want to use this bathroom when I'm done."

He let out an embarrassed chuckle. Abigale ground her hips up and down as he struggled to hold her still. He groaned.

"Okay? Sure, take your time. Your mother gave us some food, and your father a bottle of wine. I'll be out in the car."

"Oh okay, yeah-yeah. I'll be out—soon."

He listened to her heels strike the marble tiles in the hallway as she walked away. The sound of her steps was lighter, like ones that belong to a girl and not a woman. Abigale released low, hushed moans and a playful giggle. She moved again in a slow rhythm. He pulled out of her. His thick cock, less firm, glistened with her pussy juice. He quickly zipped his trousers and buckled his belt. As he finished fixing himself, she straightened her panties and adjusted her skirt down her thighs. She turned around and got in his face. Their noses touched. Her lips brushed his lips with a delicate, wet kiss.

"We're not finished, Nicholas. I want you and I know you want me."

Her breath puffed against his lips. She unlocked the bathroom door and slipped out without first checking if the coast was clear. It astonished him. She seemed to have no care if anyone caught them. He rubbed his forehead, then he turned around to the sink and splashed water on his face and washed his hands. It was a struggle to look at himself in the mirror, so he turned around and waited. He waited until it felt right to leave the bathroom.

Voices came from down the hallway. He first heard Abigale, then his mother, and finally his father and Henry. The conversation sounded as though the Rutherfords were departing. He waited in the hallway until they left, then he stepped out into the foyer. Before his mother closed the front door, he heard the crisp growl of Henry's Porsche. Soon they would be down the driveway and gone by the time he stepped out of the house. His mother looked concerned when she saw him.

"Dear, are you not feeling well?"

"Probably something I ate earlier."

"Don't tell me the Scotts poisoned you," his father said.

He stood there with his arms crossed. Nick chuckled.

"Of course not. Anyway, I'm feeling better. Just eager to get home."

There was that distinction again that struck him. This place, his parents' home, was no longer *his* home. He felt sad and liberated at the same time. His mother tilted her head and smiled at him.

"Well, it was wonderful seeing you and Colette, and with such splendid news."

"Better not keep her waiting."

"Thank you both."

He hugged his mother and shook his father's hand. Richard squeezed his shoulder. In the driveway Colette smiled from the passenger seat when he approached the car. Rather than taking her home to her parents', they headed back to his apartment at Crest Tower. She expressed she wanted to be with him, even if they didn't have sex and only cuddled. She touched his shoulder and played with the hair at the nape of his neck as he drove. Every time he glanced at her, she had a warm smile on her face. Although he wished he could be alone, it felt good to be with someone who cared for him the way she did. He wanted to please her, so he kept his apprehensions to himself. Whatever else the night brought on, he was anxious to get a shower first.

23

Nick met Autumn at the Ramada Inn parking lot. A hotel owned by her father. He was concerned about going inside, especially sharing the privacy of a room with her. He leaned against the driver's side of his BMW and glanced down at his watch. She was late. It was typical of her, especially when they did something other than fucking. The thought struck him and he huffed. Funny, all this time, and now it occurred to him she liked sex more than many of his guy friends. He snorted and shook his head. She finally arrived and parked with a space between their cars. She was slow to get out, and when she did, she had a long face. Her pale complexion struck him. She had on little makeup, perhaps due to all her crying. She wore a t-shirt, jean capris, and sandals. Her eyes were red, and she looked as though it had been days since she last slept.

"Hi Nick."

Her voice was hollow. She leaned against the passenger side door of her car, with the empty parking space between them.

"Hey, Autumn. Thanks for meeting me."

"Nick, you know—well, I thought you knew, I would never say no to seeing you."

His lips tightened, and he nodded.

"Autumn, I'm sorry about the phone call. I should have come to you in person."

She knit her fingers together in front of her, crossed her feet, and glanced at the ground.

"I don't think it would have mattered much. You've made up your mind."

He wrinkled his face, and his eyebrows drew together.

"Yeah. Well, anyway, we're here now, and there is something else I have to tell you."

"Oh?"

Her gaze rose to meet his. He released a heavy breath.

"I—I'm engaged. I'm engaged to Colette."

"What?"

She tilted her head, and her eyes became glassy.

"Why her? No one knows you better than I do."

He glanced at the ground, then back at her. He knew his words stabbed at her heart, and when he continued, more hurt would come.

"Um. I've known her since we were teenagers."

"Is her pussy better than mine? Does she fuck you better than I do? Or, is she smarter than me, is that it? What the fuck is it?"

He stared at her.

"Do you really love her, Nick? I want to hear you say that you love her more than you love me. Say it. Say it, Nick."

She collapsed to her knees, then curled against her car, and wept. He stepped toward her and crouched near her.

"Get away from me."

She wailed.

"Oh, Nick."

Her words slurred. He reached for her.

"Don't touch me! Don't fucking touch me!"

He stood and backed away. He rubbed his face and knit his fingers behind his head and brought his elbows together. Her body shuddered as she cried.

"Just fucking go."

Her sobs muddled her words. His heart hung heavy in his chest.

"Autumn, I'm—so sorry."

"Go."

He did as she asked. He should have called her instead. It was worse leaving her crying in the parking lot all by herself where people passing by could see her. When he got further away, and the hotel disappeared from his rearview mirror, the tears came. His vision blurred and forced him to pull over.

The afternoon sun came through the living room window. Nick lie stretched out on the sofa in his Crest Tower apartment, an open bottle of beer sat on the coffee table. No one was there to criticize him, so he joked to himself about getting an early start on the drinking. Colette had left earlier, after breakfast. He told her he would call his friends to tell them about their engagement. She seemed happy about that. He had no intention of calling his friends. Especially after receiving some scathing text messages from Sandy and Derek, admonishing him over the hurt he caused Autumn. After meeting with Autumn yesterday, he had no desire to have sex with Colette last night. He was certain she picked up on it and was angry about it. When she slept last night, he came out into the living room and sent Elizabeth a text message. Today, while he relaxed on the couch, he glanced at his phone. Occasionally, he would take a sip of beer. There was no reply from Elizabeth.

He sighed, then called Blake. He wanted to meet with Blake, to ask if he would be his best man. After he left a message, he figured he would visit his mother and hopefully get a swim in. Later, maybe even have dinner with his parents. It would be interesting to see if his father had anything new to lecture him about. He snorted and shook his head. He wanted a little space from Colette, and going to visit his parents would be a good excuse.

Elizabeth lie in bed with the covers pulled up. Her eyelids were heavy, but her thoughts kept her awake. Earlier, she drank a cup of herbal tea and did some reading, but nothing helped.

She listened to her own breathing. His name passed her dry lips in a whisper.

"Nick."

She thought of their night together at her hotel room in Madrid. Before she left for her morning meeting, she had whispered his name as he slept. He looked beautiful and without a trouble in the world. She snorted. That night was wonderful, although he was less skilled at making love than what she hoped for. He was young, after all. She questioned if it was wrong for her to want him. He seemed absolutely sure of her—of them. She was sure of herself, but unsure if she wanted to carry the weight of their relationship for the both of them, if he was unable. Then again, if he was unable, the whole thing would crumble, anyway.

"Fuck sake."

She kicked the covers off of her and strolled barefoot, in lounge pants and a tank top, to the kitchen. She flipped on the lights and reached into the cabinet for a wineglass, then into the refrigerator for the bottle of Monsant she opened earlier, and poured.

When she got back to her bedroom, all the rooms were dark again. She sat cross-legged and drank her glass of wine in the dark. The speed with which she dismissed him troubled her. She released a heavy breath. He crossed the line with that repulsive woman, Abigale. She wrinkled her face and bobbed her head. She mocked Abigale's statement from the restaurant.

"I am a friend of Josephine's, Nick's mother."

It was unimaginable that Nick's mother would be friends with such a woman. She tucked her hair behind her ear and drank. She wondered if he could get past her relationship with his father. He did show up on her doorstep. She sighed and tugged at a knot in her hair.

She tried to push Antonio from her thoughts, but he gave her some good advice in the past. He told her, when faced with a dilemma, make a list of positives and negatives, weigh them against one another, and then make your decision. Easy, right? She shook her head and chuckled to herself. She drank, swallowed, and thought.

Let's see… Nick is young. That's a negative. Hm. Let's make it neutral. He's handsome, now that's a positive, and not just handsome, he's gorgeous. He's tall, another positive. He has an amazing body, that's a positive. Okay, Lizzy, those are all physical things. Yeah-yeah I know, but they're good physical things, like his big beautiful cock. Mm. Come on, focus. Okay-okay. He's thoughtful, that's positive. Hm? Okay, maybe we should make that one neutral? He's reckless, that's a definite negative. He's athletic, that's positive. He's inexperienced? Let's just say he's had a lot of opportunities, or so it seems, but could still learn a thing or two in the bedroom. A negative. I think he would be willing to learn. A positive. Let's go back to him being young. That's a positive. He has stamina and is adventurous. What does that add up to? Who the hell knows? I'm too tired to think. Does any of this really matter?

She had a vision of Antonio nodding. She smiled and finished her wine and put the empty glass on the nightstand.

When sleep still eluded her, she fumbled and found her phone. The screen lit up her face and blinded her for a moment. She squinted at it. She was about to write Nick a text message, but there was a new message from him.

He wrote, "I miss you."

She put her palm on her cheek and had a sudden feeling that she could breathe. She read the message a second time, then wrote her reply.

She wrote, "I miss you too. I'm sorry I pushed you away."

She tapped Send, then sat her phone on the pillow next to her and gazed at it until the screen went dark.

She let out a sigh, and after a few heavy breaths, sleep found her instead.

Blake and Nick sat at one of the outdoor tables at Starbucks. They were in shorts, t-shirts and had their sunglasses on. Earlier, after Nick showered and raced out the door to meet Blake, he read Elizabeth's reply. As he rubbed his eyes and ran his fingers through his hair, Blake stared at him.

"Okay, what's on your mind?"

"Nothing really. Maybe stressed a little over my engagement."

Blake gazed at his phone. He flipped his sunglasses up, so they sat on top of his head. He looked to be preoccupied with something he was reading.

"Oh? Do you think you rushed things with Colette?"

He was silent. He sipped his latte before he spoke.

"I don't know."

His words were low, as if he hoped Blake wouldn't hear them. Blake continued to read something on his phone. Perhaps a text message.

"Sorry, what'd you say?"

He smiled at Blake, then sipped his latte.

"Nothing, it's cool. What's going on with you? Care to share?"

Blake chuckled. He took a drink of his coffee, rubbed his hands together, and leaned forward as if he was about to impart some secret.

"Nick. I've been doing a lot of thinking, and I think you helped me out, indirectly, that is."

"Oh?"

"I booked a flight to Madrid to see Marissa. We've been text messaging. I'm going to propose to her when I'm there. You and Colette inspired me to take the plunge."

He was beaming.

"Oh? Really? Does she have any idea?"

"No, she doesn't. I told her we would have a better time in Madrid than in Atlanta, which she didn't agree with. She knows I want to meet her family, so she's happy that I'm coming. What she doesn't know is, if she says 'Yes,' then I have arranged for her to fly back with me."

"Wow Blake. Congratulations, but what about your parents?"

"They totally support me. They met Marissa over video chat, and think she's wonderful."

"That's great. I'm thrilled for you."

He smiled at Blake and squeezed his shoulder. Blake nodded. There was a confident glitter in Blake's eyes. He wondered if he looked like that when he thought about Colette—or Elizabeth.

"I knew something was brewing between you and Marissa. You've been in contact with her like she's the only woman on the planet."

"She is, Nick. She is."

He looked off with a dreamy gaze and drank his coffee. Nick raised his eyebrows and wondered what Elizabeth was doing at that moment. He released a heavy breath and Blake looked at him.

"Have you and Colette set a date?"

"No, we're discussing it. She wants to get married right away. I mentioned waiting."

Blake's eyebrows rose.

"Oh?"

"She knows about Isabella, but I don't think she knows how long I have to wait before we can get a paternity test."

"Wait. She knows about Isabella, and she's agreed to marry you?"

"Yes."

"Wow, Nick. She's a keeper."

"I hope all of this doesn't fall apart."

"It won't. You'll be fine."

He reached over and squeezed Nick's arm. Nick straightened up in his chair.

"I'll be fine if you'll be my best man."

He grinned at Blake.

"Well?"

"Absolutely."

After Blake left, Nick went back inside Starbucks and ordered another ice coffee, then returned to the outdoor table where they sat earlier. He was in no rush to go anywhere. The light breeze and the shade under the table's umbrella made for a comfortable place to think.

Nick sat with his chin in his hand and elbow on the table. He smiled at two ladies who had three little kids with them. They were trying to get the kids to settle down before they would give them their cookie and juice. They sat at a larger table. The only other people there were a young couple. They looked like college students. They smiled, laughed, and teased one another. Their book bags sat on the table. Definitely students. The girl looked over at him and smiled. Then the boy noticed their eye contact and turned to the girl. He spoke fast in a hushed tone. She crossed her arms and glared at him. Nick smiled to himself and shook his head.

He glanced at his phone to read Elizabeth's reply again. Her words made him feel hopeful, but he was uncertain what he should be hopeful for. He looked at her contact information. She should be at work. He tapped the phone icon next to her office number at Nexgen Biosolutions, and listened as it rang.

"Ms. Bach's office. How can I help you?"

"Hello, this is Nicholas Evers of Hale Biotech. May I speak to Ms. Bach, please?"

There was a pause.

"Um? Mr. Evers, Nexgen assigned a new account representative for the Hale account. Would you like me to transfer you?"

"Huh? I mean, no, I still would like to speak to Ms. Bach. Is she available?"

He clenched the bench seat. Hale Biotech was probably Nexgen's biggest client. It seemed improbable that Elizabeth would give up the account unless they forced her to. His eyebrows knit together and his lips tightened. He glanced at the other tables, then took his sunglasses from above his head and put them on to hide his eyes. It gave him a little privacy.

"I'm sorry, she is in a meeting at the moment. Can I take a message?"

He tilted his head and wrinkled his lips. It seemed her assistant was giving him the brush off. He squeezed the back of his neck where the tension had settled.

"When will she be available? It's important that I speak to her."

There was another pause, and he wondered if she was standing there.

"Again, I'm sorry Mr. Evers. Ms. Bach is in an impromptu meeting that was not on her schedule. I'm not sure when she'll be available."

She sounded sincere. He sighed and ran his fingers through his hair.

"Okay. That's okay. I'll try her later. Thank you."

He ended the call before she could say anything, then sat his phone on the table next to his drink and stared at it. He wondered if she would answer her cellphone. There seemed to be something going on over there. He wanted to call his father and find out what he's been up to. A moment later, his phone screen lit up, and a designated ringtone played. It was the ringtone he selected for Colette.

"Hey. How's it going?"

"Hi. I'm good. Where are you, and what are you up to?"

"Wait a minute. Is this the nagging I'm going to have to endure?"

He laughed.

"Very funny mister, but 'yes' it is. So where are you, and what are you up to?"

She laughed, and now they were both chuckling.

"I'm at Starbucks. Blake and I were hanging out, but he took off, and now I'm sitting here by my lonesome."

He glanced over at the young college girl. She looked his way and smiled again. She probably heard what he said. He returned her smile. The boy she was with was busy digging through his book bag. The girl twirled the ends of her hair and bit her lower lip.

"Did you ask Blake to be your best man?"

"Yes, and he agreed. I knew Blake wouldn't let me down."

"That's wonderful. I called Leslie, my best friend in California, to be my maid of honor. She is super happy for us and she'll do it."

"That's great."

"Nick?"

"Yeah?"

"I've been thinking. I know our wedding day is supposed to be amazing, and it will be, but I'm not sure I need all the fanfare."

His eyebrows rose.

"Really? My mother keeps telling me it's the biggest day for a bride and everything should be done to ensure it's the best day of her life."

"Well. She's right."

She laughed.

"But, honestly Nick—I don't need all that. I just want our family and closest friends. I know your father knows a lot of powerful people and I'm sure he would invite them all to have a grand over-the-top event. Nick—"

"You don't have to say anything more. He would make our wedding day more about him than us. I don't want to think about that happening. I love your idea. Keep it small and intimate. How many people total?"

He recalled his graduation party and how he knew only a small portion of the guests. The others, he was certain, came to see his father. He snorted.

"I was thinking twenty, maybe thirty guests, at most."

"I like twenty."

"Oh, good. I was worried you might feel different."

"Like my mother said, it's the bride's big day."

"Thanks, Nick. You're so sweet. I also had something else on my mind."

Her voice got lower as she spoke.

"Oh?"

"You asked me about *when* we should get married. I've been thinking a lot about it. Let's get married right away. I don't want to wait. There doesn't seem to be any reason to, is there?"

A pregnant Isabella. A nine week wait for a paternity test. The possibility that he could be the father.

"Nick?"

"Yeah, I'm here. I was lost in thought."

"Oh? I don't mean to stress you out, but it would be nice to finish school already married, and then we can just start our lives."

"I'm stressed out, but not for that reason."

"Oh? Talk to me Nick."

The two women with the three kids finally left. He was grateful as the kids screeched and one whined.

"Colette, remember when you advised me to get a paternity test when I told you the girl I slept with in Spain was pregnant? I can't believe I'm bringing this shit up again, but I'm sorry I have to."

"Yes, I remember."

Her voice was flat.

"I can't get the test for nine weeks? She has to be that far along."

Colette was silent. Then an audible sigh came over his phone.

"I was thinking about the test when we spoke about setting a date for the wedding, but I didn't have time to bring it up. Shouldn't we hold off on getting married until we know the results?"

Again, she remained silent. She must be mulling things over. Maybe she would come around and they could put things off until they got some clarity. Her silence felt like she was aiming a gun at him in the dark, and he was waiting for it to go off.

"Nick. I can be okay with not knowing, but I need to know how you would handle things if the child was yours."

With his elbows on the table, he rested his chin in his cupped hand.

"I don't know. I hardly know Isabella."

"It was a mistake, that's all. Not an easy one to navigate, but I don't think you're obligated to be part of their lives. Is that something you want?"

"No, I don't think so."

"Nick, you sound conflicted. Will you trust me on this? Will you trust me on what *we* should do? Please know that I have your best interest at heart."

The moment felt like a post-argument with his father, where his father's voice became low and conciliatory, and his words came out slow and careful. He felt pacified again. This time not by his father, but by his bride to be. The only thing that felt right was to reach Elizabeth.

"I—I guess so."

"Nick?"

"Yes Colette. I trust you, but my mind is all over the place."

He sighed.

"I know. It will be okay. See you tonight?"

"Yeah, sure."

They said their goodbyes. More people sat at the outdoor tables. Two women exited the cafe with their drinks in hand and glanced around for a place to sit. He waved them over.

"I'm leaving."

They smiled and thanked him. He went to his car. When he sat in the quiet cabin, he took out his phone and tapped the phone icon next to Elizabeth's cellphone number. It rang for a while and her voicemail would soon answer. He held his thumb over the phone icon to end the call. If he left a phone message, he was unsure what to say. He never felt so wanting of someone and so cautious in his life.

"Hello, you have reached Ms. Elizabeth Bach of Nexgen Biosolutions. I am on an extended leave. Please direct all business related calls to Nexgen's main phone number. The number is…"

He ended the call. His eyebrows knit together and his lips parted.

"What is going on over there?"

He called her office number again. Maybe her assistant could tell him. He listened to the same recorded message as on her cellphone number and wondered if they had let her go. It astonished him how quickly things were happening. When he imagined her being escorted out of the building, he slammed his fist down on the car's center console.

After glaring out the front window, he called his father. It rang, and he assumed he would soon hear his father's recorded greeting.

"Hello Nick. Son, what can I do for you?"

His father's voice was very jovial, which made him clench his teeth.

"Can you tell me why Elizabeth Bach is no longer working at Nexgen Biosolutions?"

"Whoa son. Where is this coming from? How would I know?"

"C'mon, it's not difficult to put two and two together. You didn't want me to see her, fine. I'm engaged to Colette now, so why are you going after her?"

"Hold on a second, Nicholas."

He listened to his father's muffled voice speaking to someone at the office. He knew what was coming next.

"I'm sorry Nicholas, I've got to run to a meeting. We can continue this conversation later."

There it was.

"Sure."

He tapped the phone icon to end the call. Fuckwad. He ran his fingers through his hair, then started the car's engine. He hoped Elizabeth would be home.

~

It was early evening. Nick fought rush hour traffic on his way to check on Elizabeth. As he sat in the Lakewood Estates' guest parking lot, he thought about what he might say to her. When he first arrived, it surprised him how full the lot was, but he found a spot near the back. On his way over, he stopped by his apartment to put on a button-up shirt and trousers. He checked his look in the car's rearview mirror, then fussed with his shirt collar and finger-combed his hair. Satisfied with his appearance, he released a heavy slow breath, then got out of his car.

He crossed the parking lot and started up the walkway. When he reached the street, he saw an elegantly dressed woman at Elizabeth's door. Something about her looked familiar, but she faced the door. The woman pushed the doorbell button several times as if she were eager for Elizabeth to answer the door. His eyebrows furrowed. He moved closer to the tree that stood where the corner of the street and walkway met. The woman pounded on the door with an open hand.

"Hello. I know you're in there. I'm not leaving, so you might as well answer the door."

His shoulders stiffened. The woman's voice. It was his mother's voice. The woman stepped to the edge of the porch to look into the windows. When her head turned, his eyes widened. It was definitely his mother. She must have been to the salon. Her hairstyle was shorter and colored. Nothing like what he was used to.

His mother faced the door once again and pressed the doorbell button a few more times. She stepped back from the door as if she finally acknowledged that nobody was home. When she stepped down the porch steps, her heels clicked on the concrete. He hurried back across the parking lot, but his mother appeared on the walkway, and all he could do was squat alongside his car.

She passed through two rows of parked vehicles and walked straight toward where he had parked. His heart pounded. She was three vehicles away from where he hid. She slipped between the cars. He sighed. His mother climbed inside a silver Mercedes SUV. He shook his head and imagined if they both arrived at the same time. There would definitely be questions, and knowing her, he would have to provide the answers. He recalled glancing at the silver SUV when he entered the parking lot, and never would have guessed it belong to his mother. He stayed down and waited for her to drive away. After a while, he wondered if she would wait for Elizabeth to come home.

The sun had almost set. Car lights pointed down the row where he had parked. His mother waved to signal that she was leaving. She turned left toward him so the other driver could take her spot. Fuck. He duck-walked on bent knees to the back of his car and wedged himself between the rear bumper and the hedges. He peeked around the side of his car. After she passed by and was far enough away, he stood. The man who took her spot stared at him, and probably wondered what he was doing hiding behind a car. He dug out his keys and pushed the trunk release button, then grabbed a light jacket that he kept in the trunk and closed the lid.

He got in his car and waited for the man to disappear up the walkway. When no one else came, he sighed. He gripped the steering wheel tight and hoped to God that Elizabeth was okay. He needed to talk to his mother. To know why she was there. Tonight, he had a date with Colette, so there was nothing else he could do.

24

Nick hurried up the sidewalk to The Meridian Club. His navy sports jacket and silver and brown striped tie swayed with each stride, while his burgundy loafers scuffed the concrete. When he got inside, he buttoned his jacket, stood there with parted lips as he took in the elegant space. Several enormous ceiling light fixtures composed of many various sized glass spheres hung by fine filaments. They floated like giant, illuminated raindrops above the deep purple plush sofas. Couples lounged comfortably on the sofas in front of long, slender, shiny black lacquered tables. They chatted one-on-one or in small groups. A live jazz band played at the front of the house. He scanned the space until he spotted Colette. She sat toward the back at one of the smaller tables with dark emerald green plush club chairs.

As he made his way past the bar, a woman who stood facing away from him made him pause. She chatted with the bartender. He licked his dry lips. She wore an elegant black cocktail dress, and her long wavy dark chestnut hair flowed down her shoulders and back. The way she moved her head and her shoulders held him there.

"Elizabeth?"

Maybe his voice was too low to compete with the surrounding chatter or the music from the speakers overhead. He was about to call out to her again, but she turned and she was someone else. His breath caught and his shoulders softened. He blinked his eyes as if to chide his own vision and went to the tables toward the back of the club. He sat down across from Colette.

"You're late."

He was about to say something, but she inclined her head and put her finger on her cheek. He stood and gave her a peck. When he tried to kiss her lips, she covered his mouth with her fingertips.

"Sit dear."

She sounded like his mother. He sat down on the club chair across from her.

"No kiss? I thought we were going to have a romantic night out?"

"We will. Next time, don't keep me waiting."

"Fair enough."

He raised his eyebrows, then broke his gaze from hers and glanced around the restaurant and lounge.

"This is quite a place. I'm impressed with your choice."

"I can be chic and classy, when I need to be."

"And who would have thought Colette Scott liked to go slumming."

"Sarcasm? Hah! This is far nicer than most of the pubs you and your friends spend your time at."

He chuckled, but she was right.

"They probably wouldn't let my friends into a place like this."

They both laughed, and she shook her head and smirked at him.

The server arrived in a tight black t-shirt and slacks. Her shirt molded around her large breasts and narrow waist. He sensed Colette's gaze, so he kept his eyes on the server's face. She leaned over and placed in front of both them tall glasses of clear liquor with lemon wedges and a maraschino cherry riding on top of ice cubes. She then took Colette's empty cocktail glass. He was about to protest, but Colette held up her hand to silence him. After the server left the table, He wrinkled his face.

"What's this?"

"I ordered us both a Tom Collins. I told her not to bring them out until *you* got here."

"Lovey. How thoughtful, but you're one drink ahead of me."

He raised an eyebrow as he looked at the Tom Collins, then at her. She grinned, tucked her hair behind her ear, then took a sip of her drink. He waited for her answer.

"It was only a cranberry juice and tonic."

He raised an eyebrow.

"Really? That's all it was?"

She glared at him.

"All right, I believe you."

She cocked her head and her lips formed a crooked smile, which faded as quick as it appeared.

"So, how was your day?"

It struck him, and probably her as well, that both of them would hear that question a lot after they got married. He shifted in his seat and tilted his head as he contemplated the question.

"It was good. Got some great news."

"Oh, yeah?"

"Blake is going to propose to Marissa."

She beamed.

"That's wonderful."

"Yeah, Blake told me when we were out getting coffee. Apparently, our engagement influenced his decision to take the plunge. Crazy, right?"

"Not that crazy. We're a beautiful couple embarking on a beautiful future. We should be on the cover of some magazines."

He chuckled.

"What? It's true."

She crossed her arms.

"Ok-ok, I'll concede that we are a good-looking couple. I'm not sure about us landing on any magazine covers."

She smiled and turned her head from side to side.

"I don't know, Nick. I don't think you believe in us."

He tilted his head and smirked at her.

"Huh? That's not nice."

"Sorry, dear, but you've got to convince me."

She shrugged and took a sip of her Tom Collins. There was that motherly tone again. His shoulders tighten. He leaned toward the edge of the table and looked into her eyes.

"Colette, I am really sorry about being late. I feel bad about you sitting here by yourself on my account."

He raised his eyebrows, then took a sip of his Tom Collins.

"Not bad."

He smiled at her. She uncrossed her arms, but the corners of her lips tightened as if she struggled not to smile.

"Yeah? There it is."

She smiled.

"Fuck you."

They both laughed and drank. Then she held up her glass.

"I think we should toast to Blake and Marissa. Let's hope and pray she says, 'Yes.'"

He raised his glass to meet hers.

"To Blake and Marissa. That's very thoughtful of you, dear."

They both took a healthy drink. This time he referred to her as *dear* and wondered how she felt about it. Thoughts of her parents, Dale and Irene, crept in. They appear to have a great relationship, and one with Colette. He felt all alone when he thought about his parents.

"Nick, are you okay?"

Her voice sounded far away. He had been looking down at his cocktail. The pieces of lemon had fallen through the ice and now swirled at the bottom of the glass. Music from the jazz players up front came through the ceiling speakers and filled the silence between them.

"Nick?"

He looked up at her. Her eyes looked sad and concerned.

"Huh? Sorry."

"What's on your mind?"

"Ah? I was thinking about our wedding. Do you think we're moving too fast?"

She sat up straighter and the tenseness in her eyes returned.

"Why do you say that?"

"We have a difference of opinion about where to live, and we didn't—"

"Nick, I told you not to worry about that. It will *all* work itself out. You and I are very easy-going people. Plus, your father went to great lengths to secure us a beautiful venue. The Windsor Estates is exactly what I asked for and he came through for us on incredibly short notice."

He shifted in his seat.

"I understand that, and I'm grateful for all he's done…"

He wanted to spit. His father had come through for them, but it could also be something in the future that his father could hold over his head.

"… but can we please talk about your desire to live on the west coast? You have a year left of school, that's fine, but beyond that—living there—I'm not sure how I feel about it."

She crossed her arms. Her eyebrows drew together, and her gaze hardened, then fell to her Tom Collins. She twisted the cherry by its stem that floated atop the ice cubes. She then brushed her fingers through the ends of her curly honey blonde hair. A soft sigh passed her lips. She looked up at him.

"We'll work it out."

She sounded deflated. He gripped his thigh and his face felt warm and flush. He wanted to drag out their engagement so he could be at ease when their wedding day came.

"What the hell. You're right, we'll be fine."

He blurted the words he thought she wanted to hear. Anything to take away the pain and doubt that formed in her eyes. He took a healthy drink of his cocktail and motioned for the server to come. They had one more drink, then they headed out for a walk around town.

An invisible space hung between them, even when she took his arm and put her head on his shoulder. The beautiful downtown Atlanta lights from the SkyView Ferris Wheel to the street lamps lining Centennial Olympic Park should have softened the mood to a romantic one. Instead, they agreed to call it a night and get a good night's rest for their big day tomorrow.

He walked her to her car. After she drove off, he returned to The Meridian Club. He sat at the bar a few seats down from the woman who reminded him of Elizabeth. She started the conversation. He learned her name, Silvia. She moved to sit next to him. Silvia appeared to be around Elizabeth's age. She played with her long, dark chestnut curls. Silvia's gaze made him feel like he was the only other person there, and her smile warmed him. As the night progressed, he could have taken her back to his apartment.

"It wouldn't be the same," he mumbled.

She stared at him.

"I'm sorry, I've got to go. It was nice meeting you."

He paid for their drinks.

"Please stay a little while longer."

He kissed her hand, thanked her for her company, and then departed.

Two horses trotted and played with one another in the fenced-in field which was part of the Windsor Estate's grounds. Colette smiled as she watched them and thought about her and Nick.

"Hold still, dear," the makeup artist said.

The makeup artist had Colette face the window so she would have soft, even light to work with. Colette fidgeted.

"Sorry."

"Hush."

She peered out the window at the grounds. It was an amazing day. A perfect blue sky with few clouds. She was deeply thankful for Richard Evers for using his influence to secure the Windsor Estate on such short notice. They were all very gracious in allowing her to pick the location. She wanted something elegant, yet country. When she found the property with the attached horse stables, she knew she had found the right place. Nick had smiled when she told him about it.

"There. Have a look," the makeup artist said.

She turned to the full-length mirror and beamed at her reflection as she stood radiant in her wedding dress. The hairdresser and two other women fussed about her to make sure everything was perfect. A knock came at the door. One woman who helped dress her peeked outside. She glanced toward the door. The woman had a big smile on her face. She opened the door and Colette's father, Dale Scott, stood in the doorframe in his tuxedo. His eyes widened when he saw his daughter in her wedding dress.

"Oh."

That was all he seemed able to say. The women laughed. He entered the room and held Colette's hands and kissed her on the cheek. There were smiles all around.

"My dear—dearest Colette. You look absolutely beautiful."

He spoke as if he were out of breath. His eyes became glassy and a tear ran down his cheek.

"Oh, dad."

Her eyes became glassy.

"No-no. You two stop that this instant," the makeup artist said.

She hurried to her kit on the table near the window. One of the other women grabbed a box of facial tissue and stepped in front of Dale to catch Colette's tears. Her father moved back to give them space, then took out his handkerchief, dabbed at his own tears, and blew his nose. Wonk. His eyes went wide. The women burst into laughter, which made Dale laugh. Colette shook her head and laughed with them.

The makeup artist touched up her cheeks and fixed her eyes.

"Dad?"

"Yes."

"Have you seen Nick?"

"Yes, he looks very handsome in his tuxedo."

"Did he look nervous?"

"Ah? Well, a little. Hell, I'm nervous."

He chuckled.

"Okay."

"Honey, I'll be waiting outside the door."

"Yes, please," the makeup artist said.

The makeup artist made a shooing gesture.

It had been a week of silence, with only memories of Elizabeth. Nick drew his eyebrows together and his lips tightened into a straight line. It was a beautiful day. A light breeze blew around the columns at the side of the grand building. He told Blake that he needed some time to himself. Everyone was waiting. Soon the wedding procession would start and he would have to go back inside. A few birds sang and he could see in the distance a couple of horses running together in the fenced area of the estate. When he paced around, all he could hear were his oxfords on the stone pavers. Outside, he felt alone, but safe. He had left his tuxedo jacket inside and leaned against a column.

Twice, he saw Blake behind the glass panel door. Blake would give him a thumbs up, and he would return with a thumbs up and a smile, which faded when he turned around to gaze out onto the estate. He wished he could stay out longer to lose himself in his thoughts, but he imagined Blake would soon appear, tapping his watch for him to come inside. He closed his eyes and breathed in the fresh air, and wondered if Elizabeth was okay.

He took his phone from his pocket and read her last text message. She never replied. The signs said that whatever they had was over. He thought there had been something. He snorted and raised his eyebrows.

The door opened behind him.

"It's time buddy."

Blake stood in the open doorway with a confident smile that faded as soon as he saw Nick. He stepped outside and shut the door behind him.

"What's up?"

Nick struggled to look at Blake, and instead, he glanced off in the distance to gaze at the horses. The two horses trotted alongside the wooden fence.

"Talk to me Nick. What's going on?"

His vision blurred and his eyes burned.

"I'm sorry, I've got to go."

"What?"

He turned to Blake and huffed.

"I can't be here. I'm not supposed to be here."

"What? I thought this was what you wanted."

"Blake, it's terrible for me to put this on you."

Blake held his arm.

"Wait—wait a minute. What do you mean?"

"I need you to tell everyone I'm not coming. Can you do that for me?"

Blake's eyes were wide, and his mouth hung open.

"Hang on, just wait a minute here. Are you sure about this? Everyone is waiting. Everyone is expecting you."

Nick's eyes burned. He imagined the astonished faces, their parents' anger, Colette's confusion and embarrassment. He dragged his fingers through his hair.

"That's the problem, Blake. Everyone is expecting me. They're *always* expecting me."

He glanced away. His shoulders stiffened, and his face wrinkled into a tight scowl. Blake huffed.

"Did your father pressure you?"

Blake's gaze burned into him, and he must have seen the answer in his eyes.

"Fuck! Fucking A, Nick."

Blake shook his head and stared at the ground.

"Please, can you tell them? Can you do that for me?"

Blake sighed and nodded. Both men hugged, and Blake patted him on the back. Nick took long strides down the walkway to where he had parked his car. It occurred to him then, the fact he drove his own car, may have been prophetic. When asked who he was riding with, he always had a satisfying answer, only to end up driving himself.

He drove down the lane where the wooden ranch style fence ran parallel to the road. The two horses he had seen earlier galloped alongside the fence as if they were escorting him. When the fence turned direction, the horses slowed and trotted off into the field. He dug his phone out of his pocket and turned it off. The calls would come soon. His eyes burned, and the tears came. He cried for Colette, their friendship, and her love for him.

25

A week passed, and the demand for explanations had cooled to a bitter simmer. It would be a long time, if ever, when his parents could accept his decision to leave Colette on their wedding day. His father was furious, and left him several berating phone messages, which he could only bear to listen to portions of them. He only talked to his mother, who cried and told him how disappointed she was. He heard nothing from Dale and Irene Scott, or Colette. It would surprise him if they ever let Colette speak to him again.

When Nick walked down the hallway to his Crest Tower apartment, the building owned by his father's company added to the weight he carried. He imagined his father would soon have him removed. After he entered his apartment and put his things on the kitchen island, the silence added to his emptiness. Every sound he made seemed amplified, especially the door to his apartment when it clunked shut. It sounded final, like a prison cell door lock that hammered into place. He closed his eyes and pinched the bridge of his nose, then took a deep breath and tried to calm himself.

"Fuck."

After he sat his car keys on the counter, he groaned and went to the refrigerator. He was thirsty, but he needed something more than water. In the refrigerator was his last bottle of beer. The sound of humming came from the bedroom. It was a sweet feminine voice. His eyebrows knit together and he cocked his head. Whoever was there must have heard him come in. His stomach knotted.

"Hello?"

No answer, but the humming continued. He sat the bottle of beer on the island and crept down the hallway to the bedroom. The humming grew louder and clearer when he got to the bedroom. His lips tightened and his jaw flexed. The voice had a richer tone than Colette's.

"Hello?"

He stepped into the bedroom. A blouse and shirt lie carefully folded atop his dresser. Heels clicked on the adjoining bathroom tiles. Abigale emerged in a pink and purple lacy bra and panties, sheer nude-colored thigh highs, and beige pumps. His lips parted.

"Hello Nick."

Her voice was soft above a whisper. She sounded delighted, as if this was a routine for him to come home to her. Her eyes were bright and her lips were curled into a devilish smile.

"Uh?"

"These are new. I got them just for you. Do you like them?"

She drew her fingertips around one of her breasts and made circles with the other hand on her thigh. She raised an eyebrow.

"Of course, you do."

She went to him and stood close enough that he could feel her breath on him. The scent of her perfume captured him. They gazed into one another's eyes.

"Abigale, I don't know what—"

She put her fingertips to his lips.

"Shh. It's okay Nick. You've been through a lot. Let Abby take care of you."

"Abby?"

She touched her lips to his. The tip of her tongue teased at him until he parted his lips to let her in. Her tongue tasted of sweet wine. She caressed the sides of his face as they kissed and left her body available for him to put his hands anywhere he liked.

"Touch me Nick."

She spoke into his open lips. His hands settled at her waist. She moved closer so their bodies touched. He moved his hands down her body, over the strip of lace that disappeared between her bare buttocks. When he squeezed her flesh, he knew in that moment he belonged to her. She wrapped her arms around his shoulders and kissed him deep. He slipped his fingers under the cup of her bra and squeezed her breast. She unclasped her bra and tossed it on the floor. There was a hint of frustration in her eyes. He realized, in that moment, that she would have liked him to take his time and savor stripping her of her new lingerie. He gave her a flirtatious smile.

She squealed when he lifted her. Her legs wrapped around his waist and she giggled like a girl before they kissed again. Her breasts mashed against his broad chest, and her long curls fell over their faces. He carried her to the side of the bed and sat her down. She unbuckled his trousers, slipped his briefs down, and took his cock into her mouth. He sucked in a sharp breath as she cupped and massaged his balls as she worked her mouth over him. He unbuttoned his shirt and tossed it on the floor. His cock was firm from their kissing, but after she put her mouth on him, he hardened to stone. He closed his eyes and his body swayed. He tried not to think about Autumn, but she always wanted to suck his cock, even when he was asleep or not in the mood. His eyebrows drew together.

"Wait."

He held her shoulders and stepped back to free himself of his trousers and briefs pooled at his ankles. She slipped off her heels. Her shoes made delicate hollow thuds when they landed on the carpeted floor. She stood, bit her lower lip as she gazed into his eyes. He adored her girlish gesture. He wanted to believe that it came from an honest, innocent place. She shimmied playfully as she teased and lowered her panties. He found a condom in the nightstand drawer and rolled it over his cock.

He went to her and seized her by the arms. They kissed rough and wet. Her panties slipped down her legs, caught at the knee briefly, then settled around her ankles. She barely stepped out of them before he spun her around and bent her over the bed. He held her hips and slipped his hand between her legs. She was slick, wet, and ready. He imagined she pleasured herself in his bathroom before he got home. She made a surprised grunt when he plunged his full length inside her. His hips slapped her buttocks as he fucked her. She grasped handfuls of the bedsheets and held on.

"The guy you were with—at the restaurant—Bruno. Did he fuck you like this?"

He grunted as he thrust into her. Her moans grew louder. He lifted her hips, and she balanced on her toes. She cried out as he rode her from behind. After a moment, he slipped from her. His cock arched upward and glistened wet with her juices. He turned her around and mashed his open mouth to hers, then he held her in his intense gaze.

"Get on the bed."

She got on the bed and opened her legs to him. Her gaze only shone excitement. She seemed unaware of his anger. Regardless, what did she have to fear from him? He climbed on top of her and their bodies joined again. He fucked her hard. She made no complaints and only released cries and moans of pleasure. When he slowed, her lips curled into a half smile. His eyebrows drew together, and he fucked her harder.

"Did he? Bruno? Did he fuck you like this?"

She nodded as she cried out. Her orgasm seized his cock. She nodded again in quick succession. He wanted to hurt her. To stab his cock into her cunt. Her cries grew loud enough to carry throughout the apartment and maybe through the walls. He groaned as his climax rose.

It disgusted him, the various men who were entertaining her cunt. Henry, her husband, should be the one to have her. But maybe he knew his wife slept around, and as boring as Henry seemed to be, maybe he was thankful.

"I want to fuck that little whore cunt of yours."

"Nicholas!"

Her eyes widened.

"Oh! Oh! Yes! Yes-yes!"

Her voice crackled in a surprised tone, then she groaned. He held her legs wide. She grasped his thighs as he drove into her. She licked her shiny lips. Her face smothered by her long blonde curls.

"Open your dirty little cunt. Hold yourself open."

"Nicholas!"

Her tone was that of a woman who found a boy masturbating. Her eyes widened.

"You heard me. Hold your cunt open."

"Nick."

"Do it."

She reached under her thighs and held herself open as he continued to fuck her. The condom wrapped around his cock glistened with her wet climax. Her inner muscles bound tight around him. Her eyebrows knit together, her mouth hung open, then her tongue circled her lips as he plunged into her with long strokes. She tilted her head back and cried out.

His chest heaved, and his body curled over hers. Before he came, he pulled out, tore the condom off, and held his breath as he shot his pearlescent stream into her open cunt. He sheathed his entire length inside her, then held her hips tight to his own until he filled her with all that he had left.

Her wide-eyed shock turned to moans of acceptance, then to exhilarated laughter.

"Oh Baby. You fucked me so good. Oh Nick, don't stop fucking me baby."

She ran her fingertips over his chest and down his abdomen. That was the first time she called him *Baby*. He held his face in a painful scowl. His anger, a weary tempest, subsided when he realized she was laughing. She laughed, exhilarated, as though she had survived a bungee jump. He had ventured into hell. He moved his hips slowly in and out, but his cock softened with each thrust. She rested her arms behind her head as if she were lying out on some soft grassy field, watching the clouds float by.

Now he was a whore, like Elizabeth said. Now he was nothing.

He lay spent and naked in bed. His cock hung lifeless in the crease between his hip and thigh like a deflated balloon. He watched her dress. She told him how good he fucked, and that he was a naughty boy for coming inside her. Her period had come recently, and she told him not to worry. She said she enjoyed feeling him come inside her without the condom, and the risk of him possibly impregnating her added to the thrill of them being caught. If he could get hard, he knew she would be ready for more. As he lie there, he gazed at the ceiling light fixture, and felt sick. It was all a game. A game of who would tag Abigale's pussy first. His madness pondered the question. Would it be Bruno, her husband Henry, not likely, or yours truly, Nicholas Grand Fuckwad Evers?

Her heels clicked on the tile floor when she went to the bathroom to fix her makeup and fuss with her hair. She hummed the same song that he heard when he came home. When she came back into the room, she stood at the foot of the bed and fussed with one of her earrings. Her blouse, buttoned low, hung open, her cleavage visible. She had left her bra off. Her nipples pointed through the white semi-sheer silk fabric. A glossy line of his semen traced down the inside of her thigh.

"Mm. Nick. You're such a pretty sight."

He pulled the sheet over his waist. She smirked, then walked out of the room. Her heels clicked on the hardwood floors in the hallway and kitchen. Shortly after, the front door of the apartment creaked open and then crashed shut.

~

In the illuminated visor mirror, Josephine inspected her makeup. She blinked her eyes several times. Although, today she managed not to cry, she hated how tense her eyes looked, with the awful redness around the eyelids. There was nothing she could do, so she touched up her lipstick instead. She flipped up the visor, closed her eyes, and hoped a brief minute or two would reduce the strain.

It was silent inside the cabin of her silver Mercedes SUV. There was only the faint sound of a car that passed behind her. The parking deck for the Crest Tower apartments was more than half empty.

She had picked up some lunch for her and Nick on her way over. He never gave her or Richard an answer why he ran off on his wedding day. Without his father breathing down his neck, maybe he would talk to her.

"Nick, my dear Nicholas."

She took in a deep breath, then got out of her car. From the back of the SUV, she retrieved a white handled shopping bag with gold foiled letters scrolled on it. She had picked up a couple of salads and one of his childhood favorites, chicken fingers. After the tailgate closed and the SUV's alarm chirped, she started for the short skyway that attached the parking deck to the apartment building. Above the alley, the skyway linked both structures at the apartment complex's second floor. Her heels clacked on the concrete and echoed among the dull, cool, gray walls.

Down the slopping ramp, a blur of white caught her eye, then red brake lights. A white Mercedes convertible with its top up headed down the ramp. Before it turned toward the exit, she caught the license plate: *CHEEKY*. It was Abigale's car. She fought the urge to shout. It was useless to cry out after her. Her arms were too full to retrieve her cellphone, so she huffed and stood there for a moment. Her face wrinkled, and her hands balled into fists. She marched to and then across the skyway. Her heels made a loud, rhythmic staccato on the concrete. When she got to the elevators, she braced herself and tried not to cry. She and Nick were going to have a totally different conversation. Whatever they were up to, it was obvious Abigale was having an affair with Nick.

A knock came at the door. Nick lie in bed, still naked as Abigale had left him. The sheet covered his waist and one of his legs. His forearm rested over his eyes. The knock came again, and he sat up on his elbows. He rubbed his eyes and pinched the bridge of his nose, then groaned. Fuck sake. Abigale got the building manager to let her into his apartment. Now she needed him to open the door for her. Her gall astounded him. The knock came again. He went to the dresser and fished out some shorts and lumbered to the front door. She was damn persistent. He tilted his head. This was getting absurd.

"All right! All right! Abby, I'm coming! Keep your panties on."

He huffed and wondered if she even put them back on, and if she did, she would probably have them off soon enough. Whatever she left behind, he hoped she would retrieve and be on her way. He grabbed the doorknob and swung the door open, then his mouth dropped.

"Mother?"

"Abby? Really, Nicholas?"

Before he could reply, his mother pushed her way into his apartment. He stepped out of the way. She marched into the kitchen. Her heels were sharp on the hardwood floors. She sat the bag from the restaurant on the kitchen island and dropped her handbag next to it. He closed the door. Although he wore shorts, he felt naked in front of her.

"I saw her leaving. What were you two doing?"

Before he could answer, she stormed down the hallway to his bedroom, and he followed her. She stood frozen as she looked at the unmade bed. His stomach knotted. She then went to the bathroom. Her heels clacked on the tile floor and echoed on the tile walls. She appeared with Abigale's pink and purple panties clenched in her fist. His eyes widened and his lips parted.

"Um?"

"Don't *um* me, Nicholas."

She threw Abigale's panties, and they hit him in the face. He caught them as they fell into his arms and tossed them on the floor near the wall.

"How long have you been sleeping with her?"

She crossed her arms and glared at him.

His mouth was suddenly dry.

"Is she the real reason you ran out on Colette?"

"Um? No."

"Are you going to tell me what is really going on, or do I have to piece it together? I think it's getting clearer by the moment."

Her tortured gaze was one he had never seen before. Then her voice broke.

"Tell me Nicholas! What the hell is going on?"

Her words, mixed with tears, came out muddled. She held her hands to the sides of her head, with a look as though she were going crazy. He had never seen her so hurt, and could only imagine her expression when he fled on his wedding day. He stepped toward her, wanting to embrace her, but she held her hand up to stop him.

"No. Start talking."

She waved her hand as if to coax the words out of him.

"Yes. I slept with Abigale. It was a mistake. I'm sorry. My life is a mess."

She pushed past him with a sickened expression, and he followed her back to the kitchen. Another moment in his bedroom where he fucked Abigale would probably have been too much for her. At the kitchen island, she pulled some tissue from her handbag, dabbed under her eyes, and wiped her nose.

"Nick, your father and I had great plans for you. We had everything laid out for you to have a wonderful life. When you proposed to Colette, she was the missing piece we thought would lead you to a happy family life. Why did you have to go against us, and why with Abigale, for God's sake? If it was just sex, why not mess around with Autumn? You kept *her* around long enough. Your father and I were worried you would eventually marry her. But now—now with Abigale. I was always worried your little crush on her would develop into something more when you got older, and now it has. Are you proud of yourself? How will you ever look Henry in the eye, or shake his hand?"

He looked at the floor between them and turned his head slowly from side to side.

"No, I'm not proud of what I've done. As for Autumn, I ended things with her before I started things with Colette. You're right. I kept Autumn around too long, led her on, and hurt her bad. I doubt we can be friends."

He leaned against the kitchen island and ran his fingers through his hair and squeezed the back of his neck before he met his mother's fiery gaze.

"Here, I brought you some lunch."

She pushed the handled bag from the restaurant toward him.

"Uh. Thanks."

"I was hoping for us to sit and talk about Colette, but now I can't even look at you."

"Oh, stay. Please."

"I'm sorry Nick. I can't. Not now. Not today."

She rolled her eyes and dabbed at more tears.

"Goodbye Nicholas."

She grabbed her handbag and opened the door.

"Goodbye. I—"

The door clunked shut. He sniffled and his eyes burned. Although he was hungry, he put the bag of food his mother brought him into the refrigerator and grabbed his last bottle of beer. It was a San Miguel 1516, a pale Spanish lager. He opened the bottle and took a few sips, then went out onto the balcony.

He leaned over the railing with his chest against his folded forearms and sipped the beer. He gazed out onto the horizon, first in the distance toward the Atlanta skyline, then at the nearby park below. When he looked straight down to the sidewalk behind the Crest Tower apartment building, his gaze held. It was four stories down. He swallowed and wondered if a fall from that height would do him in. His eyes burned from seeing the pain he caused his mother. Her words and her tears caused him to knot up inside. He respected her firm guidance, but wondered if his parents understood his pain, his wants, his needs. They always seemed to think they knew, but they never asked him, or they dismissed his wants as flights of fancy.

A tear dripped from his chin and blew away in the air like a random raindrop. His eyes blurred. He took a healthier gulp of the San Miguel 1516 and almost emptied the bottle. No one was on the sidewalk below. Before he let go of the beer bottle, he gave it a slight push so it would go further out from the side of the building and miss the sidewalk. It seemed to take forever to hit the ground, as if it hung desperately in the air. The bottle landed on the soft shoulder that ran along the sidewalk. It remained in one piece, bounced, slid, then rolled down an incline into a man-made runoff. He raised his eyebrows. The bottle should have been in a million pieces. A faint text message alert came from his phone on the kitchen island. Two more alerts came. He wiped his wet cheeks, sniffled, then went back inside.

26

On the kitchen island in his Crest Tower apartment, Nick's phone beckoned; the screen illuminated with new messages. Several were from Blake. Before he could read them, a call came through. Blake's name appeared. He tapped the screen.

"Hey Blake. How's Madrid? Are you engaged yet?"

He released a weary chuckle.

"Not yet, but thanks for asking. I've been trying to get a hold of you. Where have you been?"

"Sorry, I haven't been checking my phone."

He glanced at the wall clock in the kitchen, then closed his eyes and pinched the bridge of his nose.

"Well, you fucking should."

His shoulders tensed as he listened to Blake sigh, then huff.

"At this point, you can delete my messages and I'll fill you in."

He wrinkled his lips and his eyebrows drew together.

"Sure."

He walked to the couch and plopped down.

"The hotel where I'm staying is down the street from where Elizabeth's friend Gabriella works. I ran into her. Nick! Elizabeth is in Madrid. I thought you would like to know."

He sat up on the couch.

"What?"

"Yeah! Marissa and I were sitting outside at a cafe near the hotel and Gabriella walked by. She gave me a second glance, because you know, I'm terribly good looking. Long story short, I told her you couldn't reach Elizabeth, and you thought she lost her job, etcetera, etcetera. Anyway, she tells me that Elizabeth is in Madrid. She probably flew out the day you last tried to reach her."

"Okay? Okay, that explains some things."

"Gabriella was reluctant to tell me at first, so I had to work my charm on her."

He rolled his eyes.

"Yeah, sure. I'm sure Marissa loved to see you do that."

Blake's laughter came over the phone.

"Actually, I told Gabriella you were very concerned, and she understood. Gabriella wasn't comfortable giving me a phone number for Elizabeth, but I thought I would let you know first that I found her."

"Thanks Blake. I owe you big."

"That you do."

He sighed and listened to Blake clear his throat.

"So, what are you going to do now?"

"I might have to book a flight to Madrid."

"That would be awesome to have you here. I could use your support."

"Nervous?"

"Yes. I didn't think I would be, but since I got here, I've been waiting for the right moment."

"I see. Well, you've got my support. Don't start the fireworks until I get there."

"Really? You're really coming to Madrid?"

There was relief in Blake's voice. He snorted and smiled.

"I'll leave as soon as I can. I'll send you a text message when I get my flight arranged."

"Great. Adiós pal."

"Bye Blake."

He held his phone in his lap and gazed at the screen even though it went dark. He tapped the screen and brought it back to life, then cleared out

Blake's old messages. An unread text message from an unknown source caught his eye. He tapped to read the text message.

The message read, "Hi Nick, this is Jenna, Elizabeth's former assistant. She'll be taking some time off. That's all I know. One of the last things she had me do was book her a flight to Madrid. I thought you might like to know."

He looked up from his phone. Blake was right to admonish him. He should have checked his messages. He gazed off at nothing in particular, then wrote a reply.

He wrote, "Thanks Jenna," then hit Send.

᪥

Nick took the first flight he could get to Madrid. He landed in Spain and sent Blake a text message that he arrived. He looked around the arrival area for Blake and finally spotted him. Blake grinned at him as though years had passed since he had last seen him. Blake looked older, or maybe he stood a little different, maybe a little taller. He was unsure, but he liked this new version. He was happy for his friend. The two men embraced and patted each other on their backs and shoulders.

It was near midnight in Madrid. Blake was quiet most of the ride to the hotel. Nick welcomed the silence. There would be plenty of time tomorrow to catch up and to see Marissa after she got off work. They both peered out of the taxi's windows at the night traffic and the passing city lights.

He closed his eyes. Between the flight and the taxi ride, fatigue had set in. There was a growing feeling of closeness to Elizabeth that came over him. He wanted to hold her and it seemed the closer he physically got to her, the more anxious he became. He needed time to figure out how he would handle things. A day with Blake to discuss everything is what he needed.

᪥

Blake and Nick sat outside at the cafe, where Blake and Marissa saw Gabriella. They were in t-shirts, shorts, and sneakers, and planned for a casual day. They sipped at their cups of coffee and ate chocolate con churros, like they had when they first met up with Elizabeth and Gabriella. Blake looked more comfortable than the first time they visited Madrid. He looked like he belonged. Nick never thought to ask Blake where he and Marissa would live, if everything worked out, and they got married. He always assumed Marissa would come to the United States. That assumption made him feel foolish and naïve. Madrid was wonderful. Blake and Marissa could have a great life here.

He smiled, sipped his coffee, and glanced at the people that walked by.

"I'm really glade you came," Blake said.

"Me too. I needed to get away. I never really got to thank you in person for covering for me at the wedding."

Blake snorted.

"You're welcome. You know—whatever it is—I would do what I can for you. Of course, that was one big mess. It made me doubt what I should do regarding Marissa and me."

Nick wrinkled his lips, and he ran his fingers through his hair.

"Man, I'm sorry Blake. I hope I didn't fuck up things for you. Where's your head at now?"

"It's right here."

Blake slipped a small velvet-covered box from his pocket and flipped it open to show him the engagement ring he got for Marissa. He grinned at Blake.

"Damn, that's beautiful."

Blake closed the box and put it back in his pocket.

"Thanks. I hope she likes it."

"Blake, Marissa is going to love it! Why the hell are you carrying it around with you? Why not lock it in the safe in your room?"

"I'm waiting for the right moment. It has to be perfect. Plus, I don't trust the room safe. Paranoia, I guess. The only time I locked it in the safe was when Marissa and I went dancing. I didn't want to lose it."

He nodded at Blake.

"So, what are your plans to make the right time happen?"

"I've been thinking about that. I've stopped by the restaurant where she works, had lunch, and waited for her shift to end. The place is nice. The vibe feels right. I want to propose to her there, while she's at work. What do you think?"

Nick wrinkled his lips, rubbed his chin, then he slowly nodded.

"Sounds great. I like it. Did you meet her parents?"

"Yes, I did, and they are wonderful people."

"Did you speak to Marissa's father?"

"No, and I'm glad I didn't."

"Oh?"

"Yeah, my plan was to get Juan Miguel to translate my intensions to Marissa's father. He informed me that getting a father's blessing to marry his daughter is not a tradition in Spain, and they frown on it."

Nick grimaced. Blake shrugged.

"Who knew, right?"

"Yeah. You better rethink your plan to propose to her at work. We need to find you a romantic spot that she'll love."

Blake's face lit up.

"I have just the place. El Retiro Park. She took me there the first time you and I came to Madrid. I remember her face lit up. She was so excited and happy to take me there."

He remembered visiting the Puerta del Sol with Elizabeth. She told him it was the square where the streets originated from, and she said that it could be their starting place. His heart warmed, and he smiled.

"Great idea, right?"

He woke from his reverie. His gaze had trailed off to peer at the people on the sidewalk, but he brought his attention back to Blake and smiled.

"Sounds perfect."

Blake finished eating.

"How long do you want to hang out here? There's no telling if Gabriella will pass by. Maybe it was a onetime thing."

Nick sipped the last of his coffee. He glanced up and down the street. There were a few women in business attire, but none of them were Gabriella. His eyebrows drew together, then his face softened.

"I came to Spain not just for Elizabeth, but for you and Marissa. It would be sad not to see Elizabeth, but I want you to know I'm here for you and Marissa. So, it's all good."

He smiled at Blake, but inside he was desperate to find Elizabeth.

"I'm sure you'll get to see her."

"Care to go for a walk? Maybe in the direction Gabriella went the day you spoke to her? She said she worked close by, right? We know she works for a newspaper here. She can't be too difficult to locate."

Blake nodded.

"Sure, I'm down. I'm happy you're here. With Marissa and Juan Miguel at work, there's no one to hang out with."

"Great, let's go."

Nick paid the check, and they strolled down the sidewalk.

~

Nick and Blake looked for any signs on the buildings, which there were none. Even if there were any, they would be in Spanish. After they crossed a side street, they decided they would go only a few more streets, then either try to ask someone, or try again another time. Although Nick agreed to try another time if they were unsuccessful, he knew he would search for Gabriella by himself if he had to. He needed to find Elizabeth. That's all that mattered, and hopefully Gabriella knew where she was staying.

A woman stood to the side of some curved steps that led up into a nondescript gray stone building. She wore an abstract printed dress that fell above her knees. The breeze lifted her long, dark curls. She smoked a cigarette and appeared to be reading something on her phone. She wore dark sunglasses, but when she placed them on top of her head, Blake grabbed Nick's arm.

"Hey, that's her!"

Gabriella put the cigarette to her lips and used both hands to type something on her phone. Nick glanced up at the building. It looked like all the others. He and Blake would have easily passed by it.

"Gabriella!"

He waved and called to her. Blake waved as well. She smiled and dropped her cigarette on the sidewalk, then stepped on it. She beamed when she saw them.

"Nick!"

Her voice was sweet, high, and musical. As he and Blake approached, she walked toward them and gave him a big hug and a kiss on both cheeks. He looked at Blake with a broad smile. She then gave Blake a brief hug and two quick kisses on each cheek.

"It's so nice to see you again."

She grinned, her eyes were on him, and occasionally she glanced at Blake. Blake stood there with his arms crossed and rocked back and forth, alternating his weight on either leg.

"Great to see you, too. Blake said that you work around here."

"Yes."

She pointed up the steps to the building behind her. He nodded and smiled. Then Blake, who was looking around, turned to Gabriella and smiled as well.

"Blake mentioned I was looking for Elizabeth. She left her job and condo, and frankly the country. I only had her work numbers, which were disconnected. Do you know where she is? Do you have a phone number where I can reach her?"

She smiled as if she were waiting for him to ask her that very question.

"Yes, of course. Lizzy is staying with me."

There was her nickname again. The name he desperately wanted to call her to know that he was close to her heart. He wondered why Elizabeth left without giving him a phone number where he could reach her.

"Has she said anything about me? Do you think she would want to see me?"

He put his hands in his pockets, and his arms stiffened. He braced for Gabriella's answer and was thankful he wore his sunglasses to hide his tired eyes. She shifted her stance.

"Politics, was what she said. They took some important accounts from her because of politics. As far as I know, she hasn't quit her job, nor did they fire her, but her company was very accommodating to allow her to take a leave of absence. Do you mind?"

She held up her pack of cigarettes. Both young men shook their heads no to not minding that she smoked, and no, to her offer for a cigarette. Nick suspected his father had something to do with Elizabeth's situation. Blake wrinkled his face while Nick stood without a word and seethed.

"Did Elizabeth say why they were being so nasty to her?" Blake asked.

Nick looked at both of them, then his gaze wandered briefly into the street.

"I'm sorry, I don't know. She didn't say."

She held her hands up and looked as baffled as both as both of them. After she lit her cigarette, she took a long drag. She tilted her head and touched her pinky nail to her teeth. Her eyes moved from Blake to Nick.

"Can we go to your place? I really need to see her. It would mean the world to me."

"Let's exchange numbers and I will speak with her tonight."

"Please?"

"Lizzy and I have a rule, especially when it comes to men, not to give out each other's contact information."

He sighed. Blake patted his shoulder.

"All right. Fair enough."

They exchanged phone numbers. He also gave her his room number and the name of the hotel where he was staying. She said she had to get back to work. They thanked her and headed back to the hotel.

27

Elizabeth sat on Gabriella's burgundy velvet sofa with her feet tucked under her. She had a plate of cheese in her lap and a glass of Port on the end table. The latest copies of El País and Vogue Spain sat on the cushions next to her. She always admired Gabriella's apartment, with its exposed brick, rough rustic wooden beams, and faded mahogany floors. It was vintage modern chic. The only elements with clean finished lines were the white painted balcony doors, the fireplace mantle, and the crown and base molding.

She lifted the glass of Port and took a drink while she went through the new email messages on her phone. Before her last trip to Madrid, she put out some job feelers for opportunities in both the United States and in Spain. Two companies in the US were interested. She would set up some interviews and maybe even cut her stay in Spain short, but there was one company in Madrid that wanted to meet with her. She would entertain that possibility first. The faint sound of the door as it clunked shut echoed from down the hallway.

"Hola."

The voice was Gabriella's. Her heels clacked on the hardwood floors.

"Hola," Elizabeth replied.

Gabriella stood in the entranceway with a broad smile and bright eyes.

"What?"

"You're not going to believe who I saw today."

Elizabeth sat the plate of cheese and glass of Port on the table and sat up.

"Who?"

Gabriella's eyes brightened. Irritated, Elizabeth held up her hands.

"Well?"

"Nick! Nick Evers."

She shifted on the sofa.

"What?"

"Yes, I was out having a cigarette, and they came up the sidewalk. Nick shouted my name. I was so surprised and happy to see him. His friend, Blake, too."

"Did Nick say why he was in Spain? Was there a girl with him?"

"No, no girl. Why?"

"He was to be married to a girl named Colette. He should be on his honeymoon, unless he's come to Spain for his honeymoon."

Gabriella tilted her head, and her eyebrows drew together. She sat at the other end of the sofa and took off her heels.

"I don't understand."

"Neither do I."

Elizabeth stroked the side of her face and neck.

"He said he had been trying to contact you. Does he not have your phone number?"

"Only my work number. I wasn't sure if I should give him my *personal* cellphone number."

"Why?"

She shrugged.

"I needed time to figure him out, I guess."

Gabriella's eyebrows rose.

"Nick gave me his phone number, and the name of the hotel where he's staying, including the room number."

Her eyes were bright with anticipation. Elizabeth picked up her wineglass and took a drink. She stared off into the room at nothing in particular. Gabriella huffed and scowled.

"Well? Call him."

Gabriella stood with her hands on her hips. Elizabeth raised her eyebrows and wrinkled her lips.

"I have moments where I'm all in, and I want to be all in, then I am scared that I'm headed down a dead end."

"Oh Lizzy, take a chance. Here's my phone if you want to read his text message."

She dropped her phone on top of the copy of El País, then picked up her shoes and headed down the hallway. After a moment, Elizabeth heard her in the kitchen. She hoped Gabriella would bring the bottle of wine out to the living room. She picked up Gabriella's phone. The name on his contact profile was 'Nicky Evers.' She shook her head and smirked.

He wrote, "Hi Gabriella. This is Nick Evers. It was great seeing you again. Please tell Elizabeth I need to speak to her. I would really appreciate it."

She wrinkled her lips and raised her eyebrows. They were going out tonight for dinner. She would think about her reply, if any. She picked up her empty glass of wine and the small plate with two pieces of uneaten cheese and headed to the kitchen. Once she found out from Gabriella where they were going tonight, she could figure out what to wear.

After a couple of hours of getting ready, they sat at a nearby restaurant close to Gabriella's apartment. They enjoyed small meals of fresh fish, rice topped with a tomato sauce and a fried egg, but they were out mostly drink and relax.

"I've been thinking about Nick. I—or rather we—should send him a text message."

"Great. I think *you* should send Nick a text message, then *you* both can communicate directly."

Elizabeth huffed.

"I'm not ready for that."

"C'mon Lizzy, be courageous."

"Please Gabriella."

Gabriella made a sour face. Elizabeth countered with her best puppy dog eyes.

"Please?"

"All right, all right."

Gabriella took her phone from her clutch handbag.

"How does this sound? 'Hi, Nick. I spoke to Elizabeth. She's surprised that you are here in Madrid.'"

"Okay, great. Ask about his wedding or honeymoon."

Gabriella's eyes narrowed.

"How about, 'She thought you should be on your honeymoon with Colette.'?"

"Send now?"

"No, make it sound more like you."

Gabriella tilted her head and wrinkled her lips. She shrugged, then added to the text message.

"Okay, how's this? Keep in mind I work for a newspaper, I'm supposed to be nosey… 'Who's Colette? Sorry, don't answer that. It's none of my business.'"

"Perfect. Enough nosey, but not too pushy."

Gabriella pressed the Send button. Elizabeth shifted on the bar stool, then sipped at her cocktail. Gabriella shook her head and appeared to fight the smile that formed on her face. It was useless. She smiled despite herself.

"Now what, Lizzy?"

She raised an eyebrow, then shrugged.

"Now, we wait."

Gabriella's phone chimed with a new text message alert.

"Oh!"

Both women stared wide-eyed at each other.

Nick's reply said, "Colette and I were engaged, but we split up. She's not the one for me. I've been trying to reach Elizabeth, that's why I came to Madrid to find her. Please tell her."

Although Gabriella read Nick's message aloud, she reiterated part of it.

"Nick says he came to Madrid to find *you*. He said to please tell you. Okay, I did, now what?"

"Yeah, I heard you the first time."

She shifted on the bar stool. Gabriella laughed and grinned.

"Are you nervous, Lizzy?"

"Shut up."

"Please remember, I'm helping you. Now, what do we write next? Oh, Nick, I can not wait to be swept up in your arms and for you to take me to bed."

"You better not say that."

Gabriella held her phone away from her.

"Why? Is it not sexy enough?"

"Just don't reply."

"Are you going to be nice to me?"

Her shoulders slumped, and she cocked her head.

"I'm always nice to you. Please don't reply. Just let it drop until I can think."

"We are thinking now and if you order us more drinks, we will think even better."

Elizabeth wrinkled her lips. Gabriella shrugged, as if her suggestion was a serious one.

"I have to say something. How about a simple, 'I will let her know.'?"

"Sure. Fine."

Gabriella tapped the message and hit Send before Elizabeth could protest. She then waved to the bartender. After they ordered another round of drinks, Gabriella leaned toward her.

"If you change your mind and want to pour your heart out to him, I have him right here."

She waved her phone and laughed while Elizabeth shook her head.

Nick wanted to hide in his hotel room and order room service, something he would have never done. Blake squished the idea and demanded he go out with him and Marissa for drinks and dancing. His room was down the hallway from Blake's, and he knew Blake would pound on the door to get him to come out. He dragged himself to the bathroom to get a shower. If going out would help him get his mind off of things, he welcomed it. He worried Isabella might be there, but he was relieved when Blake told him it would only be the three of them. He considered visiting her, but worried it might only add confusion to an already stressful situation.

Before he could think too much about things, he was in the taxi, dressed for a night on the town with Blake and Marissa. Both he and Blake wore button up shirts, sports jackets and casual linen trousers. Marissa had on a sexy little black dress. He recalled her wearing more colorful outfits. Maybe it was something Blake got for her. She looked stunning and more mature than when he last saw her.

At the club, he hung out at the bar while they danced. It was nice to see them get along so well. He looked at his phone and wondered how long it would take Gabriella to speak to Elizabeth. After he sat and finished his beer, he received a new text message notification. It was from Gabriella.

She wrote, "Hi, Nick. I spoke to Elizabeth. She's surprised that you are here in Madrid. She thought you should be on your honeymoon with Colette. Who's Colette? Sorry, don't answer that. It's none of my business."

He ran his fingers through his hair and chewed on his lower lip.

He replied, "Colette and I were engaged, but we split up. She's not the one for me. I've been trying to reach Elizabeth, that's why I came to Madrid to find her. Please tell her."

After he hit Send, he stared at his phone. Was she even with Elizabeth? He chewed his bottom lip. A text message alert came over his phone.

Gabriella replied, "I will let her know."

"Fuck, that's all?"

He closed his eyes and pinched the bridge of his nose. They must not be together. Relax, he told himself. Elizabeth went through some tough shit at work, cut her some slack.

There was a brief pause in the music. Blake and Marissa bounded up to him. They fought to catch their breaths and their faces glistened with perspiration. He put on a smile.

"You two look like you're having a great time. I feel like I'm cramping your style."

Blake squeezed his shoulder.

"Nonsense."

Both Blake and Marissa took sips of their drinks while they caught their breaths. He leaned back against the bar and sipped at a fresh bottle of beer. Blake gazed at him. He raised an eyebrow.

"What?"

Blake chuckled.

"You look like you could use something stronger than that beer."

He snorted.

"It doesn't matter. What can I do about anything? I guess I just need to go with the flow."

"Good. Maybe you should. I don't enjoy seeing you stressed out. You used to never let shit bother you. That was my thing."

He smiled and glanced at Blake.

"Does this mean you're going to join us on the dance floor?"

"Yes, Nick, yes," Marissa said.

She smiled and tugged at his arm, then pouted when she was unable to pry him from the bar. He smiled and shook his head. Before he could protest further, Blake grabbed his other arm, and they all moved to the dance floor.

Club goers packed the dance floor, and there was little room to move, but the three managed. He smiled despite himself, as he saw how at ease and how much fun they were having. Tomorrow, Blake would spend the day with Marissa under the guise they would meet Nick and Juan Miguel later, and have dinner some place nice. That was the story Blake told Marissa.

Nick and Juan Miguel waited with the photographer, Daniela, in El Retiro Park, behind the Monument to Alfonso XII for Marissa and Blake to arrive. It was the spot where Blake wanted to propose to Marissa. Daniela took a few pictures of Nick in the area where Blake was to propose to Marissa, so she could get her camera's exposure settings dialed in. Although she spoke mostly in Spanish, with a few English words, he could tell by her eyes and her body language that she flirted with him. A few times, he tugged on Juan Miguel's arm to drag him into the frame. She usually gestured for Juan Miguel to stand off to the side. He finally gave up and let her take pictures of him.

"Okay, sure-sure."

Juan Miguel chuckled as he watched Nick pose. He also kept an eye out for the couple, as the three of them were supposed to be hidden until after Marissa said, "Yes." Providing she would say, "Yes." In the morning when Blake and Nick had breakfast, Blake's joy and hopefulness struck him. His own personal apprehensions crept in, but he avoided sharing his worries with his best friend. It mattered little now. Juan Miguel spotted them as they strolled up the walkway. The couple held hands, and both smiled as they approached.

"Hurry, date prisa," Juan Miguel said.

He and Daniela ducked behind some hedges, and Nick hurried to join them. Juan Miguel grinned and Daniela covered her mouth. Her two cameras dangled from straps slung on her shoulders. Nick chuckled and shook his head as they hunched over. The hedge was tall enough to hide him, and he was taller than them.

The couple stopped at the entrance to the towering monument. Blake held her and they kissed. No one could hear what they were saying. Nick smiled to himself and pinched at the hedge needles. Juan Miguel and Daniela whispered in Spanish.

Earlier, Nick sent a text message to Gabriella to let her know he would be at El Retiro Park for Blake's proposal. He also gave her the name of the restaurant where they would celebrate at if Marissa said, Yes. Gabriella replied, sending her best wishes to Blake, but said nothing about Elizabeth. He struggled to be positive for his best friend on his big day. God knows, he owed Blake big time for his wedding catastrophe. If all he had to do was smile and cheer, by God, he would do that for Blake and Marissa. As he watched his friend, he felt small.

Juan Miguel gasped when Blake went down on his knee. Daniela hurried and slipped around the hedge, ready with her one camera that had the longer lens. Marissa squealed when Blake showed her the ring. She nodded yes before she could bring herself to speak. Nick smiled as he watched them. Daniela was already moving in and taking photographs. Juan Miguel and Nick stepped out from behind the hedges to clap, cheer, and congratulate the couple.

Daniela gave Nick her business card before she departed, which brought a broad smile to Juan Miguel's face. She promised to have the photographs ready for the couple to review by tomorrow. They gave Daniela a goodbye hug, and she disappeared down one of the park's paths with her two cameras slung over her shoulders.

"Let's go celebrate! I've got us a reservation at a very nice restaurant here in the park."

"Wow? Thanks buddy."

Blake and Nick hugged. Everyone was hungry. They followed Juan Miguel through the park to the restaurant.

Joyful laughter from the table where the newly engaged couple and friends dined drew the attention of the other patrons at El Pabellón. Nick wondered if Blake and Marissa would ever let go of one another, or if they would drink and eat with only their free hands. They held hands on top of the white linen-covered table to show off Marissa's ring. She smiled and bashfully shrugged. Her giddiness was palpable and contagious. Every time she grinned, everyone else would grin. Juan Miguel and Nick took turns making toasts to the couple.

After they ate, the three men shared old college stories. Marissa waited for Juan Miguel to translate, after which she erupted with laughter. Nick kept things clean. He avoided mentioning any of Blake's past womanizing. He smiled as he watched Blake and Marissa interact. They are going to be a great couple. The dessert that Marissa ordered to share with Blake arrived. Juan Miguel and Nick skipped dessert and ordered drinks instead. While they waited for the server to return, Nick excused himself from the table.

He stood outside the men's bathroom and checked his phone. He had new text and voice messages. The ones from his parents, he ignored for the moment. Soon, though, they would contact Blake and then he would have to fill them in on where he was. There was a new message from Gabriella, and one from an unknown source. He tapped on the one from Gabriella.

She wrote, "Please congratulate Blake for me on his engagement. I wish him and Marissa the best."

There was nothing after that. No mention of Elizabeth. His eyebrows drew together, and he huffed. He closed her message and looked at the list of new unread messages. The one labeled unknown caught his eye. He hesitated before he tapped it. His lips parted when he read the first four words.

The text message said, "Hello Nick. It's Elizabeth. I had to surrender my business cellphone. You can reach me at this number. It's my personal phone. I'm sorry I've been out of touch. There's been a lot going on in my life, and it seems yours as well. I thought you were marrying Colette. I'm sorry to hear things didn't work out."

He raked his fingers through his hair and squeezed the back of his neck. His eyes burned as he read Elizabeth's text message.

He wrote, "Elizabeth, where are you? I've missed you so much. I need to see you."

His thumb hovered over the Send button. His message sounded desperate. He huffed and tilted his head. Knots formed in his shoulders and neck. There was nothing left for him. All he could be was sincere. But he had been sincere. Doubt crept in. He locked the screen of his phone, his message unsent. His eyes felt wet when he blinked. Out in the dining room, Blake, Marissa, and Juan Miguel waited for him. He glanced at the bar. The seats were half filled with a mix of Spaniards and foreigners. His phone chimed with a new text message alert. It was from unknown again.

The message read, "Hi."

He glanced across the bar to consider how he might reply, but there she was, at the end of the bar. He blinked twice. She appeared like a ghost. Elizabeth sat there with a warm, subtle smile. She ran her fingertips through the ends of her long, dark chestnut curls. Light reflected off the mirrored wall behind the glass shelves where the bottles of various liquors sat. Her crystal blue diamond eyes sparkled. She wore an elegant, strapless, black cocktail dress. Bracelets adorned her forearm. She rested her chin on her fingertips. Her cellphone sat on the bar in front of her.

Two older couples, who looked like foreigners, maybe even tourists, were at the bar. Both men stood behind the seated women they accompanied. All four of them chatted, laughed, and drank. They must have hid her from view. His chest pounded, but it was a moment where he felt he could suddenly breathe again. His lips curled into a tight-lipped smile, then he slipped his phone into his pocket. He moved magnetically to her, his eyes never left hers. He would die if she vanished.

She stood when he was at her side.

"Elizabeth. I thought I would never see you again. I missed you more than you can imagine."

"I missed you too."

They wrapped their arms around one another in a sudden hungry embrace, then she touched his wet cheek, while he had his arms around her waist. Their lips met in a moist desperate kiss, and their breaths became one. Her eyes were glassy when she looked at him. He grinned at her through his tears.

"Stop that."

She patted his chest. She ran her thumb over his cheek to wipe away the tears, then took a tissue from her handbag and dabbed under her eyes. He chuckled softly.

"Blake, Marissa, and Juan Miguel are here. Will you please join us? Because if you don't, I'll have to explain later where I disappeared to. I'm not losing you this time."

She laughed, then nodded.

When they walked out into the dining room, Blake saw them first, and he clapped. Marissa and Juan Miguel looked confused until they saw Nick holding hands with this mysterious and gorgeous woman. They glanced at Blake, then clapped as well. By the time they got to the table, everyone in the restaurant looked and spoke in hushed tones.

Nick introduced Elizabeth. Everyone gave her a warm greeting. Juan Miguel apologized, but he needed to leave. He kissed both Marissa and Blake on both cheeks, then shook Nick and Elizabeth's hands before he departed.

Marissa showed Elizabeth her engagement ring. Her eyes brightened and her tone was sweet when she spoke to Marissa in Spanish. Nick smiled as he watched the both of them. Blake gripped Nick's shoulder and leaned toward him.

"I'm so happy you found her."

"Me, too."

"If you could see your face. If that's not love, I don't know what is. It's a good look for you. Of course, it begs the question, what will you do about it?"

Both women glanced at the men with looks of curiosity.

"What are you two scheming up?"

"Nothing. We are enjoying the moment."

Blake raised his glass to make a toast.

"To a wonderful evening, and the company of beautiful, intelligent women."

They all picked up their cocktail glasses.

"Salud everyone."

After the group finished their drinks, Nick got the check, and they all drifted out into El Retiro Park. Marissa and Blake walked ahead to give Nick and Elizabeth some privacy. Elizabeth looped her arm around Nick's. Loose stones on the pathway crunched under their feet. The air was warm with the pleasant scent of the trees and shrubs. Nick was on top of the world, but shadows lurked in the back of his mind. He worried how long things would last.

"Stay the night with me."

He was afraid to look at her. He braced for an answer that might crush him. They both gazed ahead as they walked. She was quiet. As they got closer to the park's entrance, their footsteps on the loose stones was replace by the city's evening traffic. His thoughts raced. Before she could answer, he spoke.

"Even if I can only watch you sleep."

The corner of her lips curled up.

"That's sweet, but I have to tell you something."

His shoulders stiffened, and his eyebrows drew together.

"I'm actually leaving tomorrow afternoon. I had this long-planned trip to Peru to visit Machu Picchu."

"The ruins in your photographs?"

"Yes. I've had this trip planned months before we first met."

"I see."

"After my visit there, I'm heading back to Atlanta. I've got to find out if I still have a job."

He raised his eyebrows and chuckled.

"Me too. I bet I'm not the first son to be fired by his father."

"I doubt that's going to happen. Things will work out."

He snorted.

"I'm not sure I want things to work out at Hale."

"Oh?"

He stopped, and she turned to look at him. She still held his arm.

"Elizabeth? Whatever your plans are, I want *you* to stay the night with me. Will you stay with me?"

She squeezed his arm.

"Okay."

28

The boutique hotel where Nick stayed was far less extravagant than the one near the Neptune Fountain and the Prado Museum. Although the hotel lacked a dining hall and a swank rooftop pool and bar, it was cozier with a casual vibe.

He opened the balcony doors when they got to his room. The faint sound of a distant car horn and tires on the cobblestone street below filtered into the space.

"Sorry, no beautiful street music."

Elizabeth stood with her arms crossed. She smiled and shrugged.

"You can't have everything."

"Yeah, that's true."

He sighed. She sat on the sofa. There were a few clothing items slung over the back. She eyed them briefly, then her gaze fell on one piece.

"I couldn't decide what to wear."

She ran her hand over the slender, dark teal tie that lay on the back of the sofa.

"This looks familiar."

"I wore it the first time we had lunch together. It seems like a lifetime ago. I hoped it would bring me luck."

She smiled as she gazed at the tie.

"That was a nice lunch meeting, but I have a confession."

"Oh?"

She laughed.

"What? What's so funny?"

"That day, I had Jenna call me and pretend there was an emergency at the office. Terrible, I know."

She rolled her eyes.

"That was downright rotten."

He smiled and shook his head.

"If it's any consolation, I do that with all my new clients. Jenna calls me forty-five minutes into my lunch meetings."

"Oh? I'm a client?"

She chuckled and wrinkled her lips.

"Don't be silly. Most of my clients are rather boring, and many of the new ones ramble on, so I need a means to make a polite get-a-way. In your case, I didn't know what to make of you. I had to be cautious. You might have been psycho? You looked awfully edgy to me. Or it could have been worse."

He sat and slid in next to her, then put his arm on the back of the sofa.

"And now?"

"Oh, it's much, much worse."

Her breath caressed his face as she spoke. Their lips pushed together, soft and warm. Their breaths were the sound of a gentle tide on a moonlit beach.

She brushed her fingertips against his cheek. She unbuttoned his shirt, slow and methodical, until her fingers could venture in to caress the contours of his chest and glide down his ribs. He slipped off his shirt. Light from the table lamp highlighted the peaks of muscle in his upper body, from his broad shoulders, his full chest, flat stomach and strong arms. Her gaze travelled his body from his navel to his lips, to his eyes. Her lips parted as she drew in a breath.

He kissed her neck and shoulder while he unzipped the back of her strapless black cocktail dress. She put her hand on her chest to keep her dress in place. It was more of a tease than a modest gesture. She reached down to remove her heels, but he stopped her.

He slipped off her pumps. When his fingers circled her sheer nylon covered legs, his cock stiffened. His soft linen trousers yielded and did nothing to hide his enthusiasm. She pushed him back onto the sofa and pressed her stocking covered toes against the bulge in his trousers. He sucked in a breath.

She unbuckled and unzipped his trousers and, when she pulled down his briefs, his cock sprung free. It astounded him how hard she made him. She tugged his pants and underwear to the middle of his thighs, then she stood and slipped free of her black dress. Her bracelets glimmered and chimed as they rode up and down her forearm. His lips parted at the sight of her, in her coffee-colored sheer stockings held up by a pastel pink garter belt. Below her garter belt was the biggest surprise. She wore no panties. Her sex was smooth shaven except for a triangular patch of delicate chestnut hairs on her pubis.

She straddled him as he held the back of the sofa and armrest. He lay there in an awkward position with his pants and underwear half down his thighs. Her gaze told him that there would be no more waiting and no more games. Her hips flexed and her velvety sex slid over the length of his cock. His thick, long cock lurched with every stroke of her slick, wet folds. She ground her clit against his rigid shaft. With each movement, he sucked in and held his breath. Her gaze penetrated his as she moved her hips with increased speed.

He caressed her thigh and massaged her breast. Her smooth skin, the firmness of her muscles as they flexed within his grasp, and the texture of the sheer nylon stocking drove him to the edge. He groaned and muttered.

"Fuck."

He reached for his sports jacket and retrieved a condom from the pocket. She took it from him, removed the wrapper, and rolled it over his cock, then raised her hips and mounted him. He slipped inside her with ease. She moaned as she took in his full length. As she moved, her heavy breaths turned to soft moans. Their fingers interlaced as her body rose and fell atop of his. It took only a moment before her body tensed and trembled, and then she climaxed.

He held her buttocks and stood with his cock still inside her. She gasped wide-eyed with excitement and wrapped her arms around his shoulders.

Their open mouths met and tongues tasted one another's desperate desire. He pinned her to the nearest wall and fucked her there.

"Oh, fuck me," she cried.

After she came, she kept her arms around him and kissed him deep. His climax followed close behind hers and his thighs trembled. He struggled to hold her while his cock jolted within the grasp of her inner walls.

He slipped free and lowered her. They embraced against the wall. His heart hammered and heavy breaths passed over his lips. They kissed. Then he grimaced.

"I think I got an ass cramp."

She burst out laughing. Her laughter echoed on the plaster walls.

Afterwards, they showered together before they slipped into bed. She curled her body into his and he held her until her breathing became heavy and she drifted off to sleep. He breathed in the scent of her hair and gazed out into the shadowy gloom. She would leave him tomorrow. He could talk her into having breakfast with him, but there would be no way she would cancel her trip to Peru. Tomorrow, he would think of something. He kissed her shoulder and the back of her head, then he closed his eyes. Something good had to come. Tonight, though, she was there in his arms. That was all he ever wanted.

When he woke in the morning, she was gone. His chest tightened until he heard her peeing in the bathroom. When she stood at the sink, he joined her. They gazed at their reflections. His behind hers. She wore his dark teal tie knotted loosely around her neck and it hung between her breasts. With his hands on her hips, he placed soft kisses on her shoulder like spring raindrops. His arousal grew and touched the base of her buttocks.

She rummaged through his toiletry case and dug out a condom. She slid it over his swollen cock, then she turned back around and leaned over the sink. He ran his fingertips down her spine, caressed her ass cheeks, then parted them and eased into her.

After breakfast, she got a cab, and he watched her disappear again. She had taken his dark teal tie and told him she would keep it as a memento. He smiled when he thought of her sassy expression when she spoke about the tie.

They agreed to get together when they both got back to Atlanta, but he thought he could do better than that. The wait would be unbearable. He needed to see Blake, and soon. The first thing he would do when he got back to his hotel room was to look into flights to Peru.

29

"What's the big secret? Why do you need hiking boots and outdoor clothing? Are you planning a trip to the mountains? If so, I'm down. Where are we going? Peñalara? Pico Almanzor?"

Blake crossed his arms and shifted his weight from one leg to the other. Nick remained silent as he sat on the bench in the sporting goods store's shoe department.

"Well? Nick? Are you going to give me a hint?"

He smiled as he slipped on a pair of hiking shoes the salesman brought out. He was an older gentleman, who treated them with patience and smiles. Blake was sure they annoyed the man, and probably rolled his eyes every time he had to service tourists, especially impatient Americans. The salesman stood back while Blake pelted Nick with questions. He finally answered.

"I'm actually going alone, but I don't hope to be alone when I get there."

"Oh, goodie, a riddle."

Nick sat with his finger inside the heel of the shoe and struggled to get his foot into it. He looked up and chuckled.

"I told you I had an awesome night with Elizabeth. She told me last night after dinner that she was leaving the next day for Peru."

"Did she tell you why?"

"She had the trip planned for some time. I guess she didn't expect to be coming to Spain. Anyway, she's visiting Machu Picchu. It's the site of ancient Inca ruins."

Blake stood with his hands on his hips, and nodded with his eyebrows knit together, then he pursed his lips.

"Don't you have a picture of Machu Picchu in your bedroom?"

"Yes."

"Wait, a second. Didn't you buy that picture with Colette?"

Nick sighed, and he wrinkled his lips.

"Yes."

His eyebrows rose, and he grinned. Nick raised an eyebrow and gazed at him.

"Don't you see? It's fate. Okay, I get it. You're going to Peru to meet up with Elizabeth."

His mouth hung open, and his eyes were wide as if he won some game show prize, while Nick's shoulders slumped.

"Okay, now you know. Will you help me pick out some clothes?"

"Sure buddy. What about your plane ticket?"

Nick smiled.

"I booked my flight after having breakfast with her."

"Does she know what you're up to?"

"Not yet. I wanted to make sure I could get a plane ticket first."

"That's sensible."

Nick stood and nodded to the salesman that he wanted the hiking shoes. The salesman, whose English was a little slow and choppy but serviceable, told him he would hold the box for him while he finished shopping.

~

After Nick and Blake left the sporting goods store, they sat at a nearby restaurant for lunch. Nick had until that evening before his flight departed. While they waited for the food to come, he checked his phone. Among the barrage of messages from his parents, there was one from Elizabeth.

She wrote, "I had a wonderful time last night, and this morning. I'm at the airport waiting to board my flight. Thank you again for offering to see me off at the airport, but it wasn't necessary. Did you get together with Blake? I can't wait to see you again. Xo."

He smiled, then wrote, "Would you like some company?"

A new text message alert from her surprised him. She never replied that quick. He imagined her waiting with nothing else to do.

She wrote, "That would be amazing. It's around a twelve hour flight, are you sure?"

He replied, "Will you wait for me?"

She wrote, "Yes! Get your airline ticket and you can stay with me."

He replied, "Great. Send me a message when you get there, and I'll let you know when I arrive. Have a safe flight. Xo."

She wrote, "Can't wait! I've been wanting to see Machu Picchu with someone special. I'm happy that someone is you. Have a safe flight, too. Speak soon. Xo."

He grinned and his eyes became wet and glassy.

"Dude, are you okay?"

He glanced up at Blake. Blake had his phone out as well and was probably sending text messages to Marissa.

"I'm good. In fact—I'm better than good."

Blake's eyebrows rose.

"Oh?"

"She's at the airport waiting for her flight to Peru. I asked if she would like me to join her, and she said, 'Yes.'"

"That's awesome. I'm so happy for you. You know, I worried you were wasting your time."

He snorted and turned his head from side to side. His lips curled into a soft smile. Blake gave him a reassuring smile. Everything he needed to do before his evening departure raced through his mind. There was one last thing he wanted to do.

~

Nick and Blake headed back to the hotel. On their way, a storefront caught Nick's eye.

"Hey, let's go in here and have a look."

Blake looked at the store windows and wrinkled his lips.

"Are you sure you have time?"

He glanced at his watch.

"We have time. I want to get something for Elizabeth."

"Oh okay, sure. That sounds nice."

"You know, I was never good at choosing gifts for girls. You always have a better eye than me. Maybe you can help me pick something out?"

He shrugged as he held his shopping bags from the sporting goods store. Blake winked at him.

"Sure, I got your back."

Blake held the door and they went inside.

The jewelry store was narrow but deep. The mirrored walls and all the glass displays gave the store's interior a larger appearance. Long rectangular cases lined both sides, and toward the back were two semi-circular cases. Customers of various stripes, some in business dress, others in casual traveler's attire, conversed with the jewelers on the other side of the cases. The male jewelers wore dark gray or navy suits, and women wore elegant but simple black dresses, some cut shorter than others. Necklaces, wristwatches, bracelets, earrings, and more, filled the displays with black velvet covered shelves.

Blake walked ahead to assist him in finding a gift for Elizabeth. A lovely looking older woman, perhaps his mother's age, greeted them with a warm smile.

"Hello and welcome," the woman said.

He smiled at her and assumed she knew they were Americans.

"Hello," he said.

He gazed toward the back of the store. Large framed pictures of couples, men in tuxedos and women in brides' gowns, hung behind the semi-circular cases in the back. He knew what the cases contained—engagement and wedding rings. He wanted to go straight to them. Then Blake waved him over to one of the nearby counters.

"Look at these bracelets. These are really nice. She wore bracelets at dinner, so you know she likes them. I don't think she wore a necklace."

His eyebrows rose at his friend's keen observation.

"Yeah, those look very nice. I never remember a time when she wore a necklace. Does that mean she doesn't like them?"

Blake shrugged.

"Who knows? Maybe, maybe not. I'm only going by what I've seen her wear."

He wrinkled his lips and sighed.

"Let's keep looking, but keep those in mind."

"Got it."

He went to the opposite side of the store to look at the wristwatches, where there were no free jewelers to assist him, so he could look around undisturbed. As he inspected the ladies' watches, he thought it was too much to get her a watch, and it would be less romantic. She had a nice Rolex already. It was a ridiculous consideration. When he reached the far end of the counter, there were the displays of engagement and wedding rings.

A stunningly beautiful woman behind the counter smiled at him. She had big dark brown eyes, full lips, long, dark hair that descended in curls past her shoulders, and a body of a runway or swimsuit model. She was tall with long legs and a well balanced, proportionate figure. The scoop neckline of her dress revealed the tops of her breasts.

"Hello. How are you today?" she asked.

As beautiful as the woman was, he found himself drawn to gaze at the selection of rings.

"Hi. I'm well, thank you. I would like to see your engagement rings."

"Certainly. The ones you see here are his-and-her matching sets for both the bride and groom. The single engagement rings are in this other cabinet."

The woman gestured, and he moved to look into the other glass case. He bumped into Blake, who was now at his side.

"Wow, you're down here?"

"Yeah, let's just say you and Marissa inspired me."

He winked at Blake, but Blake was smiling at the beautiful woman behind the glass counter. He elbowed him.

"Ahem?"

Blake turned to him. The woman caressed her forearm. Gold bracelets adorned her long slender arms. Her eyes were bright, inviting, and attentive. She waited to answer their questions, if they had any. Blake looked as though he had a few questions for her, which unnerved Nick.

An older gentleman came over and touched the woman's arm. He whispered, but Nick caught the woman's name, Clara. As Clara and the older gentlemen conversed, Blake elbowed Nick.

"Did you see her?"

He spoke in a hushed tone.

"Yes, Blake."

He smiled. His gaze split between Blake and the engagement rings.

"Fuck Nick. I've never seen such a beautiful woman. At least, not in person. What is she doing here?"

He snorted and he wrinkled his lips.

"Blake, she works here, okay?"

"Sure, yeah-yeah, I get that, but why?"

"How am I supposed to know? Besides, aren't you forgetting about Marissa?"

"Ah? No, of course not. A guy can look right?"

"Sure, look, if you don't end up creeping her out. And try not to drool on me."

Blake snorted and chuckled.

"Can I help you find something?" The woman asked.

He looked up, but the woman, Clara, had addressed Blake, who stood there with wide-eyes and a grin.

"You certainly can," he said.

"We have many beautiful engagement rings. Please have a look and if you would like to see something, I would be happy to show you."

Nick shook his head. Clara came forward so her hips rested with the top edge of the glass display and she leaned over toward Blake. She peered down at the neat arrangement of rings. Nick glanced at Blake. Blake's eyes were on something other than the rings.

"They are very splendid," Blake said.

She glanced up at Blake. She wore a mask of professionalism, but Nick was sure she knew what she was doing.

"Which ones would you like to see?" She asked.

Blake was speechless. Nick snorted. He brought his focus back to the rings and Elizabeth. He spotted two he thought matched her taste or, at least, would look good on her. Now he had to wait for the side-show to end.

"Well, you see, my friend has trouble choosing gifts for ladies. So I'm actually here to help *him* out."

Blake patted Nick on the back.

"That's right, and so far, you have done a wonderful job. Can I *please* look at these two rings?"

He pointed down into the display and gave Clara a polite smile, then glared at Blake.

"Beautiful. Your friend already knows what he likes."

Blake tilted his head and smirked. Although she addressed Blake, her gaze was all on him. She unlocked the case and removed the two rings. He knew right away which one of the two.

"It's the pear-shaped one. That's the one."

Her eyes widened, and her lips parted.

"Oh? So quick."

She glanced at Blake.

"I see your friend *knows* what he wants."

Her eyes glinted as though she was the one Nick was going to propose to. She held the ring by its delicate loop and presented it to him. Nick held the ring and examined it. He tried to imagine Elizabeth's ring size. He would rather the ring be too big. That was also the advice he heard when he and Colette shopped for her ring. He sighed and pushed the memory from his thoughts.

"See how it looks on her finger?" Blake said.

Nick was sure Clara's fingers were thinner than Elizabeth's. He only wanted to see it on Elizabeth's finger.

"That won't be necessary. I'll take it."

Clara's face brightened.

"Wonderful. I think it's one of our more beautiful rings. She'll love it."

He was sure Elizabeth would love it too, but more than that, he wished he could be sure she would say, "Yes."

Before his flight to Peru, he planned on spending the rest of the day with Blake. Blake wanted to go drinking, but he talked him out of it. He promised Blake they would get together when they got back to Atlanta. So a light dinner and a single beer or glass of wine was all he wanted and hoped Blake would choose some place mellow where he could think and relax with his best friend.

30

When the plane touched down in Cusco, Nick took out his phone. He read Elizabeth's text message she sent hours ago when her plane landed. It reminded him of the first time when he followed her to Madrid. This time, she would be there waiting for him. He smiled through his sleep stupor and rocked his shoulders up and down to work the knots out of them. As the plane taxied toward the terminal, he sent her a text message that he had arrived.

While he waited to deplane, he received a new text message alert. She sent a welcome to Peru greeting along with her hotel information and room number. There was excitement in her words, as much as there was for him to read them.

The terminal was bright, clean, and modern. He lumbered his way through until he found where the taxis were waiting. She told him it was a twenty-minute ride to the hotel, which he was grateful for. To his dismay, the taxi was a compact car, which cramped his knees, and jarred his tailbone as the driver navigated the streets of Cusco. He wished he had been more selective and jumped into a Toyota or some other midsize sedan. He had no clue who manufactured the tiny boxy car he rode in.

When they finally arrived at the hotel, he was eager to jump out of the car, but fought tingly, blood-starved legs as he climbed out from the back seat. The driver opened the trunk, and he removed his luggage. He paid the driver, who smiled, then sped away. He was eager and joyful to see her again, just as much as he was eager and joyful to lie in bed when he got to the room. She had a seven-hour jump on him. He imagined she had time to settle in, get something to eat, take a nap, and relax before he got there.

She greeted him with a broad smile and held the door for him to enter her room. Their embrace was immediate and their mouths opened to receive one another's kiss. After they made their amorous greeting, he stood back from her to take her in. His eyes widened. She had her hair tied back and wore lightweight thermal leggings, a matching zip-up top, and thin ankle socks. If they were in Atlanta, she looked dressed for an autumn jog in some city park. It was the most casual he had ever seen her. She had traded her astute sense of fashion for clothing he could imagine a journalist might wear on a faraway excursion. Her casual appearance put him at ease. Only when he thought about the ring, he became anxious.

"You look great. You always look great."

He grinned at her.

"And you look beat."

She laughed.

"C'mon and get settled in."

Her eyes were bright with an honest, child-like enthusiasm. She rolled his carry-on out of the way while he took his jacket and shoes off, then they both sat on the sofa.

"I trust what's in your bag is not a tuxedo and oxfords."

He chuckled, rubbed his eyes, and shook his head no.

"Okay, I'm anxious to see what you packed."

He thought of the ring, and he struggled to keep his composure.

"Are you okay? You're not drunk, are you?"

He tilted his head and wrinkled his lips.

"Of course not. I'm happy to see you and probably a little giddy from the flight to get here."

She nodded, but he knew she already knew this.

"Fair enough. It is near midnight. Did you know we are an hour behind Atlanta's time?"

"Oh? That's interesting. No, I didn't."

"I got you something to eat, since it's too late to go out, and we have an early morning start ahead of us."

She went to the room's small table where a plastic bag sat. She took out some bottles of water and a container. He joined her at the table.

"It's causa. It's potatoes, chicken, and spices."

"It looks like some sort of dessert."

"It's cold like potato salad. It's good."

She smiled as she watched him eat. When he raised his eyebrows and nodded, she chuckled. She rested her chin on her palm. He squeezed her thigh under the table.

"I'm sure you can't wait to hear about what we're doing tomorrow. We have a lot of traveling to do."

He raised his eyebrows, but his mouth was full, so he just looked at her.

"We'll catch an early morning train to Aguas Calientes, where we can get a shuttle to take us to the ruins."

He swallowed.

"As long as it's relaxing, I'm good."

"The next couple of days after we visit Machu Picchu, we can explore the city of Cusco."

"Sounds wonderful."

All he could think about was his proposal. He could do it now, here in the hotel room. He shook the idea from his thoughts. Pins crawled up his back. He needed to sleep, besides the time had to be right, and it had to be grand. The food had sated him and made him even more drowsy. Sleep weighed on him like a heavy blanket.

"Thank you for that. I don't know about you, but I'm ready to crash, especially since we have to get the train first thing in the morning."

"That's right. All you'll need to worry about is getting a shower and getting dressed in the morning. I already packed a backpack for us with water, snacks and whatever else I thought we might need."

She stood, and he hugged her around her waist. He lifted her shirt and kissed her stomach. She squealed when he lifted her off her feet and carried her to bed.

~

Elizabeth held Nick's hand and guided him to the first lookout area of Machu Picchu. As they got closer, his eyes widened.

"Oh."

The view was the same spot as the photograph on display in her condo. She tugged his arm and put her head on his shoulder.

"Magnificent, isn't it?"

"It's incredible. Amazing for such a place so high in the mountains."

He felt the small jewelry box through the cloth of his pocket. She retrieved her camera from the backpack and took a couple of photographs of him with the ruins. They switched, and he photographed her. An older Australian gentleman greeted them and offered to take their picture. The man took a picture of them with her camera.

"Would you mind taking one more of us?" Nick asked.

He stood in front of her and gave the man a wink. The man's eyebrows drew together, but then he smiled.

"Sure, I don't mind."

He gave the camera back to the man and whispered.

"Please wait to take the shot. You'll know when."

The man took the camera and nodded.

Nick returned to Elizabeth, but with his back to the gentleman who held her camera.

"I love you Elizabeth."

Her eyes brightened.

"Nick, I love you too."

He moved to her side so that they would be in profile for the camera, then he got down on his knee and opened the small jewelry box.

"Elizabeth, will you marry me?"

She covered her mouth with both hands. All he could see were her wide eyes.

"You are the one I want to be with. I knew there was something special about you the first time we met. I know that sounds crazy, but I can't go a day without thinking about you. I want you in my life, more than anything I've ever wanted."

Other visitors made it to the lookout point, but they stood back, silent, and surrounded the couple. They waited breathlessly with him for her answer.

The pear-shaped diamond ring glittered in the early light. She gazed at the ring, then at him. Her head moved in a slow nod. There were a few gasps from the small crowd.

"Yes—Nick Evers—I will marry you."

Camera shutter clicks came from the crowd. He was unsure if the Australian gentleman was the one who took the pictures or if other people took pictures as well. He slipped the ring on her finger, then he stood and they kissed with cheers from the crowd. She held both sides of his face, and he wrapped her in his arms. The gentleman with her camera took a few more shots and congratulated them. He gave Nick a nod and a wink.

All day Nick felt light on his feet, even for a full day of climbing stairs and navigating the stone ruins. It was silly to ask someone to pinch him. Instead, he touched the stones often as if to make sure they were real, that in fact he was there with her and they were now engaged. The stones of the ruins fit together perfectly, each one made for the other. He felt the same way about her. She smiled and laughed at his amazement and curiosity. The pear-shaped ring, in its proper place, glittered on her finger. He never felt so bold, so confident. They shared kisses and held hands as they followed the thread of visitors among the ancient ruins.

Their journey back to the hotel, the shuttle, the train, the taxi, was long but held a cherished note of euphoria. That night, they made love, in the shower, on the bed, on the sofa, even on the small dining table in the room. Their joy carried them over the waves of the day's fatigue until, at last, they collapsed on the bed in each other's arms. He thought of tomorrow, when they would venture around the city of Cusco. He looked forward to the days to come with thoughts about Atlanta, his family, his friends, and his eventual announcement to them all. His father's resentment, which he knew would come, no longer mattered in the moment. A bigger concern was how his mother would take things.

Elizabeth took his hand and drew it to her chest as she slept. The ring pressed into his hand and he smiled and kissed the back of her head before he drifted off to sleep.

31

Nick and Elizabeth strolled the narrow streets of San Blas, Cusco's old colonial quarter. They stopped at a quaint little restaurant and bakery to get something to eat. The restaurant had five small, round black lacquered tables with white plastic molded chairs. All were empty except for one. Two girls sat with an older woman. A short, smiling Peruvian woman greeted and directed them to come inside.

Colorful decorative plates hung from the white plaster walls. On the back counter, where Elizabeth placed their order, were rows of wicker baskets filled with various types of bread in different shapes and sizes. They picked a table and sat as the woman prepared their meals. Elizabeth smiled at the woman and the two girls seated a table away from them. The girls were probably college freshmen, maybe even seniors in high school. That age, and that time in her life, seemed so long ago. The older woman, possibly Nick's mother's age, could be their mother or an aunt.

The girls giggled and snuck glances at him. They glanced maybe once at her. She smiled at them. They whispered among themselves, while the older woman enjoyed her meal and ignored them. She too had glanced at Nick, but only once, and gave Elizabeth a polite smile. The ring was on her finger, but Nick was without one. She wondered if the girls or the woman noticed. His voice woke her from her thoughts.

"Sorry, what was that?"

"I said we got lucky—with the weather. Doesn't it rain here a lot?"

"Yes—yes it does."

She looked out at the sun-soaked street and nodded as she ate. She smiled at him. He devoured the chicken and rice dish she ordered for him. His appetite for food, for sex, for life, made her smile inside. She gazed at her engagement ring. It was truly beautiful. She was engaged. The thought of it now—it being her turn—gave her pause. She loved him; she was sure of that, but wondered if it was the best thing for the both of them.

"What will you do when we get back to Atlanta?"

His gaze met hers.

"I won't go back to Hale, so I'll be looking for gainful employment. I have savings and investments. We won't be starting out with nothing if you're concerned about that."

"You say that as though you already believe your father is going to cut you out. Do you?"

He scowled, and his gaze left hers for a moment.

"I really don't know, but you should know I'm not afraid to do what needs to be done for us to have a great life together."

The corners of her lips turned up in a subtle smile. His words were what she needed to hear, but his actions were what she needed most. She admitted the engagement ring was one defining action. She raised her eyebrows and took a spoonful of his rice. He watched her eat as he sipped the Peruvian cocktail she ordered for him, called a pisco sour. She mused at the subtle facial expressions he made when he drank it. She sipped at her cocktail as well. He tore off a piece of bread and glanced at her.

"What else is on your mind?"

She brushed her curls over her shoulder and glanced at the other table with the two girls and the woman. They ate and seemed preoccupied with whatever conversation they were having.

"What about your mother and sister?"

"They love me. They'll come around. As much as my mother was heartbroken about me walking out on Colette, I know deep down inside she wants me to be happy."

He sounded confident about his mother, but there was pain in his eyes when he said Colette's name. Elizabeth sighed.

"And your friends?"

"Blake supports me, and that's all that matters. I've ended things with Autumn, which was a long time coming. Derek hates me because of Autumn. He's got a thing for her. Peter and Sandy, I'm not sure where they stand. They were friends with Autumn, too. They might hate me as well, but all I can do is move forward and do the best I can."

Her lips tightened. Under the table, she rotated the engagement ring around her finger.

"What about you?"

She raised her eyebrows and stroked her upper arm.

"If I still have a job at Nexgen, I'll continue there until I find something new. I doubt it would be good for me to stay there long term, even if I wanted to. Since they took me off the Hale account, at least I won't have to face your father, or Dale, or anyone else there. It's a relief. I guess."

She shrugged. His lips tightened and his eyebrows knit together, then he huffed.

"I understand the shit between my father and me, but that should have never come your way."

She snorted.

"Isn't that a bit naïve? How did you think things were going to play out?"

He cocked his head. She was about to cross her arms, but that would have given the appearance that she was chiding him. She instead took a sip of her cocktail, folded her hands in her lap, and rotated her engagement ring around her finger.

"I guess I didn't think things were going to turn out the way they did, for you, for me. All I know is that we can be great together. You're strong and beautiful. You're the only one for me. All I needed was for *you* to give *us* a chance."

The tension in her shoulders eased. Her heart softened, and she nodded despite the deep fears that lingered inside her. His words—beautifully spoken from sensuous lips—from a handsome man, a younger man. As she took in his words, she caressed the ring's large, pear-shaped diamond. Its sharp cut facets felt serious, maybe even dangerous.

"What do you say that we enjoy the rest of our day exploring Cusco, and we'll figure out the rest later?"

He smiled at her suggestion and held up his cocktail. She sat up, took her glass and they toasted to a wonderful day together.

Nick stirred under the covers. He reached out, but the bed was empty. The bathroom. Elizabeth must be in the bathroom. He tugged at the sheets to cover his shoulders and fell back asleep. When he awoke an hour later, he expected her to have returned to bed. Maybe she was getting them something to eat. He sat up on his elbows and rubbed his eyes. Even with the curtains partially drawn, the angle of the sun brought more light into the room, and had roused him from his slumber.

"Lizzy?"

His voice sounded dry and hollow. He sat on the edge of the bed to first clear his head.

"Lizzy?"

He stood, rubbed his eyes with the palm of his hand, and lumbered to the bathroom. When he turned on the light, her things were missing from the vanity counter. His eyebrows drew together. Her luggage was gone as well. There was a note on the small dining table.

Dear Nick,

I'm sorry I left without saying goodbye, but I need time to process things. I've gotten so accustomed to steering my own ship and in order to have a relationship with you, I have to surrender the part of me that has protected me for so long. Please understand. Another thing that's been on my mind is your family. If your family never accepts us, I worry the eventual stress on you would cause you to resent me. Please speak to your family and try to resolve any differences. You're smart and charming. I know you'll find a way to win them over. You need to have an understanding with your family in order for us to move forward.

Love, Lizzy

Her stealthy departure forced him to consider how he left Colette on their wedding day. He dropped into a chair at the table and tugged a fist full of his hair. He swallowed the dry knot in his throat. His eyes watered and tears glided down his cheeks.

32

The morning sun blazed through the BMW's windows. Nick's eyes narrowed even though he wore his dark wayfarer sunglasses. His body jostled over the bumps in the road with a numbness and detachment. He called Elizabeth and left a message when he arrived back in Atlanta. He promised her he would speak to his parents and give her space. The wait to hear her voice and to see her again was almost too much to bear.

He stopped by his apartment at Crest Tower only to find it occupied by a new tenant. The building manager told him they moved his things to storage in the basement per Dr. Richard Evers' instructions. There was no official lease agreement with his father or Hale, so what could he do? He stormed to his car in the parking deck, dumped his luggage in the trunk, and sped away as if the place was on fire. He clenched the steering wheel and shook his head as he drove with no destination in mind. Elizabeth was the last person he wanted to tell what had happened to his living situation. It would prove, yet again, to the both of them that his father still had control. He turned onto I-75 and headed toward his parents' home. It was the only place he could go, as Blake was still in Spain, and the rest of his friends had blocked his text messages. He also wanted to confront his father about his apartment, and he needed it to be face-to-face.

A text message alert came over his phone. He glanced at it, but ignored it until the third alert sounded. He realized it might be Lizzy, so he picked up his phone. The last three messages were from Blake. After he got off the expressway, he pulled into the parking lot of a strip mall.

He tapped the first message from Blake.

Blake's last message, "Nick, read my messages. Importante!"

He huffed.

"Okay?"

Blake's previous message, "Nick, hello?"

He shook his head.

Blake's first message, "Nick, sit down before you read this. I found out from Marissa that Isabella had had a miscarriage. We're going to see her tonight. I didn't know what to feel or think. Maybe it's not my place to feel or think anything. I wanted to let you know as soon as I could. Sorry I couldn't tell you in person. I'm here if you need me."

His eyes blurred with tears, and he blurted out an audible breath. He put his head back on the headrest and closed his eyes. A sadness came over him for Isabella. He wept through tears of guilt and grief. Guilt that he should feel any sense of relief, and grief that she lost the child she wanted regardless of who the father was.

People walked to and from their parked cars to the shops. He wondered if anyone saw him crying in his car. After he wiped away his tears, the numbness returned but for different reasons, and his headache lingered. Any anger he had subsided into an odd feeling of hopeful acceptance. He still wanted to hear his father's explanation, but then he would be on his way, and he would be okay with that.

~

The BMW's tires growled softly over the stone pavers as Nick drove up the driveway to his parents' house. There was an abandoned stillness in the air as he went to the front door. He pressed the doorbell button. After only a few minutes, which seemed like an eternity, he turned to his car, ready to leave, but then the door opened and his mother stood there. At first she looked surprised, then a weary smile appeared on her face.

"Oh, Nick."

"Hello mother."

She wiped away a tear, hurried out of the house, and embraced him.

"It's great to see you. I was so worried."

"I'm sorry I worried you, but I needed time—time to myself. Is dad home?"

"Yes."

His shoulders knotted, but he steeled himself—for Elizabeth.

"Come inside so we can talk."

She looped her arm around his and they went inside. He followed her to the sitting room where he announced his and Colette's engagement. It made him ill to look at the sofa where they sat. He was thankful when she brought him a bottle of beer and poured herself a glass of wine. He worried he would need a lot more to drink before the day was done.

"Your father's in the basement, in his golf room. I imagine he's playing on that damn thing."

Nick glanced at the hallway that led to the basement. His father's golf room was one of his favorite places to sneak off to. Now it was the last place he ever wanted to visit.

"Are you aware that I have no place to live? The building manager at Crest Tower told me they moved my things to make room for a new Hale employee."

"Yes, your father and I argued over it, but I got him to agree that you can move back home."

"Mother, you know I can't move back. He wants me to find a place, and that's what I'll do."

"At least stay here until you can think things over."

He looked down at the bottle of beer, but he had little desire to take another drink.

"Son, we need to talk about something more important."

He looked up at his mother.

"Oh?"

She sat her glass of wine on the coffee table, went to the fireplace mantle, and returned with something hidden in her hand. When she sat next to him on the sofa, she opened her hand. In her palm was the engagement ring that he got in Spain for Elizabeth. His heart sank.

"Elizabeth came to the house to talk to your father and me."

"What? Why—"

She raised her hand to hush him.

"As you might imagine, your father stormed off, but I wanted to hear what she had to say."

He felt hollow. She examined the ring and its facets sparkled. He wanted to take the ring from his mother and thrust it into his pocket, out of sight.

"This is a beautiful ring, Nick. I don't have to ask how serious you are about Elizabeth."

Her gaze was softer than when he first returned from Spain, and mentioned his interest in older women.

"Elizabeth was very gracious and respectful. She is quite an elegant woman. I wanted to hear what she had to say about your relationship, especially after she showed me the ring and told me about your time together in Spain and Peru."

He shifted in his seat, but said nothing, eager to hear what else Elizabeth told his mother.

"Elizabeth wanted to know what I thought, or how I felt, about you two being together."

She touched her fingertips to her chin. He brushed his fingers through his hair and stared at his mother.

"I have to say, at first, before I knew her, I thought it was absurd that you were having some misguided crush on this woman, but when I met her, the way she spoke about you and how much you care for her, I—"

She peered at the ring between her fingertips. A tear caressed her cheek. He brushed it away with his thumb. She smiled, patted his leg, then she took his hand and turned it over and placed the ring in his palm.

"She's special, and this belongs on her finger."

His mother closed his hand around the ring and kissed him on the cheek.

"But what about my father?"

"This isn't about your father. It's about you. Go talk to him, but don't forget your heart."

His mother spoke as if she were giving him advice that she wished she had gotten long ago. He wondered if she ever loved his father. They stood and embraced.

"Thanks mom."

She patted his chest and wrinkled her lips. Her eyes held the confidence he needed. He put the engagement ring in his pocket and went down the hallway to the basement. It felt as though gravity increase with every step as he descended the stairs.

The sharp crack of a golf ball being driven down a fairway startled Nick when he opened the door to his father's golf room. He stood in the doorway. His father watched the projected ball on the screen as it flew down the virtual fairway. When it landed, he let out a heavy sigh.

"I told you Josephine, I'm not changing my mind. The subject *is* closed."

Nick was silent. His father turned around, and his eyes widened, then narrowed and his brow furrowed.

"Nick. Good to see that you're alive. What brings you around?"

He was certain his father already knew.

"I don't have a place to live. You instructed the building manager to remove my things."

His father wrinkled his lips and stood there with his hands rested on the grip end of the golf club.

"Hale hired some new overseas employees, and we needed the space. Things weren't working out, and I grew tired of your antics. You seem to know what's best for you, and you've steered your own ship. Well, Nick, you're now out in open water. Best of luck to you."

"So you're cutting me out?"

"Let's be honest Nick, you were never really in."

Nick huffed. He wanted to protest, but there was some truth to his father's words.

"I'm sure your mother told you that Ms. Bach stopped by. I was busy, so I let your mother deal with her."

His jaw tightened and his shoulders stiffened as he watched his father hit the ball, then he huffed.

"It's funny. Elizabeth wanted me to restore our relationship, but I doubt that's possible. There is one thing I will leave you with. We are engaged. Regardless of how you feel, I love her and she loves me."

His father stared down the projected fairway as his ball landed in one of the sand traps. He said nothing and only appeared to be contemplating his next swing. Nick walked out, and as he climbed the steps, only the dull metallic sound of the door latch striking home echoed in the stairwell.

At Il Fasto, Nick sat at the same table where he and Elizabeth first had lunch. He rubbed his hands together under the table, then dried his moist palms on his pant legs.

"Sir, would you like another glass of wine?"

The waiter startled him.

"Um? Yes, thank you."

As the waiter filled his wineglass, he glanced around the dining room and stared at the front of the restaurant with a hope and a prayer that she would walk in at any moment. After he left his parents' house, he called her cellphone, but only got her voicemail. After he left a voice message, he also sent her a text message echoing what he had said. He was on his way to her place when she replied. She wrote, "Meet me at two o'clock where we first had lunch."

It was twenty minutes after, and still no sign of her. It made him smile when he discovered she put the reservation under the name "Lizzy." Sunlight poked through an overcast sky and brightened the white linen-covered table tops near the windows. He took the engagement ring from his pocket. It sparkled between his fingertips. Its diamond cast tinted rays of light on the white tablecloth. His lips curved into a soft, tight-lipped smile. When he glanced out the window, there she was. He drew in a sudden breath. She smiled and waved. He beamed and his heart sang as he watched her walk up the sidewalk.

Acknowledgments

It's been a long journey to write, edit, and publish my debut novel, Kilómetro Cero. My deepest gratitude to my family and friends for their patience, support, and encouragement.

About the Author

Winner of a Literary Titan Award for his debut novel, Kilómetro Cero, and INDIEFAB Awards finalist for his short story collection, Tooth and Talon, James Walter Lee is an American author who writes literary and general fiction, and in the genres of thrillers, horror, and romance. He owns and operates two publishing imprints, Zennea Press and 2nd Sight Press. He holds a Master's in Fine Arts from The New York Academy of Art and a Bachelor's in Fine Arts from the College for Creative Studies. James is also an avid photographer and lives in Pennsylvania. For more about James Walter Lee, please visit jameswalterlee.com.

Follow author James Walter Lee
Goodreads: James_Walter_Lee
BookBub: james-walter-lee
TikTok: @jameswalterlee
Instagram: jameswalterlee
X: JamesWalterLee

www.ingramcontent.com/pod-product-compliance
Lightning Source LLC
LaVergne TN
LVHW100512110826
845146LV00002B/607

* 9 7 9 8 9 8 8 5 1 5 3 0 2 *